Rachel Hore worked in London publishing for many years before moving with her family to Norwich, where she taught publishing and creative writing at the University of East Anglia before becoming a full-time writer. She is married to the writer D. J. Taylor and they have three sons. Rachel is a *Sunday Times* bestselling author and her previous novels include *One Moonlit Night* and *A Beautiful Spy*.

Praise for

RACHEL HORE

'This complex, thoughtful novel features two interlocking stories in different timeframes. Themes of family, self-determination and passionate love make for a dramatic, warm-hearted, wonderfully written read'
Daily Mail

'A gorgeous tale – I raced through the pages.
A new book by Rachel Hore is always a
treat and this is no exception'
Tracy Rees

'Packed with secrets, heartbreak and lies'
Yours

RACHEL HORE

The Hidden Years

**SIMON &
SCHUSTER**

London · New York · Sydney · Toronto · New Delhi

First published in Great Britain by Simon & Schuster UK Ltd, 2023
This paperback edition first published 2024

1 3 5 7 9 10 8 6 4 2

Simon & Schuster UK Ltd
1st Floor
222 Gray's Inn Road
London WC1X 8HB

Simon & Schuster: Celebrating 100 Years of Publishing in 2024

Simon & Schuster Australia, Sydney
Simon & Schuster India, New Delhi

www.simonandschuster.co.uk
www.simonandschuster.com.au
www.simonandschuster.co.in

A CIP catalogue record for this book
is available from the British Library

Paperback ISBN: 978-1-3985-1799-8
eBook ISBN: 978-1-3985-1797-4
Audio ISBN: 978-1-3985-1798-1

Typeset in Palatino by M Rules
Printed and Bound in the UK using 100% Renewable
Electricity at CPI Group (UK) Ltd

In loving memory of
Elizabeth Anne Castell Taylor
(1932–2022),
a child of wartime.

'Perhaps it would be better if she could find the knack of realising what things are worth having and trying for, for then the desire for them would carry her on.'

ADVICE TO A GRANDDAUGHTER
(taken from my grandfather's diary)

One

June 1966

The clock above the porter's lodge of Darbyfield University was half an hour ahead of the time showing on Belle Johnson's wristwatch, but whichever was correct, she had been waiting ages for her lift and the blazing noonday sun was doing nothing for her hangover. Passers-by glanced curiously at the attractive student with her overstuffed rucksack and a guitar in a canvas case. At nineteen she was tall, lean and supple in faded jeans and a loose-fitting T-shirt. Her long smooth dark hair was parted in the middle, a tiny plait on each side holding it back from her drawn face. One of her chestnut-brown eyes was slightly larger than the other, which gave her an appealing look – or would have done had she not been scowling.

Belle tapped the watch, but the second hand wouldn't move, and she frowned. Her parents had given her the delicate gold timepiece on her eighteenth birthday with the instruction to 'look after it'. Possibly it hadn't liked being left in a puddle of wine after last night's party. She sighed as she unfastened it and slid it into her rucksack. Hopefully it would dry out. Then her lips curved at a secret thought. Perhaps time wouldn't matter where she was going.

'Hello, stranger!' The accusing voice broke through her thoughts and Belle looked up, shading her eyes against the sunlight until Carrie's earnest round face came into focus.

'Oh, hi,' she mumbled. Her friend looked as neat and conventional as ever in an A-line cotton skirt and spotless white blouse. Although it was a Saturday it was exam season and Carrie clutched a folder under her arm labelled, 'The Enlightenment – First Year Revision Notes' in her even handwriting.

'What have you been up to, Belle? I haven't seen you in ages and I've knocked on your door ever so many times.'

'Sorry.' Belle shrugged. 'I've been in the library. And exams, of course. Hey, how's History going, by the way?' Belle felt bad at keeping Carrie in the dark, but then she hadn't told any of her friends what she'd been doing for the last week – or about her big decision.

She barely heard Carrie's response as she glanced anxiously up the road for the twentieth time. The cars continued to pass without slowing.

'Belle? I said, who are you waiting for?'

She forced her attention back to Carrie's troubled face and relented. 'Listen, I'm sorry I haven't been around. I was going to write, honest. I'm going away for a while. In case anyone asks, the rest of my stuff's in the landing cupboard and I've handed in my key.'

Carrie's pale blue eyes widened in concern. 'You've cleared your room? Why? Where are you going?'

'I'm off to Cornwall.'

'*Cornwall*? But that's hundreds of miles away. What about exams?'

'I've only one left – Monday afternoon – and it hardly counts.'

'You're going to miss an exam?' Carrie's voice rose to a horrified squeak. 'Belle, you can't.'

Something inside her snapped. 'I can. It doesn't matter.'

'But they might not let you back for your second year.'

Belle shuffled her feet and looked away, her roaming gaze taking in the old red-brick arched gateway, the cropped grass of the quad beyond, students trailing about in chattering groups in the sunshine, bags of books slung over their shoulders. A busy, familiar scene. She'd thought Darbyfield University was where she'd wanted to be, had been ecstatic when she'd won a place to read English. How proud her parents had been. But now ... well, life looked different.

'So when are you planning to come back?' Carrie asked, folding her arms. '*If* you are coming back, that is. What about the Summer Ball?'

'I don't know yet.' Belle felt a stab of annoyance at Carrie's inquisition, while admitting it was unfair of her.

Carrie had been her constant friend at university, indeed the first friendly face she'd met after she'd driven up from suburban Surrey the previous September. Belle's father had hefted a box of books onto her desk, remarked that her modern hall of residence was luxury compared to the shabby hostel *he'd* endured as a student in London ('But that was 1930, Dad!' she'd groaned), then bid her an abrupt goodbye with a quick peck on the cheek and an, 'I'll leave you to it then.' She'd gazed down at the upright, tweed-jacketed figure with the salt-and-pepper hair marching purposefully towards the porter's lodge, and longed for him to look up and give a final wave. But he didn't and sighing, she turned back to the room, feeling rather alone. She ought to make up the narrow bed and unpack. Instead sounds of activity drew her out to the corridor. There a petite girl with brown bobbed hair and delicate features was fetching a bottle of milk from the communal fridge. She looked up at Belle and gave her a shy smile. 'Hi, I'm Carrie. I'm just making tea. Would you like some?' And Belle's loneliness had lifted.

Now she was biting her lip, wondering what to tell Carrie of her recent adventures, when the toot of a horn interrupted her thoughts and they both turned to see an ancient yellow car judder towards them in a miasma of fumes and tinny pop music. The young man at the wheel was grinning. Belle sighed with relief. 'Finally, Gray!' she exclaimed. Carrie just stared.

Happiness filling her, Belle gripped her guitar as the car ground to a halt. Gray leaned from the window and Belle's heart leaped to see his tangle of corn-coloured hair, white teeth gleaming in his thin tanned face, sharp blue eyes twinkling above a hawkish nose.

'You're late,' she admonished, trying, but failing, to sound stern.

He smiled lazily and patted the car door. 'Couldn't help it. Trouble getting the old girl going!' *Oh, that smoky drawl.* 'Chuck your stuff on the back seat.'

Seeing that he wasn't going to help or apologize, Belle wrested the rear door open, then pushed her luggage inside next to some boxes and a grubby holdall. When she turned to say goodbye to Carrie, her friend was still staring at Gray and Belle giggled, for her mouth was a perfect O of amazement.

'Carrie, darling, this is Gray,' she said and gave her a hug. 'Now, promise you won't worry about me.' She closed her eyes, breathing in Carrie's clean, soapy smell.

'I can't help worrying,' Carrie said in a small voice. 'Be careful, Belle, won't you? And stay in touch.'

'I'll write, of course.'

Carrie hissed in Belle's ear, 'I don't know where you found him, but he's gorgeous.'

Belle laughed and gave her a brief final squeeze. Then she gathered up a pulsing transistor radio and a punnet of cherries from the passenger seat and climbed in next to Gray.

'All right, love?' Gray pushed back his hair and smiled at her. 'Have a cherry.' He offered the punnet through the window to Carrie, who shook her head shyly and backed away. He popped one in his mouth and gunned the engine into life.

Belle waved to Carrie as the car leaped forward, but by the time they'd swung round the corner she'd all but forgotten her. Her mouth was full of ripe cherry and her heart was singing. She'd thrown off all her troubles. For a while, at least.

Or so she thought, as she dropped a fruit stone from the window.

Belle was still too young to have learned that your problems have a habit of coming along with you.

Two

Belle had known Gray for precisely a week.

She'd been out in the Derbyshire hills the previous Saturday with the Rambling Club, the university society she most enjoyed. There were a dozen of them, a mixed bag, their president a serious-faced Chemistry postgraduate named Duncan, who'd been brought up in the Cairngorm mountains and found the Peak District summits gentle in comparison. They were nice, ordinary young people, any of whom Belle would have felt happy introducing to her parents. The exercise and the peace and beauty of the countryside made her feel free; she could lose herself for a few hours.

That day's walk had involved strenuous climbing, then on the way down the weather had suddenly worsened, the rain coming down in sheets, and they'd taken shelter in the mouth of a shallow cave. The rain passed and they'd pressed on, finally reaching the village station they'd started from, but were annoyed to discover that their train back to the city had been cancelled. The next one wasn't for an hour. The rain clouds had gone, however, and everything looked fresh, the early evening sky gleaming peach and gold.

'Why don't we stop at that pub we passed?' Duncan suggested and they retraced their steps.

Outside the Black Dog, a sandwich board advertised live music, a group called 'The Witchers'. Belle felt exhausted, every bone aching from the day's endeavours, so she gladly stuffed her waterproofs into her knapsack and followed the others through the ancient oak doorway.

She loved the atmosphere of the pub at once. It was old-fashioned spit and sawdust, with rough floorboards, horse brasses decorating the walls, and a scattering of wooden benches, tables and chairs. The low-ceilinged space was loud with talk and laughter, busy as one would expect for a Saturday evening. In one corner two empty chairs and a microphone had been set up on a low dais, ready for the live act.

'Belle, what are you having?' Duncan gave her a friendly nudge. He was a good-looking, athletic young man with a scruff of short dark curls and a steady, brown-eyed gaze. He was always especially kind to Belle, who was the only girl in the group and its youngest member.

'Sweet cider and crisps, please.' She handed him some coins and while she waited for him to order, looked round at the other customers. Some seated around tables were dressed for walking, like themselves, while over by the window a group of brawny youngish men stood nursing pints as they waited their turn at a dartboard. Local farmers, no doubt, from their physiques and weatherbeaten faces. Belle's attention roved to a very different party by the far wall, close to the dais, half a dozen people a few years older than herself sitting around a long table, engaged in eager conversation. She stared at them with fascination, the men with longish hair, the girls in floaty dresses and ropes of beads, bright, alien figures in a Peak District pub. The blond head of a man facing her was bent to the task of rolling a cigarette, but suddenly he threw back his head and laughed at some joke, and she caught a flash of his white teeth and felt a stab of attraction.

'Your drink, my lady,' she heard Duncan say and she smiled her thanks.

Thirsty, she took a large gulp of cider, which went down the wrong way so that Duncan had to slap her back. By the time she finished coughing there were signs of activity across the room. The blond man, lithe in a white shirt and jeans, and a lanky mouse-haired one with a thin, peaky-looking face and round glasses, were taking up position on the dais with their guitars. After a shuffling of chairs, some patient plinks and plonks of tuning up and a few exploratory chords, they began to play a beautiful intricate harmony and the chatter in the room died away.

'Are you okay now?' Duncan whispered, concerned.

Belle nodded vaguely, transfixed by the music. She crept forward with her drink to hear better, just as the duo began to sing. The song was a lament, something about love among the willow trees, sad but droll, too, sung with merriment in the singers' eyes and a chorus with a beat that made her tap her foot. Her gaze could not leave the blond singer's face with its sleepy blue eyes, which he closed when he sang the tenderest lines. His warm, full-throated tenor voice teased and charmed. The other man's was higher, reedier, but attractive in its own way, and the voices wove in and out of each other in perfect harmony.

When the song was over there was a burst of applause, and then they struck up another tune that had a swing like a country dance. Belle joined in as people clapped in time. After this the blond man spoke. 'Thank you, everyone, for your appreciation,' he said in a slow lazy voice and Belle hung onto every word. 'I'm Gray Robinson and this here is Stu Ford. We're The Witchers and we'd like to thank Frank there behind the bar for having us here this evening. Cheers, Frank. Now without further ado we're going to sing a love song.' Gray gazed round the room as he struck an opening chord and Belle, to her amazement, felt his eyes rest on her briefly. 'It's a bit sad, I'm afraid, but, hey, that's the way it goes sometimes.'

Here someone at the back of the room shouted 'Ahhh' and there was laughter and Gray smiled in a laid-back fashion. Belle breathed in deeply. Again he glanced her way and she stared back at him in surprise. Then he closed his eyes and began to sing, by himself this time, a plaintive ballad about a summer romance blown away by an autumn breeze.

'I don't usually like folksy music,' someone said in Belle's ear. 'A classical man myself, but they're good, aren't they?' It was Tim, another of the ramblers, a stocky, rather ponderous lad, who'd regaled Belle earlier out on the hills with an account of his ambitions to be a barrister. She was sure he'd be a good one because he could talk so much.

'They're wonderful,' she murmured back. 'Sshh, I want to listen.'

Tim ignored this and glanced at his watch. 'We'll have to be moving soon. It's not long till the train.'

'Mmm. We've got plenty of time.'

Thankfully, Tim took the hint and stepped away, leaving her to concentrate on the song. It faded and segued into another. After several more, Gray announced a short interval. Stu leaned his guitar against the wall. Someone passed them pints of golden beer and Stu carried his to the table where they'd been sitting. Gray took several gulps of his then set the glass on the floor and picked up his guitar. As he adjusted the strings, his gaze strayed over towards Belle.

On a mad impulse, with a leap of courage she'd never known she possessed, Belle walked over to stand before him. He rested his arms on his guitar and smiled at her.

'I . . .' She felt suddenly self-conscious.

'Love the gear,' he said, pointing to her muddy walking boots and she smiled.

'I love your music,' she mumbled and he nodded his thanks.

'Um, I'm Belle. We have to go to catch our train in a moment,' she went on. 'We're from Darbyfield University. But I wanted to say . . . about loving the songs, I mean. And that I hope we won't seem rude, leaving early.'

'Hey, no offence, I promise,' Gray said. He sipped his beer then played a few chords, staring at her all the while.

'Tell you what, Belle. We're playing in Darbyfield tomorrow. The Kaleidoscope in White Horse Alley. You know it? You should come.'

'The Kaleidoscope. Okay.' She didn't know White Horse Alley, but she'd find it.

'Gray?' Another of his friends appeared and glanced curiously at Belle before asking him, 'Another pint?'

'Yeah, why not. Hang on, I owe you a quid . . .'

'See you tomorrow then, hopefully,' she broke in quickly, her courage running out. She returned to the others at the bar and shouldered her knapsack then cast Gray a final glance. He was helping Stu tune up, but he smiled at her and gave her a wave. Light with happiness, she waved back. She'd see him again, she vowed.

The following evening at eight, Belle found The Kaleidoscope in a cobbled backstreet that she had never known existed. It was a Sunday evening and the city was quiet. A hand-drawn arrow sign pointed down to a basement beneath a bookshop, in the window of which lay a dozen dusty volumes with curling covers and titles such as *The Way of the Yogi* and *Capricorn's Daughter*. She sniffed at an exotic smoky scent that coiled through the air.

The same sandwich board advertising The Witchers was propped up on the narrow pavement and Belle pretended to study it, twisting her fingers in her hair as a group of young people flowed round her and down the steps on their way inside, trying to pluck up courage to follow them. She'd never been into a club on her own before. She'd failed to persuade

Carrie to come because Carrie was revising, all her friends were, so she was here on her own. Eventually, she trod carefully down the narrow concrete steps. At the bottom she pushed open a rough wooden door and found herself in a dimly lit, claustrophobic space that smelled strongly of malt and tobacco smoke. A group of lads in turtlenecks and ankle boots who were clustered around the seedy bar with pints and cigarettes looked up briefly at her entrance, but otherwise no one took any notice. She gazed about, feeling out of place. Then, thankfully, she spotted Gray. He was standing with Stu and the others near a tiny corner stage where their guitars and two chairs were set up.

Gray hadn't seen her. He was talking animatedly, gesturing as he related some anecdote and Belle waited uncertainly, unable to take her eyes off him but too shy to approach. Someone bumped into her and beer sloshed over her arm, an apology was muttered. She dabbed at her jacket with a handkerchief then walked hesitantly across and hovered at the fringes of the group. At last, Gray noticed her and broke off his story, smiling as he stepped across to greet her, bending to kiss her cheek as though he'd known her for years.

'Folks,' he said, turning to the group, 'this is Belle.'

'Hi.' She smiled round at them nervously and they all nodded with varying degrees of enthusiasm. Gray stayed with his arm round her waist, in a way that was friendly rather than possessive, took a sip of his beer and continued his story.

'Then the guy said ...' It was something about an argument regarding payment for a performance – and Belle leaned against Gray, quietly dazed, unable to believe that she was suddenly part of this world. Except she wasn't, of course. Gray had merely made it seem so. No one else spoke to her or offered her a drink and her fingers felt horribly sticky from the spilt beer. Suddenly Gray raised his eyebrows in response to a signal from a man behind the bar. He withdrew his arm. It was time for The Witchers to tune up.

As the act got underway, once again the liquid notes of the guitars, Gray's lazy voice and Stu's plaintive high one played havoc with Belle's emotions. Some of the songs she remembered from the evening before, but the intimacy of this smaller space suited them better, and the audience, dedicated fans who'd come for the music, listened attentively and were warm in their appreciation.

There was no interval and late in the performance Gray took a draught of his beer. 'Now,' he said, 'I'd like to sing you a song I've never tried in public before. It's called "Silverwood" and it's about a place that's special to me.'

Silverwood, Belle thought with surprise. The name sounded familiar but she couldn't think why. She listened closely to the words. '*Down a winding lane, hidden by silver trees, it calls to me, place of freedom by the river that runs to the sea, it calls to me. Dancing waters, rolling hills, all the beauty you can see, it calls to me, it calls to me. Silverwood.*' It was light but heartfelt and she liked it. Silverwood. It definitely stirred a memory.

There was a round of enthusiastic applause, then they played what seemed to be an old favourite called 'On my Wagon'. Finally, after a hearty sea shanty with Stu as a rousing encore, it was over.

Belle waited for Gray to finish talking to the fans swarming round him, wondering self-consciously what she should do, whether she was merely making a fool of herself by hanging about. One of the girls in Gray's group of friends, willowy and fair-haired with dreamy eyes, smiled at her vaguely and Belle smiled back and it was this single friendly gesture that made her decide to wait and see what happened. To look less like a spare part she went to the bar.

'What'll you have, Miss?'

'Er, a bitter lemon, please.'

She felt the man's prurient eyes on her as he filled a glass. 'Belle?'

She turned with relief to see Gray. 'Oh,' she burbled. 'You were wonderful.' He smiled as though this was simply his due. He paid for her drink, watched as the barman drew him a pint, then steered her back to where two tables had been pushed together, round which Gray's friends had gathered. She sat quietly on a bench close to Gray as Stu and the others discussed the performance. Gray simply listened, sipping his beer, a faint smile on his face. When Belle finished her bitter lemon someone fetched her another, which tasted a bit different, metallic, but she didn't complain. It made her feel happy, more relaxed. Time flew past, more strange lemonades were drunk. The barman called last orders and soon afterwards the lights flickered, a sign that they should leave. Their group, all eight or nine of them, tumbled up the steps onto the dark street. Belle's world swayed a bit then righted itself. She shivered, fastened her jacket against the cool of the night and murmured regretfully to Gray, 'I ought to be getting back now.'

He gripped her wrist. 'Don't go. We're moving on some-where. Where're we going, Stu?'

'Just back to ours, I suppose.'

Gray looked at her enquiringly as the others waited.

'I don't think I should,' Belle said weakly. 'I'm in the middle of exams and I've got revision.'

'Oh, I see,' Gray murmured. 'That's a shame.' He loos-ened her hand. 'Anybody remember *exams*?' He appealed to the group in a teasing voice. There were shaken heads and laughter. 'I'll see you around then, I guess,' he added with a rueful moue.

It was so embarrassing it hurt. They moved off, leaving her standing. All her joy drained away.

'Gray?' she called miserably in a small voice. 'Gray?' He swung round and his face lit up with a grin.

'Coming?'

She'd get up early and revise before the afternoon's exam. 'Yes.' She smiled and hurried towards him. He shifted the guitar on his shoulder, took her hand and tucked it under his arm as though it belonged there.

The party, if that's what it was, went on for the rest of the night. Gray and Stu's flat comprised a clutch of small rooms on the third floor of a concrete apartment block with a broken lift, but they'd made it homely, the yellow-painted walls dec-orated with posters and colourful strings of bells. Everyone sat or lay around on big floor cushions, the guys smoking pot and drinking beer. The willowy girl with the dreamy eyes was called Chrissie and appeared to be Stu's girlfriend. She dished out steaming plates of vegetable stew and fried rice which people ate hungrily. A strange, throbbing music played faintly in the background. Gray sat facing Belle, strumming his guitar quietly, keeping his eyes on her as he tried out snatches of song, and soon she was busking along, experimenting with harmonies, which made his eyes light up.

'You have a lovely singing voice,' he told her.

'Thank you. I play a bit, as well,' she said, eyeing his guitar longingly, but the odd background music had faded away and when invited to try the guitar she felt exposed. 'No, I'm not very good really,' she lied. 'I'd just embarrass myself.'

'Go on. Try.'

She settled the instrument in her lap, pushed back her hair and strummed a soft chord or two, liking the tone – it was a far better guitar than hers – then, forgetting she had an audience, began to play.

'"Blowing in the Wind",' Gray said promptly with a grin and they sang it together, and soon others joined in. Then she sang 'Michelle' solo – she loved the reference to 'my Belle' and had worked out the chords from listening to the Beatles record. There was a flutter of applause and, flushed with success, Belle returned the guitar to Gray.

Stu lit a joint and handed it round. Belle tried it, too, but choked on the fumes and hastily passed it on. Instead she lost herself in Gray's gaze as he played, which had just as mesmerising an effect on her as breathing in the scented smoke that hung in the air. He had a way of making her feel special, as though she mattered to him. No boy had ever looked at her like that before. It felt extraordinary, overwhelming.

'You all right?' he murmured, finally putting his guitar aside. She felt his fingers in her hair, gently tugging and stroking it, and they leaned into one another until their foreheads touched. Presently she lifted her face to his and he kissed her mouth gently, then again more deeply, and she sensed her whole body opening up to him. She shifted so that she was leaning against the wall next to him with her head on his shoulder and his arm round her. Maybe it was the food, the warm, druggy atmosphere of the room, the hypnotic music that had started up again, or all of these, but after a while Belle sank into unconsciousness.

~

'Hey. Belle, it's eight o'clock. Wake up.'

It was like surfacing from deep water. She blinked in pain and confusion against a sharp ray of daylight streaming in from the window. Gray was crouching before her and the tea he offered had a herby fragrance.

'Don't you have an exam?'

Her mind began to clear. Gray looked concerned and she was touched given his mockery of the night before. 'It's at half past one.' She took the cup and sipped from it cautiously, her nose wrinkling at the bitter taste.

'No need to rush, then.' Gray kissed her brow, rose lightly and went to the kitchen. She finished the tea and, headache receding, stretched to ease her stiffness. In the morning light the room wore a murky, run-down air. Several bodies under blankets lay gently snoring. There was no sign of Stu or his girlfriend. A delicious smell of toast was filling the room.

Revision! Belle climbed to her feet. She rummaged for her jacket and shoes then hurried into the kitchen.

'I need to go.'

'Stay for breakfast,' Gray commanded, holding out a plate of buttered toast.

'I can't. Honestly.'

'It'll only take you a moment.'

She took a slice and ate it while she shuffled on her shoes. Gray lounged against the kitchen doorway, watching with arms folded.

'Goodbye,' she breathed, standing before him. Was this it? Would she ever see him again?

'Bye.' His smile was teasing. As she brushed past him he reached and pulled her close and kissed her thoroughly, until she had to drag herself away. As she fumbled the flat door open, dizzy, he said, 'Hey, my Belle.' She turned, expectant, but all he said was, 'Good luck this afternoon!'

She forced a smile. 'Thanks,' she said and pulled the door to behind her. As she tottered down the stairs she tried to dismiss a voice that sang in her mind to the rhythm of her feet, *Is that it, then? Is that it?*

Somehow Belle ploughed through a couple of hours' revision in the library then, in the tense silence of the exam hall, scrawled some banalities on John Milton's apocalyptic language and the use of stock characters in Ben Jonson's plays. Then she was free. She trailed out with the other English first-years, dazed in the sunlight, and sat with them in the union bar as they compared answers, but her thoughts were elsewhere.

'Are you all right, Belle?' someone asked.

'Of course,' she said. 'I was up half the night, that's all.' *Just not revising.* They seemed suddenly so young, her fellow students, so dull next to Gray and his friends. After a while she excused herself and ambled back to the hall of residence, intending to lie down.

Reaching the first-floor landing she sniffed at a smell of smoke and was surprised and delighted to find Gray sitting cross-legged on the floor outside her room. He'd taken off his shoes and was smoking a roll-up.

'How did you find me?' she gasped, as he pinched out his cigarette and jumped to his feet. Despite their late night his skin glowed as though he'd slept well and his jeans and shirt looked freshly laundered.

'Easy. I asked around.' His husky voice and lopsided grin played havoc with her insides.

Inside her room, she watched anxiously as he prowled about, touching the strings of her guitar, squinting at a volume of country and western music that lay open on the carpet, examining her posters of Snoopy and the Beatles. But all he said was 'Nice'. Then he picked up a photograph from the desk.

'These your folks?'

She nodded. 'Dad, Mum, my little sister Jackie.'

'You look the perfect family.'

'What do you mean?' She couldn't tell if he was being wistful or sneering.

He set down the photo and put his arms round her. 'Oh, Belle, you're so pure,' he whispered, smiling at her wonderingly. He was compact, wiry, only a little taller than her five feet eight, and she stared directly into his piercing blue eyes, feeling the warmth of his body.

'I'm not at all pure,' she said, indignant.

'Yes, you are. Don't be cross. It's a compliment. It's something I like most about you.'

She smiled uncertainly. 'I'm not annoyed. I don't know quite what you mean by pure. It sounds boring and I certainly don't want to be that.'

'You're really not boring. Very interesting, in fact.'

He pulled her to him and she closed her eyes as he kissed her, his tongue exploring her mouth. She kissed him back, then, after a second's hesitation, led him to the narrow bed and drew him down close beside her. She would show him that she wasn't 'pure'.

It was not her first time – recalling with embarrassment a drunken fumble with an angelic-looking first year Engineer after a party in freshers' week. She'd wanted to lose her virginity – get it over and forget about it – but he was inexperienced as well, and although he hadn't meant to, he'd hurt her. They'd avoided one another since. After that, she'd dated two or three others, but never for long.

Gray was prepared and clearly knew exactly what to do. He was gentle and patient with her and she found herself responding passionately, soon lost in widening ripples of pleasure. Afterwards they lay panting in one another's arms. 'That was beautiful,' he whispered, his gaze lost in hers.

'Am I still pure?' she asked, smiling.

'Oh yes, very.'

She made a moue. He raised himself on one elbow and traced the contours of her face with his finger. 'I'm serious,' he said wonderingly. 'It's like nothing bad has ever happened to you. So sweet and perfect like your room and your perfect family. When I saw you in the crowd that first night I couldn't look away. Your spirit shines out of your eyes, you know. That's what I mean by pure.'

'That's ridiculous. I'm not like that,' she said hotly. 'You don't know me. I—'

'No, don't spoil it.' He stroked her hair, then bent and kissed her eyelids and she shivered with delight.

At that moment came a knock at the door and they froze. 'Belle, are you there?' Carrie's muffled voice. She rattled the door handle. *Thank goodness I locked it.* Belle began silently to giggle. Gray smiled. After a moment Carrie's footsteps retreated and Belle felt ashamed. Carrie was her friend after all. She got up and visited her tiny ensuite bathroom.

When she returned Gray was lying on his side, examining a pile of books on her bedside table. '*Ignorance and Self-Deception in Troilus and Cressida*?' he read aloud. 'Heavy stuff.'

'It's wrong for me, though. I thought that English Literature here would be exciting, but it's not. It's taught in such a boring way and some of the lecturers are so old. I don't think they've read anything published since Charles Dickens.'

'Why stay, then? Life's too short.'

'I'm lucky to be here, Gray. I worked hard for it.'

He nodded. 'Fair enough, but sometimes the things you want you find you don't want.'

She bit her lip and wondered if he might be right. 'What about you?'

'What about me? I do what I care about. Music. I hated school, got out as soon as I could, left home – there was just me and my mum – did this and that for a year or two then got together with Stu. It's been good, but it's changing now he's got Chrissie. Feels weird. It's Stu's flat and I need to find somewhere new.'

'Where?'

'Cornwall to start with. Silverwood.'

Again, recognition stirred. 'The place in your song. It's in Cornwall?'

'Yeah. It's this huge house in the middle of nowhere. I spent some time there last summer. I need to go back, work on some songs in peace. I've got so many ideas.'

'When are you going?'

'Saturday.'

'Next Saturday?' Belle breathed, staring at him in dismay. *That was in five days' time.*

'I'm just waiting for my car brakes to be fixed.'

'You've got a car?'

'Yeah. Is that bad?'

'No, of course not, it's great.' None of her friends had cars.

She sat up slowly, her movements heavy with disappointment. What was she doing here with him if he was going away? Did he see her just as a pleasant way of passing the time? She'd only just met him, but she'd fallen in deep and she'd thought he felt the same. What an idiot she was. But when she glanced down at him he was looking thoughtful.

'Come with me,' he said at last. 'To Cornwall.'

'What?' Her spirits rose. Maybe he did feel the same as her. Then they sank again. 'My last exam's on Monday. It's not an important one, but ... Can you wait till I've finished?'

'Unfortunately not. I've got a booking in Falmouth on Sunday night. It's a shame because I thought ...' He paused.

'What?'

'Well, Stu can't make it, so first I thought I'd try solo. But then last night you sang for me. You've a great voice, really soft and touching. I've been thinking. You could try doing one or two of the songs with me. We've a few days to practise.'

'Me? Sing with you? I couldn't.' She laughed in disbelief.

'You. Could. Yes.' He tapped her collarbone with his finger in time with his words then smiled at her astonished face. Then he sighed. 'It's a shame about that exam.'

'Yes. Look, I'm really tempted.'

He smiled. 'Don't look so serious, love. It's up to you. I just thought ... well, why don't you come round to the flat tomorrow and we'll talk. And ... other things!'

She kissed him. 'Okay!'

After he'd left, Belle locked the door and lay on her bed for a long while, brooding. Her mind and body thrummed with joy at the memory of Gray. He'd come into her life so suddenly and with such force that he'd torn it apart. She'd listened to many love songs, read many romances, but despite all the boys she'd dated, she'd never experienced the force of love for herself.

But now Gray was moving things along without giving her

time. Cornwall. A wonderful house. Being with him. Singing with him. It was all too tantalizing. Yet the exam, only to test her written English skills, but still. And afterwards she had plans. Parties. The Summer Ball next week. She'd paid the deposit on a backpacking holiday in Wales with the ramblers. Though she'd need to earn some money to pay for that. How long would he be in Cornwall? She should ask.

She was reluctant to say no to the opportunity. Maybe once he left Darbyfield she'd never see him again. Perhaps this was irrational, but she'd always had that fear when people said goodbye. She couldn't afford to follow him down on the train, and she could hardly ask him to come back and fetch her after her exam. Perhaps she could hitch? But he wanted her to learn his lovely songs right away and sing with him on Sunday!

She sighed, turned over and pulled a pillow over her head. Everything about her life here seemed colourless now. Tomorrow's exam. Mediaeval English, for heaven's sake. It meant mugging up paragraphs of Chaucer and writing out modern translations. Boring, boring, where was the magic in that? Whereas Gray filled her heart and mind with life and excitement. *You have to work for what you want,* her teachers had told her.

What had Gray said? *Sometimes the things you want you find you don't want.* Well, she didn't want Mediaeval English and, to be honest, she didn't like any of her studies. The course was a disappointment and she didn't know if she even wanted to come back after the summer holidays. Monday's exam, though, she'd never missed an exam in her life. But Gray, if she turned away this opportunity to be with him, there might never be another. She sat up, blinking, and glanced round the room, seeing it now with his eyes.

Pure, he'd called her. Now she understood. Her teenage posters, the spider plant on the desk, fairies on a flyer for a student production of *A Midsummer Night's Dream* – ordinary middle-class things, like everyone else's. Her eye fell on the photograph of her family. As he'd remarked, they looked perfect, two parents, two daughters, everybody smiling for the camera.

One thing Gray was wrong about, though.

He'd said nothing bad had ever happened to her.

Sometimes she felt that something had. Something that had struck at the roots of her confidence and made her careful, diligent, watchful.

She picked up the photograph and slid it into the drawer of her desk. 'Silverwood,' she said to herself. She was going to Silverwood and she wouldn't be pure any more.

Three

Evening was falling by the time they came to a gap in a line of silver birch trees and Gray nudged the yellow car between rugged stone gateposts. They bumped along a rutted drive with tangled undergrowth on either side. This opened out into a park of rough grass where they passed two goats staring at them over a wooden fence near a tumbledown shed, then Belle caught her breath at the imposing mass of the house before them.

'Gray, it's huge!'

Gray laughed. 'I told you.'

Silverwood was a beautiful, broad-shouldered building of Cornish granite, its particles of quartz sparkling in the waning light. A wisteria still in glorious flower crept across the frontage and here and there sash windows stood raised to welcoming effect. The building must have sustained damage at some time, as if a demolition ball had chipped the top right-hand corner, but Belle didn't have a chance to see properly before they drew close.

A campervan was parked on the gravel area before the house and Gray pulled up alongside it. Belle stared at its gaudy hand-painted decoration of flowers and trees. They stood together for a moment looking around, relishing the tranquil atmosphere, the smell of smoke coiling from Gray's cigarette failing to mask a glorious scent of earth and sap.

Only the sound of a flute or recorder, inexpertly played, broke the peace of the evening, then it stopped abruptly and the bold face of a young man with short brown curly hair appeared at an upstairs window, 'Hey!' he called down, a degree of surprise in his voice.

'Hey!' Gray called back. 'I'm a friend of Francis's. We've come to stay for a bit.'

'Sure. I'm Arlo. Go in round the side. I'll come down.' The young man withdrew.

'How does Arlo fit in?' Belle murmured as they made their way towards the left-hand side of the house.

'No idea. He wasn't here last year, but then people come and go.'

Something dawned on Belle as they turned the corner to see a brick wall with an arched doorway open before them. 'Gray,' she hissed, 'does anyone know we're coming?'

'Well no, they don't have a phone, do they?' he said, offhand.

She stopped dead. 'Surely we can't just turn up,' she said in dismay.

Gray gave an uncertain grin. 'I'm sure it'll be okay,' he said and walked on. She followed reluctantly. His way of dealing with the world was obviously different from hers, and she had little choice but to go along with it.

In other ways Belle was glad of his laid-back nature. The drive down had been fun. Twice in her life she'd been with her father when the family car broke down and he'd treated it as a personal affront, endured with barely suppressed rage that made the rest of the family cower. So, when after an hour that morning, clouds of steam had begun to rise from under the bonnet, forcing Gray to pull into a layby, she was wary. Yet he remained remarkably unbothered. They simply waited for the engine to cool before he hefted a canister out of the boot and poured water into the radiator. Then off they went again. All without fuss. 'It's always happening,' he sighed. 'Costs too much to fix.'

They laughed and sang the rest of the way to Cornwall. At lunchtime they stopped at a pretty village near Bristol to buy bread and cheese and cheap cider from a shop. They sat on a bench by a wide babbling stream to eat, threw the crusts to a family of swans, then crossed by stepping stones to a grassy island where they lay curled up in each other's arms and dozed for a while.

They'd talked on the journey, too, mostly of music and the place where they were going, Silverwood, on the north side of the Helford Estuary.

'It belongs to a guy called Francis Penmartin,' he said. They had met last summer at a folk music festival in Falmouth and Francis had invited him to visit. Gray had ended up staying several weeks, getting inspiration from the landscape, writing songs. 'It's magical and they've a good thing running there.' He spoke in awe of a woman called Rain and her amazing vision for the place, how people lived there together in harmony, away from the evils of the capitalist system. They grew much of their own food and made their own clothes, and there was no television or anything, though there was electricity, and everything was very spiritual and close to the earth. He'd loved it. He could be himself there and nobody bothered him.

Belle listened, spellbound, thinking it sounded like heaven. 'How long are you planning to stay?' she asked him, not daring to say 'we' yet in case it sounded too possessive.

Gray braked suddenly to avoid hitting a dawdling car in front, then the engine strained as he swerved and overtook it. Belle clutched onto her seat. 'I don't know yet. Depends how things go, what turns up.'

She glanced at him, puzzled. 'But don't you have to get back sometime?'

'Maybe. Need to fix up some gigs.' He shrugged and stared at the road ahead. 'Let's have some music, shall we?'

Belle switched on the radio and tinny pop filled the air. She rested her head against the window and watched the passing landscape, lost in her thoughts.

So far Gray had volunteered only vague details about his background and had asked nothing more about hers. They had passed several days in a happy haze of lovemaking and music with not much time given to talking. Only now was Belle finding that he was completely unlike anyone she'd known before.

Most significantly, Gray appeared to live on impulse. He was serious and purposeful about his music, but otherwise he liked to be free of other people's expectations and she both admired this and was shocked by it. All her life she'd been ruled by routine. Neither she nor her sister had been allowed morning lie-ins, even on Sundays. Time had to be usefully employed, her father said, the days plotted out, the trajectory of school, exams, university, work, marriage and children her expected path. Now she was dazzled by a man who she suspected had none of these things in his sights, but who lived for the moment and got by. He was twenty-two, she'd discovered, and she looked up to his superior experience. Unlike any boy she'd dated, he'd had to make his own way in life, to hustle. He wore an air of detachment that intrigued her. Maybe she'd be the one to penetrate it. The thought was thrilling. More worrying were thoughts of her family. She hadn't told her parents what she was doing. She'd write as soon as she could, she decided.

The tinny music was fading and when Belle shook the radio, it died altogether so instead she began to sing one of the songs they'd been practising together. Gray smiled and joined in and soon their voices were weaving together in harmony. With the windows wound down and the wind in their hair, they sang with loud joy as they crossed a humped bridge over a narrow river and entered Cornwall.

Now at Silverwood they passed under the stone arch into an overgrown vegetable garden. A small terrier dog with a high-pitched bark rushed out of a door at the side of the house, his tail wagging in a friendly manner. Gray crouched down with a 'Hey, Figgy boy,' and made a great fuss of him.

'Gray, what a nice surprise!' called a gentle voice and Belle's eyes widened as a wiry woman in dungarees rose stiffly from behind a jungle of plants and flexed her back with a groan.

'Hello, Janey.' Gray straightened and beamed at her. 'It's good to see you.'

'And lovely to see you,' Janey said, with a weary smile. She tossed a handful of weeds onto a pile in a wheelbarrow. 'I'm just finishing out here. The tasks are endless this time of year.' She pushed a lock of greying hair off her narrow, tanned face and fastened her eyes on Belle. 'And who's this?'

'I'm Belle,' Belle said politely. 'I hope it's all right that I've come. Gray said—'

'Yeah, sorry I couldn't let anybody know we were coming,' Gray mumbled.

'Never mind, you're here now.' Janey looked thoughtful then said, 'I'll throw some extra pearl barley in the pot for supper and we've more than enough carrots and potatoes.'

'You are a marvel, Janey.' Gray flashed her a charming smile and she looked pleased.

'Yes, well, rather an untidy one.' She gestured at her grubby clothes and worn rubber boots.

'Janey keeps everything together here,' Gray remarked to Belle.

'I try,' Janey said, with a sigh, 'but it's a challenge. Especially with Rain being away.'

'Oh? Where's she gone?'

'Wales. Some conference or other, I don't know exactly. I can't keep up.'

'A conference? How grand!'

'A pow wow, then. With some guru I've never heard of. You know Rain. She's taken Angel, of course. Angel's her son,' Janey told Belle. 'He's just turned seven and we love him to bits. Listen, why don't you two make yourselves tea. I won't be long.'

Figgy the dog, who'd been sitting panting, leaped up at their approach and led them into the side entrance, through a lobby full of muddy footwear and into a huge old-fashioned kitchen beyond. Here he lapped water from a bowl by the sink then trotted outside again. Belle gasped to see the walls, which were painted a cheerful blue with puffy white clouds. 'So pretty! Like the summer sky.'

'Yeah, nice,' Gray said vaguely. He filled a kettle at a large chipped white sink under a rear window with a view of a mossy courtyard, then set it on a hotplate on the ancient range.

'I can't believe this place. Everything's so old!' Belle said. She peeped under the lid of a saucepan at some unappetizing-looking cold stew.

'That's part of its charm. Pass those cups, will you?' Gray selected one of a row of dusty glass jars on the wooden work-top and shook some of the dried leaves it contained into an old tin teapot. Belle obediently fetched two wonky pottery mugs from the draining board and wiped them dry with a ragged tea towel.

Whilst they waited for the kettle to boil, Arlo, the young man who'd greeted them earlier, sauntered in, his strong bare feet swishing on the flagstones. He grinned at Belle, hitched up his blue cotton trousers and yawned lustily. Since he didn't make polite conversation and Gray's expression was guarded, it was left to Belle to be friendly. 'Hello, I'm Belle and this is Gray,' she said, putting out her hand.

The young man shook it, then he and Gray nodded at one another. *Gray doesn't like him*, Belle noticed.

She had never heard the name Arlo before. He reminded her of pictures of the god Pan she had seen in books, bright-eyed, boyish, muscular and full of vitality. She liked his open, friendly expression and the crisscross pattern of the drawstrings at the neck of his shirt whose whiteness empha-sised his tan. 'Gray,' Arlo said, 'I've heard of you. You're the singer, right?'

Gray raised his eyebrows. 'Right. I was here last year.'

'Yeah. Sorry to have missed you. I was in India. Sirius said your music's amazing.'

'Is Sirius here?'

What odd names everyone had, Belle thought.

'He's somewhere about.'

'Belle sings, too,' Gray said with a grin. 'You should come and hear us in Falmouth tomorrow night.'

'I'd like that. Do you need a flute-player?' Arlo asked eagerly.

'Sorry, no.' Gray's voice was firm, and remembering Arlo's off-pitch efforts earlier, Belle suppressed a smile.

'All right.' Arlo shrugged, apparently not offended.

When Gray poured the tea delicious scents of raspberry and ginger filled the kitchen. As they sipped it, Belle asked Gray, 'Where are we going to sleep?'

'There are lots of bedrooms,' Arlo waved his hand airily

as he drifted out of the kitchen. 'Janey will sort you out. See you later.'

Janey came in shortly afterwards, directed Belle to sit and rest, and swept Gray off, talking non-stop, to locate a suitable bedroom. On their return, Arlo appeared in a pair of wooden clogs and clopped about helping Gray unpack the car, whistling as he went. Belle hung about outside in the fading sunlight, finishing her tea and vaguely wondering about the purpose of four wooden buildings in front, arranged in a horseshoe near the walled garden. They were too big to be sheds and their broken windows and front doors suggested human rather than animal use. Her gaze moved to a hen coop near the goatshed where several chickens pecked about in a run. Nearby, against the boundary hedge, there was a wooden shelter with a corrugated iron roof. Half of it was full of neatly stacked logs and beside these stood the skeleton of a big elderly motorbike, components of which lay strewn over the concrete floor like bits of a jigsaw puzzle.

The air was still warm and swifts swooped about overhead with high-pitched whistles, catching insects. Drifts of cloud tinged with orange and mauve filled the sky. Darkness was gathering under the trees. From somewhere in the house came the faint chatter of a radio. Belle closed her eyes and felt a sense of deep peace. She was with Gray. Silverwood was lovely. Janey seemed friendly. So did Arlo. She would be happy here, she thought.

Just then a distant chugging sound started up. Then a man's deep hearty laugh came from somewhere in the house, and when she looked up she saw a light come on at an upstairs window and a sagging scrap of curtain move across with a rasping sound.

From there her gaze was caught once more by the damaged top-right corner of the building. Belle crossed the drive to take a closer look and saw that an attempt had been made to repair the damage with stone of a darker colour.

A sharp pain as she tripped on something hard. 'Ouch!' She glanced around to see bits of rubble poking up from the undergrowth. It was getting too gloomy to see, but she squinted ahead, trying to make out the bulk of a ruined building stretching at a wide angle from behind the house. She stepped towards it, but barked her shin on a fallen tile, yelped again and retreated.

'Belle?' She heard Gray's voice as she returned to the front of the house and gazed up to see him framed by an open window. 'There you are. Come on up!'

'Hang on.' She stood for a moment, struck by a fragrance of woodsmoke in the air. Where was that coming from, she wondered.

Out of curiosity, she tried entering the house at the front, climbing several steps to a giant pair of double doors, but the bronze doorknobs would not turn. Indeed, they gave every impression of having been stuck for years, so she made her way round through the arch to the side entrance.

The kitchen was full of steam and delicious herby smells coming from the saucepan on the range. Janey was bustling about, preparing vegetables. She had changed into a long cotton skirt and a smock top and was chatting to Arlo, who was setting plates in a pile on the long wooden table.

'. . . and whatever your book says, the protein in goat's milk is more easily digestible. Hello, dear,' she addressed Belle. 'Dinner's on the way.'

'I'll come and help, but I need to find Gray first.'

'No need to do anything on your first evening. You get yourselves settled.'

'You are kind.'

'We're nearly ready, anyway,' Arlo added cheerfully, placing a knife on a board next to an enormous wholemeal loaf as lopsided as the house. Next to it was a slab of butter on a pottery dish and a couple of dusty wine bottles labelled 'Blackberry, '65'. Janey pointed the way to the stairs with her ladle. Belle threw her a grateful smile and slipped away through the far doorway into the shadowy depths of the house.

She walked through a spacious panelled hall smelling heavily of incense. This, she thought, must be from several Indian rugs, pools of bright colour on the scuffed floorboards. Several doors opened off; she'd have to explore later. She went to a broad staircase that rose from the centre of the hall. 'Gray?' she called up, craning, but there was no answer. She started to climb, two steps at a time, and when she reached the first landing called out to him again. Hearing his answering voice she continued upwards.

On the second floor she followed Gray's shouted 'In here!' into a large airy bedroom, not at the front of the house from which he'd summoned her, but at the back. She found him resting barefoot on an old mattress, one of two pushed together on the floor under an open window, arms linked behind his head, staring up at the ceiling where a moth was fluttering around a dimly lit bulb. He grinned at her when she entered. She glanced about, a little disappointed. She'd hoped for a bed at least.

'I suppose we use our sleeping bags,' she said wistfully.

'Ah, fortunately, no,' he said, his face brightening, and scrambled to his feet. 'Janey said something about a linen cupboard.' He squeezed her waist as he passed and brushed her lips with his, then she heard him humming as he cantered down the stairs.

Hands on hips, Belle scanned the room. A dustpan and brush lay near her rucksack and her guitar, so she picked them up and did her best with the dust and cobwebs. Going to the window, she paused in wonder at the sky, streaked with cloud and tinged with shades of gold, crimson and purple. She leaned on the sill to stare, then glanced down and frowned, trying to make sense of what she saw in the gloom. It seemed that two angled wings extended behind the main house, but only the left-hand one of these remained intact. The other was the ruin she'd glimpsed earlier. Naked elevations, burned black, still thrust upwards, casting shadows across fallen masonry half blanketed with undergrowth. Only fragments of the old roof clung to the walls. The sight was deeply unsettling.

After a while she raised her head and peered out at the fields that undulated away into darkness beyond the ruins. It was hard to tell where the land ended and the sky began. And which way, she wondered, was the sea?

Just then a yellow light snapped on in the distance. It

illuminated the four squares of a window and by its glow she could make out the silhouette of a cottage. A pair of high chimneys stood out against a line of trees and smoke coiled from one into the still air. Belle sniffed and once again she could smell a woody fragrance. As she watched, the trim figure of an older woman appeared at the window of the cottage and stood as though gazing out. Belle realized with disquiet that the stranger might be able see her, indeed was staring right at her. Then the woman raised her arms and drew the curtains across in a slow, careful movement.

At the sound of footsteps Belle turned to see Gray, his arms full of bedding. 'This is the best I could find.' The pile landed on the mattresses with a thump and a draught of air.

'Oh dear.' Belle bent to investigate. She shook out a large blue eiderdown that reminded her of her grandmother's, sending up a cloud of feathers. She batted at them, coughing. The quilt was lumpy with age, its colour faded, but it would have to do, as would the pair of sagging pillows. The sheets were singles, though generously cut, and when she spread one across the makeshift bed she noticed that it was labelled in one corner in neat handwritten capitals.

'St Mary's School. Where's that, I wonder?'

Gray shrugged, uninterested. He was sitting, watching her from the windowsill, his fingers playing an invisible guitar.

She spread out the other sheet and a blanket, then knelt to tuck the bedding in around the mattresses and laid the eiderdown on top. Then she joined him at the window, leaning on the sill. Her gaze wandered once again over the ruins. Beside her, Gray picked a roll-up from his breast pocket and lit it.

'What happened down there?' Belle murmured. 'I mean, was there a fire or something?'

'I don't know. Probably.' He drew on his cigarette, then stood up and tweaked her hair. 'Come on, babe. Janey said dinner's nearly ready.'

She straightened and took a final look round the room. It really was very bare, with no pictures on the peeling wallpaper or rugs on the floorboards. At least there was a mantelshelf above the cramped fireplace and they could store clothes in the massive chest of drawers that brooded in one corner. The simple life. What else could she possibly need? She thought of something.

'Where's the bathroom?'

'There's one next door.'

'Is it just for us?'

'Something this place is not short of is bathrooms. Only problem is there's never much hot water.'

'Really?' she said, dismayed.

He laughed. 'It'll be whoever gets there first. Sometimes we have to heat water in the kitchen and bring it upstairs.'

'We're on the second floor, Gray.'

His white teeth flashed in a grin and he hugged her. 'You'd better not get yourself dirty, then,' he murmured in her ear. He kissed her lightly and let her go. 'It's a good thing I'm too hungry to do anything else right now.' He pinched out his cigarette, tucked it in his pocket and followed her downstairs.

In the kitchen, Arlo and two others were already sitting expectantly round the table. As Belle and Gray sat down,

Janey hefted the pan of stew onto the table. 'Do the introduc-
tions, Arlo,' she said. She fetched a tray of baked potatoes out
of the oven and began to dish up.

'Yeah, so this is Gray and this is Belle and, Gray, you said
you know Sirius.' Sirius, handsome and powerfully built with
a blue bandana tied in his grey-threaded hair, nodded as he
studied Belle from his seat at the head of the table but did not
smile. Next to him a slight, fair-skinned girl in her twenties
with long shiny brown hair perched on her chair with her
knees drawn up and toyed with several bangles on her slight
wrist. She wore a disconsolate expression but greeted Belle
politely enough. 'I'm Chouli,' she said in a soft cultured voice.

'Hi, Julie.'

'Chouli. With a *ch*.'

'It's short for Patchouli,' Janey explained. 'Isn't that
right, dear?'

Chouli nodded. Belle, imagining that Patchouli couldn't be
her real name, said, 'I love the pattern on your dress, Chouli.'
The girl looked pleased. She wore a floaty white gauze garment, beautifully embroidered with flowers and birds.

'Thanks. I made it myself.'

'You're so clever. I'm useless at sewing.'

'I'll teach you to embroider if you like.' They smiled at
one another.

Everyone, Belle reflected, glancing about as she split open
her potato, was comfortably clothed in their own individual
style. Sirius's coarsely woven shirt and leather jerkin were
clearly homemade. Arlo wore a plaited bracelet of bright
thread. Belle felt she was the only one who shopped at C&A.

'So what's brought you both down here?' Arlo asked as he cut bread.

Gray contemplated him, then supped a mouthful of his stew, stopped, added salt and began to eat as quickly as the heat of the food allowed.

'Gray asked me to come,' Belle rushed in, thinking Gray a little rude. 'He said it was good here, that you shared a marvellous sense of community.'

'We do,' Chouli said.

'And there's peace and quiet to work on my music,' Gray said finally.

'The vibes are great here,' Arlo said with enthusiasm. 'Rain says it's the ley lines. Any time you want to hook up to play, as I said ...'

'I think that's unlikely,' Gray said shortly and returned to his food. Belle wondered why he'd taken against Arlo. The young man seemed harmless to her.

Apart from Gray's brisk rebuttal, the atmosphere at dinner was tranquil. Janey, Belle thought, looked tired, but given the lines etched into her face then perhaps she always did. Sirius drank deeply of the blackberry wine. Gray poured some for himself and Belle, but when she sipped it she found it acid and the others laughed at her screwed-up face. For dessert, Chouli fetched a dish of strawberries from the draining board, her bangles rattling as she spooned them out into bowls. They were small but tasted sweeter than any that Belle had eaten before.

'We grow them here,' Janey told her. Most of their food, she said, was either grown at Silverwood or bought at local farms and markets. Sirius had driven into Falmouth for odds and ends that very morning. It seemed that their determination to live an alternative life didn't cover motor vehicles. Or electricity, Belle thought, noticing the pendant light.

At the end of the meal, Janey glanced at Sirius then addressed Gray and Belle. 'I think I speak for all of us,' she said, 'when I say, "Welcome to Silverwood". And you are indeed welcome.' They both murmured thanks and she hurried on. 'However, with Rain away, it's left to me to remind you that it's important that everyone here follows the rules. Not that there are many.' Here she stared anxiously at Sirius, who raised his eyebrows and nodded for her to continue.

'We try to live off grid here, Belle, which means we avoid turning on the lights much or using hot water.'

'Not that we ever pay for those,' Sirius murmured with a knowing smile, and Janey looked embarrassed.

'Anyway,' she continued, 'there's a kitty for other stuff and we expect everyone to give what they can. Anyone who's earning pays more. And it's important that we all pull our weight here. It's a great deal of work to keep the house and garden in good order.' Here her voice became plaintive. 'Rain doesn't approve of rotas or anything like that; she says we must work on an outpouring of generosity of spirit. Of course, she's right, but —'

'Some people have more generous spirits than others,' Sirius broke in and gave a deep laugh. His eyes twinkled. 'Poor old Janey. Everyone takes advantage, hey?'

'I'm sure they don't mean to, Sirius.'

Sirius leaned and rubbed Janey's shoulder. 'Never mind, love. What would we do without you, eh?'

'We understand,' Belle said, feeling sorry for Janey. She'd initially wondered if Janey and Sirius were together, but she'd noticed during the meal that it was Chouli who sat closer to him and he was gentler with her than with Janey.

'Thank you, Belle. Another thing is Angel, Rain's son. They're not here at the moment, but they'll be back in a day or two. I'm always having to remind everyone that he's only a child.'

'Oh, come on, old girl,' Sirius groaned. 'There's no need to nanny us. If we're to live a life of freedom away from the world we need to forget all this bourgeois nonsense.'

'I'm talking about drink and hash and ... well, you know the sort of thing.'

Sirius sighed. 'Of course, of course. I'm sure that these people ... Anyway, you do, Gray, you've been here before.'

Gray, who had been staring down at his empty strawberry bowl, gave a good-humoured shrug.

The conversation moved on to other things and Belle, sitting quietly listening, started to get to know the people around the table, thinking how different they were from anyone she'd mixed with before.

Janey asked how everyone had passed their day. Sirius spoke proudly about his painting. A gallery at Penzance had agreed to hang two canvases of his and he'd spent the afternoon framing them. He fetched them, one under each arm, to show everyone, and Janey particularly was fulsome with her praise. They were the size of large tea trays, acrylics, a pair of nudes in artless poses, and Belle squirmed with unease to see that they were of Chouli, though Chouli herself looked bored rather than perturbed. While knowing little of art, Belle judged them lifelike, though the trails of ivy that Sirius had painted into the girl's hair and round the borders of the pictures made them look fussy and a bit sentimental. She asked Sirius what else he liked to paint, and once he saw that she was genuinely interested, he said she was welcome to look sometime.

Janey gently asked Chouli what she'd been doing and Chouli said shyly that she'd written a poem. 'Oh, do read it out. I love your poems,' Janey exclaimed so Chouli, obviously prepared for this request, withdrew a folded piece of paper from a pocket in her skirt and everyone listened respectfully to a rhyme in praise of a meadow full of butterflies that reminded the poet of her childhood. Again, Janey was the first to offer praise and Chouli smiled with glowing eyes. Belle, brought up on a diet of Keats and Tennyson, wasn't sure what to say apart from that it was 'touching' and might make a good song.

After this Arlo and Janey offered accounts of how they'd passed the day. Arlo had been tinkering with the motorbike and writing what he called an 'artistic manifesto' which he promised to share when it was finished. Janey had set up a stall on the main road selling homegrown flowers and strawberries to passers-by, which had made one pound and three shillings for the kitty. Belle understood that this sharing of their days was part of the routine at Silverwood and felt a prickle of alarm at joining in herself. Fortunately, it fell to Gray to describe their journey down, which he did with amusing self-deprecation.

Once the washing-up was done, she and Gray made their excuses and trudged wearily upstairs. Before she edged the thin curtain along its wire, Belle paused at the open window, staring out at the night and breathing in new scents borne in on the breeze. Gray came and stood behind her, snaking his arms round her waist.

'Who lives there?' she asked, pointing to the cottage where a single upstairs light shone out.

'A friend of Francis's. I don't know much about her.'

'And where's the sea?' she asked. He pointed towards the dark distance.

'Can we go and find it tomorrow?'

'Yeah, we can,' he whispered. She shivered with pleasure at his soft warm breath on her neck, then turned in his arms to face him.

'It's perfect here,' she said. 'Everyone's so ... welcoming. Thank you for bringing me.'

'I knew you'd like it.'

'The man who invited you here in the first place ... ?'

'Francis Penmartin?'

'Yes. Where was he tonight?'

'Francis doesn't live here. He just visits occasionally. Otherwise, people come and go. I hadn't met what's his name, Arlo, before, or Chouli, but Janey and Sirius are here all the time and so usually are Rain and her son.'

'Janey's such a sweet woman.'

'She is, yes.'

'Why don't you like Arlo?'

'Did I say that?'

'I guessed.'

'I don't not like him, just … he's a bit out of it.'

This puzzled Belle, but she couldn't get Gray to pinpoint what he meant. She sensed that he wasn't interested in other people in the way that she was. For a moment her spirits faltered. Perhaps she'd taken on too much with him. Still, she did know that she loved the warm comfort of his arms around her. She pulled him down beside her and snuggled up close to him. 'I think I'm going to love Silverwood,' she whispered.

'I thought you would.' She could see his eyes glinting in the darkness and smiled as he began to sing quietly, 'Silverwood, Silverwood,' and again she experienced that bolt of recognition.

Later, as she was drifting off to sleep, she remembered why.

~

It had been three or four years ago, a wintry Sunday, and Belle was blissfully alone in the house, having refused to go out to lunch at the home of one of her father's teaching colleagues, her excuse being that she had too much homework. She'd grilled cheese on toast, then turned on the electric fire and settled with the plate in her father's armchair. A pile of choral music belonging to her mother lay at eye level on a nearby shelf. Looking closely, she noticed a small book with a coloured spine hidden under it. Curious, she eased it out. It was a guidebook about Cornwall and she turned the pages as she munched, looking at the black-and-white photographs of beaches, quaint fishing harbours and ruined engine houses. There was a map glued into the book at the back and when she started to unfold it, a scrap of card fell out onto her lap. She picked the card up, dusted off crumbs and turned it over.

It was a black-and-white snapshot of a young woman standing by a jagged black rock on a sandy beach. She was bare-legged and carried a jolly-looking infant in gingham knickers and a mob cap. The baby, she thought, was possibly herself, but the woman definitely wasn't Mum or Aunt Avril or, indeed, anyone she recognized.

There was a faint pencil scrawl on the back: 'Kynance Cove, 1948'. She'd have been eighteen months that summer. Belle stared at the picture a moment longer then knitted her brows and put it aside, turning her attention to the book with renewed interest. Why was it in the house? She was sure she'd never been to Cornwall and her parents had never mentioned doing so. 'Kynance Cove' was listed in the index and she turned to the page referenced and read the description. It was one of the best-known Cornish beauty spots, she learned, with 'serpentine rocks that take their name from their resemblance in gloss and colouring to snakeskin'. There was a photograph of the cove opposite the text and Belle gazed at it longingly. With those jagged rocks it was wilder and more characterful than any of the gentle sandy beaches she'd visited on family holidays in Dorset.

She finished her toast then flipped to the map inside the back of the book, finding the cove at the southernmost point of the county. Cornwall, she mused, looked like a pair of giant jaws – quite sinister – with Land's End at the tip of the upper one and Kynance on the lower. Just north from Kynance someone had made a pencil dot near Falmouth and labelled it with one word, something like 'Silverwood'. But there was no mention of Silverwood in the index. Perhaps it was too small a place. After Belle refolded the map she turned to the front of the book and was surprised to see that the title page had been torn out – there was only a ragged remnant. How odd.

Another thought struck her. Rising, she went to a bookcase on the other side of the room and pulled out the oldest and scruffiest of the family photo albums. She knew there was only a single photograph of her as a tiny baby before the toddler pictures began. There it was. She was lying in a cot, the lens of the camera reflected in the sheen of her large dark eyes. She'd once pointed out that there were many more pictures of her sister Jackie at the same age and had been slightly mollified by her father's reply, 'We didn't have a camera when you were born. Someone else took that one and gave it to us.' Belle compared the picture of her as a newborn to the older baby in the beach photograph, then examined later photographs of herself in the album. The same whorl of dark hair, high forehead and rosebud mouth. Surely the infant on the beach was herself, she concluded.

Later, when her parents and sister returned, her father good-humoured after a well-cooked roast dinner, she showed them the photograph she had found and asked who the woman was. Her father's joviality disappeared in an instant. 'Where did you find that?' he snapped. 'Have you been snooping about?' Stunned and confused, she explained how she had come across the guidebook, while her mother examined the print with an expression of quiet distress.

From across the room Jackie's eyes met Belle's, telegraphing the message *Now you're for it* before she disappeared upstairs, leaving Belle to the mercy of their father's change of mood.

'I don't think Belle's done anything wrong, dear,' her mother said gently.

Her father sighed. He sat down in his chair by the fire, passed his fingers through his sleek hair and managed to compose himself. 'We met some friends on the beach there, didn't we, Jill? I can't remember their names. The wife was very keen on you, Belle, as you can see.'

'Yes, that's it,' Belle's mother said quickly. 'I can't remember who they were either.'

Her parents glanced at one another briefly.

'I didn't know we'd been to Cornwall,' Belle said hastily to cover the silence.

'Well, we did. A short holiday. We were lucky with the weather, I seem to remember. Now if you don't mind, I'd like a few minutes' peace to sit and read the paper.'

And so the matter was closed.

But not quite. When no one was looking, Belle tucked the photograph into her jeans pocket and escaped upstairs to her room. She took down the cardboard treasure box she kept on the top shelf of her wardrobe. It contained, among other things, her secret diary, a Valentine's card whose sender she'd never discovered, and a silver christening bracelet which she didn't dare confess to her parents she'd accidentally bent out of shape. She added the photograph to the pile in the box then picked up the bracelet. She'd damaged it years ago when she'd tried to adjust it to fit onto her wrist. There were no photographs of her christening in the album downstairs, she realized, only of her sister's.

Belle returned the bracelet to the box and the box to its hiding place then sat on the bed feeling troubled and unsettled.

From time to time over the past few years she'd taken out that photograph and studied it. The guidebook, however, mysteriously vanished.

She'd decided to forget the matter, not to investigate further. Instead she had striven to be the hard-working elder daughter who liked to please and, despite the occasional teenage rebellion, had largely managed to do so. But sometimes she felt on edge, as though she were walking a tightrope over an abyss, a tightrope that was fraying and might one day break, sending her tumbling into the unknown.

Beside her, Gray stirred in the darkness. 'Are you awake? I've remembered where I read the name Silverwood before,' she whispered and told him.

'That's weird,' he sighed and she had to agree, but he meant for a different reason. 'Silverwood shouldn't be on a map. It's too mysterious, like the lost island of Atlantis or Shangri-la.'

Four

Belle woke late the following morning to the sound of Gray's guitar. He was sitting on the top stair outside their bedroom, already dressed and quietly working through his songs for the evening. She lay half dozing in the warm gloom, listening to him sing and play, knowing she ought to get up, too, but she'd slept deeply last night after the long journey and their lovemaking and was still pleasantly tired. After a while the room began to warm up in the morning sun. Gray went downstairs in search of breakfast and she pushed back the bedclothes and reached for her jeans, which lay where she'd stepped out of them the night before like the shed skin of her old life.

She found Gray in the cool of the kitchen pouring deliciously scented coffee from an earthenware pot. He smiled at her dreamily, and passed her a brimming mug, then began to saw at the loaf of last night's homemade bread.

'Is there any milk?' she asked.

'If you like goat. Personally, I don't.'

The squat rusty fridge hummed in a corner, plugged into an overloaded wall socket. Belle opened it, took a bottle of milk from the door and sniffed at the contents tentatively, then put it back, deciding to have her coffee black. She glanced with curiosity at several jars and plastic pots marked 'yoghurt', 'yeast' and 'vegetable stock' in black pen. No meat and nothing looked very appetizing. Bottles of homemade beer and white wine were packed in round them, which she had to move to ease the butter out. The butter, at least, smelled as though it had come from a cow.

'We'll sit outside,' Gray called and she followed him through a scullery containing an elderly twin tub – that must have been the noise she'd heard the previous evening – out to a sunny courtyard behind the house. There a wooden table and chairs were arranged on the cracked flagstones by a line of drying clothes. Nearby Chouli lay stretched out on a rickety sunbed, her face half-hidden by an enormous pair of sunglasses, her dress rolled up above her knees. A white garment she'd been embroidering lay abandoned by her side.

'Hey, d'you mind if we join you?' Gray asked.

Chouli raised her sunglasses briefly and blinked. 'Go ahead.' They settled themselves at the table with their breakfast. Belle felt self-conscious talking to Gray while Chouli was there listening and was relieved when after a few moments Chouli batted at a bee that was bothering her, then got up and stalked off inside, muttering something about finding Sirius.

'Did we upset her?' Belle asked anxiously. Gray merely shrugged.

'Shall we practise your songs?' he asked after they finished eating and when Belle nodded, went off to fetch his guitar. However, he was delayed in the kitchen by Janey for Belle heard the rhythm of their voices. She was glad to be able to finish her coffee in peace.

Really, on a beautiful summer's day like today, this place was perfect, she thought, shading her eyes to look across the courtyard. It was enclosed on two sides by the wings of the house, the ruined one to the right, the entire wing to the left. She saw that it was only the upper floors of the latter that were joined to the main house, forming a bridge. If she walked underneath it was probable that she would reach the vegetable garden and the side door to the kitchen that acted as the main entrance to the house. Janey had told her last night that the wing itself was blocked off. No one had used it for years.

Before her, where the courtyard ended, lay an expanse of rough pasture and, in the distance, a fence and trees. Beyond that, she knew, were fields and the cottage she'd seen last night from their attic. And then maybe the sea? Or was it still the river estuary here? Gulls flew skirling overhead and Belle longed to explore. But Gray had returned and was pulling up his chair beside her, slipping the strap of his guitar over his head. He grinned at her, a soft expression in his eyes, and began to play. She had no trouble coming in to sing at the right time and the words came naturally to her. Even though she had only three songs to sing with him, she was still a little nervous for she'd rarely performed in public. Guitar exams were bad enough.

She didn't have long to wait to see the sea. Early in the afternoon a breeze got up and puffs of cotton wool cloud raced across a sky of depthless blue. Belle trailed behind Gray and Sirius along a narrow path that ran between hedges, listening to snatches of their conversation, which was about music, singers and groups she hadn't heard of. She didn't mind, though. She was feeling at home already, wearing a light, floaty dress that Chouli had lent her and straw sandals, though she was beginning to regret these as the ruts in the path turned to mud when they passed into shadow under the trees and there was some unpleasant evidence that cows had walked this way.

Ahead was the cottage, and as they drew near, Belle studied it with interest. It was a plain, white-painted house with tall chimneys, approached on its other side by a narrow lane. The tiles on the roof were covered with yellow lichen and window boxes on the downstairs sills were heaped with bright petunias. Washing danced in the breeze on a line in the rocky fenced garden and a black and white cat sat on the doorstep licking its paw.

'Is it right that a friend of Francis's lives there?' she asked Sirius as they left it behind, the path starting to turn steeply downhill.

'Mrs Kitto. A very old pal of Francis's. Shall we say she keeps an eye on us.' Sirius had a dramatic way of speaking to her, emphasizing words unnecessarily. He didn't do it with Gray or Arlo and it felt patronizing.

Belle laughed nervously. 'That sounds a bit sinister.'

He rolled his eyes. 'Oh, very sinister. If there's anything

wrong we're supposed to go to her. More often it's the other way round. She's always complaining about something – that we're making too much noise or that Figgy chases her effing moggy.'

'Isn't Francis in charge?'

'Yes, but he lives in Falmouth. You might see him tonight at your happening.'

'You're coming, I hope,' Gray said.

'Wouldn't miss it for the world, dear boy. I think Chouli and Arlo will be there too. Not Janey, though. There's always something she wants to do here.' Belle had noticed that Sirius wasn't very kind to Janey.

'That's a shame. Can't we persuade her?'

'You can try.'

Although he'd answered her questions readily enough, in some ways Sirius explained little. An undercurrent flowed beneath his words. Belle was curious about Francis and why he didn't live in his own house, and she was intrigued by the relationships between the different inhabitants of Silverwood. She glanced at Gray, who appeared his usual good-humoured self. Again it struck her that such matters had no interest for him. He was wrapped up in his music – and, she felt with a leap of happiness, in her. The smile he flashed her now was as warm as ever.

The path down turned steeper and Gray stretched out his hand to take hers and help her over the rough bits in her unsuitable shoes. The air was warm and smelled of coconut from the yellow gorse bushes that bordered the route.

At the bottom of the valley they came to an unusually

wide lane, made up for vehicles. They turned right onto this and soon, with a leap of pleasure, Belle could see the estuary ahead, a vast sheet of twinkling dark blue. Dropping Gray's hand in excitement, she gathered up her skirts and broke into a run.

The lane passed down between trees and undergrowth and then opened out onto a shingled beach where water lapped against a stone-slabbed slipway. The tide was in and several sailing dinghies bobbed at anchor offshore. Belle took off her shoes, tied a knot in her dress and danced over the gritty sand to the water, thrilling to the breeze and the gentle movement of the waves. The chill of the sea when she paddled in was a shock, but it quickly felt refreshing. She turned to see that Sirius and Gray were still engaged in conversation by the slipway where she'd left her shoes. She began to splash along the shoreline, stopping occasionally to pick up a shell or pretty pebble. When a gust of wind caught her hair, she raised her head to smooth it back and gazed about.

The hillside rising on either side of the cove was green and lush with tangled undergrowth, but something caught her attention. On a headland the remains of a low grey concrete lookout point crouched above the sea. Her eyes narrowed. It was a remnant of the war, she knew, but were military operations also responsible for the strips of pocked concrete that still covered the further parts of the beach? The place was deserted at present apart from herself and her companions, but the wide lane that had led them here, the pillbox, the stretches of concrete, suggested that armed forces, boats and military vehicles had once passed this way.

Now only ruins and ghosts were left, and the melancholic sound of gulls crying in the wind. The war: part of her parents' world. It had ended more than twenty years ago, was ancient history to her generation. Her father often complained that Belle and Jackie had no idea how lucky they were being brought up without the terror, disruption and restrictions that had blighted his life. She could just about remember Mum needing her ration book when she went to the butcher's, but that was all.

It had seemed paradoxical that her father, who'd experienced the war, now took against people who marched in protest against nuclear weapons. 'Long-haired layabouts,' he'd growl, 'getting in the way of ordinary folks' business and wasting police time. The atomic bombs falling on Japan brought the war to an end, people forget that.' Poor Dad; so many things made him angry. But the world had moved on and it was the turn of her generation to shape the future. Still, Belle felt a sudden rush of guilt. She ought to ring home sometime or write and explain where she had gone. Her mother wrote to her regularly at university about matters such as Jackie's new black-patent party shoes or the next-door neighbour's bronchitis and asking anxiously after Belle's health, and Belle always telephoned them once a week from the porter's lodge to tell them that she was working hard and eating sensibly. They'd be worried if in a few days' time they hadn't heard from her.

A gasp and a splash beside her made her turn, laughing, to see Gray hopping about, his jeans rolled up, grimacing at the cold water. Once he'd recovered, he drew her to him.

He smelled of salt and smoke. She felt herself melt into his embrace and all her sombre thoughts flew away.

The trouble with the downhill walk to the beach was that it meant a long climb back. Sirius, bulky and unfit, breathed heavily and needed frequent rests, and since he and Gray were still in conversation and Gray kept stopping to wait for him, Belle found herself far ahead. When she reached the cottage there was a woman in the garden unpegging the washing. Belle saw immediately that hers was the trim figure she'd seen silhouetted at the backlit window the evening before. What had Sirius said her name was? Something unusual. The woman caught Belle's eye and stared at her, then a frown crossed her face. She laid an armful of clothes onto a pile in a wicker basket, smoothed her print cotton dress and walked across to speak to Belle over the picket gate.

'We haven't met before, have we?' the woman said. 'Are you staying at Silverwood?' She looked Belle up and down with a bright-eyed gaze. Her grey hair was cropped short with no pretension to fashion, but it suited her small features and round face. It was a characterful face and her eyes were shrewd. She was well spoken and held herself very upright.

'Yes, I am,' Belle said warily, remembering what Sirius had said about this woman being difficult. 'We only arrived yesterday. I'm Belle.'

'Belle. That's a pretty name.' The woman clutched the palings of the gate, seemingly unable to take her eyes off her. 'I'm Mrs Sylvia Kitto.' After a moment she said, 'And your other name?'

'My surname? Johnson.'

'Belle Johnson.' Her hand flew to her mouth. 'Goodness. Do you come from round here, may I ask?'

'N ... no. I live in Surrey, though I'm at Darbyfield University.' She was finding Mrs Kitto's behaviour odd. 'It's the first time I've been to Cornwall.' She stopped and corrected herself. 'Well, the first time I remember. Do you know a beach called Kynance Cove?'

'Of course.' She sounded cautious. 'It's a lovely place and not far from here. Why?'

'Apparently I went there as a baby.'

'As a baby,' Mrs Kitto repeated faintly. 'So that would be ... when?'

'Nineteen forty-eight.'

'Ah. That's very interesting.' Mrs Kitto stared again at Belle, then broke her gaze, apologizing for appearing rude. 'Kynance is beautiful, but like many parts of the coast, there can be strong currents.'

'I'd like to go some time.'

At that moment they were interrupted by the arrival of the others. Sirius was puffing hard, red-faced from the effort of climbing, but Gray was hardly ruffled. Belle noticed at once how Mrs Kitto's mood changed. She'd been friendly to Belle, if a little odd, but at the sight of Sirius she crossed her arms tightly and her manner turned chilly. Sirius ignored her and toiled on ahead. Gray nodded and smiled, then walked on a short way before waiting for Belle to catch up.

'It's nice to meet you, Mrs Kitto,' Belle said, turning to go. 'Goodbye.'

'Belle?' She paused and looked back. Mrs Kitto wore a concerned expression. 'Come and see me properly sometime. I can tell you about Kynance Cove and other good places to visit.' She sounded eager. 'If you like, that is.'

'Thank you,' Belle murmured. 'I'll come.'

She continued on her way, puzzled. Mrs Kitto seemed nice enough but still, there was something about her that Belle couldn't put her finger on. The invitation had not, she thought, been a simple act of friendliness. There was something else she'd seen in the older lady's eyes. It was recognition.

That night the sound of an owl awoke her and as she lay listening, she was visited by another memory, one older than last night's, a memory she'd tried to suppress.

It had been just after Easter at home in Surrey, her sixteenth birthday. Belle had finished the last crumbs of a chocolate egg in her bedroom while listening to a single on her new gramophone. She remembered the song clearly: it was called 'Island of Dreams'. Later, she was going to the cinema with some pals from school to see *Summer Holiday* for the second time, starring fresh-faced Cliff Richard, and then on to a club, though her parents didn't know about that bit. She'd promised to be home by ten, and if she managed to appear sober that was the only thing that mattered.

She was lying on her back on the rug, her head resting on a cushion, her feet against the bed, singing along to The Springfields using a hairbrush as a microphone. She loved singing and enjoyed her guitar lessons. Maybe one day she'd play in a band.

It was a sunny day and the window was open. The school timetable pinned to her noticeboard fluttered in the breeze. The song faded and as she pushed herself up to restart the record, she heard the thud of the front door closing below. Her own door clicked open in the draught and she froze as the sound of voices reached her from the hallway. One of them was Aunt Avril's unmistakable piercing tones.

She lowered the needle and The Springfields' bright notes blotted out the sound. One more listen, she thought, flopping down on the bed, and she'd go and say hello. She liked Avril, who was her Mum's lively older sister, while being wary of her sharp eye. If Belle's shoelace was undone or she had a spot on her nose, Aunt Avril would alert her to the fact. She probably thought she was being kind. Perhaps it was her and older Uncle Vic having lived in the Far East with servants and no children that made her so exacting. Their house reflected this – full of ornaments from their travels that Belle and Jackie were not allowed to touch.

Belle's bedroom was at the back of the house and this time when the record ended, the voices floated up from the garden.

'Why is it young people like that frightful racket?' Aunt Avril was saying.

'Some of it's quite tuneful,' her mother replied in her soft voice. Belle rose and went to the window, intending to call hello. The women were standing near the house, Jill's dark brown head touching Avril's fair one as they admired the magnolia tree coming into luscious pink and white bloom.

'So, sweet sixteen, eh?' Aunt Avril said clearly. 'She's a lovely girl, Jill. A credit to you.'

'Do you think so?'

'Yes, really. Considering that—'

'Shh, Avril!' Her mother's head snapped up. She shaded her eyes to stare up at Belle's window. Just in time Belle backed out of view, but there was no stopping her aunt.

'You mean you haven't told her?' Aunt Avril lowered her voice, but not by much.

'For heaven's sake, Avril,' said her mother. Then something inaudible. Belle crept back to the window, straining to hear.

'Oh, Jill, does he?' Aunt Avril's whisper was clear. 'Surely after all these years . . .' The women drifted away down the garden out of earshot.

Belle slid to the floor. What did their words mean? Something was wrong, she gauged that much, but what it was she couldn't imagine.

She lay curled up on the bed for a while, trying to make sense of what she'd heard, but she couldn't. She must have been mistaken, she thought eventually, sitting up. They were an ordinary family really. Her father was strict and irritable and her mother wouldn't let her wear make-up, but everyone she knew complained about their parents. Her sister Jackie, at eleven, was too young to be a useful companion while being annoyingly blonde and blue-eyed like her pretty aunt. Sometimes Belle argued with her parents, stomped around and sulked when told what to do and was rude to her sister. But if anyone were to ask – which they never had – whether her family loved her, the answer would have been a resounding 'of course'.

Yet Aunt Avril, with a few careless words, had sent her

confidence tumbling. For a week or two after that, Belle brooded on what she'd heard, but she could not pluck up sufficient courage to ask her mother what they'd been talking about. In the end she tamped the matter down in her mind and tried to forget it. If there was a secret to be uncovered then she didn't want to know about it.

It was funny, Belle thought now, lying in the darkness next to the sleeping Gray, but she'd never connected the two memories before. There was something about the atmosphere of Silverwood that made her wonder if they were related. And why had 'Silverwood' been pencilled onto a map in an old guidebook? It would suggest that something important happened here a long time ago.

Five

Late September 1939

Imogen Lockhart found the train journey to Cornwall with her small charges long and arduous. The younger boy, Michael, dwarfed by an oversized blazer, had cried at being parted from his mother who was waving from the platform as the smart brown and cream carriages of the Riviera Express pulled out of Paddington. His older brother, Nicholas, was slumped in his seat, pale and listless. Given the general air of uncertainty since the outbreak of war, their distress was understandable and both boys were still thin and scabby from measles. They had been handed into the care of a stranger and even Imogen, a friendly young woman with the energy and colouring of a young lioness, struggled to amuse them.

It had taken lunch in the restaurant car to cheer them up, and many games of Hangman, then Beetle, which had annoyed the other passengers in their compartment because

Michael shrieked with excitement whenever he threw a six and could therefore add a leg to his hand-drawn insect. Finally the die tumbled through a hole at the back of the seat and could not be extracted, which led to a noisy squabble between the brothers as to whose fault it was.

To top it all they were delayed at Exeter for a whole hour owing to an accident further down the line. Only after Plymouth did the boys' spirits rise again, when Imogen lowered the window as the train crossed the bridge over the Tamar with a long joyful whistle, and they counted the sailing boats spread like butterflies across the wide expanse of the estuary and smelled the fresh scent of the sea.

As they clattered through Cornwall the boys parroted the strange names of the stations they passed through and kept asking Imogen how long it would be before they reached Truro. Their excitement was infectious and Imogen, too, gazed out with pleasure at the rough fields, hedges and moorland and the slate-roofed houses. She'd never travelled so far southwest before. At Truro she was to hand the children over to a teacher from St Mary's School and then she'd be free. She would stay in the city overnight and return to London by the morning train.

'The Fanshawe-Hicks boys are ten and eight years old,' Mrs Arnold from Mother's Little Helpers had trilled down the telephone. She had one of those loud, upper-class voices bred from generations of calling 'tally-ho' across the English countryside. 'They're an old Norfolk family, though this branch lives in Hampstead. Major F-H is away with his unit and his wife feels unable to leave her ailing mother in order to take the boys down to Cornwall where their prep school's been evacuated. They couldn't travel with the main party because of illness.'

'How far into Cornwall are we talking about?'

'The school's somewhere called Silverwood, near Falmouth, on the Helford Estuary, but a master from the school will relieve you of the little brutes at Truro. Mrs F-H will pay for you to stay somewhere inexpensive, then you'll have a few hours in the morning to look round the city before you hop back on the train. I hear it has an attractive cathedral.'

'I'll do it.' Imogen wasn't bothered about the cathedral, but she liked small boys, having been brought up with her cousins who had lived close to the Lockharts in a rambling house in the Hertfordshire countryside. She was an only child and Uncle Geoffrey and Aunt Verity's three boys – she was the same age as the middle one – had been glorious fun after the claustrophobic atmosphere of her own home. Her parents, her father an academic, her mother a librarian, had met and married in their late thirties and after Imogen was born and the whole nasty business of nappies and feeding was out of the way, her mother had turned to writing crime fiction. She was delighted whenever her younger sister Verity said she'd have Imogen, who would, Verity said, 'civilize the boys'. The boys' behaviour had not improved in the least in the company of their girl cousin. Instead Imogen had quickly become a tomboy who enjoyed climbing trees, making dens and wearing shorts instead of dresses.

These idylls became less regular when, at the age of twelve, she'd been packed off to a strict boarding school where Imogen's father complained that she learned little except how to ask awkward questions. Now, aged twenty, still grieving for her dear father who had died two years ago from an allergic reaction to a bee sting, and her mother now a successful but reclusive author, Imogen had entered a period of aimlessness, never settling to a job for longer than it took for another to appeal to her. Working for the Mother's Little Helpers Agency, run by Mrs Arnold, was something she stuck at because she liked the variety and unexpectedness of the tasks. One day she might be making cardboard pirate hats for a children's birthday party, the next she'd be entertaining a mischievous pair of toddlers while their mother was in hospital. Mrs Arnold was good at making the best of her girls' talents. A train ride to Cornwall with two young boys couldn't be too painful, Imogen had concluded.

It was late afternoon when the train slowed to a halt at Truro with a shriek of brakes and an acrid stink of burning rubber. Imogen passed down the boys' gas masks and satchels from the luggage rack – their trunks had been sent ahead – brushed crumbs from Michael's blazer and straightened Nicholas's tie before whispering, 'Be brave' and shepherding them down from the train.

For a moment they stood bewildered on the platform, then a stocky, amiable-looking young man in a tweed suit with leather patches on the elbows materialized from a cloud of steam like an eccentric saint and strode purposefully towards them, a beatific smile of greeting on his chubby face.

'Miss Lockhart, I presume?' he said, tipping his hat.

'That's right.' Imogen liked him at once.

'I'm Ned Thorpe, the boys' housemaster at St Mary's. You

must have had quite a journey. Ah, Fanshawe-Hicks Major, sir. We meet again. And this young fellow must be your brother Michael. Shake paws?'

He bent to offer little Michael his hand with a solemn expression, but his eyes twinkled, which made Imogen warm to him. 'I'm head of Brooke House, Michael, which as you probably know is yours and your brother's, so we'll be seeing a lot of one another.' Michael managed to shake Mr Thorpe's hand but was lost for words and his vulnerable expression tugged at Imogen's heartstrings.

'They're tired, poor dears,' she said. 'I'm afraid we've kept you waiting. The train ahead came off the line apparently.'

'So I was told, but I had a new Miss Christie novel with me so I assure you I was happy.'

'Oh,' Imogen brightened. 'Do you like whodunnits? My mother writes them. Have you heard of Norah Gentles?'

'I have, but I've never read one. I must look 'em out. Now, have you your tickets handy?'

Ned took the tickets and Imogen's small suitcase from her so that she could hold the boys' hands. They stuck close to his capable figure as he forged a way out onto the busy station concourse where parents were marshalling children, elderly ladies were dawdling and porters loading cases into taxis. Ned stepped out of the path of a luggage trolley and drew Imogen and the boys to a quiet corner.

'I suppose I should say goodbye now,' Imogen said, 'unless you can drop me at my hotel. It's the Godolphin. Do you know it?' The boys stared up at her with dismay. Michael made an odd noise in his throat and squeezed her hand tightly.

'Ah,' Ned said sheepishly. 'I could, but I was hoping we might have a little talk first.' He looked uncertain then continued. 'You see, there's something I'm supposed to ask you, Miss Lockhart, that is, if I liked the look of you ... which I do, of course.' Here he had the grace to blush. 'It's a special request.'

'What sort of request?' she said suspiciously.

He glanced at his watch then said, 'I'll tell you what, let's discuss the matter over tea. You boys will be hungry, no doubt?'

He led them to a crowded café where they secured the last free table and while the boys drank milk and wolfed down saffron buns, Imogen sipped tea and he explained.

'Regrettably our matron, Miss Edgecumbe, has just been taken to hospital with an attack of something.'

'I'm sorry to hear that.'

'The thing is, we don't have anyone suitable to manage the sickbay while she's away and the head wondered whether you might stand in until we know what's happening. It's likely to be only for a day or two, we imagine.'

'I'm not a nurse, Mr Thorpe.'

'No, but the head was speaking to the boys' mother on the telephone this morning and she recommended the agency you're with and said you have first-aid training and appeared to be very capable. Which no doubt you are!' Again that charming smile, but he rolled his eyes humorously and she couldn't stop herself smiling back.

'I'm very flattered, but the training I have is minimal. There was a rubber doll that we breathed into and I can fit a good sling, but that's about it.'

'I'm sure that won't matter. We have only three boys in the sickbay at present and there's nothing seriously wrong with any of them. In fact, one, I'm sure, is faking it. It's the inter-house cross-country run tomorrow, you see.'

'I don't blame him then,' Imogen laughed.

'There you are! You have the touch of sympathy he'll need. And a woman's always best at dealing with homesickness, I find.' He glanced at Michael as he said this. 'Not that we'll be having any of that, Fanshaw-Hicks Minor,' he said sternly and Michael returned a fearful look.

'Where's your handkerchief, Michael,' Imogen said gently. 'You've grown a milk moustache.'

Michael wiped the back of his hand across his mouth and Imogen sighed.

They were nice boys, these two, but it was hard on Michael starting at the school so far away from home. His mother could hardly dash down to Cornwall to visit at a moment's notice, especially with a war on. His pleading eyes were on her now, as though waiting for guidance.

'I suppose you'd like me to stay,' she said to him and he nodded, his scabby cheeks flushing with colour.

'All right,' she told Mr Thorpe. 'I'll square it with the agency in the morning.'

'That's marvellous. Thank you so much. The head will be relieved and I'll find myself in good odour.'

'I'm happy to hear that,' she said teasingly, then remem-bered. 'Blow. We should telephone the hotel. Oh, and cancel my railway ticket.'

'I can do all that for you now if you'll wait here,' he said, rising, and she gave him the return ticket. 'The hotel's the Godolphin, you say? I shouldn't be long.' And he went off to sort matters out.

'So I'll be coming with you to the school,' she told the boys.

'That's ripping,' Nicholas said solemnly. 'I won't mind being sick if you're the matron. The old one is nice but she's awfully strict.'

Michael jumped up and hugged her, smiling all over his face.

'England, home and safety,' Ned cried as the elderly black Hillman car pulled up outside the school. They climbed out. It was after six and the crisp autumn air rang with the sound of children's voices.

Imogen gazed up in admiration at the broad-shouldered grandeur of Silverwood House. It was rather beautiful with the shards of quartz embedded in its pale granite stone twinkling like tiny stars in the fading light. Its name, however, must have come from the line of silver birch trees they'd passed by the gate.

A movement caught her eye and she broke into a smile, for now she saw that there were little faces at some of the windows.

Suddenly, as though at some signal, the double doors at the front flew inwards and Imogen straightened as three older boys in uniform sauntered out and down the steps. They approached with confidence and introduced themselves to Imogen politely, each shaking her hand. At Ned Thorpe's command they gathered up Nicholas and Michael, together with satchels and gas masks, and escorted them indoors. Ned followed them carrying Imogen's case, while Imogen hesitated on the gravel forecourt to take in more of her surroundings. Sharp gusts of breeze tossed the canopy of restless beeches and oaks that sheltered the park and a solitary small plane with British markings growled far overhead. Otherwise all was tranquil. Nearly a month had passed since hostilities had been declared, but apart from the plane in the sky and the sandbags stacked against the house, it was difficult to believe that a war was on.

During the car journey she'd learned from Ned that in peacetime St Mary's Prep School was based near Sevenoaks in Kent. Francis Penmartin, the owner of Silverwood House, was an old boy. Over the summer, when war became a certainty and Kent a likely target of enemy bombing, he and the head had executed a long-hatched evacuation plan. It had been a rush to convert opulently furnished bedrooms and shabby attics to plain, clean dormitories. A grand drawing room had been cleared of sofas and mahogany bookcases in order to accommodate eighty boys and a dozen staff for assemblies and school productions, and the long dining room was now rammed with trestle tables and benches, the original ancestral table pushed to one end from where the masters could survey the pupils as they ate. The head's wife had taken charge of hiring domestic staff and the Herculean task of making blackout curtains for the windows of the entire house. Ned himself had cut short a walking holiday in the Swiss Alps to help organize the building of wooden cabins in the grounds as extra classrooms and the transfer of desks, beds, blackboards and the like from the old school to the new. The school's usual premises in Kent was down on a list to become a military billet.

'The move's been a success, on the whole,' Ned had said cheerfully on the winding road to Silverwood, swerving to avoid an army lorry coming in the other direction. 'We've no proper games pitches yet, and the groundsman and his assistant decided to stay put in Kent, but the boys have taken to the sea air. Indeed, rather too many of them seem to think they're still on holiday!'

When Imogen entered the hallway, she saw immediately what he meant. A dozen round-eyed boys of varying sizes, the youngest ones already in pyjamas, had gathered on the broad staircase to see the new arrivals. Imogen couldn't help smiling up at them and most had smiled back. There was no sign of the Fanshawe-Hickses among them. Ned dismissed the horde with an amiable wave, so they retreated reluctantly as far as the landing, then he strode across the hall to where a door labelled 'Headmaster' stood ajar. He knocked and stood aside for Imogen to enter. She found herself in a large comfortable study that smelled pleasantly of old books, for shelves of leatherbound volumes lined the walls from floor to ceiling. A further door, currently closed, bore a sign that read 'Library'.

Nicholas and Michael were standing meekly in front of a huge desk behind which the head, a tall, spindly man in his fifties with a long face and sparse, plastered-back hair, was regarding them sternly through a tiny pair of pince-nez. '... wish to make your parents proud of you,' he was saying.

'Ah,' he greeted Imogen, rising briefly from his seat. 'Miss Lockhart. Our temp-or-ary matron, is that right, Mr Thorpe?' He pronounced every syllable in 'temporary' in a pompous manner.

'I did manage to persuade her, sir, as you can see. Miss Lockhart, this is Mr Forbes.'

The headmaster's hand, when Imogen shook it, felt dry and papery and she didn't warm to him one bit.

'Thank you, Mr Thorpe,' he said importantly. 'Perhaps you'd take this pair of ruffians and find them some supper. I'm sure our new matron will see how they are later.'

Nicholas and Michael trooped out silently behind their housemaster, leaving Imogen and Mr Forbes alone together.

'Please, sit.' He gestured to an ornately carved chair with a tapestry seat before the desk and Imogen duly perched on it. She met his eye squarely, determined not to let him have the better of her.

'I understand that I might only be needed for a day or two,' she said.

'Ah, that was indeed the case, Miss Lockhart,' Mr Forbes said, rubbing his chin, 'but since Mr Thorpe left to fetch you from the station, everything has changed. It seems that Matron requires an urgent operation to extract her appendix, so I imagine that it will be a while before she is able to return to her duties. Mrs Fanshawe-Hicks, the boys' mother, kindly furnished me with your agency's telephone number so I've been speaking to your Mrs Arnold. She was hearty in her recommendation of you. Very hearty indeed. Said you were particularly good with young boys. All her mothers remark upon it. So I'd like to offer you the post of matron here on a short-term basis. Until our worthy Miss Edgecumbe is well enough to return.'

'It seems that it's been arranged to everyone else's satisfaction,' Imogen remarked crisply. *No one imagines that I might have a life in London.*

'And yours too, I trust, Miss Lockhart,' Mr Forbes said, fiddling with his pince-nez. 'As I'm constantly reminding my dear wife, there is a war on and we are having to do things that we might not choose to. You must agree that this is a very pleasant place to be evacuated. Beautiful gardens.' He waved towards the window. 'And the sea not far away. I imagine you'll be happy here.' He rose from his chair. 'If you'll accompany me, I'll show you your quarters.' He opened the door for her, then she followed his spindly figure up the stairs to the second floor. 'There's a telephone extension in the sickbay,' he said over his shoulder, 'but it's strictly for school matters only. However, you'll need to use it in the morning, I imagine, to iron out details with the agency.'

Imogen nodded, compliant. Mr Forbes was very forceful and she didn't have the energy to ask questions tonight. If truth be told, she liked the look of Silverwood House, and would be pleased to be here for a few days. She would keep an eye on little Michael and Nicholas, too, having quickly become fond of them. And it wasn't as though she had urgent personal commitments in London. She'd been living as a lodger in someone's spare room and since Ginny was currently away, she wouldn't be missed. Maybe, too, at Silverwood, she could forget her heartache for a while.

Six

It was after nine in the evening when Imogen slipped out for some fresh air before bed. The last few hours had been relentless. Mr Forbes had shown her the sickbay and its three sad-eyed inhabitants, and the matron's room next door. There were two bathrooms nearby, one of which had been designated for the invalids. Miss Edgecumbe, being the only woman occupying this end of the corridor, had apparently bagged the other and defended it against all comers, which meant that Imogen had it to herself.

Once the headmaster had left her in peace, she administered doses of prescribed medicine to a small queue of boys who'd appeared in their pyjamas, then busied herself with her bedbound charges, making sure they were comfortable. Her heart had melted at the sight of them. Two were among the youngest in the school and, after doses of acrid linctus for coughs and sniffles followed by rosehip syrup to take the bitter taste away, needed only hugs and reassurance, which she willingly provided. The third boy was a lanky twelve-year-old with knobbly knees, bitten nails and an expression of frustrated boredom. He had an infected cut on his foot from a razor shell and although this was beginning to heal, he wasn't yet ready to risk the hurly-burly of the dormitory. None of the boys was faking illness to miss the cross-country race, Imogen decided. Perhaps Ned Thorpe had been joking.

She settled the younger boys down to sleep, then changed the older one's dressing and played Ludo with him for a while before drawing the blackout curtains and retreating, leaving the interconnecting door of the sickbay open in case she was needed.

Matron's room was as Miss Edgecumbe had left it that morning, with a faded photograph of a young soldier displayed on the bedside table, two nurse's uniforms and a pitifully small number of personal clothes in sober colours hanging in the closet. A vivacious young maid with corkscrew curls appeared in the room with shepherd's pie and fruit cobbler on a nicely laid tray for Imogen's supper. She remained to change the bedsheets, chatting all the while in her thick Cornish accent as Imogen ate at a small desk under the window. Her name was Kezia and she was the eldest of four girls, daughters of a local miller and his wife. She'd answered the advertisement to work at the school because, 'I'm fed up of girls. Boys, they be dirty and noisy but these ones here, they're polite and friendly and you know where you are with them.'

Imogen grinned. 'I went to a girls' boarding school,' she said. 'Girls can be sly.' She'd been regarded warily at school at first because she was so angry at being sent there. All this was in the past now. She had one good friend, Monica, whom she heard from occasionally, but that was all.

'That's not to say I didn't love my sisters, mind you,' Kezia continued, 'but they can be wild as foxes and my mam expected me to look out for them, and I said to myself, Kezia, you must get away.'

'I don't blame you,' Imogen replied with feeling, sensing that Kezia, with her forthright nature, would be a useful ally in this predominantly male household.

She'd just finished eating when Ned Thorpe appeared in the open doorway.

'Hello, are you allowed in the ladies' quarters?' she asked cheerily and he looked embarrassed.

'Probably not.' He stood aside as Kezia bustled out with the tray. 'I came to find out how you're getting on. The Fanshawe-Hicks boys, thankfully, are both asleep.'

'Exhausted from their journey, I expect. All's well here, though I don't know where anything is. I'll go through the medical supplies in the morning.'

'I'll show you around quickly downstairs if you like.'

'That would be helpful.'

The tour of the main building was a swift one because it was growing dark, but first Ned took her to look in on little Michael. The child was asleep, but tears glinted on his cheeks.

'He wanted his teddy bear, but I had to confiscate it,' Ned whispered after they withdrew. 'The other boys would rag him otherwise.'

'Poor boy,' she sighed, thinking it a shame because he must have cried himself to sleep.

'It's part of growing up,' Ned said briskly. 'He'll be as right as rain in a day or two. You'll see.'

Downstairs he showed her the refectory and the assembly hall – all as he had described. In the old drawing room at the front of the house, the school's honours boards hung in splendour on either side of the fireplace imparting a certain air of formality. In the classrooms they visited, the dusty blackboards looked out of place on walls papered with designs of fruit and flowers or Chinese junks and mountains. 'Anything really messy like art and which stinks is taught in the prefabs outside,' Ned said with a smile.

'Where do the masters live?' Imogen wanted to know.

'Wherever they can. There are married quarters in one of the wings, but as a single man and head of Brooke House I'm right in the fray of the main building here.'

'Quashing the midnight feasts and the practical jokes?'

'Something like that, though to tell the truth there's not much in the way of high jinks. The fresh air exhausts them. Be prepared for me to come and wake you up if any boy's sick, of course.'

'I suppose that's what I'm here for,' she sighed.

They smiled at each other. Imogen liked Ned's warm, open smile, feeling at ease with him as she had with her boy cousins as a child. Less so with another teacher whom they met on their rounds. 'Miss Lockwood, this is Oliver Dalton, the Deputy Head,' Ned said stiffly. 'I expect you're prowling the corridors looking for miscreants, are you, Dalton?'

'Actually, I'm on my way to the common room.' Dalton was a tall, lean, good-looking man with sleek dark hair, chiselled features and a reserved air. 'It's good to meet you, Miss Lockwood. I hope you're being well looked after.' Imogen felt his keen, brown-eyed gaze on her as though he was stripping her secrets bare and thought he'd be good at keeping discipline. She stared back at him, finding him attractive, but was determined not to be cowed by his formal manner. At the same time, his near-black hair and very pale skin reminded her painfully of Tony, the recent boyfriend whom she was fighting to forget.

'Mr Thorpe is doing a grand job showing me round, Mr Dalton. I'm sure I'll be happy here.'

Ned said nothing after Dalton continued on his way and she glanced at him curiously.

'Mr Dalton is very formidable,' she hissed. 'I think I'm a teeny bit frightened by him.'

'That's the job of a deputy head,' Ned replied. 'Head of discipline. Couldn't do it myself.' He didn't smile and his tone told her that he wasn't friendly with his fellow teacher, but he was either too well bred or too professional to say so to Imogen who was, after all, an outsider.

Finally, he left her in the big hallway. 'Regretfully I have to mug up on Ancient Egypt for the Lower Seconds. All those pharaohs have similar names! I say, perhaps I should borrow some of your bandages to explain about mummies.'

'You can think again,' she said, smiling. 'I need my bandages. And I don't want any nightmares about mummies among the boys tomorrow night!' She wagged her finger as she spoke.

'Only joking! Goodnight and sleep well.'

'Thank you, and you. I'm nipping outside for some fresh air first. See you tomorrow.'

It had been a long day. The evening air was cool, refreshing, and puffs of cloud were stained purple and navy against a darkening sky. Imogen's weariness began to drain away. Although it was late September, she noticed how much light there was late in the evening here, more than London. That made her think of August evenings, before the outbreak of war, when she and her landlady Ginny sprawled on cushions on the flat roof behind Imogen's bedroom drinking homemade punch, talking and laughing, until the harassed woman upstairs, whose husband worked early shifts, shouted for them to 'put a sock in it' so that he could sleep.

That was little more than a month ago, but it felt like another life. Imogen sighed and let the memory slip away. Here, the extraordinary peace of the place already had her in its grip. The peace wasn't silent. Rooks cawed sleepily in their high roosts and blackbirds called urgently to one another across the garden. The last rays of the setting sun reflected on the windows of the three wooden cabins on the lawn. She crossed the well-trodden grass to peer into one and, in the dimness, was filled with awe to see shelves packed with the neatly arranged equipment of a science classroom. The names and purposes of the odd-shaped glass vessels and the chemicals in the lines of jars were mysterious to her. There had been no such things at her school; instead they'd had rooms of sewing machines and pots and pans, and she felt a stab of regret at the paucity of her education.

She folded her arms against a cool breeze that had begun to blow and hurriedly retraced her steps, but as she approached the house, she was surprised to see a curtain flicker at an open window on the second floor. Then part of a face and a hand appeared and something flew through the air and landed at her feet. So much for Ned's belief about no late-night high jinks. She picked it up. It was a paper plane. There was something written on the wings in rounded letters and she unfolded the paper to read the words: 'We think you're prettier than Matron.' She heard a giggle and looked up, but though the curtain trembled in the breeze she could see no one so she called up sternly, 'Go back to bed, boys!' and went inside thinking wistfully that she might indeed be younger and prettier than Matron, but Miss Edgecumbe with her nurse's uniform was undoubtedly more qualified for the post.

Seven

'Imogen, how's young Porter today?' It was several days later that Ned stopped Imogen in the hall as she emerged from the head's study.

'I've spoken to the doctor and was just telling Mr Forbes. The good news is that he slept well and his headache's gone so he can attend classes today. The bad news is it's strictly no games until next week. Not after a concussion like that.'

Ned's face fell. 'Our best prop forward, but it can't be helped. Lyndhurst will have to step up to the plate.'

'I have to warn you that Lyndhurst came to me yesterday complaining about a sore knee.'

Ned sighed. 'I know you think rugby is a nasty dangerous game, but it's character-building.'

'Character-building my foot,' she said, wagging her finger. 'They're still only children, Ned.'

Despite these grumbles, now that she'd settled in, Imogen found she was enjoying the job more than she'd expected.

Not least because, despite the tightly regulated air of the school, she was queen of her own domain. Of course, there had to be a routine – medicines must be administered at set times, sick boys fed, bathed, monitored – but she was in charge. She alone of all the school staff did not have to attend morning assembly or evening prayers. Meals were brought upstairs to her and if she needed short periods of time off the cheerful Kezia was often available and delighted to cover for her. 'My sisters are always getting ill, they are, so I'm used to it.'

Yesterday, however, the unexpected had happened when a lively top-year boy, Jonathan Porter, had knocked himself out on a marble mantelpiece while horsing about in his dormitory. Having already refreshed her knowledge of first aid with the help of a government pamphlet Imogen found in the sickbay, she knew exactly what danger signs to look for when he came round and was relieved that all he had was a slight headache. To be on the safe side a local doctor had been summoned, and Imogen had telephoned Porter's parents to explain and reassure. All in all she felt that she'd handled the situation as well as she could and had kept her nerve.

'Imogen, listen,' Ned glanced around to check they were alone, then lowered his voice. 'I wondered whether you have any time off next weekend? I'm free on Sunday afternoon and am rather keen to explore the countryside. It's always nicer to have a companion.'

'I'd love to, but do you think we should?' Imogen whispered back. 'I mean, won't we be ribbed by the boys if we're seen going off together.'

'Ah, I've thought about that. We could set off separately and meet up.'

'That sounds fun! I love a bit of intrigue. I'll see if I can wangle Sunday afternoon. I could make up a picnic if you like. Cook won't mind.'

Ned beamed. 'That would be marvellous.' Just then the hall clock began to chime and he leaped to attention. 'Good Lord. Lower Three will be waiting for their maths test. Must dash.'

Imogen watched him tear off with a spring in his step, his black gown flying. She liked him immensely and the thought of an outing together in the countryside was an attractive one. The downside of Silverwood was it being so isolated. Even if she could persuade someone to drive her to the nearest town, there wasn't much point. Cinemas and theatres were closed for the moment and everywhere was likely to feel subdued. It was sensible to make the best of the good weather instead. If only she had some suitable shoes. Maybe Miss Edgecumbe had a pair.

$\sim$

Imogen set out past a field in which she glimpsed a circle of standing stones. The lane was muddy and she was glad she had found a pair of stout walking shoes her size in Matron's wardrobe. Ned was waiting for her at a stile, as agreed, and she smiled to see the colourful checked cap atop his good-humoured face . He shouldered her canvas haversack, which was heavy with the picnic, and strode ahead whistling and at first she had to walk faster than was comfortable to keep up. She called to him crossly.

'Slow down. You're not in the Alps here!'

'Sorry.' He paused for her to catch up.

After that he kept stopping to wait for her, though she waved away his solicitous hand at the stiles they came to. 'I can manage, you know.' But she smiled to see his rueful expression. They fell into an easy pace together and enjoyed the sunshine and the soft grass of the path as they crossed the fields, turning upriver to skirt the silver band of water glimmering below. Their talk was mostly of their surroundings as they passed through shaded woodland and followed a stony winding footpath down into a hidden valley, the hills on either side bright with autumn colours. After a while they came out onto a headland with views of the river and its wooded opposite bank and found a long flat rock to sit on that was warm from the sunshine.

Imogen unfolded several paper packages and arranged them on a tea cloth between them, then poured tea from a vacuum flask and passed Ned a cup. They sat together companionably eating sandwiches and Cook's scones, spread with cream and jam, and enjoying the sights and sounds around them, the soft lowing of cows, the twitter of starlings from a stunted hawthorn bush. Sharp gusts of chilly wind blew, but these were refreshingly welcome after their exercise.

'It's difficult out here to believe that things are other than normal,' Ned sighed.

'I was thinking that. There's nothing to suggest we're at war. Those little boats out there look so tranquil.'

'A perfect hideaway for enemy spies. I suppose heaps of things are going on behind the scenes, but we don't hear about them.'

'They certainly don't make the press.'

Imogen always made time to browse through the news-papers, including the local one. They were delivered each morning to the staff common room and over the course of the day became crumpled, their pages detached, from being passed around or tossed to one side. So by the time Imogen got to them they usually needed reassembling and smoothing down.

She smiled, remembering the first time she'd ventured into the common room, after lunch earlier in the week, how half a dozen male heads had snapped up, eyes blinking at her in astonishment before everyone pretended that they hadn't really noticed a woman in their midst and returned to their cups of tea, their marking or conversation. She'd felt irritated, knowing perfectly well that she was entitled to be there, but Ned explained to her later that Miss Edgecumbe had never ventured inside and that the teaching staff were used to the common room being a male preserve. 'Old fogeys,' he said. 'Even the married ones treat it as a gentlemen's club.' He urged her not to worry and she'd laughed and said that she didn't give a fig.

'I like to know what's going on in the world and I like male company,' she'd said. 'If I want to sit and read the papers and discuss the news I will. I'm sure they'll get used to me.'

'I gather one or two of my colleagues in the staff common room are having to temper their vocabulary,' Ned said now with a twinkle in his eye.

'If so, then at last I'm a civilizing influence! My aunt always hoped I'd turn my boy cousins into proper gentlemen, but instead they turned me into a hoyden.' Imogen spoke wistfully, for she rarely saw them these days. Bob and Paul were of an age to be called up, and Bob was already away at sea.

'You're not in the least bit a hoyden,' Ned said solemnly.

'I think it's important to be oneself, don't you? And I've always disliked girls who simper.'

'You certainly can't be accused of simpering.'

'I don't want to be called bracing either, mind you.'

'Bracing is pretty awful, I agree.'

'There seem to be a lot of unpleasant things for girls to avoid to be.' Imogen shared out the last dregs of the tea. 'A bluestocking is another.'

'A gossip, a scold. A great-aunt called my sister a Plain Jane, which she's definitely not.'

'That is wounding. And it's the sort of thing a young girl can't forget. Do you just have a sister or are there more of you at home?'

'I've an older brother, Vaughn, then there's Margaret and I'm the youngest.' Ned paused. 'I don't remember my father well – he was killed in Flanders – and my mother brought us up on her own on a shoestring in our small house in Sussex so we had to find our way in the world early. It was easiest for me because I knew what I wanted to do. I loved school and wanted to teach. Then I had a spot of luck. The aforementioned great-aunt made good because she died and left Mother some money which she spent on sending me to college.'

He spoke lightly, but as she studied him she sensed sadness. Ned was a cheerful soul and gave every impression of being fulfilled in his work, but his upbringing must have been shadowed and difficult and despite the 'spot of luck', his achievements hard won.

'What about the others?'

'You really want to know?'

'Yes, yes. I'm an only child and I always longed for a brother or a sister. I was close to my cousins but it wasn't the same. So I'm interested. Tell me.'

'All right. Well, despite Great Aunt Ethel's gloom and doom about her looks, Margaret married a splendid clergyman she met at a church social and they have three children.'

'You're Uncle Ned!'

'Two are little girls – a nice change after wall-to-wall boys here.'

'And your brother?'

'Vaughn has never quite found his place. He was very close to my father and the one most affected by his death. Mother got him into the lower reaches of the Home Office through a family friend, but he couldn't stick to it and left. He was looking for something else but last week I had a letter from Mother saying he's been called up. She's terribly upset. With cause, I think. Vaughn's awfully sensitive, I don't know how he'll get on in the army. Our school had a cadet force and he was hopeless. Never anywhere on time, frequently losing kit and didn't listen to instructions. He was always in trouble.'

'That is worrying for you all,' Imogen agreed. 'But as we were saying, there doesn't seem to be much happening yet on the military front.'

'No, thank heavens. What about you? Are you doing what you like in life?'

She broke off a bit of scone as she considered the question. 'Right now I'm perfectly happy being here in this beautiful place away from the hullaballoo of London, but working for Mother's Little Helpers is hardly a proper job, is it? Dashing around after other women's children. I only put up with it because I'm not doing the same thing every day.' She yawned. 'Sorry, it's the busy last week catching up with me.'

'And the fresh air.'

'Gallons of it, isn't there? Smashing. No, I can't stay here for long, Ned. I'm enjoying it, but as soon as Matron is back on her feet then I'll be off.'

'I'll simply have to hope that Matron has a long period of convalescence. It's nice having you around the place, lightens everything up. Some of my colleagues' wives are good sorts, but they're older.'

Imogen smiled. 'That's a lovely thing to say. But don't get used to me, I was always going to be temporary.'

'Will you go back to London afterwards?'

'Yes. I need to earn my crust and I want to make myself useful somewhere. Don't know where yet. Everyone says the Wrens because the uniform's flattering, but I'm not bothered about silly things like that.' She picked some burrs off her skirt and smoothed away the creases.

'There must be something you could do here in Cornwall. They're advertising for land girls, I notice.'

'That doesn't appeal. I'm terrified of horses. I fell off one once and couldn't get back on. Didn't like the way it rolled its eyes at me.'

Ned laughed. He had a nice laugh, natural and not too loud.

'I wish I knew what I did want to do, though. You wanting to be a teacher, I envy you that certainty. I expect I'll get married one day and have children, but I want to do something before that to prove myself to myself. Do you understand?'

'Perfectly. But I'm afraid that these decisions will be out of our hands for the moment. Even for me. School teaching is a reserved occupation for now and Mother begs me not to volunteer. But who knows what the future holds if the war goes badly?'

'Don't.'

They were both silent for a moment, then Imogen pushed the last half of scone towards him. 'Have this. I'm stuffed. Then we ought to be getting back, I suppose,' she said, shaking crumbs from her lap. 'I didn't like the look of Tom Beaumont's throat earlier. Kezia's a dear, but she might be hesitant about ringing the doctor and he won't thank me for calling him out on a Sunday evening.'

It had been a perfect afternoon, she reflected as Ned took the knapsack and they retraced their route. A flock of geese flew over the river, their melancholy honking echoing through the air. All around birds were singing and the low autumn sun turned the silvery river to shimmering gold. Clouds of dancing midges were the only irritation. When they reached the stile from where they'd started, Ned returned the bag to her and said gravely, 'I've enjoyed this afternoon very much. Would you like to do it again sometime? Or if I find an excuse to go into Falmouth, perhaps you'd like a meal out?'

She studied his face, but saw only kindness and friendliness there. That was all she needed at the moment, a friend.

'I'd like that,' she said. Then she said goodbye and set off alone along the lane back to the school. Ned would take a different route and arrive later so there would be no gossip.

At the bend by the field with the circle of stones, she glanced back to see Ned leaning on the stile lighting a cigarette and squinting up at the sky at a tiny plane passing seawards overhead. She stared at it . 'One of ours, isn't it?' she called back and he replied.

'Yes, wonder where it's off to?'

How different Ned was from Tony, she thought as she continued along the lane, finally allowing herself to remember. Tony Wyndham had been her first and only boyfriend. Sophisticated, ten years older than her, she'd met him six months ago. She'd been looking after a pair of little girls while their mother was away tending a sick relative, and he'd been living as a lodger in the family's house. The week Imogen had expected to stay there had become two and she'd sometimes found herself in Tony's company in the late spring evenings after she'd put the children to bed. That spark between them was not to be denied. Once the father had returned from work, she and Tony went out together to bars, once a nightclub.

They continued the relationship after the job finished. She was intrigued by him. He was dark and saturnine, like Oliver Dalton, the deputy head. Tony rarely laughed, but his slow, cynical smile and narrowed eyes, the graceful way he smoked his Turkish cigarettes, fascinated her and she was drawn into his arms as though into a trap. He seemed amused by her chatter – and she talked too much when she was with him.

And then suddenly, shortly after war broke out, she received a letter from him saying that he was going abroad. *Sorry I could not say goodbye in person.* She was left bewildered. For a week or so she was in shock and could barely stop crying until, one morning, she woke up and felt better. But she couldn't stop thinking she might bump into him and if she passed a particular bar where they used to go she'd feel a pang of expectation. Once she was sure she saw him in the street with a tall redhead on his arm, but when she hurried in their wake to check, they crossed the road and she lost them.

Ned was completely different from Tony, more like a brother, and she was glad of that. She didn't need to think when she was talking to him – no, that sounded insulting, she laughed to herself. What she meant was that she could act naturally around him. He didn't make her feel self-conscious in the way that Tony had and that was restful. She'd enjoyed their afternoon and looked forward to another outing with Ned soon. Oliver Dalton, however, who reminded her so much of Tony, was another, more complicated, matter.

Boys were playing football out on the rough grass using jerseys as goalposts when Imogen turned into the grounds of Silverwood House. The younger ones waved as she passed and she waved back, smiling, and smiled too at Oliver Dalton who was on duty. He acknowledged her with a grave nod and she shivered again at his likeness to Tony as she hurried past into the house and up the stairs. Here she found that Tom Beaumont's sore throat was much better and that he and the only other occupant of the sickbay were playing a noisy game of Snakes and Ladders with Kezia, so all was well.

Eight

June 1966

The pub where Gray and Belle were to perform on Sunday evening was an old timber-framed building most unoriginally called The Ship, but since it was sited right on the sea front in the port of Falmouth the name was at least fitting. Sirius parked the garish campervan in a side street and Belle, Gray, Arlo and Chouli clambered out, Belle rather shaken by the drive. It had been a hair-raising journey along winding country roads. She'd clutched the strap above her window tightly at every bend to save herself being flung from her seat and at every screaming gear change, every jolting pothole, her eyes had widened in fear. She'd been convinced that the vehicle was going to fall apart under her. Gray, too, had looked alarmed, but the others were obviously used to it. Arlo in the front sang tunelessly under his breath and Chouli sat next to Belle in the back with her eyes closed as though meditating or simply pretending she wasn't there. Trying to make conversation, Belle had asked her why Janey hadn't come, but Chouli had only opened her eyes, shrugged and said, 'I don't know. Things to do.' Belle saw that her pupils were larger than usual, her gaze unfocused, and wondered if she'd taken something. She smelled faintly of incense.

As they made their way round to the pub entrance, Belle loitered to take in the breathtaking view of boats of all sizes moored across the bay. The sky had been a clear summery blue when they'd set out, but now clouds of a threatening gunmetal shade were rolling in from the sea and a sharp breeze penetrated her thin cotton dress. She shivered and pulled her denim jacket around her. As she followed the others into the warmth of the busy old pub, she noticed with alarm a flyer pinned to the door, advertising 'The Witchers'. The *Witchers*! They weren't The Witchers. They were one Witcher and a shy girl no one had heard of!

Waiting at the bar, while Gray explained the change of personnel to the manager, an untidy middle-aged man with thinning hair, she felt annoyed with him for not being clear about her role and cross with herself for not having thought to ask. It hadn't occurred to her before.

'I'm sorry, mate, but Stu Ford is unwell. Fortunately I have Belle here, a very talented friend who's agreed to step in.'

He sounded convincing and Belle put on her bravest voice to greet the manager when Gray introduced her. The man looked her up and down with his piggy eyes, said she was pretty enough anyway, which enraged her further, and asked what they wanted to drink. She took the lemonade he poured and followed Gray across the low-ceilinged room to a corner set up for them to perform. 'That was embarrassing,' she whispered. 'You didn't tell me we were being advertised as The Witchers. Won't the crowd mind that it's me instead of Stu?'

'We're not famous enough for anyone to care. Don't *worry*, Belle.'

Belle sighed, feeling out of her depth. While Gray tuned up, she adjusted her mic and waited beside him sipping her drink, trying to calm her nerves. The room was filling up, the air turning warm and smoky. There were all sorts: a few salty old tars, a gang of young people dressed like herself and Gray, two well-dressed older couples – on holiday, she guessed. At a table by one of the diamond-paned windows, Sirius, Arlo and Chouli were conversing with a soldierly-looking older man over glasses of beer. Or rather Arlo was talking animatedly, whilst Sirius sat back listening, his small mouth twisted in a slight smile, and Chouli sat in a now familiar pose, knees bent up like a fairy creature on a toad-stool, turning a cardboard beer mat over in her slim fingers.

'Are you ready?' Gray whispered and Belle nodded. He began to strum an introduction to the first song and gradually the noisy crowd settled to become a sea of expectant faces.

'I'm Gray Robinson,' he breathed into the microphone, 'and this is Belle, and we're The Witchers. Thank you for coming to hear us tonight.' And he launched into the first song, the hearty sea shanty Belle had heard before, she joining in the chorus.

There was plenty of applause at this, and Belle began to

grow in confidence. By the time the piece she'd feared most came around, the plaintive love song she'd heard in the Black Dog at their first meeting, she was enjoying herself. She closed her eyes as she sang a wandering descant above the tune, putting all the feeling she could into it, and after it ended her eyes flew open in astonishment at the enthusiastic clapping. Gray smiled at her warmly and moved on to a ballad where her only job was to hum in the quiet bits of the chorus, before a more challenging song with a singing part over the top that Stu always played on his flute.

When afterwards they mingled with well-wishers and their glasses were replenished, Belle's spirits rose. She could still hardly believe that she was here, that she'd sung with Gray and was glad she'd had the courage for she wouldn't have missed this experience for the world. While Gray mingled with his fans, Sirius and Arlo made room for her at the table and she found herself seated next to the soldierly-looking man.

'Francis Penmartin,' he said lazily, offering his hand, which she shook. He was in his sixties, she thought, clean-shaven with neat straight hair and an open face.

'Penmartin? Then ...'

'Yes, I'm your landlord. Not that anyone pays a bean in rent, mind you. No, it's good to have someone looking after the old place. And my nephew, of course.' Here he nodded at Arlo.

'Oh, I didn't know,' she said in surprise, looking from Arlo to Francis Penmartin. Now she saw touches of likeness. They both had wide-spaced hazel eyes and a similar strong frame, though Arlo was more muscular. Arlo's face clouded under her eye and he turned his attention to his drink.

'Being a free spirit,' Francis went on, 'he won't thank me for saying, will you, boy, but he's my heir. I have no children of my own, so he'll have Silverwood when I'm gone. Though what he'll do with it, I don't know. Sell the place, I expect, and fritter the money on rubbish. There's no money to do anything with it as it is and it needs substantial repairs.'

'Oh, I'd never sell it.' Arlo was suddenly animated. 'I'll keep it as it is and everyone can carry on living there.'

Francis laughed. 'Arlo is an idealist. He thinks money is evil, that we should live in a society where people do things freely for each other and live in harmony.'

'And what's wrong with that?' Arlo protested.

'Nothing. If everyone were like you, but they're not.'

'I apologize if this sounds rude,' Belle asked, 'but why don't you yourself live in Silverwood House?'

Francis laughed. 'It's a fair question, but there's no great mystery. It's just that it's too big for me. I'm happy here in the town. I moved out in 1939 to give my old prep school a safe haven and never went back. Best thing I ever did. I prefer living in Falmouth and frankly Silverwood is a burden. I never married so I rattled around in the place. After the war I let it out to a colony of artists, but eventually there was only Sirius left.'

'And then Rain came with Angel and Janey.' Until now Sirius had been listening in silence. 'And before we knew it we were The Silverwood Project.'

'That's what you're called?' Belle asked. 'I didn't know.'

'No, I just made it up, but it's not a bad name, is it?'

'I don't like it.' Arlo frowned. 'It sounds ... industrial.'

'Have it your own way. What would you call it?'

'Silverwood. Just that. It's a lovely word. Like in Gray's song.'

Belle cast a look at Gray, who was deep in conversation with a bearded young fan at the bar. He noticed and smiled at her.

'It is a magical place,' Francis said, 'I'll give it that.' He produced several pound notes from his wallet and Arlo fetched another round of drinks. Chouli sipped hers then brought a tiny glass bottle out of a cloth bag she carried and began to paint her fingernails white, the chemical odour of the varnish mixing unpleasantly with the smells of smoke and malt in the room. Belle stared at her, fascinated. Even in this crowded place, Chouli sat in her own private world. Was there something the matter with her? she wondered.

She examined her own nails, plain and unvarnished, the ones of her right hand longer than those of the left, as befitted a right-handed guitarist. Gray's, she knew, were the same. She glanced across at him, but he was still talking, so she sipped her beer and tried to relax, glad that the performance was over without her making a fool of herself. She'd enjoyed singing and once she'd got into it had forgotten about the other people in the room. Perhaps Gray would ask her again. But surely not. He and Stu were The Witchers and this was a one-off.

'You were good tonight, Belle,' Sirius said, breaking into her thoughts, and the others chorused agreement. Even Chouli looked up and smiled.

'Thank you. I was a bundle of nerves.'

'Was it your first time performing?' Arlo said.

'Yes, outside school. Did it show?' she asked anxiously.

'You looked a little nervous at first,' Francis said, 'but when you started singing you were fine.'

'Once you've done it a few times it'll feel natural,' Arlo added.

Sirius gave a sudden harsh laugh.

'What?' Arlo asked.

'You sound like an expert.'

Arlo flushed. 'All I meant ...'

'Sirius, don't ...' Chouli said, revealing that she'd been listening all along, and smiled at Arlo who gave a helpless shrug, then took a long draught of his beer.

Being an outsider, Belle felt uncomfortable at the air of tension without fully understanding it. It was interesting that Arlo was Francis's nephew and that explained his presence, though she remembered that Gray hadn't met Arlo before and wondered how long Arlo had lived at Silverwood. She found Arlo boyish, a little young for his twenty years, but it was mean of Sirius to be crushing. Now Arlo stepped unsteadily over the bench and went off in the direction of the bathroom. In his absence, Francis asked Sirius how things were in the house. Sirius's answer was a noncommittal growl. 'Quiet with Rain away, but otherwise everything's all right.'

'When's she back?' Francis asked, but Sirius wasn't sure and there was a short silence.

'Have your family owned Silverwood a long time?' Belle asked Francis politely.

He smiled at her. 'Generations, yes. The first Francis

Penmartin built the house in 1711. The family fortunes have been sliding downhill ever since. And the house never really recovered from the war.'

'What happened to the wing at the back?'

'Ah yes. An unexploded bomb finally went off just after the war ended. The evacuees had returned to Kent and thankfully no one was hurt. But the bomb destroyed the wing, as you'll have seen, and for some footling reason I was never granted compensation to pay for its repair.'

'The school.' Something teased her memory. 'Was it called St Mary's?'

'Yes, it was. How did you know that?'

Belle explained about the name marking the bedsheets.

'I shouldn't think they'd want them back now,' Francis smiled. 'Not after you lot have slept on them.' There was laughter at this.

At that moment Arlo returned. As he clambered clumsily back into his place, his hand knocked a framed photograph from the wall to the floor with a thud. Belle reached down and brought it up, relieved to see that the glass was intact. The photograph was black and white, rather faded, and she glanced at it as she hung it back on its nail. Seeing that it was of a sinking naval ship she studied it more closely. The stricken vessel was breaking up as it sank beneath a boiling sea. Smoke and flames rose from one of the funnels. It must have been a horrifying sight. As she straightened the picture she noticed the two others arranged next to it, clearly taken at the same time. An overloaded lifeboat, its oars cutting through the stormy water. Men with desperate expressions on their oil-covered faces being hauled from the water into another ship nearby. She shivered and turned away.

As she sat down again she thought to ask Francis, 'Did you live here in Falmouth during the war?'

'Yes,' he said sharply. 'I was too old to be called up. Why?'

'I didn't mean to accuse you.' She'd touched a tender spot. 'I wondered what it was like, that's all.'

'Oh, I see. You may think we would have been out of the way here in Cornwall, but as a busy naval port with a large dockyard for repairs, Falmouth played a huge part. We received many refugees after Germany invaded the Channel Islands. And Falmouth was bombed heavily in 1944, shortly before D-Day. That was a particularly terrible time.'

'We were down at the beach near Silverwood this afternoon. Did something happen there?'

'Ah, you mean the remains of the hard. The Americans launched their craft from there for D-Day itself. That's what that's about. Not that we knew exactly what was going on at the time, just that something obviously was – engineering projects, thousands of troops gathering, mysterious practice manoeuvres – but of course we weren't to ask questions.'

Belle's gaze returned to the photograph she'd replaced on the wall. She'd never been interested in the war before. Again she remembered that it was something her parents went on about in boring, predictable ways. She and her sister shouldn't waste food. In the war they'd have eaten everything on their plates and been glad to have had it. There had been no nonsense then about which clothes were fashionable; you were glad to have a warm winter coat. She shouldn't be

friends with that German girl in her class, her grandmother
would be horrified. Belle wasn't sure exactly what her father
had done in the war. Joined the army late on. Didn't like to
talk about it. Was particularly grim on Remembrance Day.
Said he wanted to forget the whole thing.

Now, here in Cornwall, her interest was piqued. Reminders
were all around her, these photographs, the gun turrets and
the concrete hard on the beach from which thousands of
troops must have departed for Normandy, and she'd learned
that a school had been evacuated to Silverwood. Her gaze
drifted to the window where the sea gently lapped against
the harbour outside. If she tried very hard she could imagine
boatloads of refugees arriving, seeking a safe haven. Seeing
the place where it happened brought the past frighten-
ingly to life.

Nine

June 1940

Imogen boarded a bus into Falmouth one morning to buy
fresh medical supplies – sticking plasters, in particular, got
used up quickly on the succession of scrapes and grazes that
boys were prone to. She also had a shopping list from Cook
who'd run out of various cupboard items, and needed to visit
the draper's for royal blue thread to mend blazers which were
always getting torn.

Queuing up at the various shops took most of the morning, but after the final item, blacking from the ironmonger's,
she decided that shopping was thirsty work and followed a
cobbled passageway towards the water's edge, battling gusts
of wind, to find her favourite tea shop with its views of the
wartime harbour, the gun turrets on the headlands and great
fish-tail barrage balloons bobbing in the breeze.

She was quickly served by the proprietor's adolescent

daughter and sat by the window with a cup of tea. Staring out over the choppy, iron-grey sea at the boats, she was glad for a moment of peace and reflection. Her busy life at Silverwood left her little enough time for this.

She'd been there, what, eight months now. Eight months! If she'd known from the start it would be that long she'd have been on that morning train back to London in the twinkling of an eye. Though then she'd have missed so much. New friends, a beautiful environment and, above all, getting to know the boys – eighty of them and she knew them all by name. To many of them, especially those who had not seen their parents for all that time, she was a surrogate mother, always ready with a soothing word, a hug, and a willingness to play endless card games when the weather was too stormy to go outside. There had been an embarrassing moment one Sunday when she'd played hide and seek in the house and had emerged from a dusty boxroom with cobwebs in her hair just as Mr Forbes was passing with a pair of prospective parents in tow. 'This is our under-matron, Miss Lockhart,' he'd said briskly. 'She likes to enter the spirit of things with the boys.' He'd swept by, his gown blowing in a draught, but not before she'd seen the hard glint in his eye. Later, though, she heard that the parents had liked the school particularly for its air of fun, so no more was said.

Matron, Miss Edgecumbe, had returned to work early in November after her operation, but her doctor specified 'light duties' so Mr Forbes invited Imogen to stay on as under-matron for the same money. It had meant moving into the next bedroom along the corridor, but this was a pretty room with the same view of rolling fields, the gardener's cottage where the new groundsman and his family lived, and clouds sailing in from the sea. After giving it a good clean and lighting a fire in the small grate, Imogen was perfectly content.

Miss Edgecumbe herself was a more difficult proposition. She was a slender woman with mousey curls framing a round face and sad, wide-spaced brown eyes. Whatever blows life had dealt her Imogen could only guess at, though the loss of the young man in the photograph must have been one and a passing reference to ailing parents left behind in Kent was another. It wasn't easy to determine her age – early-forties, perhaps. Her recent illness had left its mark, though she was growing stronger, but the real problem so far as Imogen was concerned was the woman's lack of self-worth. This led her initially to be suspicious of Imogen's presence. Imogen had to tread a tricky path between taking the initiative where it was needed – helping lift sick children or bags of linen, for instance – and being careful to follow Miss Edgecumbe's exact instructions. There were several occasions when she had to bite her tongue, such as when Miss Edgecumbe ordered her to remake all the beds in the sickbay because their understanding of 'hospital corners' clearly differed. It had taken a few weeks for them to come to an accommodation about everything, but they'd got there.

Imogen sipped her tea and smiled as she recalled a defining event in their relationship. It had been Miss Edgecumbe's birthday, two weeks into December. Nobody would have known had not Mrs Edgecumbe received a card in the post. Imogen, in search of some medicine, had knocked and put her head round the open door of the bedroom just as Matron was reading it, the morning light falling on her face, betraying an unusual expression of tenderness. On seeing Imogen she'd looked startled and pressed the card to her chest.

'It's your birthday,' Imogen said brightly. 'Happy birthday.'

'You're very kind,' Miss Edgecumbe said, then surprised Imogen by saying, 'I'll be forty next year – too old to enjoy birthdays.' She certainly looked older than thirty-nine. 'The card's from my parents. They're the only ones who remember.'

'I sometimes think that as adults we enjoy others' birthdays more than our own,' Imogen said tactfully. 'Are you doing anything to celebrate?'

'Not a thing,' Matron said with a sigh and stood the birthday card on the dressing table. 'Now, what was it you came in for? Oh, kaolin and morphine. Here's the key to the cupboard. I hope the whole school doesn't go down with a bug.'

'They won't. The wretched boy has confessed that he ate a mouldy meatpaste sandwich as a dare. Honestly!'

After she'd administered the medicine and locked it away again, Imogen settled the child to sleep and went down to the kitchen where she informed Cook that it was Matron's birthday. The result was a little cake with a single candle that came up with the supper tray together with a simple handmade card signed by as many of the staff as Imogen had been able to muster. The mix of embarrassment and delight on Miss Edgecumbe's face was a sight to behold. After that she was as exacting as ever, but stopped treating Imogen with suspicion and sometimes they sat together in Matron's room in the evenings to drink their cocoa and chat.

Matron had been a VAD at the tail-end of the Great War, but after her fiancé was killed and her hopes of marriage were dashed, she trained as a nurse. 'A splendid career for a girl,' she said, her eyes gleaming. She'd worked primarily at London's King's College Hospital, but a few years ago she'd seen an advertisement for her current role and had fancied the change. A look of sadness had crossed her face as she said this and later Imogen brooded on what secrets Matron might be concealing. A star-crossed affair with a married consultant, perhaps? After all, Miss Edgecumbe, with her sweet face, was not unattractive.

Imogen's thoughts moved on to other pals she'd made at the school. Ned was her great buddy, though they continued to be careful not to be seen alone together as the older boys might be merciless in their teasing. Then a letter arrived from his mother to break the news that his elder brother was missing, believed captured by the Germans after the defeat of the British Expeditionary Forces at Dunkirk.

'I don't know how Vaughn will survive a prisoner-of-war camp,' he confided in Imogen. 'They won't treat them as well as we would.' Dear Ned, he was convinced of the decency of his own side and the wickedness of all Germans. She supposed she thought the same, but she had lived in London and knew a wider range of mindsets. Once, with her old flame Tony, she had got caught up in an ugly altercation between the Blackshirts and the police. She'd also known a very nice German couple who lived on the ground floor of her building and whose windows had been smashed by drunken thugs one night shortly before war broke out. She feared that what

Tony said was true: that in wartime the worst of the bullies and criminals rose to the surface 'like scum', though she wouldn't have expressed it as coarsely as that.

Poor Ned, he really was cast down. She'd heard no news of her cousins and ought to write to Aunt Verity to ask. She'd do that tonight, she decided now. Somehow time rushed away these days. She was always occupied, the evenings caught up with mending the endless piles of boys' clothes: torn collars, lost buttons, worn seats of trousers, socks with holes. These were the jobs she hated most. Anything to do with the boys themselves she loved and she thought at least some of them loved her back.

She was about to summon the waitress to pay when the door of the tearoom opened. She looked up as a shadow fell across her table.

'Miss Lockhart.' A soft male voice. She blinked and realized that the tall man who'd entered was Oliver Dalton, the deputy head. 'What on earth are you doing here?'

'The same thing as you are about to, I imagine,' she said, stung by his peremptory manner. 'Having a cup of tea.'

He removed his hat and his narrow face softened in a rather charming smile. '*Touché, mademoiselle.* I'm sorry, I didn't mean to accuse you of anything. It was simply the surprise.'

'Apology accepted.' She grinned. 'I thought I might be in trouble for playing hookey, like one of the boys.'

'Not at all. It's like I said ...' He smoothed his thick dark hair and looked worried, so she melted.

'I was only teasing.'

'Oh. I see.'

She noticed for the first time a weariness in his good-looking face. 'Would you join me?' she said. 'I can always manage more tea.'

'I will. Thank you.' He pulled out a chair and sat down opposite her at the small table in a graceful, lounging pose, his scarf still looped stylishly round his neck. The young waitress was already hovering and he smiled at her as he ordered fresh tea for two and a toasted cheese sandwich for himself.

Imogen waited until the girl hurried away, then fixed dancing eyes on her companion. 'Before you ask what I'm doing here, I had long shopping lists from Matron and Cook and now I'm filling in time before catching a bus back in time for lunch.'

'Oh, I understand.' Oliver paused then leaned forward with a sigh, his forearms resting on the table. 'I don't have a reason for being here.'

She raised her eyebrows enquiringly.

'That is, well . . .' His eyes met hers and she was stunned to see his were shining. He blinked then said in a husky voice, 'I've had some bad news this morning, Miss Lockhart. Rather a shock. My brother's ship has gone down, and apparently he didn't make it . . .'

Her hand flew to her face. 'Gosh, I'm so sorry.' *You, too,* she thought, but at least Ned had the consolation that his brother was possibly alive. 'So . . . aren't you going to go home? Um, I mean, where do your people live?'

'Are you asking, why have I come to Falmouth?' Oliver paused as the waitress placed a steaming toasted sandwich in front of him, but he stared at it, unseeing. 'I didn't know what to do,' he said, meeting her eye, 'where to go. My parents are dead and there were only the two of us boys. So when the head told me to take the day off I hitched a lift here. It was somewhere to go. I like Falmouth. I've been mooching about, watching the ships and thinking about Andrew.' He shrugged. 'There will be people to write to, but it's not as though there's a funeral to organize or anything.'

'Gosh, I see.' Poor man. It was a pity that he was alone in the world.

'A chap needs family at times like this, but apart from my pa's unmarried brother in Edinburgh I've practically no one. Odd, isn't it? The four of us were so close when growing up and I never felt the lack of relations. My mother was French and there are some cousins in Paris we used to visit, but that's no good to me now.'

'I suppose not. I can still hardly believe that the Germans have got Paris.'

'In the end, everything's happened very quickly, hasn't it?' He checked under the top of his sandwich then wiped his fingers. 'Holland, Belgium, Denmark, all fallen to the enemy like dominoes. And now France will go the same way.'

'Do you think it'll be us next?' she said in a low voice, though there was no one near them to overhear.

'We should be prepared.' He took up his knife and fork.

She watched as he ate, then he lit a cigarette and took a long drag on it, gazing out of the window, a faraway expression in his eyes. In profile he was as handsome as a matinee idol, she thought, surprised by a tug of attraction. Whether he was thinking about his brother or the course of the war, she didn't know, but she was glad to have this time with him. All these months at the school and she'd never spoken at length with Oliver. Any conversation had been about practicalities. Whether Jenkins Minor's mother needed to be informed of his swollen ankle (yes, Imogen had insisted), or if the groggy inhabitants of Dormitory Four should be further punished after raiding the tuckshop for an illicit midnight feast (no). She'd found him strict and sarcastic. Presumably this was necessary given that he was in charge of discipline, but perhaps also a cover for shyness. He was a bit of a loner among the staff, and Imogen had worried that he didn't approve of her. Today, though, he was revealing a softer, more appealing side, and she felt closer to him as a result.

'Was your brother older or younger than you?' she asked, hoping it would help him to talk about Andrew.

'Younger by two years. Twenty-five.' Which made Oliver twenty-seven. 'He joined the Royal Navy after leaving school. The only thing he ever wanted to do. We were brought up on the water, my father kept a boat at Wroxham on the Norfolk Broads. Andrew loved sailing. I grew out of it, but he never did.'

'Do you know what happened?'

'No, except that he was on the *Glorious*.'

'The aircraft carrier that went down off the Norwegian coast?' She'd read about it in the papers. 'That's terrible.' She imagined the black, icy water, the huge ship foundering.

'Ten days ago it happened, but the telegram only arrived this morning.'

'That is a long time for a telegram.'

'Or possibly they've only just found him.' His voice sounded dull, then he roused himself. 'Still, perhaps somebody in charge will get round to writing to me.' He stubbed out his cigarette, sipped his cooling tea and stared out of the window. She felt desperately sorry for him. He wasn't an easy-going, clubbable type like Ned, and she wondered if he had anyone to talk to apart from her. Well, she didn't mind, she was glad to know him a little better. She hated any kind of stiffness or formality in relationships at work. It made her jumpy. And she was rather intrigued to penetrate the air of enigma he carried.

She followed his gaze. The sparkling water of the harbour was dotted with small craft of many shapes and purposes, fishing trawlers, motor launches, sailing dinghies. Further out, bigger boats lay at anchor. She watched a ferry carve its way through the water towards a nearby quay, sending waves that set the little boats bobbing and a misty spray that coated the café windows. The sight of it all bucked her spirits, but glancing at Oliver Dalton's unhappy expression immediately made her feel guilty.

He became engaged by something he saw behind her and she turned in her seat to see. On a quay near the docks there were signs of activity around a small, greasy-looking ship set low in the water that was edging its way to a mooring. Its decks were crammed with people, subdued, dark-coloured silhouettes – it was like a painting of lost souls in the land of the dead.

'What's happening there, do you think?' she asked Oliver urgently.

'I don't know.' He narrowed his eyes and after a moment said, 'Let's go and see. Perhaps we can help.' He left some coins on the table and nodded to the waitress as he reached for his hat.

Outside, Imogen followed as he hurried in the direction of the quay, several hundred yards away. Above the sound of the wind she could hear shouting. Others, too, were being drawn to the scene like filings to a magnet. Soldiers, a couple of nurses carrying blankets, but also other ordinary people like themselves. When they reached the boat it had been secured and the crew were struggling to lower the gangplanks. The ship's hull was black with oil and tar and so, Imogen saw with dismay, were the huddled men crowding to disembark. The nearer gangplank was locked into place and the weary passengers began to shuffle down it onto the quay where a pair of soldiers with clipboards were trying to extract information from them before letting them pass.

'Where should we take them?' somebody cried.

'The Princess Pavilion,' a nurse called in reply. 'There are buses coming.'

Imogen knew the Pavilion. It was an attractive Victorian teahouse in gardens nearby. She hurried to assist a slight young man, little more than a boy, who had staggered and fallen as he'd stepped onto the quay.

'Thank you,' he muttered as she helped him to his feet, gazing with pity at his reddened weeping eyes. He had a blanket around his shoulders and Imogen could see that he was covered in oil from head to foot. Oil filled the creases on his face and he stank of it. 'Come with me,' she told him.

She turned to look for Oliver. Behind her he was marshalling several other poor wretches. An officer with a loud voice was shouting instructions and they joined the column of exhausted tar-coated figures limping their way along the quay to where a bus had drawn up. This was quickly filled, however, and left as they approached.

As they waited for another she asked the young man his name. 'Albert Waters,' he mumbled. 'Where is this?'

'Falmouth,' she said, surprised.

'Where the hell's that?'

'Cornwall. Where have you come from?'

'St Nazaire. A ship called the *Lancastria*. We was blown apart. I thought I'd copped it. Couldn't find me mate, don't think he made it. How do I find out?'

'I don't know, I'm afraid.'

The boy had started to shudder with cold or shock, or both, and Imogen wrapped his blanket tighter round him. Another bus arrived and she urged him onto it. 'It's not far where you're going, a couple of minutes away,' she reassured him. A handful of bystanders were gathering to stare now. A woman in a headscarf darted forward and thrust a bread roll into one of the men's hands with a heartfelt, 'Bless you, my lovely.'

Imogen and Oliver, lugging her shopping, hurried to the Pavilion on foot, she struggling to match his long strides. Along a road overlooking a beach they turned steeply uphill through a beautiful garden filled with exotic trees and plants. At the top lay a U-shaped pavilion with delicate arched colonnades around a green with a bandstand. Here, men discharged from the buses queued for food or sat exhausted on the lawn. Local women were bringing out bowls of steaming soapy water and towels to wash off the oil. Imogen went to help. She noticed Oliver speaking to one of the officials, who directed him inside the pavilion building.

Around Imogen, other helpers were offering pasties, sandwiches and hot drinks to the weary men. Some turned away the food. 'Me stomach's full of oil you see, Miss,' the big muscular man she was aiding told her, his teeth flashing pale in the black mask of soapy scum that covered his face.

'It must have been an awful experience.' She waited as he splashed clean water over his head, then passed him a towel.

'Bloody terrible, if you don't mind me saying, Miss,' he said as he scrubbed at his thick hair. He was, she saw now that the oil was gone, well past his first youth. 'We was crammed onto the *Lancastria* like sardines. One of the last boats out of France, she were, so I suppose they didn't like to turn men away. Then these bloody Dorniers flew over. Lobbed bombs down the funnels, they did. Blew the boat apart. I was on deck, one of the lucky ones, if you get my drift. Thrown clear. It was hell. Everywhere you looked bodies alive and dead, men screaming and grabbing what they could to stay afloat, sometimes each other. Seemed like for ever till we got picked up. Never thought we'd get back home, but here we are. A dog's dinner, whoever organized the whole dang thing, if you ask me.'

'It sounds like it. I'm glad you're safe,' Imogen said. 'If you go inside I think they'll give you something clean to wear.' And she left him towelling himself, fetched more hot water and moved on to the next oily victim, a wiry youth sitting cross-legged on the grass wolfing down the last of a sandwich. He was glad to submit to her ministrations.

It was midday now and the sun beat fiercely down. Imogen paused briefly in her work, shaded her eyes and saw with dismay that another bus had arrived and was disgorging more tired, filthy men. Several officers in uniform had set up a table by the pavilion and were organizing the onward transmission of those who'd been fed and cleaned up. 'They're mostly going to the barracks,' a friendly lieutenant told her when she asked.

Later in the afternoon, she wearily collected her bag of shopping to go home. Oliver had left earlier, having done all he could, but agreed that she should stay on as she was still needed. She'd liked feeling useful, she reflected as she waited for her bus, and being in the thick of it all, something she appreciated about life at the school. And she'd valued spending time with Oliver. Because of his loss, he'd allowed her to break through his reserve. Then she remembered how he'd reminded her of her old flame Tony and told herself to be careful. She might be drawn to aloof, mysterious older men, but she had been hurt badly and she didn't want to risk that happening again. Oliver wasn't like Tony, though; no, not really.

Back at Silverwood she found Matron in an irritable mood, despite Oliver having explained her absence. Really, she thought, the woman could manage perfectly well without her.

Over the following weeks and then with the holidays

upon them and only boys whose parents either couldn't or wouldn't take them to look after, Imogen brooded. It was time she moved on. Her experiences that day in Falmouth had decided her. There was war work to be done. And now she knew what it was she wanted.

She spoke about her idea to Ned. 'The hospital at Truro takes student nurses. I can't stay here for ever, Ned, do you see? I'm not needed here, not really. There are more important jobs that I can do.'

Ned, hands in pockets, hair untidy as usual, looked crestfallen, his usually cheerful face creased in a frown. 'I understand, though don't do yourself down. The school's a better place with you here. The boys love you.'

'They like Matron well enough.'

'Not in the way they love you. And I know it's self-ish, but I'd miss you.' His expression was tender, but she remained unmoved.

'And I'll miss you, Ned, but we can go on being friends. Truro's not far away.'

'I'd like that,' he said softly, 'for us to go on seeing one another. It's a bit ... monastic here otherwise.'

'We can't have that. A tonsure wouldn't suit you.' She spoke lightly, realizing that his interest in her was turning into more than friendship. Ned was such a nice man, but she didn't feel the same tug of attraction that she felt every time she saw Oliver across the staff room or passed him in the corridor.

Since that dramatic day in Falmouth she hadn't encoun-tered more of Oliver than chance meetings, but she recognized that her feelings towards him had grown and that was another reason for her to move on. Although plainly wrapped in his unhappiness, he always spoke to her warmly now and she felt very aware of him physically. She found herself taking more trouble with her dress, pinned back her unruly hair and even wore a touch of face powder. Yet he never sought her out and on one awful evening of self-examination in July, she lectured herself to stop mooning after him. He clearly wasn't interested. She had other things to do, and anyway she'd only end up getting hurt.

Her decision taken, she wrote to the Royal Cornwall Infirmary in Truro, endured a tough interview with the matron there, then, when she was offered a probationer position, went to see Mr Forbes to hand in her resignation. He would be sorry to see her go, he said, but agreed that they would manage. A few days after that she went upstairs gloomily to pack up her things and to say a sad goodbye to as many of the boys as she could find. She spent a few weeks with her mother in Hertfordshire, a time that tested the patience of each of them, then it was time to move to the nurses' hostel in Truro to begin life as a student nurse.

Ten

June 1966

'I saw a cockroach earlier, disgusting thing,' Janey announced on Thursday morning, coming into the kitchen from the garden with a colander of freshly picked pea pods to find Belle and Gray eating toast and plum jam at the table. 'It waved its feelers at me then scuttled under the fridge.'

'Eeugh!' Belle said, and with a sudden loss of appetite laid down her toast.

Janey dumped the colander on the draining board and placed her hands on her hips. 'We need to turn the kitchen out. You'll have to help, Belle. Arlo's on weeding duty this morning and Sirius has gone to get petrol.'

'Okay,' Belle nodded. 'You, too.' She nudged Gray.

'In a bit.' He scowled. 'I'm eating my breakfast and then I've got something to do.'

Janey had patiently explained early on how the system

worked. Each inhabitant at Silverwood was responsible for cleaning their own bedroom and bathroom. This left many reception rooms and common areas such as the corridors, hall and stairways, and all of them, in theory, helped with those.

In practice it was a different matter.

Belle had already noticed that everyone was purposeful, but some only in pursuit of their own personal interests. It was obvious that Janey kept the whole show running with Arlo as her assistant, but even Arlo had to be given precise instructions and rarely took the initiative. Sirius could be relied upon to run errands in the van or do household repairs if asked at least twice. Chouli's role was mainly to be decorative, but she was handy with light cooking or mending clothes. Otherwise she could be found embroidering, sunbathing or seeking advice from a deck of well-thumbed Tarot cards. She had given Belle a demonstration the day before, laying the cards out on the kitchen table with the melodramatic air of a fortune teller at a fair, but Belle didn't understand. There was something so vague about Chouli's pronouncements about the Queen of Pentacles or the Eight of Cups. Belle was sure they could be interpreted to underpin any outcome. 'They're not meant to be predictive,' Chouli said patiently. 'They're like signs on a journey to help you recognize opportunities or pitfalls,' but Belle was still confused.

What was being made clear was that Belle's role at Penmartin was to help with the housework. She didn't really mind, but she didn't see why Gray should escape.

On Monday, with her agreement, Gray had stuffed some of the money they'd been paid by The Ship into the biscuit tin on the fridge that acted as the kitty, but this appeared to have been his sole contribution so far to the maintenance of the household and it was beginning to annoy her. Instead he'd spent his time practising his music, sometimes inviting Belle to join him. At other times she took her own guitar to a remote part of the grounds to play by herself. Occasionally she was joined by Figgy, who sometimes howled along, but mostly preferred to lie in the shade asleep with only his ears twitching to show that he was still alive. Figgy was strictly speaking Janey's dog, found half-dead on a London street in a cardboard box, but it wasn't an exclusive relationship.

Her own was, however, and it was blossoming. Belle loved waking late in the mornings to find Gray sleeping next to her in the tangle of bedclothes. Then she'd snuggle up close, breathing in his salty smell, and draw her finger along his long narrow flank until she felt him stir and he would turn to her, pulling her on top of him, murmuring endearments while her hair fell over his face as they kissed. After their lovemaking they lay sated in each other's arms then squabbled like an old married couple about whose turn it was to fetch the tea. Belle wondered how she'd fallen into this delightful state so quickly and completely while her friends at university were just dating.

It was hard to get out of bed in the mornings when there wasn't a set routine. In term time at university there had always been early lectures and at home her mother put breakfast on the table at eight and cleared it away at half-past. At Silverwood, apart from their duties, and the communal evening meal, everyone organized their own lives.

Today, since Belle wasn't used to sitting around doing nothing, she didn't mind submitting to Janey's orders.

Gray finished his toast then wandered outside rolling a cigarette. Belle sighed.

Janey was already clattering about emptying cupboards and crowding the worktops with cans of food. 'We won't get much use out of him,' she said curtly. 'Men, they're all the same. Come on, make up some washing soda, if you know how.'

'I do,' Belle said, stung, though in truth only because she'd seen her mother do it.

'Good. The soda box is in the cupboard under the sink. That's the one. If Rain comes back to find cockroaches we'll never hear the end of it.'

'Who is Rain exactly?' Belle asked as she measured soda crystals into a cracked pudding basin.

'What do you mean, who is she?'

'I mean I know she's in charge here, but ...' Belle poured tepid water from the kettle over the crystals and stirred the bubbling brew, sneezing at the fumes.

'Nobody's in charge here, we're all equal. Rubber gloves are in the drawer ... no, that one. And a cloth. Thanks. You can wipe down the tins.' Janey snapped on some gloves and dived into a cupboard with a damp cloth. She began to scrub away with the energy of a dog digging out a rabbit.

Belle watched then gingerly dabbed a cloth into the soda and applied it with distaste to a grimy tin of luncheon meat.

Janey emerged and sat back on her heels, wiping her forehead with her sleeve. 'Rain started it all at the beginning of last year,' she said, a fond look on her face. 'We met in London. I needed a spare room and Rain had a flat on Ladbroke Grove. Nobody paid any rent because it was condemned. They were going to build a main road through the property. Rain welcomed me in. She's so inspiring, full of ideas. We talked and talked about finding somewhere in the country where we could put them into practice, then she met Arlo at a protest march and he said his uncle had this place.'

'But who is she, where does she come from?' Belle was curious at the way Janey spoke of her, with so much awe.

'Rain? She's just Rain. She's such an amazing person. Whereas most people just talk about ideas, she carries them out. She says that one day she wants there to be a whole network of places like Silverwood across England so that we can show everyone the best way to live.'

'The best way. What is that?'

But Janey had moved on to the next cupboard and didn't hear. Soon she was emitting little cries of 'Oh no, flour beetle!' and 'What a waste!' over rotting packets of dried pulses which she gathered up and tossed into the kitchen dustbin.

Belle sighed and watched a dozen ants scurrying round a hole under the worktop. 'Should I put these tins back now I've cleaned them?'

'We need some newspaper to line the cupboards first. Try Sirius's studio. He always has a stash.'

'Will he mind me nosing about?' She'd noticed him go in and out of a room off the hall, but hadn't actually seen inside it yet.

'He won't know, will he, because he's not here. Go on.'

Out in the hall, Belle opened the door of the studio cautiously to find it in semi-darkness, for swathes of velvet curtain had been drawn across the windows. It was actually a long drawing room that occupied half the front of the house. The air smelled musty with a sharp top note of turpentine. Belle tried to switch on the ceiling lights, but none of them worked so she stumbled over furniture to pull back a curtain and turned to survey the room now lit by a strip of sunlight.

Her nose wrinkled with distaste. What had once been a lovely gracious room was now a messy artist's studio. Paint-splattered dustsheets covered the floor and much of the furniture. An easel bearing a half-finished self-portrait stood in one corner. Jars full of brushes occupied the magnificent marble mantelpiece where once vases of flowers and porcelain statuettes might have stood. Sirius's paintings, some framed, lay stacked against the walls. Rolls of canvas lay across the covered form of a grand piano. Screwed-up sketches, old paint tubes, discarded reference books and unwashed crockery littered the floor.

Eventually she spotted the newspaper, laid higgledy-piggledy in a basket like a giant rook's nest, filling the fireplace. She picked her way across and gathered up a yellowed paper that had tipped into the grate. She was about to return to the kitchen with it when she noticed a headline: *First Evacuees Arrive.* She squinted at the date. *1939.* Over twenty-five years old! It was a local paper and she unfolded it and stood in the ray of sun to read the article. A photograph showed two bewildered small girls with labels round their necks. It was a shame to burn it or wipe paintbrushes on it. She tucked it into the bottom of the pile and picked up some recent editions instead that would do nicely for the kitchen shelves.

Sitting at the kitchen table later in the morning Belle tapped her chin with her pen and frowned, unsure how to proceed.

'*Dear Mum and Dad,*' she'd written. '*Yes, a letter from me, what a surprise! The reason I'm writing is to let you know that university has finished but I won't be home for a while.*'

Nothing about her current circumstances would draw anything but concern from her mother and anger from her father. She couldn't possibly tell them that she had missed her last exam and run away with an itinerant musician, nor that she was living the bohemian life in a tumbledown house with a bunch of what her father would undoubtedly call layabouts. She did, however, want them to know that she was alive and well. In the end she wrote that she was 'on holiday' in Cornwall with friends, that she was practising her music, that the beach was nice and she had been into Falmouth and sung in a pub. Then she hurriedly sent her love to her sister Jackie, scrawled her name and folded the letter into an old envelope that she'd found in a drawer that had once contained seeds.

While she was doing this Arlo wandered in from the garden. 'Hello. Seen Janey?' he asked.

'She's gone into Helston with Sirius to get supplies,' Belle replied. She'd licked the edge of the envelope but failed to get it to stick so she tucked the flap inside. 'I don't suppose you can sell me a stamp?'

Arlo yanked opened a drawer full of bits and pieces of paper and string and scrabbled about in it.

'Here. Janey's secret stash.'

'Thank you. I'll give her the money.'

'She won't know. Who are you writing to?' Arlo settled himself at the table next to her and regarded her through narrowed eyes.

'My parents.' She hadn't been alone with Arlo before. He'd not shaved, she saw, and the shadow of a beard gave him an older, saturnine look that for some reason put her on her guard.

'Mummy and Daddy, eh?' he said in a mocking voice and she gave him a level look.

'They don't know I'm here,' she said. 'They'll be worried.'

His gaze softened. 'I wish mine were worried about me.' He sighed, scratching at a stain on the table with his thumb.

'Aren't they?'

'They're not together any more. In fact, I've no idea where my dad is.'

'And your mum?'

'Moved up to London a couple of years ago with her new boyfriend. I wouldn't have gone with them even if she'd asked me, but she didn't.' He said this sadly and Belle could only guess at the resentment behind his words. 'I lived with Uncle Francis.'

'But one day this place will be yours, is that right?'

He nodded, this time with pride. 'The Penmartins go right back. We're a part of this land and it's a part of us. There's a sacred place here, did you know? A well, it's been here for ever. Down the side of the house beyond the vegetable garden. I'll show you if you like. It had been mostly buried by earth but I dug it out.' He looked proud at this.

'Okay, show me.' Belle was intrigued. She followed him out, zig-zagging between the rows of vegetable beds to a doorway in the wall at the far end. Beyond lay a large rocky outcrop and built into one side was a recess with damp walls growing with ferns, like a shallow cave, whose entrance was framed by a pointed brick arch like the entrance to a tomb or a shrine. It didn't look to Belle like her idea of a well, but Arlo beckoned her to duck and look inside. 'Careful, it's slippery,' he said, too late, as she stumbled on a slimy rock.

She craned her neck and saw near the back a rippling pool on which floated petals and leaves.

'Isn't it a spring rather than a well?' she said, looking back at him. She edged inside, crablike, crouched and trailed her fingers in the water and was surprised by its iciness and the force of the pulse where it poured from the rock.

'I suppose so, though Francis calls it a well.' He sank down beside her and picked a little pebble with a hole in it out of the pool. 'Lucky stone!' he grinned and showed it to her.

'It looks like a Polo mint!'

His smile faded.

'I didn't mean it's not lucky.' She sighed. 'Does this spring ... well, I mean ... supply water for the house?'

He shook his head. 'We're on the mains here. Maybe it did in the past.' He half rose and backed out of the shallow cave and she followed with care then straightened.

'Why do you say it's sacred?' she asked him.

'These wells usually are.' He held his lucky stone to his eye and looked through it at her, then slipped it into a trouser pocket. 'Many are linked to saints, but Rain says we need to look back before Christianity and that they're inhabited by nature spirits.'

Belle frowned, but he looked serious. 'Nature spirits. Is that what you believe?' she said eventually.

'I don't know.' He narrowed his eyes, looking even more like Pan. 'Both ideas sound strange. Whoever put this arch here probably backed the saint idea, but the inhabitants of Cornwall go back much further to prehistoric times.'

'In which case I hope they were good spirits,' she said.

'Rain says not always. Ancient people had to make sacrifices to them. Little gifts and promises, I mean.'

'Not human sacrifices,' she broke in, shivering.

'I would hope not. But this is a magical part of the world. There are ley lines and a ring of standing stones in the next field, and Rain says their power is still there if we only allow ourselves to believe. When midsummer comes we'll have a ceremony at the stones. I missed last year's because of being in India. These stones, they're ordinary boulders, but they were positioned there on purpose by somebody. There's a legend that they were people turned to stone for dancing on the Sabbath. Something like that, but they must be ancient, too.'

'What kind of ceremony do you mean?' Belle's skin prickled.

'I don't know, to be honest.' He began to scratch at a patch of yellow lichen on the arch. 'Like I said, I wasn't here for it last year.'

'Was Gray?'

'I don't think so.'

'Arlo,' Belle said hesitantly. 'It is safe, the ceremony? We won't be . . . releasing anything awful?'

He stilled his hand and stared at her through those narrowed eyes. 'Yeah, 'course it's safe. Rain says it's to honour the spirits. Pay our respects.'

Belle shivered. 'I still don't like the sound of it.' She gazed around at the trees, a gull soaring overhead, then back at the house, trying to shake off her odd mood. When she met his eye again, Arlo's expression was watchful, unfriendly. She blinked at him uncertainly.

He turned on his heel without speaking and started back towards the door in the wall. She followed him back inside the garden where he paused before saying, 'Hang on,' and crossed to enter a small greenhouse. She waited in the doorway while he inspected a line of leggy tomato plants. She breathed in. 'I like the smell,' she said. 'My dad grows tomatoes.'

'Yeah?' His usual good mood had returned.

She watched as he nipped unwanted shoots with quick fingers. 'Arlo,' she said. 'Is that a family name, like Francis?'

'No, there's never been an Arlo, but I don't mind, the Francises weren't always nice. The one who built Silverwood was a complete criminal, made a fortune from piracy and wrecking.' Arlo began tying up one of the plants, the tip of his tongue showing between his teeth as he concentrated.

'Was your uncle born here?'

'Yes, and my mum, but she left and, like he said, he cleared out during the war to make room for his old school. They paid him rent which he was glad of and, anyway, he was worried that they'd billet soldiers here who'd ruin the place.'

'It's a lovely place to be at school,' she said. 'All this gorgeous countryside and the sea.'

'The school mucked about with it a bit, but in useful ways. I'll show you.'

They walked together across the garden and under the arch to the front where he explained about the prefab buildings.

'These old shacks. They were classrooms. No one ever got round to taking them down. Rain uses this big one for meditation and stuff, and the others are full of tools and supplies.'

'You didn't attend the school?'

'Francis wanted me to go, but it had returned to Kent by the time I was old enough and my mum said no, it was too far away.'

Something occurred to Belle. 'How old is your uncle?'

'You do ask some questions! Sixty-five. My mum's twenty years younger, before you ask.' She'd annoyed him again, but that's what she'd wanted to know.

They returned to the kitchen where she started to assemble lunch for everyone while he filled the kettle and spooned tea into a pot, whistling to himself, miles away.

She sliced the bread, thinking furiously. She felt on edge with Arlo, unsure, while at the same fascinated. She couldn't work him out at all. He was basically friendly towards her, but she also realized that she annoyed him. That stuff about the nature spirits, for instance. He hadn't liked her questioning it. And he took his heritage ridiculously seriously. It must be strange, though, to know that you were bound to a place like Silverwood and would inherit it. All that history behind you; it would be a heavy responsibility.

She was about to speak, to try to make amends, but just

at that moment they heard the distant vibrations of a vehicle coming up the drive and before long Sirius and Janey entered, carrying their purchases.

'Here's the important stuff.' Sirius set a crate of beer on the floor and went out again.

'Fruit for jam,' Janey said happily, laying a large cardboard box of overripe strawberries on the table and batting at some tiny flies darting above the decaying flesh. The fruit's sweet smell began to fill the kitchen. 'Your job for the afternoon, Arlo. Wash and hull them, cut out the worst bits.'

'Yes, ma'am,' Arlo said, inspecting the fruit. 'Any sugar?'

'There are several packets in the airing cupboard.' Janey saw his raised eyebrows. 'To keep it dry, of course. This place is so damp,' she explained to Belle, her lined forehead creasing even more. 'What with that and the cockroaches it's a constant war.'

Belle nodded. 'I'll help, if you like,' she said to Arlo and as she hoped, he accepted gratefully. Then she remembered. 'Though I'd better see if Gray has any plans first.'

'Of course, must ask Gray.' Arlo's voice was heavy with irony and her heart sank.

Out in the hall she followed the muffled sound of Gray's guitar into a sitting room at the back of the house where the French windows stood open to the courtyard. He was lolling on a tattered chaise longue, his eyes closed as he played, and she leaned against the door jamb watching him, affectionate but irritated at the same time. He was so obviously lost in his music, frowning slightly as he stopped to replay a series of chords that didn't sound right. Finally, he sensed her presence, opened his eyes and stared right at her. His gaze softened and he set his instrument aside.

'Hello, you. Am I wanted?'

She came to sit beside him and laid her head on his shoulder. 'Only by me. Gray,' – she sat up – 'you never came to help.'

'Sorry, I got caught up. What time is it?' He yawned.

'Lunchtime.' She sighed.

'I'm sorry, you must feel a bit abandoned. What have you been doing?'

'Lots of housework. Oh, and talking to Arlo. Did you know about the sacred well behind the kitchen garden?'

'No.'

'There is one. He showed me. He made it sound a bit spooky.'

'I'd better have a look sometime.'

'And I'm going to make jam with him this afternoon. Do you mind?'

'You can do what you like.' There was an unpleasant edge to his voice.

'Really?'

'Make jam. Go on.'

He combed his fingers through his thick hair. 'Tomorrow, though, let's go out.'

'Where?'

'Where would you like to go?'

'I don't know.' A thought struck her. She sat up. 'Actually, I do. There's a beach called Kynance Cove. I was talking about it to the woman from the cottage, Mrs Kitto.'

He nodded slowly. 'I've heard of it all right. I'll look it up on the map, but yeah, why not?'

'So you don't mind about this afternoon?'

'Why would I mind?'

She glanced around in case they were overheard.

'It's just . . . I *know* you don't like Arlo, that's all.'

'What makes you think that?'

'Your tone of voice now for a start.'

'I hardly know the guy. He's a bit full of himself, that's all. And what's he doing here? Sirius does his art. Rain's in charge of everything. Janey, well, we all know how hard Janey works.'

'What about me? And Chouli.'

'Chouli's with Sirius and she sews things, and you're with me and you . . .'

'Gray, are you saying that's all I do, be here for you?'

'You sing,' he said. 'Don't put yourself down.' Then he smiled. 'Listen.' He picked up his guitar. 'This came into my head last night.' He struck a few chords and began to sing a haunting tune: *'By moonlight you come to me, running with silver, and lay your hands on me.'* He stopped. 'That's as far as I've got, but I'm working on it.'

'It's lovely.'

'It's inspired by you, Belle, so I hope you do like it.'

'I do, very much.' Touched, she leaned over to kiss him, but pulled back, aware of a movement outside. Perhaps it had been a bird, she thought, going over casually to see. It was only Arlo. He'd sat down on a sunbed to eat a sandwich.

*

'Jam jars are in the nearest hut. There's a box of them on a shelf and they'll need washing and sterilizing.' Janey was firing out instructions.

'How do we sterilize them?' Arlo wanted to know.

'Mum puts them into a warm oven,' Belle told him.

'That's right,' Janey said. 'I'll leave you to get on.' She went outside to weed the lettuce beds.

There was some argument and a little laughter between the two of them. Hulling the strawberries and discarding the bad bits was a messy business and in washing off flies and bits of grass Arlo made the berries go soggy.

'It won't set easily if you do that,' Belle groaned.

'I'm not having sodding insects in my jam,' he said.

'What's worse than finding a fly in your jam?'

'Finding half a fly. That joke is so boring. Now, what do we do next?'

'Boil the fruit with the water and lemon juice in the pre-serving pan. And Mum warms the sugar in the oven.'

'Janey didn't say that bit so let's not do it. Where's the lemon juice?'

'In the lemon.' Belle rolled it across the worktop to him, but Arlo looked put out. She went to unhook the large pan from a wooden rail by the range with a feeling of suppressed rage.

He perked up once they got the pan on the stove and stirred the mixture eagerly. 'I never did any cooking at home. Mum did it all. I don't mind it when it's fun like this.'

'Didn't you make sweets as a child?' Belle asked. 'I can make peppermint creams and coconut ice and fudge. I don't suppose there's a cooking thermometer anywhere? We've got to heat the jam to a high temperature or it doesn't set.' She opened several drawers and rummaged around. There were an awful lot of rusting implements that served no obvious purpose, but not a thermometer. She'd have to guess. After the jam had been bubbling away for some time she slopped some onto a saucer and placed it in the fridge to see if it would set. When she closed the door the fridge began to make an alarming chugging noise, and, noticing again the grubby and overloaded socket, she asked, 'It is safe, the wiring here?'

Arlo shrugged. 'Nothing bad's happened yet.'

'How is it you don't pay for electricity?'

'Sirius did something to the meter. He's clever that way.'

'But that's stealing!' She was shocked.

Arlo frowned. 'What if it is? It's not hurting anyone.'

'But surely ... Oh, for goodness sake, I'll go and get the jars.' She left him licking spilt jam from his finger.

It was gloomy in the hut, but the air smelled pleasantly of the grain Janey gave the chickens and she felt calmer out here. The windows had been boarded up, presumably to keep the place dark and cool, so she left the door open a crack and filled an old wooden crate with a dozen lidded jars and a large Kilner.

Outside, Belle pushed the door shut with her hip then hesitated, her eye on the hut that Arlo had said was Rain's workroom. The windows here had curtains and she put down the box and stood on tiptoe to peep inside. The large room was sparsely furnished. At one end was a kind of shrine with candlesticks beside it and a wood carving of a dancing man playing a flute who looked a bit like Arlo. She wished she could see better so glanced guiltily behind her then tried the door. It was locked. Disappointed, she returned to the kitchen. Only to find that Arlo had disappeared.

She sighed angrily. Presumably he was fed up or else had decided that the jam was ready. Examining the saucer in the fridge she concluded that it wasn't. She washed the jars with angry movements, sterilized them in the oven and finished the job herself. It was strange, she thought, as she spooned the hot jam into the jars, how the pair of them got on well initially that afternoon, but then she'd annoy him or he her. Was it her fault? He'd definitely resented her comment about the electricity, but then she had basically accused everyone of stealing. On the other hand he'd been downright rude when she'd made simple suggestions. Why was it so difficult to read people? She'd met Gray and fallen for him immediately, but was only now starting to get to know him. Arlo was more difficult, unpredictable.

'Smells delicious, Belle,' said Janey when she came in from the garden, her brow damp with perspiration and her flyaway hair escaping its knot. 'Well done. Arlo given up, I take it?'

'He was here most of the time,' Belle said, unwilling to make more trouble.

'Give me strength,' Janey said and picked up the kettle. 'Tea?'

Despite Janey's friendliness, Belle felt a little in awe of her. It was her competence, the way she knew how to do everything and fought her way to getting it done. She was a similar age to Mum, Belle thought, yet very different. Belle's mum wore dainty print frocks and heeled shoes and kept her dark hair neatly cut and set. Old dungarees or oversized smocks and trousers were Janey's usual wear and her hair was greying and unkempt. She could have been pretty if she'd bothered, with her deepset blue eyes in her tanned face, her small straight nose, and her wide mouth set in a natural smile, but a perpetual worried expression had carved lines on her forehead and around her eyes. Belle liked her, though, and appreciated her kindly interest.

Sitting across from one another at the table with mugs of herb tea, Belle answered her direct questions shyly, how she'd been feeling before that she'd chosen the wrong path in life until she met Gray.

'What do you want to *do*?' Janey's gaze was piercing.

'I . . . I don't know.' The thought made her throat swell.

Janey patted her arm. 'Don't worry. I don't mean to interrogate you. You're still very young, dear. Something will sort itself out.'

'I've only just got here. It still feels like a holiday. Too early to start thinking.'

'And I've set you to work. Poor you.'

'No, I don't mind that, really I don't. It's good to have something to contribute. And it's so kind of you all to have me. It's restful here.'

'Is it?' There was a steely tone in Janey's voice and a hard look came into her eyes.

'Well, yes,' Belle said, uncertain. 'Everybody's very nice and . . .'

'I'm glad you think so,' Janey said crisply. 'I find them complete pains in the backside sometimes.' She drained her cup.

'I'd better get on with some sorting out upstairs.' Belle was shocked at her words and to see the bitterness in her smile.

Once the jam had cooled, she tightened the lids on the jars and since she couldn't find any labels wrote the date straight onto the glass with a black felt pen. Then she washed up and cleaned the range, which was awash with spilt jam.

When she went upstairs to look for Gray she found him asleep on their bed. She sighed and quietly retreated. The afternoon was wearing on so she purloined a piece of stale flapjack from the kitchen and wandered outside chewing it, thinking she'd go down to the beach again. In the back courtyard she found Chouli sitting cross-legged on a sunbed sewing sequins onto a T-shirt. Belle told her where she was going and ambled off.

The afternoon air was treacly with heat and she was glad of the breeze on the beach. Glancing about to make sure that she was alone, she peeled off her jeans and blouse and splashed into the water in her underwear. The cold made her gasp, but after a moment she became used to it and swam about briskly until she felt warm. Then she lay floating, looking up at the sky, watching the gulls and the odd cloud glide across the sun, finding it calming. Gentle waves wafted her to the shore and her head bumped onto sand. She sat up in surprise, shaking water out of her eyes and blinking, then carefully got to her feet and walked back over the shingle to collect her clothes. As she pulled on her sandals, the skin on the back of her neck prickled. She was being watched. Her eyes scanned the edge of the beach where the treeline began, but she could see no one. Had she imagined it? No, there was a movement, a patch of red, then it was gone. She shivered. She sensed that she was being followed by someone who did not wish to be seen.

Belle sat on a lump of concrete and waited for a while, tossing pebbles into the sea and glancing about, but no one appeared. Perhaps she'd imagined that someone was there. She trudged up the beach to the path. She was tired now after her swim and the walk uphill felt strenuous. Reaching the top of a hillock she had a sudden view of the path far ahead. There, that same patch of red. A man's shirt. Arlo's, yes, she was sure it was Arlo. She blushed to think that he'd seen her cavorting in her underwear. Perhaps that's why he hadn't declared himself – he too had been embarrassed. Or had he been spying on her? How had she been stupid enough to assume that she was alone?

She waited until he'd disappeared from view before resuming her climb. She wouldn't dare confront him about the matter in case she made a fool of herself, but she was wary of him now, more than ever.

When she paused wearily by Mrs Kitto's cottage, Belle saw that the gate and the back door stood wide open, then her eye was caught by something small and blue lying on the path. It was a purse. After a moment's hesitation she entered the garden and picked it up then stood in the tiny covered porch, peering into the hall and the kitchen beyond. The black and white cat was sitting on the table, washing its paws.

'Hello?' she called out softly, hoping Mrs Kitto would hear. The cat blinked at her. It was then she noticed that a set of keys had been left in the door. 'Mrs Kitto?' she said, this time louder. 'Are you there?' Again there came no answer. She was thinking about simply leaving the purse on the hall shelf and withdrawing when she heard a movement from deeper in the house. Some instinct alerted her to investigate. She slipped off her sandy shoes and stepped inside.

'Mrs Kitto?' she called. This time she heard a muffled, 'In here.' She followed the sound through a door into a sitting room where she was momentarily blinded by the sun streaming through the window. Then she made out the form of Mrs Kitto half lying on a high-backed sofa, propped up by cushions.

'I'm so sorry,' Belle started to say. She moved until she could see the woman more clearly.

'Don't be.' Mrs Kitto's voice was faint and her face ashen. 'Fetch more water, would you?' She held out a cup.

Belle did as she was bid, filling the cup with ice-cold water at the kitchen sink. Mrs Kitto sipped the water noisily with a shaking hand then passed the cup back to Belle and sank back, her eyes closed.

'Should I call someone?' Belle said with a prickle of panic.

Mrs Kitto mouthed, 'No. Migraine. I've taken some tablets.' She raised a feeble hand and pointed. 'Curtain, please.'

Belle shut out the worst of the dazzle then picked up a fallen pill bottle from the floor and set it on the side table at Mrs Kitto's elbow. 'Poor you,' she murmured.

'Feel better in a bit. Just have to lie here.'

'I'll stay with you,' she said, hovering.

Mrs Kitto dipped her head slightly and her lips shaped, 'Thank you.'

A damp flannel. That's what people did for headaches. Back in the kitchen Belle found a clean tea cloth, soaked it, wrung it out and folded it into a band which she took to Mrs Kitto and laid across her forehead.

'Nice, thank you,' the woman whispered.

'It's a good thing I came in,' Belle said. 'I was passing and saw your purse on the path.'

'Thank you. Stupid me. Scrabbling for the key. It came on while I was on the bus and I only just got myself home.'

There was a silence during which the cat strolled in and began to rub itself against the sofa, purring.

'Oh, Smudge. It's feeding time. Belle ...'

'Of course.'

'Tin in fridge. Give her what's left. And make us some strong tea. The doctor says no caffeine, but it seems to help.'

By the time Belle carried in mugs of fragrant tea, Mrs Kitto's face was beginning to look a more normal colour. She tucked a crocheted rug around Mrs Kitto's knees and, aware that her own clothes were damp from swimming, knelt on the floor by the fireplace. She took a sip of tea and glanced about the room. A pair of china dogs occupied the wooden mantelpiece on either side of a vase of dried flowers. A collection of porcelain thimbles filled a tiny set of shelves on the white painted wall. Several photographs in frames stood on a low, glass-fronted bookcase next to the window, but in the dim light she couldn't see who they were.

Mrs Kitto set her mug on the side table and looked up, smiling at Belle. 'Thank you. That was very welcome.'

'Are you feeling better?'

'The pills are beginning to work. I don't get the headaches very often, but when I do . . . Phew.'

Belle nodded to show she understood, but Mrs Kitto was still looking at her, a soft expression in her brown eyes. 'You don't need to stay, but I must say it's nice having you here.'

Belle smiled. 'It's fine.'

'I'm glad to meet you properly, but sorry I'm not at my best. I don't usually expect guests to make their own tea.'

'I don't mind at all.'

'How are you getting on at Silverwood?'

'I've only been here a few days. It's okay, though.'

'They're a funny lot. That Rain especially.'

'I haven't met her. She's away somewhere.'

'I warn you, she has some strange ideas. And I feel sorry for her little boy amongst all those eccentric adults. Of course, it's wonderful surroundings for a child to grow up in, but I don't think he sees anyone his own age.'

'Doesn't he go to school?'

'No. Rain teaches him herself.'

'Oh, I didn't know.'

'I only do because Francis tells me. We speak quite often.'

Mrs Kitto had become talkative, obviously feeling better, but now a wave of pain crossed her face and she closed her eyes once more.

'Would you like more tea?'

She moved her head to indicate no, then adjusted the damp tea towel on her forehead. She whispered, 'Tell me a bit about yourself, Belle. It'll distract me nicely.'

'What shall I tell you?'

'What brought you here?'

'Oh, well, Gray did. Do you know Gray?'

'The singer with the corn-coloured hair? I've seen him with his guitar as I've walked past the house to the road.'

'Yes, he was here last year as well.' Belle went on to explain how she loved music and how she had first heard Gray perform. 'He sang a song about Silverwood and made it sound magical.'

'It is,' Mrs Kitto said wistfully. 'A beautiful place. I'm lucky to live here. Francis has been kind. Listen, I wonder if you'd mind fetching some biscuits. There's a tin in the pantry. The one with roses on it.'

When Belle returned with a few ginger biscuits on a plate she found Mrs Kitto in a stronger state. They ate for a moment in silence.

'You know,' Mrs Kitto said, brushing away crumbs, 'I've been wanting to speak to you properly since we first met. The truth is that you remind me of someone Francis and I used to know. Ridiculous, such associations, but when I saw you the other day I was immediately drawn to you.'

'I thought you looked at me ... well, strangely. Who is it I remind you of?' Belle picked a bit of cat hair off the rug and watched it float away. Secrets and strange associations could be creepy, but not when Mrs Kitto was speaking because she was such a kindly person and Belle felt comfortable with her. She wondered privately what might have happened to Mr Kitto and glanced over at the photographs on the bookcase, thinking one might be of him. Mrs Kitto noticed the direction of her gaze.

'The middle one. Would you like to fetch it? Yes, that one. Bring it here.'

It was a studio portrait of a young woman in a nurse's uniform. Belle passed it over. 'Dear Imogen,' Mrs Kitto said, studying it with a sigh. 'We need a bit more light, don't we?'

A pause while Belle adjusted the curtains again.

'That's better. This is my friend Imogen Lockhart in 1940 as a student nurse.'

Belle took the photograph from her and angled it towards the light. Imogen was smiling gently. Her fair hair was pinned back under her nurse's cap, but it was possible to see that it was wavy and abundant. She had an open face with large friendly eyes, a broad forehead and an intelligent expression, but her features and her skin were so smooth and unblemished that Belle thought the print had probably been touched up by the studio.

'She's lovely,' Belle said politely and handed it back. 'But I don't think she looks like me. For a start she's fair and I'm dark.'

'I suppose I remember the real live Imogen. It's the shape of the face and the line of the eyes. You move in the same way as her, too.'

'I'm not able to judge that,' Belle said, laughing. 'How do I move?'

Mrs Kitto thought a moment. 'You hold yourself very upright when you walk,' she said, 'and you swing your arms and move your whole body. Don't look so worried, it's attractive.'

Astonished, Belle murmured, 'I don't do it on purpose.'

'Of course not. We can't help these things. Imogen told me once she'd been sent to have deportment lessons at school to make her walk with more ladylike daintiness, but they didn't work.'

'How did you get to know Imogen?'

'Let's say that we worked together during the war.' Her eyes twinkled.

'Were you a nurse, too?' Belle wanted to know. Mrs Kitto was back to her normal self.

'Aha. If you'd be good enough to make us another pot of tea now, I'll tell you more about it.'

Eleven

December 1940

'Nurse Lockhart,' Sister Chapman called over the rattle of Imogen's trolley. 'After you've finished in the sluice room, take this box of bandages back to stores. They're the wrong size. And remember to ask for a receipt this time.'

'Yes, Sister,' Imogen sighed, and continued on her way.

The only good thing about shutting herself in the sluice room to wash the bedpans and urine bottles was the pleasure of her own company for a few minutes. The job itself was disgusting and she took care not to breathe through her nose as she snapped on rubber gloves, ran water in the sink and reached for the carbolic solution. She'd learned the hard way to be thorough in this task. Sister often inspected the students' work and had sent her back more than once to scour the insides of the bedpan handles or wipe the sink round again and Imogen had had to bite back a retort, sigh and reapply herself to the task until everything was spotless. Today, as ever, she was racing against the clock. There were still too many jobs left to do before it was time to serve lunch to the patients.

A few minutes later the door opened and her pal Sarah Summers poked her small pointed face around it. 'Skates on, Lockhart, there are still two beds to make up. Oh, and Sister's on the warpath. One of the thermometers has vamoosed.'

'Nothing to do with—' Imogen began to say, but the door had already closed. She wiped her forehead with her sleeve then noticed with dismay that she'd forgotten to remove her starched white cuffs before she'd set to work. Too late now, but if Sister noticed . . . She was sure that Sister gave her the worst jobs because she didn't like her. Twice, since she'd started on the wards, she'd been called to Matron's office for a wigging, once for oversleeping and missing the beginning of a shift, the other for answering back too often. That was something else she'd learned not to do. Sister was always right.

There were times, though not often, when Imogen regretted her choice of war work. She'd never had to survive on so little sleep before, not even during the week of the great sickness bug at Silverwood the previous winter when half the school was bedridden. The shifts here were long. She'd started at nine this morning, and after a three-hour break this afternoon into which she'd have to fit some study, she would resume until eight in the evening, though if she hadn't finished her allotted tasks, it might be later than that. The night nurses would never take on the day staff's work.

She set the last enamel bottle upside down on its rack, cleaned all the surfaces and made sure that everything was in its place before changing her soiled apron and rushing out of the door, only to bump straight into Sister Chapman. 'Is there a fire in the sluice room?' Sister asked, her high-pitched voice dripping with irony. 'Or a haemorrhage?' These were the only two situations when nurses were allowed to run.

'No. Sorry, Sister.'

'More haste, less speed. Go and help Nurse Summers. Mrs Pascoe needs adjusting again. And don't forget the bandages.'

'Yes, Sister.' Mrs Pascoe was a mountainous woman who'd broken her leg when she'd slipped on her daughter-in-law's newly washed kitchen floor. The limb was in traction and clearly uncomfortable because she was always asking for her position to be altered.

'Oh, and Nurse ...'

Imogen turned, eyebrows furrowed. 'No, I haven't seen the thermometer, Sister,' she said.

'The thermometer has been found. I was only going to say, don't look so worried, you'll upset the patients.' And to Imogen's surprise Sister Chapman cracked a smile. Only a tiny smile but then she only had a small mouth, which was usually pursed as though an ill wind had fixed it that way.

Imogen smiled back. Wonders would never cease, she reflected as she walked briskly across the ward to where Summers was pulling the screens round Mrs Pascoe's bed. 'Lucky escape there,' she whispered to her pal. 'Now, Mrs P, we'll soon set you right.'

Sarah Summers was Imogen's roommate in the nurses' hostel and although the young women were from different backgrounds and unlikely to have met in peacetime, they liked and watched out for one another. Summers was from Falmouth, a clever girl from an ordinary background – her father was a radio operator in the Merchant Navy and currently away at sea, no one knew where. She hadn't ever left Cornwall. Her childhood sweetheart was a Royal Navy marine called Sam and she kept a snapshot of him in uniform at her bedside. He was leaning on a sea wall, a mischievous grin reaching from ear to ear.

Imogen helped Summers pull Mrs Pascoe up on her pillows, a not inconsiderable task, and Mrs Pascoe yelped at the too-sudden movement. Finally, the woman said she was comfortable.

'Nurses!' Sister appeared round the screen. 'Why this cacophony?'

'They're doin' all right, Sister,' Mrs Pascoe said. 'It's my fault. I get this pain, see. Right here under me sit-upon.' The patients were always on the side of the nurses.

'I'm sorry to hear that, Mrs Pascoe. Nurse Lockhart. Bandages. Go.'

Imogen replaced a fallen magazine, found Mrs Pascoe's spectacles for her, then hurriedly left her friend smoothing the bedclothes. She hefted the large box of dressings from the desk onto a spare trolley and sped off with it through the green daylight of the corridors to the back lift that took her down to the surgical stores.

At least she knew the way now. After three months she still made mistakes if sent off somewhere new. The hospital was a jumble of buildings around the original Victorian block with its tall chimneys and pointed gables. On the day of her interview with Matron back in the summer, she had entered via a gracious foyer past a marble bust of the hospital's founder and remembered thinking how grand and splendid it all was. She'd never visited that foyer since, instead using the nurses' entrance approached by a path under a low arch from the nurses' hostel nearby.

Downstairs, she exchanged quips with the storekeeper, pocketed the required receipt and hurried back up to the ward, wondering how she was going to find time to clean the floor before serving lunch. When she returned she knew it was too late. Matron had arrived and with Sister formed a stern reception committee.

'I asked you to sweep the floor earlier, Nurse.' Sister Chapman's smile was long gone. 'Why isn't it done?'

'I...'

Matron raised her eyebrows in admonition so Imogen tossed the storekeeper's receipt into a wooden tray on the desk and stomped off to fetch the broom, her face burning.

Early evenings were the rush hour. Patients had to be washed, bedpans proffered and beds remade. The blackout screens must be put up and the curtains closed, all before the night shift commenced.

By eight o'clock Imogen was so tired that she could hardly walk in a straight line back to the hostel. After a depressing supper of tinned sardines, tepid mashed potato and cold rice pudding she stumbled back to her room and lay down on the creaky iron bedstead with her forearm shielding her eyes, too tired even to read. She must have fallen asleep, for she came to when someone was shaking her. It was Summers. 'Imogen, we're going out, remember?'

'Are we? Oh, heavens, so we are.' There was a dance out at a nearby barracks. Laura Jevons, a vivacious nurse with long-lashed dark eyes, a toothy smile and a smoky laugh, had organized a party of them to go. An officer friend of Jevon's was picking them up in his jeep. Imogen, who'd been sitting on the fringes of the group at supper the night before, hadn't realized she was included.

'You'll enjoy it once we get there.'

Groaning, she swung her feet to the floor and reached for a suitable dress. A brush pulled quickly through her hair, a slick of lipstick, her old coat and she'd have to do.

Outside, the fresh air of the winter evening woke her fully and by the time they arrived at the dimly lit barracks, she realized that Sarah Summers was right. The whole thing felt like a splendid adventure. Soon, in between dances in a Nissen hut warmed by the heat of their bodies, Imogen was sharing an illicit nip of whisky with Sarah and trading banter with some of the officers. By the time the band put down their instruments at midnight, she was thoroughly enjoying herself. She said goodbye firmly to a beefy, red-faced lieutenant who'd been shadowing her like a Labrador dog and followed the other nurses back to the jeep.

'I'll never be able to get up tomorrow,' Sarah whispered as they tiptoed back to their room in stockinged feet to avoid waking the house sister. 'It's all right for you having a day off.'

'Hard cheese,' Imogen laughed.

Tomorrow was a Saturday and at last hers and Ned's

days off had coincided, so Ned was coming to Truro to meet her. It was the first time they'd seen each other since the summer. Despite their promises they'd been poor correspondents, both too busy to write each other more than the odd postcard. However, earlier in the week Imogen had received a telephone message to say that he was free on the Saturday she'd suggested and he'd be arriving on a particular train. She was looking forward to seeing him and hearing all the news.

The next morning the view of the city from the window was shrouded in sleety rain. After breakfast Imogen borrowed Summers's brolly, wrapped her coat round her warmly and ventured out into the street where the gutters were streaming with water. She dived into a shop and bought toiletries and a pair of thick lisle stockings, then dodged puddles and potholes as she made her way to the railway station. There, as arranged, she waited for Ned in the café where he'd taken her with the boys when they'd first met. She rubbed the condensation from the window and looked out, but there was no sign of him so she lingered patiently over her tea. Finally, she picked out his rain-coated figure hurrying across the concourse. She smiled tenderly for he presented a comic figure, having forgotten to remove his cycle clips. Soon he was inside, hanging his dripping coat and hat on the stand by the door and beaming all over his face.

'You are soaked,' she gasped, seeing his sodden trousers.

'Cycling to the station was not the best of ideas,' he said with a twinkle.

'You must warm up. Let's go over there,' she said, eyeing a free table near the gas fire. She gathered up her belongings. Soon they were sitting by the hissing flames with Ned's gloves drying on the guard and the scent of wet wool rising around them.

He brushed his forearm against the table and flinched. 'Ouch. Sorry, I came off at one point taking a bend, it was so slippery.' He rolled up a sleeve and showed her the wound.

'Oh, that's nasty,' she exclaimed. 'May I?' She took his hand and turned the arm gently to examine the long graze on his forearm that was beaded with dried blood. 'Wiggle your fingers,' she commanded and he obliged. 'I don't think anything's broken but you'll have a horrid bruise.' She felt the pulse on the underside of his wrist quicken under her touch and couldn't help noticing the gold hairs on the back of his hand, the smoothness of the skin, his strong fingers and short clean nails. She heard him swallow. Embarrassed, she released him.

'It sounds as though I'll survive. Thank you.' He kept his voice level and his eyes focused on his sleeve as he refastened the cuff.

'I should have stopped you coming,' she said awkwardly. 'The weather is awful.'

'No, you shouldn't.' His eyes met hers. 'We've tried often enough to meet. Can't allow a little bit of rain to put us off.'

The waitress arrived with fishpaste sandwiches and a fresh pot of tea and the awkward moment was broken. Imogen fiddled with the cups and saucers then they set upon the sandwiches, eating hungrily and eagerly swapping news.

Imogen described how hard she was working, how by comparison being under-matron at St Mary's was one long holiday.

'We have lectures in the afternoon but I keep falling asleep. Let's hope my brain absorbs the information somehow because there are exams after Christmas.'

'Can't you mug it up from a textbook?'

'Too tired to read. I go over the same page time and again and don't take anything in. I should be studying today, Ned, not gallivanting with you.'

He laughed. 'A cup of tea and a sandwich is hardly gallivanting. Anyway, you need some time off. You look tired, if it's not rude of me to say. What are you doing at Christmas?'

'I'm on duty,' she sighed. 'So are most of the junior pros. We're the workhorses, you see. Still, everyone says Christmas Day is fun in the wards. The rumour is that Matron's actually tracked down some turkey. What about you lot?'

Ned made a face. 'I'll be on duty, too. You'll remember from last year that it's the masters with families who have time off. A few of the boys are going home or to relatives, but it's different this year with the Blitz. Families are scattered. Anyway, the trains will be packed with servicemen. I don't mind. It would be nice to see my parents, I haven't been home since the summer, but I won't regret missing the ghastly annual sherry party with the neighbours!'

'Stiff last year, didn't you tell me?'

'Stiff was the word. Everyone moaning about short-ages and not understanding that teaching is a reserved occupation, which is why I wasn't in uniform. Actually, we've lost a couple of teaching staff that way recently. Bit of a nuisance in that now I'm now having to teach Latin, not one of my strengths. One of them's Oliver Dalton, so I'm now temporarily deputy head.'

'Oliver, he's signed up?' She felt a pang, whether of sadness or relief. So he'd gone. Would she ever see him again?

'Left a few weeks ago. I had a chat with him before he went. He looked less gloomy than he'd done for months. It's the loss of his brother that decided him. Said he felt he'd copped out by being a teacher in beautiful surroundings while his brother had made the ultimate sacrifice. Made me feel I've copped out myself.'

'Those boys need you, Ned. Anyway, I thought you'd be turned down for active service.'

'I would. The effects of that childhood brush with polio, but I expect if I pushed it ... Well, teaching's a valuable job and someone has to do it.'

'They do. Don't beat yourself up about it, Ned.'

'But here are you doing your duty splendidly. I must say, I'm envious.'

'Sometimes I think I'm just a glorified skivvy,' she sighed, then smiled. 'But strangely, I love it!'

'What do you like about it?'

'Even the skivvying feels important. I understand why the wards have to be spotless and everything shipshape so the patients avoid infections and receive the best possible care. And they're pathetically grateful. They can see how hard we nurses work. There are some stupid antiquated rules, though.

Do you know, we're not allowed to speak to the doctors, not even the medical students? Only Sister can. And I was torn off a strip once for not leaving the bed castors all facing the same way.'

'It sounds like the military. Kit inspections and so forth.'

'Don't get me started on uniforms. Collars and cuffs, snow-white and starched. Most impractical. And it took me weeks to learn to pin the cap on properly. At least the cape's warm. And it's nice the way we're treated when we're out and about. If they realize we're nurses, people are respectful. Sometimes I meet an ex-patient – we're not supposed to talk to them, but of course it would be wrong to be rude so you find yourself listening to how their lives are going and whether their stomach ulcers are still giving them trouble . . . I'm sorry, Ned, I'm babbling.'

'Not at all. It's interesting. And your eyes light up when you're talking about it. I like that!'

The conversation moved on, the pair exchanging bits of news. Imogen explained that she was due some leave soon, and thought she'd visit her mother for a few days. Ned said that the Fanshawe-Hicks boys were thriving, and that the maid, Kezia, was being teased for being courted by a local farmer's son.

'I know. She writes to me sometimes, dear thing. So does Miss Edgecumbe, which is kind of her.'

Finally, the waitress came to clear their table.

'Should we order more tea?' Ned wondered.

'No, I'm swimming in it.' She inspected his gloves on the fireguard. 'I think they're dry. What about the rest of you?'

'Not bad, I'd say. What shall we do now? It's hardly a day for a walk by the river.'

They decided on the cathedral, which neither of them had visited before. 'It's funny,' Imogen said, 'but there's never time to do anything like that. I haven't been to a church service for months. Haven't thought about it, to be honest.'

'While I, of course, never miss a day, if you count morning assembly at Silverwood. Though a few of the boys have joined the choir at the parish church and sometimes it's my turn to escort them on Sundays.'

'That's a lovely thing for them to do.'

Ned paid the bill and they buttoned themselves up against the weather and sallied forth, Ned brandishing the umbrella and Imogen holding his arm.

It was chilly in the cathedral, but at least it was dry. Several other people had obviously had the same idea for it was busy, and sounds of conversation were transformed into something musical, taken up by the great airy space. Ned and Imogen walked about separately, examining the memorial stones and the statues, each lost in their own thoughts. They spent some time together in a side chapel, which was all that was left of the ancient parish church that the cathedral had replaced.

'It has a lovely atmosphere,' Imogen whispered as they sat down together in the cathedral nave and watched the activity around, 'and the coloured windows are beautiful.' As she spoke, the organ started up with a few parps and squeaks, and then they were stunned into silence by a joyous shower of notes that cascaded around them. 'A Bach fugue, I think,'

Ned whispered when she asked if he knew, 'no idea which one, but it's a fine instrument.' The fugue stopped abruptly and a familiar hymn started up.

'I wish I knew about music, but I don't,' Imogen sighed. 'I love it. I can sing, sort of.'

'You've got a lovely voice.'

'Thank you, so do you.' She remembered how they sang together on their walks, practising the rounds that the boys often enjoyed. Ned had a fine tenor voice.

It was restful sitting with him with all the beauty around. She knew that if she encouraged him, their friendship would deepen and turn to something else. She remembered his reaction to her touch when she'd examined his injured wrist and the way his eyes had rested on her. The thought made her aware that they were sitting close together now. She carefully shifted away an inch or two. If she allowed things to develop then it would be serious with Ned and she didn't want that at present. Her life was filled with work at which she badly wanted to succeed and, anyway, she didn't know how she felt about Ned. Not with the warmth of desire she'd begun to feel in Oliver's presence, that was certain. No, she mustn't dwell on Oliver; he'd obviously not been interested in her. Anyway, he was gone, heaven knows where to what fate.

And Ned? She glanced at his dear, friendly face, his eyes closed as he listened to the music. He was a beloved friend, there was no doubt about that, but she felt determined to keep it that way. Anyway, at present it was more important to do her duty as a citizen than to marry and she was lucky to be mostly enjoying that duty.

The sleet had eased when they left the cathedral and a pale wintry sun had emerged from the clouds, making the wet streets sparkle. They joined a short queue for the Regent Cinema and took their seats in the musty auditorium just as the newsreel was starting. It was sobering, sitting in silence, watching awful scenes of the aftermath of air raids in British cities, with the falsely cheery voiceover reassuring the audience that Britannia was unbowed. When the lights went up she whispered, 'We are lucky down here. Hitler doesn't appear to be interested in Truro.'

'Thank heavens for that,' Ned murmured back.

'I hadn't realized that things were so bad in London. I hardly see a paper, there simply isn't time, and you know how I used to like keeping up. It's the first time I've been to the pictures in months.'

'Me, too. Ah, here we go.' The lights had dimmed and the screen leaped into jaunty life. The film was a light comedy set in sunny Texas with no mention of bombs or rationing and Imogen became so caught up in it, laughing, that the time seemed to pass in a flash.

'That *was* good for me,' she remarked as they gathered coats and umbrellas and rose to leave.

'I thought you were enjoying it,' Ned said. 'Absolute rubbish, of course, but Jane Wyman's a very pretty girl.'

'If you like those kind of looks,' she said, a touch of primness entering her voice, then she saw he was teasing and smiled back. 'The film was just what I needed, Ned,' she said. 'I haven't laughed so much in ages.'

They were standing outside now, buttoning their gloves

against the cold. It was getting dark. The air was crisp and smelled metallic and the sky had an odd yellow tinge as though it was trying to snow.

Ned turned to her, his lips pressed together in regret. 'I must be getting back. God knows what the trains will be like. Mine was packed coming up.'

'And there's the cycle ride at the other end. I hope you have lights.'

'I do. Not that they're much use with all that tape on them.'

'You must go carefully. I'll walk with you to the train.'

'That would be lovely.' He gave her his arm and they climbed the hill to the station where they found there would be a wait, so they had tea in the platform café. It was crowded with men in uniform and the only free table was by the door, which admitted a blast of cold air every time it was opened, but the tea was hot and reviving.

Ned kept looking round at the servicemen with their kit bags, an unhappy expression on his face. Imogen guessed what he was thinking – that he should be one of them – and her heart went out to him. She reached and squeezed his hand briefly and whispered, 'Don't. You're doing what is needed, Ned. Honestly.'

'Do I give myself away so easily?' He sounded grumpy.

'No. It's only because I know you.' She met his eye with a look of kindness and his face cleared and he smiled. 'You mustn't worry. Think of all the good that you do.'

'Dear Imogen, you always say the right thing. How I wish we had longer together today.'

'It's rotten, isn't it?'

'It's so difficult to meet.'

'I know. And it's going to be worse when I'm on nights. It's on the cards, you know.'

'Poor you. You will find time to write?'

'I'll do my best, but I hope you'll forgive me for being erratic. It's bad enough finding time to answer my mother's letters. Do keep sending me postcards, though. The little sketches you draw make me giggle, especially the one of Mr Forbes.'

She was keeping it light and saw the disappointment in his face.

'And I love hearing about you, of course!' she added quickly.

'Of course.' But his eyes were sad. Then he brightened. 'Oh, I almost forgot.' He dug his hand in his pocket and brought out a small, flat package wrapped in brown paper. 'It's for Christmas.'

'Oh, Lordy, I haven't got you anything,' she wailed as she took it from him. 'There's been no time for Christmas shopping.'

'Don't worry, I understand.' He sighed and looked up as a train came in at a further platform. 'I'd better go.'

He left some coins on the table and she followed him out and across to where the little shuttle train from Falmouth had just arrived. They waited while it disgorged a seemingly endless load of passengers and was made ready for its return journey.

'Goodbye, Im. Happy Christmas.' Slowly Ned brushed her cheek with his fingers.

'And to you, dear Ned.' Feeling suddenly very fond of him, she hugged him tightly then flushed and before he could say anything, muttered, 'You'd better go. Goodbye.'

You fool, she told herself as she hurried through the crowds, out of the station and down the road past the rows of sandstone terraces. *You'll just encourage him*. But hugging him had seemed the right thing to do at that moment. She slid her hands in her bag to find her gloves and encountered the package that he'd given her. It was obviously a book, but she decided not to open it until Christmas Day. Ten days to go. She ought to buy something for her mother. If she passed West End Drapery on her way back to the hospital, she could see if they had a nice scarf or a box of handkerchiefs.

~

'Merry Christmas!' the nurses on the new shift called to one another at breakfast in the hostel, their excited voices belying their bleary eyes. Like a flock of awkward ducks they stepped outside into snowy darkness, sliding and shivering their way to work where they hung up their dripping capes and changed their shoes. The atmosphere on the ward felt instantly different from usual. Some of the more able male patients had hung up paper chains and holly the day before and the night nurses seemed unusually reluctant to leave their posts for they would miss the fun.

'Here come our nurses,' birdlike Miss Evans trilled cheerfully over her neck brace. 'Happy Christmas, lovelies!' Her greeting was echoed around the ward by a dozen other women. Everyone managed to look bright and lively, except poor Mrs Bowen lying with her face to the wall, unable to move even if she'd wanted to, which she didn't, for the army truck that had crushed her on a country road and left her with broken ribs had killed her youngest, a baby of two. Imogen was taking special care of Mrs Bowen and it was to her that she went first to ready her for the day.

The early part of the morning was the usual blur of activity – emptying bedpans, washing patients and changing bedding, but the atmosphere was more relaxed than usual. Matron had taken the day off and the house doctors arrived before lunch full of fun, wearing garlands of tinsel and taking turns like schoolboys to bat an escaped balloon. Sister, however, was as beady-eyed as ever. 'Christmas doesn't mean dropping standards, Nurse,' she grumbled regarding a tea stain on Imogen's apron, but even Sister managed a smile when she pulled a cracker with Jeannie, at sixteen the youngest orthopaedic patient, in for an operation on her club foot. Then there was Christmas dinner – the much-anticipated turkey and a Christmas pudding that contained little dried fruit and was smothered with bland custard. The nurses were looking forward to theirs later.

At two o'clock, the doors were opened and visitors poured in with cries of joy and bags of gifts for their loved ones. Imogen stayed on a little to be part of it. After all, it was more cheerful than the nurses' hostel and she witnessed many touching family scenes that left her feeling wistful. What would her own mother be doing today? Mrs Lockhart had written to say that she might have Christmas dinner with Aunt Verity and Uncle Geoffrey, but that none of Imogen's cousins would be home. Perhaps Imogen wasn't missing much there then.

Back in the hostel by three, she and the other nurses

listened to the King read his Christmas Message on the wireless in halting tones. 'Why's there a sound of running water behind him?' Summers wondered.

'Shh,' someone complained, but when they listened closely there it was.

'Perhaps he's on a boat,' Imogen said when the speech finished.

'Or in the bath,' Summers gurgled, overcome by her own joke.

'That's disrespectful,' pious Vera Reynolds said. 'I thought it very touching, all that about children separated from their parents.'

'It was,' everyone agreed, and they were silent for a moment thinking of their own families, whom they weren't able to see today, and of fathers and brothers and cousins and sweethearts in faraway places, some in deadly danger. Imogen put in a prayer for Oliver, hoping that he was somewhere safe.

In a quiet moment Imogen opened her presents. A pair of woollen gloves and a postal order from her mother, both very welcome. Stockings from her aunt, similarly. A comic-looking china pig, carefully wrapped, from her old schoolfriend Monica, who had a peculiar sense of humour. She set it on her bedside cabinet, resolving to send something silly back. Lastly, she undid Ned's present. She smiled to see that it was a pocket-sized guidebook to Cornwall with a map folded inside the back. 'In memory of happy days,' Ned had written on the title page, 'and in anticipation of more. Happy Christmas,

1940! Yours, Edward Thorpe.' A very formal message, she thought, flicking through the volume with a smile, but touching and kind. She would treasure the book.

She added it to several others on the bottom shelf of the cabinet. A pocket-sized New Testament, her mother's latest crime novel, several forbidding-looking textbooks and a couple of classics from the local library that she probably wouldn't have time to read.

Twelve

June 1966

'It was some time before Imogen saw Ned again.'

In the quiet gloom of the sitting room Mrs Kitto's voice faltered and came to a halt. And she sighed. 'I think that's all I can manage for now, Belle. I hope it hasn't bored you.'

'Not in the least,' Belle replied sincerely. She was puzzled about the importance of this unknown Imogen; but had become enthralled by her story and secretly disappointed that it was unfinished. 'You must be exhausted.'

'I am rather tired. I do hope you'll come again, though.'

'I will.' Belle smiled. 'Is there anything I can do for you before I go?' Mrs Kitto assured her that there wasn't so she let herself out and set off across the fields back to Silverwood, deep in thought. Mrs Kitto had told her story vividly and Belle was eager to know more.

Back at Silverwood, there was no one in the kitchen, just a

ghostly scent of strawberry jam. In the hall, the sound of Gray playing and singing was drifting down the stairs. There was no hurry to go up and disturb him. Instead, Belle opened a door she hadn't tried before. It swished inwards over a carpet and, peeping round, she realized it was a study or a library. She stepped inside.

It was really two small rooms, she quickly realized, with an interconnecting door standing open between them. In this first room a large, leather-topped desk stood under a tall window with a view across the back courtyard. Shelves stuffed with ancient leather-bound tomes lined the walls. Belle sniffed at the comforting smell of them. It was peaceful here, though with the door to the hall ajar she could just make out the sound of Gray's guitar.

The carpet was thick with dust and she sent up puffs of it as she walked about examining the titles on the spines. These volumes had dull-sounding titles indicating local manorial records, but when she passed through into the second room she discovered rows of classic novels and, on several lower shelves, an untidy collection of children's books. Recently raided, it seemed, for some had fallen onto the floor and there was a path in the dust from the hall. Angel's, perhaps, from the footprints.

Belle stooped and gathered up the fallen books, and returned them to the shelves. Finding one that she'd loved when she was little about a runaway train, she brushed the cobwebs from a careworn armchair and sat for a while, turning the pages and smiling to herself. Then she slotted it back among the others and stepped sideways to survey the shelves of classics. Dickens; all the Brontës, in a standard red livery with titles in gold; a set of John Galsworthy novels, and others by authors whose names she didn't recognize. She had never read Charlotte Brontë's *Villette* so she drew it from the shelf and turned to go. There was a second door out to the hall and she left by that. As she looked back at the rooms, each bathed in gentle daylight, she thought of them as a world apart, a sanctuary. She closed the door after her, promising to be back.

Upstairs, she told Gray where she'd been, but not about seeing Arlo at the beach, though she was more unsettled by it than she'd thought.

~

Belle was to learn much more about Gray over the course of the following afternoon. It was a Friday and they'd now been at Silverwood for almost a week. Kynance Cove wasn't far as a crow might fly, but first involved a long drive inland to Gweek where the river narrowed and there was a bridge. The journey was delightful, Belle shouting out directions with the help of Gray's battered roadmap. First they passed through the cool, watery green light of sunken lanes, where trees met in arches overhead, then, on a better road, between high hedges with glimpses of pasture and rolling fields, and finally, after the bridge, a long dash south across rough open country.

It was a perfect summer's day. They drove with the windows down and the breeze in their hair, Belle holding her breath whenever Gray took a bend too fast. Once they almost hit a farm truck coming the other way, but Gray swerved into a layby just in time and the truck rolled past with its horn blaring, leaving them both shaken. Belle shouted at Gray then and threatened to get out. After that he drove more carefully, but scowling.

'Why are you so keen to visit this place anyway?'

She hesitated briefly, wondering how much to tell him. 'I found a photograph at home of myself as a baby,' she said. 'On the back it said "Kynance Cove". So ...'

Belle hadn't told him anything more about her background, but then he'd not asked. She'd let him think the picture he'd seen in her room at university told the truth, that hers was a typical happy family. Nor had she told anyone else about what she'd overheard on her sixteenth birthday. Her anxious reaction to Aunt Avril's casual words might sound ridiculous to an outsider.

'So?' he said, waiting for her to go on.

'So I'm curious about it.' Her explanation sounded weak and he frowned.

'You don't remember being there?'

'I was much too young. A woman was holding me, but it wasn't Mum.' She tried to picture the woman's face, but it hadn't been very clear. Now she took the plunge and told him the rest of it.

'You're lucky,' he growled after a moment. 'At least there are photos of you as a child. My mum doesn't have any. Or says she doesn't. We were always moving in Darbyfield when I was a kid and she was always leaving stuff behind if we had to go in a hurry. If I complained, she said possessions weren't important. I never had many. When I left home I could fit everything except my guitar into an old army kitbag.'

'That's awful. Where did you go?'

'My dad's place for a bit. D'you see that bird?' He pointed ahead. 'The way it's hovering.'

'It's a kite, I think. Why did your mum move around all the time?'

'She never had any money. Or rather if she did, she spent it. Drink and fags, having fun. Then she wouldn't be able to pay the rent and we'd be out. We'd move in with her brother's family for a bit until they got fed up. Or a friend's. Or somewhere cheap and there'd be a reason for that – rats or damp or something. It always went wrong in the end.'

'That's so sad,' Belle breathed.

'I got away as soon as I could. Left school with five O-levels. Did odd jobs, then got in with Stu and his mates. Music was the only thing I liked and was really good at. I thought it would be easy, but it's not, it's hard.'

Belle glanced at him, suddenly aware of his vulnerability. He was concentrating hard on the road, a grim expression on his face.

'What about your dad? And what happened to your mum?'

Gray was silent for a moment and she worried that the question was too intrusive, but he was merely concentrating on edging past a man on an ancient bicycle. Accelerating, he said, 'Dad left Mum when I was five. They'd met at a dance in Darbyfield when he was stationed near there. Not sure they'd have married if I hadn't turned up. Anyway, his family have money and occasionally he'd give us some. That's how I got this car in fact. A final cheque on my twenty-first birthday, a card saying he was moving to York, and I haven't seen him since.'

He sounded bitter.

'And your mum?'

'Mum's still in Darbyfield. She's found a boyfriend who's stuck by her. He's an older man, but steady. I think she's happy at last.'

Suddenly Belle was glad that despite the problems, she at least had a stable family. She felt mean, not telling them exactly where she was when she wrote that letter. They must be worrying about her. And Jackie, her sister, it wasn't fair on her to have disappeared. On the other hand, wouldn't they have come straight down and fetched her back? She felt a pang of annoyance at her seeming inability to do the right thing.

Gray had seemed to her so grown up and independent and that was part of his glamour, but now she knew something of his story she realized that he'd been forced to grow up too fast. His air of maturity might be a veneer, she thought with dismay, a protective shell. She felt overwhelmed, not sure what to say to him for all that he'd suffered.

So she said nothing and they drove the rest of the way in silence. It was a comfortable silence, but Belle was glad to break it when she spotted a sign to Kynance Cove and called out as Gray overshot it. He reversed at speed and turned down the narrow lane towards the sea, which sparkled in the distance.

The car park was busy, but Gray squeezed the car into a

narrow space on the cliff top and they stepped out into a cool breeze, the wind tossing their hair. He grinned at her as he shouldered the canvas bag containing their towels and a picnic and she smiled back, relieved that she hadn't offended him by her silence.

Several times on the steep path down to the beach she stopped to look at the view and was transfixed by the wild glory of the scene below. The tide was out and white-tipped waves dashed against the furthest of the cruel black granite rocks that marched out towards the glittering blue. The golden sand glittered like crystal in the sun. It was so beautiful, the most beautiful place she'd ever seen.

At the bottom, Belle stopped to kick off her sandals and wriggle her toes in the warm sand, closing her eyes in ecstasy. When she opened them, she couldn't see Gray for a moment against the dazzle. There he was, trudging jauntily ahead, and she hurried after him, beyond the crowds then round some rocks to a sheltered spot where he dumped the bag and they spread their towels on the sand.

She stepped out of her dress, adjusted the straps of the bikini she'd borrowed from Chouli, and cried, 'I'm going in,' then dashed towards the sea. The water was icy and she gasped, then the pull of the tide swept her off her feet. A huge wave crashed over her and she tumbled under its spray. In a moment that seemed to go on for ever she was sucked down, rolled over, dragged over shingle and spat out, grazed, breathless and terrified onto the shore. There was Gray, in bathing trunks and T-shirt, and to her dismay he was laughing. 'Sea one, Belle nil. Come on.' He helped her up.

Every inch of her flesh smarted. She blinked and tried not to cry.

'Are you all right?'

'I . . . think so.' The waters of the estuary had been gentle by comparison. Here, on a breezy summer's day, the monstrous power of the ocean had shown itself. It had surged and swelled and roared and smashed itself against her. To her astonishment she started to laugh. It had been frightening, but now that she was safe she felt exhilarated.

'Come on,' she cried, seizing his hand. She tugged him towards the sea, but he resisted.

'No,' he said, a look of horror on his face. As she watched, this turned to shame and then she realized.

'Can't you swim?' she asked in surprise.

He shook his head, and she felt not concern or sympathy, but disappointment. Once more he'd revealed a vulnerable side. He seemed diminished in her eyes.

'It's dangerous. Can't you just paddle and I'll watch?'

She looked around. There were no lifeguards on this part of the beach, but through the dazzle of the sun she saw there were other swimmers in the water, out beyond the rolling breakers. 'I'm going to swim,' she said. 'I'll be careful.' And waded in.

This time she was used to the cold. She worked with the rhythm of the waves, bobbing under or over them, enjoying the thrill of the swell and the sense of buoyancy. She was out of her depth yet felt perfectly safe. After a few minutes she turned, treading water, and studied the beach. Gray was standing on the shore, shading his eyes against the sun. She waved and after a moment he saw her and waved back then skipped backwards from the reaching grasp of the sea. She felt sorry for him now. It was a shame that they could not share this simple pleasure, the exhilaration, the sense of isolation and smallness yet oneness of nature, the marvel of being held up by this vast rolling body of water.

Lengthening her gaze she took in the wider panorama of the beach, the gold of the sand stark against the black rock and the grassy shoulders of the cliffs above. Then she lay back, floating on the water and stared up at the sky where a gull wheeled effortlessly in an updraught and puffs of white cloud floated across a ceiling of deep blue. She closed her eyes and turned a somersault of joy, waited for the world to stop spinning, then half swam, half surfed her way back to the shore. Gray had given up watching her and returned to base to sunbathe. So much for his concern, she thought crossly as she strode up the beach.

She let her wet hair drip on him as she reached across him for her towel.

'Hey!'

She grinned as she dried herself.

'You looked like you were having fun,' he said, squinting up at her.

'I was.' She ran her fingers through her hair, sticky with salt, then lay down on her towel, wriggling herself comfortable. It was warm in the sun. She closed her eyes and saw patterns of light on her lids. Suddenly she felt a tickling sensation and sat up, crying out and brushing at the sand Gray had scattered on her belly. She pushed his hand away and he rolled away laughing. She watched him thoughtfully.

'Why can't you swim?'

Again, that shamed expression. 'Never given the chance.'

'Not even at school?'

'No.' He reached in his bag for a tin and started to roll a cigarette.

'I'll teach you if you like.'

He looked as though he was about to say something, but then shook his head and bent to his task. When he cupped his hand to light the roll-up she liked the scent of it in the salty air.

'Why not, Gray?'

He shrugged.

'You ought to learn. Suppose, I don't know, you fell in a river or something. You might drown.'

He said nothing, just picked a bit of tobacco from his lip.

'Gray?' He looked at her. 'Why won't you learn?'

'Don't fancy it,' he muttered. He lay back and closed his eyes.

God, he was infuriating. Her gaze travelled from his hawkish face over the pulse throbbing at the base of his neck, and along his pale, lean body, the whorls of fair hair on his chest, a line of it running down his belly and desire stirred in her. On impulse she leaned down and bit his forearm.

'Ouch! What the hell are you doing!'

She laughed and licked the toothmark, then pushed herself lightly to her feet.

'I'm going for a walk. Want to come?'

He sat up. 'Where?'

'Round that corner. There might be rock pools.'

'Okay.'

They clambered across rocks in their bare feet, peering into tide pools, enchanted by the miniature watery worlds they saw. Crabs the size of fingernails scuttled under stones while tiny electric-blue fish eluded the wafting arms of bright anemones. Gray crouched down, teasing a large magenta anemone with his finger.

'Perhaps I'll write a song about anemones.'

She laughed. 'What would you say?'

He smoothed back his hair. 'How about: "If I had as many arms as an anemone, I'd wind them all around you, my love."'

'Ha ha. That makes me think of Marvell and "my vegetable love should grow/Vaster than empires".'

'Anemones aren't vegetables.'

'There are flowers called anemones that you see in the woods. Mum says they're called wind flowers.'

'Now you've totally confused me. Okay, "If I had as many arms as a *sea* anemone. I'd wind them all around you . . ." He raised his hands and wiggled his fingers while widening his eyes and grinning. Belle giggled and fell backwards, landing on her bottom with an 'Ouch!'

'Are you all right?'

She nodded.

While Gray returned his attention to the anemones, she thought about the photograph of herself as a baby. Black and white, of course, but perhaps it had been on another such beautiful day that she'd been here. Funny to think of herself then, grasping handfuls of sand with starfish fingers or paddling in the shallows while clutching a grown-up's hand. She had no memory of any of this, but she smiled to see a young couple at the water's edge a few yards away. They were helping their little girl build a sandcastle, but as fast as the man upturned buckets of sand for her, the child lurched forward to demolish them. Belle looked round for Gray. He was sitting by another rock pool, examining the sole of his foot. She climbed over to look. 'I've cut it on a stone,' he said.

'Wash it in the pool,' she advised, 'the cold water will help,' and he did so. The blood swirled in patterns like smoke in the water, alarming the tiny fish, but after a minute or two the bleeding stopped. He stood up, testing his weight, then she helped him limp back to the part of the beach where they'd left their things.

'Is it picnic time yet?' he asked and sank onto his towel with a sigh. 'I'm starving.'

She rummaged in the bag, passed him a packet of sandwiches and one for herself and a bottle of lemonade. They laughed at the strange vegetable pâté she'd spread in the sandwiches, but enjoyed Janey's fruitcake; then pleasantly full, baked by the warmth of the sun and lulled by the sound of the waves, they lay down in one another's arms and fell asleep.

Belle jerked awake first, shivering with cold. Something was wrong. She sat up then leaped to her feet, shocked to see how far the tide had advanced up the sand as the sun dazzled low over the sea. 'Gray.' She shook him awake. 'We've got to move!'

He cursed and rose at once, hopping because of his injured foot. They gathered their possessions and scurried up the shrinking strip of sand. Everyone had gone from their part of the beach and Belle realized with a jolt of panic that the route round the promontory to the cliff path would be cut off by the sea at any moment. Large waves were already running across the sand and dashing onto the rocks. No one, she thought with anger, had thought to wake them and now they'd be marooned.

'How do we get back?' There was panic in Gray's voice.

'We paddle, silly,' she said, trying to stay calm. 'Come on!' She grasped his arm and dragged him towards the swirling shallows by the rock face. As they waded in a large wave reared and broke over them and they lurched, clutching each other to steady themselves. Belle, reeling, was stunned to glimpse the way they'd just come. The spot where they'd slept was already covered.

Now a huge breaker was pounding towards them. 'Run,' Belle screeched, pulling Gray onwards. They staggered around the promontory just before the wave hit. They toiled through swirling water up the main beach towards dry sand and paused to recover. Around them, families were still corralling children and rolling up windbreaks. Some glanced at Gray and Belle curiously. Gray, she saw, was limping and gasping with pain and his face was ashen. Relieved that they were safe, Belle also felt a pang of a less worthy emotion – shame. *Gray should have been the brave one, not me.*

Gray drove them home with the music turned up too loud for talking. Belle lay back with her eyes closed, lost in a disturbing daydream. Was it the savage beauty of the beach that caused strange thoughts to whirl in her mind like blood in the rock pool? Or something to do with the photograph?

She felt she was reaching, reaching for something she didn't recognize or understand. She flinched at the touch of Gray's warm hand on hers and opened her eyes. He glanced down at her, his other hand on the wheel, and smiled.

'All right?' he said.

'Yeah.' She returned his smile.

She'd got to know Gray better today; it had been wonderful for them both. She'd confided in him, sort of, and in turn he'd told her about his upbringing. On the beach, too, she'd seen his vulnerabilities and been able to help him. She no longer minded that she'd been the brave one. They'd become closer.

It was late afternoon when they turned into the drive. As Silverwood came into view Gray slowed the car.

A young boy was standing watching them from the grass by the goat pen. His white-blond hair was cut to shoulder length with a fringe and he wore an old-fashioned long blue top and matching shorts. Overall, he put Belle in mind of Christopher Robin. The child watched with large troubled eyes as they parked the car and climbed out. Then he ran ahead of them into the house.

'Angel,' Gray said. 'So, Rain is back.'

Thirteen

Belle sensed the change in the atmosphere as soon she entered the kitchen. Janey was sitting at the table drinking tea with a tall, elegant woman and she greeted Belle and Gray with eyes sparkling.

'Rain, this is Belle. And you remember Gray?' Her usual weariness was gone. She was quite transformed.

'Of course. Nice to meet you, Belle.' Rain's voice was low, mellifluous. As she rose gracefully from the table, she swept back her hair, which was long and honey-coloured. Belle was stunned by her presence, her willowy figure in a calf-length grass-green robe gathered at her slim waist. Her face was pale, oval, and her eyes a clear light blue. Belle managed to murmur a greeting in return, and Rain stepped forward and shook her hand briefly, leaving an impression of coolness and a flowery fragrance.

The woman turned her attention to Gray. 'It's so good to see you again.' Her speech was measured and she exuded calmness and strength. Gray's description of her had been far from adequate, Belle decided. To his obvious discomfort, Rain touched his shoulders and pressed her cheek briefly against his. This woman displayed a charisma and confidence that Belle had never come across before. The very air sang with it.

The boy was hovering in the background and Rain brought him by the hand and stood him before her. He peered shyly from the halter of her arms. 'This is my Angel,' she told Belle, and Belle said, 'Hello,' but he did not smile or speak. 'He'll get used to you,' Rain said, stroking the boy's hair. 'Won't you, darling?'

Angel raised his head to whisper to his mother, 'The goats are hungry. Can I give them some food?'

'Janey?' Rain said.

Janey leaped up. 'I'll cut up a carrot,' she said. Angel watched as she washed the earth from it and sliced it. 'They need small pieces, dear, or they might choke.'

Angel nodded and took the handful of pieces from her. 'Off you go,' said Rain, and he ran outside with Figgy the dog at his heels. He was quieter than any boy Belle had known and she felt sorry for him being the only child in this house of adults.

'Bless him,' Janey said, a motherly expression on her face. 'He does love animals.'

Belle wondered whether Rain was frowning because of Angel or for some other reason. 'I hope you don't mind that we're here,' she told her. She'd remembered that Gray hadn't warned anyone that they were coming.

'Oh, you're most welcome. We liked having Gray last year, didn't we, Gray? He's so talented. We love his special gift of music.'

Gray grinned his thanks.

Belle remembered: 'Janey told us you'd gone to a conference.'

'A conference?' Rain laughed. 'That is a grand word for it. We've been to Nefoedd.' She noticed Belle's puzzled frown.

'Nefoedd means heaven. It's a place in Wales. Right in the mountains. I go there to refresh my soul and ... yes, I suppose you might call it a conference. There are others like us and we talk and work together. We share the same dreams and visions about the earth. Such marvellous ideas. I'm looking forward to sharing them with you all.'

Belle smiled politely.

'The shaman was there,' Rain said to Janey, who nodded with enthusiasm. 'Such a man of peace. He led us in our meditation every day. We felt so close to him there and to one another. It's how our lives should be.'

'It sounds ... lovely,' Gray said politely.

'Oh, it was. And if I could have brought the mountain air back in a bottle I would have.' She breathed in deeply.

'I love hills and mountains,' Belle said and everyone looked at her. 'It's wonderful here, though,' she added hurriedly.

'It is, it is.' Rain gave every appearance of listening intently so that Belle felt her full focus. The others too seemed swept into her power.

And now Chouli entered the room with a delighted cry and came forward to be hugged, then Arlo who kept his distance but nodded to Rain, and finally Sirius in an overall flecked with paint and wielding a palette knife.

There was an electricity between Rain and Sirius, the air crackled with it as their eyes locked, though they did not touch. 'How was your journey?' he asked her gruffly.

'We were fortunate on the way there. A van drove us as far as Bristol and someone met us there and took us onward. Coming back was more difficult. Three different lifts then a long wait near Bodmin before this posh old lady picked us up,' she sighed. 'For some reason she made it her business to tell me how to raise my son.'

Sirius gave a bark of a laugh. 'I'll bet she regretted that.'

'I was desperate to get home, Sirius, so I was perfectly polite. She'll find her nice shiny car has a nasty scratch down one side, though.' Rain held up the pendant that hung down between her breasts and which Belle hadn't properly noticed before. It was in the shape of a woman with a narrow waist, generous breasts and hips, and raised arms. Her feet met together in a sharp point. Belle imagined it scraping paint from metal and swallowed.

'Oh, Rain, you didn't,' Janey said.

Rain just smiled.

Just then came a cry from outside and they turned to see Angel running in holding up his finger. 'A goat bit me,' he sobbed.

'Oh, Angel,' Rain said, folding him to her. 'Let me see. There isn't any blood. Did you hold the food in your open hand like this for the goat to nibble from?' The boy shook his head. 'I'm sure it didn't do it on purpose.'

'Here, we'll wash it,' Janey said and Angel went with her to the sink.

'Then I'll kiss it better,' Rain remarked, and they watched mesmerized as she did. Janey led Angel outside again to mend his relationship with the goats. 'Well,' Rain said in a sharper voice, 'what's been going on here while I've been away?'

After the evening meal, Rain led the household out into the warm evening, and the regular period of sharing the day's events with one another took on a sense of more serious purpose. They sat on blankets in a small circle on the front grass. Belle and Gray, sitting together, spoke of their afternoon on the beach, how beautiful it was, then Belle was deeply moved when Gray went on to describe her quick-thinking courage in rescuing them both from the incoming tide. 'She was amazing, weren't you, Belle?' and as everyone murmured their approval Belle flushed with happiness. She touched Gray's hand and they exchanged warm smiles.

After nearly everyone else had spoken, Rain encouraged her son to have a go. He murmured something about hating their long journey home to Silverwood then hid his face. Last of all it was Rain's turn to speak. She sat with back poker-straight, legs folded to her side, and her tone was sonorous, dramatic. 'There were several others from communities such as ours,' she said, gesturing with her hands. 'Our numbers are growing. Those who have had enough of the capitalist way of life, who wish to return to a more tranquil state to work with the spirits of nature and to share what we have with each other.' She continued to speak in this way for some time and Belle, like everyone else, was hypnotized by the sound of her voice.

Later in the privacy of their room she asked Gray, 'Do you believe all that?'

'You mean about the spirits and stuff? No, of course not.'

'Nor do I, but she's so commanding in the way she speaks. Who's this shaman person she talks about?'

'All I know is that he's American. Janey says he's from one of the tribes.'

'An Indian? Wow.'

'He's probably a fake.'

'Do you know that?'

Gray shrugged. 'No. I'm just cynical, though Sirius says he has an expensive car.'

'I suppose he has to get around somehow. I wonder who pays for it?'

'That's the question worth asking. Still, I like all the other things Rain says. About a new way of life and all that. This place is perfect for that, isn't it?'

'It is idyllic.' She went to the open window and looked out at the darkening sky. The air was cooler and a breeze had picked up. Over the estuary a mist had fallen. 'It smells of rain,' she said. Her eye fell on Mrs Kitto's cottage where the living room light shone from the curtained window and she bit her lip. She should have called on her to see how her migraine was, but today had been so full.

'I must go and see Mrs Kitto again tomorrow,' she said, turning back to Gray, but her words trailed off and she smiled, for Gray was fast asleep. It must be the sea air.

Although she was tired she lay awake for a long while, brooding on the ups and downs of the day and the ideas that Rain had spoken of. But her last thought before she slept was of Imogen.

Fourteen

6 August 1942

It had been a long hot day at the hospital. Imogen loved working upstairs on the children's ward, but today she felt particularly sorry for the kids having to endure the heat. The nurses had thrown open the windows, but the air was heavy and motionless and as there was a shortage of electric fans, they'd resorted to wiping young limbs and faces with cool flannels and making sure the children had plenty to drink. The evening offered some relief and Imogen was looking forward to going off duty and walking by the river. She checked the pulse of a baby girl asleep in one of the cots, noticing as she did so that it was half-past seven. It was visiting hour and relatives were gathered round many of the beds, anxious-looking mums and a few dads and grandparents, talking quietly, handing over gifts of puzzle books and crayons or food carefully saved from rations. The mother of this particular infant always turned up regular as clockwork, but this evening she hadn't. There was still time – perhaps she was late out of work and on her way.

'Nurse Lockhart,' Sister Peacock called as she marched briskly past with a pile of paperwork. 'We can't turn off the kitchen tap properly. It must be the washer. Will you go and find a man, please, or it'll be dripping all night.'

'Yes, Sister.' Which man, Imogen thought as she draped the little girl's sheet over her hot body. The maintenance staff would have gone home. Maybe there would be a porter around or, failing that, a reasonably able serviceman from one of the men's wards. She smiled at a youngish couple seated at the bedside of their eight-year-old daughter near the door as she hurried out. The mother, she noticed, wore a bright printed cotton skirt.

~

In a field half a mile to the north of the city, a gang of young lads were playing cricket in the evening air. The *thwock* of the ball against willow and the shouts of encouragement joined the cawing of rooks in the trees. Suddenly this tranquil scene was broken by a low rumble like distant thunder. The lad batting looked up and searched the sky. A second the length of a heartbeat and the rumble became a roar and now two enemy planes were upon them, swooping down low, spraying bullets in a deafening stutter of gunfire. The boy cried out and dropped the bat. As he ran with the others towards a hedge, one of the planes swept down past him. His eyes briefly met the gaze of the pilot and he stumbled.

The image of the man's cold, expressionless face burned itself onto his retina.

He would remember that face all his life and, in low moments, brood anew on how any human being could deliberately fire on innocent young boys playing a harmless game of cricket on an idyllic evening.

Another lad broke the spell, seizing his arm and dragging him into the shadow of the hedge where the others already lay, hunched up and terrified. One was clutching his hand, staring at it in dismay, for it was smarting and covered in blood.

The pilots tired of their sport. The planes swept upwards and on towards the city and as the boys watched, shrank to the size of small toys trailing clouds of black smoke. Moments later they heard the distant crack of gunfire and soon after that a violent explosion. Before long a great plume of smoke and flame rose above the city.

Imogen was halfway down the stairs when the windows shattered. Then came a deafening whoosh and a great force snatched her up and slammed her against the wall of the stairway. She dropped to the ground, the wind knocked from her lungs. As she struggled to breathe, the world collapsed around her in a rage of falling masonry. Her shocked brain managed to frame the word 'bomb'.

Coughing and spluttering, she pushed herself to her knees. Blinking grit from her eyes, she tried to focus in the gloom. Debris lay everywhere, smoking with dust. Cries and screams assailed her ears. Light flickered and crackled in the air above. *Fire! The children. No time to lose.* Clambering upwards, crawling over rubble, reaching blindly with sore hands, she tested each foothold until she regained the entrance to the ward.

At that moment came the crump of a second explosion, but much further away this time. She clutched the door frame as the building shivered but thankfully stood firm. Finally, she heard the wail of air-raid sirens.

You're too late, she raged silently, staring at a scene of chaos. Flames licked debris at the far end of the room and urgency propelled her forward. The floor sparkled with shards of glass that crunched under her feet. Beds and cots had been hurled across the room; some of the outside wall had fallen inwards. Under a jagged heap of bricks and plaster near the door she glimpsed part of a bedstead and, with a pang, a scrap of what looked like a woman's patterned skirt. She knew what this meant, but forged on, averting her eyes. Further into the room a child was wailing and Imogen scrambled to where a cot lay on its side against the back wall. She reached and tipped it upright to find a terrified toddler inside. 'Oh, Robbie, dear.' She lifted him up, wrapped a blanket around his shivering form and held him close. When she turned to look for a way out through the dust and smoke, she glimpsed a crumpled body lying behind an upturned trolley and gasped. It was one of the nurses, she wasn't sure who; she should stop to see, but the child was heavy. She scrunched her way across to the pile of rubble above which the ward lay open to the sky, cried for help in a hoarse voice and was rewarded by the appearance of the head and shoulders of a man on a ladder.

'Give him here, my duck,' he said as he clambered over the rubble. She stumbled to meet him and pushed the child into his arms, but when he reached to help her she backed away, saying, 'No, I'm needed here.' She turned and promptly slipped, her knees crashing down onto the lethal carpet of glass. Crying out in agony, she fought to get up.

Others were arriving. Two firemen with a powerful hose that they played on the flames. A police constable, who shot one glance at Imogen and shouted for a stretcher. She looked down at herself and saw with a shock that one leg was covered in blood. Rescue workers with shovels and stretchers were pouring through the ruins and she was scooped up, protesting, and carried away.

Outside, they set her down on the front lawn. Her friend Summers arrived, her uniform still remarkably clean and crisp. 'Let me see to that cut. Stay still.' The wound below her knee was deep, but Summers quickly cleaned and bound it. Imogen stood up carefully, testing her leg. 'I must help. Where are they taking everyone?'

'Sit down. There are plenty helping,' Summers said sternly to no avail.

And indeed there were. Firemen and rescue workers levering masonry, ambulancemen clambering to and fro with laden stretchers, local people mucking in, comforting crying children, doctors working on the injured, nurses directing where to take unhurt patients. In a shaded corner under a great chestnut tree four or five shrouded bodies had been laid, one so little that tears threatened, for Imogen knew that it was a baby, maybe the one she'd been tending before the bomb whose mother hadn't come in time and now really was too late.

She left Summers to comfort an old man in a wheelchair and walked shakily down to the nurses' hostel where she negotiated her way through a bustling crowd towards her room. There she hastily changed into a clean uniform and emerged to join efforts to find beds for the patients. Even her own was given away – to an elderly man with emphysema.

Queuing for cocoa for the patients at the hostel kitchen, Imogen suddenly recalled being slammed against the wall by the explosion. The whooshing sound that hurt her ears, her powerlessness against the force of the bomb . . .

'Nurse Lockhart?' Sister Carter's voice brought her back to earth. Imogen blinked. She saw she had reached the front of the line, but was standing motionless, clutching her empty tray. 'Are you all right?' Sister took the tray from her with a concerned expression.

'Yes, yes. Perfectly all right,' Imogen managed to mutter. 'Well, no.' She gave a sob.

'I should have a wee sit down if I were you,' Sister Carter said briskly, taking her aside. 'Or go for a walk. Get some air, then come back here to the hostel when you're feeling better.'

'A walk, yes. Thank you.' She'd return to the hospital, see what was happening. No one had said anything definite, but there were rumours that Sister Peacock and one of the student nurses had been killed, possibly the girl whose body she'd seen. She closed her eyes briefly. Why had the Huns bombed a hospital, for God's sake? Hadn't they known what it was? How barbarous and senseless.

She limped slowly up the path in the fading light towards the scene of the disaster, glad of the refreshing breeze, to find rescue workers still tirelessly shifting rubble. Several servicemen in uniform were among them; others in blue service overalls were shoring up the damaged frontage with beams and posts. She glanced towards the chestnut tree, but the bodies she feared to see again had been taken away and she was relieved.

A young house doctor she recognized stood stoutly with a clipboard, directing the movements of nurses with patients. She went to his side and asked how she could help and was amazed when a passing Sister clutching a box of files cried, 'Nurse Lockhart!' in an outraged voice. Surely the rules against speaking to doctors didn't apply in such a crisis? But apparently they did. 'Don't just stand there, Nurse,' Sister said roughly, 'we need help to move Outpatients. Come along.'

'That's what I was going to suggest myself,' the doctor murmured, apologetic, and Imogen nodded and followed Sister.

An unaffected ward was being freed up to become the new outpatients department and any equipment that had survived the bomb was to be transferred to it. As Imogen moved to and fro with boxes, she thought how lucky it was that Outpatients had been closed for the night and therefore empty at the time of the explosion – a small mercy. A team of nurses and local women were at work in the new ward, sweeping the floors and arranging furniture with an air of determination. Imogen righted an upturned chair and was restoring a teddy bear to a toy box when Sister swooped and dispatched her to wash dusty stethoscopes and forceps in order to be 'ready for the morning'.

The morning! That would show the Germans! The thought gave her strength and raised her spirits, but as she rinsed a kidney dish in a cracked sink, she was reminded that a leaking tap had been the reason why she'd left the children's ward before the bomb hit. Suddenly her mind couldn't take it in. Had that leak saved her? What would have happened to her if she'd remained on the ward? The question was impossible to answer. She stared into the mirror in front of her. Her face was blotched with tiredness, she had a smudge on her nose and her cap was askew. She hardly recognized herself.

'No slacking now,' came Sister's voice from the door. 'We've little time to lose.'

'Sorry, Sister.' She set the dish to drain with shaking hands and wondered how Sister managed to keep her uniform perfectly clean. Presumably because her job was ordering other people around, she thought, somewhat uncharitably. After all, someone had to be in charge.

It was nearly midnight when the job was done. Imogen found a torch and set off back to the hostel, though she wondered where she would be able to lay her head. Bobbing beams from other torches strafed the ground and she returned one or two 'Goodnights'. Most of the rescue workers had stood down, she saw as she passed the site below the children's ward, though there were still several male figures whose flashlights played across the rubble. She stopped suddenly, intending to ask one if everyone had been accounted for, and someone bumped into her from behind. She gasped and almost fell, but was caught in time by a strong hand.

'Sorry, Nurse,' he said. 'I was going too fast.' The voice was dark velvet. A little hoarse from the dust, perhaps, but she recognized it instantly.

'Oliver?' she whispered in disbelief. 'Oliver Dalton?'

The feeble light of his torch swept across her face. 'Good Lord, Imogen. I say, are you all right?'

'Yes,' she gasped.

'You do look a sight.'

'Hardly surprising. What on earth are you doing here?'

'I was with others from my platoon having a quiet drink in town. When the bombs hit, we raced out to help. Ghastly business, isn't it?'

'Was there more than one bomb?' She vaguely remembered now hearing a second explosion.

'Not on the hospital. I don't know where the other hit, but I saw them bring in some poor woman on a stretcher.' He sighed. 'We'll be knocking off soon, then I need to get back to base somehow or there'll be hell to pay.'

'And I must find somewhere to sleep. That is, I expect something has been arranged. Some of the patients are occupying our beds in the nurses' hostel, you see.'

'Look, let's find somewhere to sit for a moment. I could do with a smoke and, anyway, I can't just let you go.'

They found a bench in the shelter of a hedge. The sudden flame of the match revealed his face, which startled her. The army had changed him, that was apparent. He was still clean-shaven but he'd lost the Bryronic lock of dark hair that used to fall across his high forehead. The planes of his face stood out more sharply and Imogen saw in the second before the flame died that his hands, cupping the cigarette, were calloused and grazed. She smelled burning tobacco and the particular crisp scent of him. Goodness knows what she stank of – ammonia and bleach, she feared.

He drew deeply on his cigarette and sighed. 'It's a bad business, this. Why the hospital, for Pete's sake.'

'Perhaps they thought it was something else, a factory or a warehouse. I hope so as I can't bear to imagine that they would kill sick people deliberately. How many have we lost, Oliver, do you know?'

'A dozen, maybe,' he said quietly.

'That many? How awful. I was on the children's ward just before it happened, but Sister sent me away on an errand. Oliver, there was a young girl with her parents visiting. When I picked myself up after the blast and went back in, they weren't there. Or rather ...' She remembered the patterned skirt. 'They must have been.'

'Oh, that family,' Oliver said quietly. 'I'm afraid they didn't stand a chance.'

Imogen gave a choked sob. 'Margaret,' she croaked. 'That was the child's name. She'd been awfully brave. Pneumonia and pleurisy quite badly, but she'd just turned the corner ... Oh, Oliver, life's so wretchedly unfair.'

She heard his sigh of sympathy in the darkness, then came a rustle and his warm hand covered hers. 'It's damnable. Not much consolation, old thing, but it would have been instant.'

'Life's a brute, though, isn't it?'

'It's war, I'm afraid.'

'And the student nurse we lost. I saw her on the ground. It's awful, Oliver. It should have been me. If Sister Peacock had sent her out instead of me . . . Oh, Lord, they were saying in the nurses' hostel that Sister Peacock had been killed, too.'

'I'm afraid that they were right. But you mustn't dwell on what might have been, Imogen. It'll drive you mad. You were simply lucky. The telephonist downstairs was lucky, too. She was surrounded by fallen rubble and by rights should have been a goner, but by some miracle we got her out unhurt.'

'I'm glad. Nothing will stop me feeling guilty, though.' Imogen gulped down another sob. 'It's dreadful about Sister Peacock.' She felt his hand tighten on hers.

'You poor thing. This may sound rotten, but have a good cry and a stiff drink if you can. Then one simply has to pull oneself together and get on with things.'

'I know, you don't need to tell me. Let's talk of something more cheerful. How are you getting on – have they sent you anywhere interesting yet?'

'No further than North Cornwall so far. It's square-bashing and guard duties, mainly, plus building endless bloody Nissen huts.' Oliver gave a bitter laugh. 'So much for glamorous dreams of serving my country. I couldn't get an officer's commission coming in so late, so I'm lowest of the low. Private Dalton, and I'm ribbed for it. They call me The Poet.'

'I didn't know you wrote poetry.'

'I don't, but some of my platoon think I look like a poet. My looks worked all right for a schoolteacher, but not for a humble infantryman.'

'At least you're alive. One of my friends, Nurse Summers, her young man's ship was sent to Singapore and she hasn't heard from him since February. She's dreadfully worried.'

'That's sad to hear. The Far East's a bad business.'

He finished his cigarette and crushed it under his boot.

'Are you in touch with the school?' she asked him.

'Not really. Are you?'

'I hear from Ned occasionally, Miss Edgecumbe, and one of the maids – do you remember Kezia?'

'I do. Local girl. Curly black hair. Loquacious.'

'That's Kezia. We became quite pally.'

'What's Ned up to then?' Oliver's tone was neutral.

'I think he's taken a party of boys camping in West Cornwall.'

'Noble of him.'

'He really does enjoy it. Anyway, I had hoped to visit the school later in August, but now I imagine all leave will be cancelled. Oh, it's selfish to talk about a spoiled holiday when this has happened.'

'Would you think me very frivolous to suggest we meet occasionally. I'm currently based a few miles north of here so it would be a waste not to see one another.'

Her heartbeat quickened, but she answered as lightly as she could, 'I don't think it frivolous at all. Let's do that.'

Fifteen

June 1966

It was difficult for Belle to put her finger on what changed at Silverwood after Rain's return. Evening meals were produced on time and though Janey was as overworked as ever, she appeared to have more energy. The others, too. Belle found Sirius washing his van one morning. Chouli would disappear with Rain to Rain's special hut for extensive periods of meditation, and Arlo made himself more available to dig beds in the kitchen garden or take Angel to the beach. Angel, it became clear, was everybody's responsibility. The expertise of each member of the group determined their role in his education. Janey took charge of reading and writing, whilst Sirius encouraged him to draw and paint and whittle odd shapes with wood. Gray attempted to teach him guitar, Belle taught him songs she'd learned at school and Chouli helped him knit and sew. Everything else he was somehow expected to absorb from conversations with adults or from the odd selection of books in the library. He was an intelligent child who liked reading and asked questions, but Belle found him unlike any little boy she'd known before. With his roughly made clothes and long hair, he would be considered odd by other children – not that he mixed with any. He was nervous of strangers – hung back when the postman came to the door – but once he became used to Belle, he followed her around.

'What are you doing?' he asked in the kitchen one afternoon.

'Peeling potatoes for dinner.'

'Can I help?'

'The knife is sharp. You might cut yourself.'

'I have a knife that's sharper than that.'

'Do you?' She wondered if he was telling the truth, but he vanished into the hall and she heard his bare feet slapping on the wooden stairs. A moment later he returned, holding a bone-handled knife in a leather sheath which he presented to her. She pulled out the blade and examined it with alarm. It was a woodsman's knife. The handle was part of a deer antler and the six-inch blade felt sharp when she tentatively touched it.

'Where did you get this?' she asked.

'Peter gave it to me.'

'Who is Peter?'

'My daddy.'

'Oh.' Angel's father had never been mentioned before. 'Where does Peter live?'

'I don't know.'

'Angel's father lives in London, but we're not together.' Belle hadn't heard Rain enter but now she stood, barefoot like her son, in a pool of sunlight by the open door to the garden. There was something large than life, goddess-like, about her in her short toga-style dress, her skin glistening from the heat. 'Angel, I said you weren't to play with that.'

'I'm not. I'm showing Belle.'

'He wants to help me with the potatoes,' Belle explained. 'Shall I let him?'

'Teach him how to do it safely. No, not with that knife, child,' Rain said, gently removing it from his grasp. She selected a short-bladed paring knife from a drawer, gave it to Belle with a 'Thank you' and disappeared with Angel's knife inside the house.

'Do potatoes have feelings?' Angel asked Belle as she held his hands to show him how to peel safely and to cut out the eyes.

She blinked in surprise. 'I don't think so.'

'They might do but can't tell us. I don't want to eat them if this hurts them.' He shook her hands away and stepped back.

'Really, it doesn't hurt them. And you've got to eat them, Angel. That's the way nature works. We have to eat or we die.'

'Rain says that there are spirits in everything in nature and we have to respect them.'

Calling his parents by their first names sounded odd to Belle from the mouth of a young child. She'd known a girl at university who referred to her parents as Simon and Beulah, but she was pretentious and gave herself airs. Angel wasn't like that, but Belle was bothered by the lack of distance between adults and child in this house that Janey had hinted at on Belle's first day at Silverwood. Rain clearly cared for her son deeply, but she didn't treat him as though he was a seven-year-old. He went to bed only when he felt tired and was no respecter of boundaries. He once walked in on Belle when she was taking a bath (the bathroom lock was broken) and appeared puzzled when Belle asked him to wait outside. 'It's so different from our house,' she said to Gray.

'Your "perfect" family again,' he replied with a grin.

'They're not perfect,' she said crossly. 'I just don't like people walking in on me when I'm not dressed.'

'It's a bit old-fashioned, love.'

'No, it's just how I am.' She hated it when he said things like that, not least because she feared that she was stuffy and prudish, but she couldn't help feeling like this. She tried not to be hurt by his teasing. She didn't like arguments. Conflict was another thing her family were bad at because their father always had to win.

There came a rainy day when Belle was left trying to amuse Angel while the others were occupied.

'Shall we play a game?' she suggested.

'What kind of game?' he asked, his particular puzzled expression crossing his face.

'What games do you like?'

'I don't know.'

He really was a strange boy. She wondered if he had ever met other children and played the games they did. He didn't appear to have many toys, no cars or trains or guns. He had a set of bow and arrows – she'd seen him playing with it in the grounds with Arlo's guidance, shooting an empty tin off a wall. He was becoming quite good at it. Clearly, he shouldn't play with those in the house, so she suggested hide and seek. This, too, he turned out to be good at. The house was enormous and he would find the most out of the way places and could lie hidden and perfectly still for longer than any child she'd come across.

'Not Sirius's work room or people's bedrooms,' she'd said sternly to him, but that left plenty of other places. She found him in a bathroom behind a shower curtain and inside a wall cupboard on a landing. Only after accidentally treading on his foot, making him yelp, did she discover him under a scrumpled eiderdown on the floor of a spare bedroom.

After she took a turn at hiding and was swiftly found, covered in cobwebs, under a huge sideboard in the dining room, he told her she wasn't very good at it and would she mind if he did all the hiding? Belle readily agreed, though she did wonder what Rain would think when she saw her precious son all grimy. At least he was being a proper little boy for a change.

She'd been searching for him for twenty minutes now and was beginning to get bored. There were too many good places of concealment in the house behind doors, in cupboards and rambling attics. How she wished she'd narrowed the field further, she thought as she tramped wearily up and down the stairs.

It was only when she passed the doors to the library that

she stopped and frowned. One was ajar. She was sure that she'd closed it behind her after an earlier search in the game. She pushed it open and went in. The room looked undisturbed, but then she'd cleaned it herself recently and could expect no telltale footprints in the dust. 'Angel?' she called. 'I give up.'

Silence.

She checked under the desk in the connecting room, then returned to look behind the armchair. She sat down and listened carefully for a breath or a movement.

Silence.

She drummed her fingers on the wooden arms, fed up. Outside, the sun slipped out from behind a cloud, and a ray of light stroked the line of children's books on their shelves, drawing her eye. Something snagged her attention and she rose, frowning, and stepped across to look. The lowest three shelves formed a unit that was not quite flush with its neighbours on the right-hand side. Sliding her fingernails into the narrow gap there, she gripped and pulled. To her astonishment the unit swung out towards her to reveal a small daylit room. She ducked under the shelf and peered round inside.

'Angel?'

There he was, looking back at her, smiling. He was kneeling on a cushion before a low window with a deep sill where a book of fairy tales that he'd been reading lay open.

Belle crawled through the space, taking care to leave the door open, then climbed to her feet, clawed a spider's web out of her hair and stared round in wonder.

'What is this place?'

'A secret room.'

'Yes, I can see that.' The square space smelled of herbs and old wood and felt comfortably warm in the sunlight. It had wood-panelled walls and bare floorboards coated with dirt. In one corner lay a mattress piled with bedding and, to one side, a stout cardboard box, its flaps closed. 'Are these things yours?'

He shook his head. She stepped over to the bed and lifted the corner of a blanket. Underneath lay an exercise book with a pencil tucked into it, a boys' comic and a little polythene bag containing dried leaves. She picked up the exercise book and flicked through it, but apart from a few scribbled notes on the first page it was blank. The notes didn't make sense. Something about 'a vision for living' and 'Cornwall's creators', followed by a list of names of everyone at Silverwood. Her own was there at the end, to her surprise, but it had a question mark by it. Remembering the mention of an art manifesto, she guessed whom the book belonged to. The judgement implied by the question mark rankled. She crossed her name out with a savage stroke of the pencil, then closed the book and threw it back on the mattress.

'How did you know about the room?' she asked Angel. He didn't reply. There was, she saw, something scribbled on one of the flaps of the box against the wall. The box was dirty, the cardboard soft with age, but she could read the words 'Bandages Size 2' on it. With some distaste she lifted the flap to see it contained not first-aid supplies but old books.

'Angel?' she repeated, glancing at him. His cheeks were flushed with shame.

'I came into the library one day,' he mumbled. 'I wanted a book to read, but the shelves were open.' He hesitated then went on. 'I heard someone there so I ran away in case ... in case it was a ghost. But it wasn't. I waited in the hall until someone came out.'

'Who was it?' She knew the answer before it came.

'Arlo.'

'Arlo,' Belle echoed. He'd know about the room, given that it was his family's house.

'He didn't see me. When he'd gone I went in again and the shelves were shut, but I looked behind the books and found a metal thingy sticking out and I pushed it down and it let me in.'

'It's a clever place to hide.' She wondered what the room had been built for. Perhaps it was a priest's hole, like she remembered from a history book. No, built in 1711, the house wasn't old enough.

'You won't tell anyone, will you?' Angel stared anxiously at her. 'About me being here.'

She sat down on the mattress. 'What are you frightened of?' she asked gently.

'I'm not frightened of anything.'

'Except ghosts,' she said with a laugh.

'Yes, ghosts. I've never seen one, have you?'

'No, I don't believe in them.' That wasn't entirely true, but she was keen to allay Angel's fears. She shivered. If ghosts did exist then Silverwood was exactly the sort of place she might see one. 'I won't tell anyone that you know about this place,' she said carefully, 'but I'm worried about you being in here. Suppose you get stuck.'

'I won't. Look.' He jumped up and went to the entrance and, to her alarm, pulled the door closed with a click. 'See,' he said, showing her, 'there's a thingy this side, too.'

She saw with relief that there was indeed a catch on the door, and when she tried it, the door disengaged and she could push it open. 'You don't shut it when you're in here, do you? I mean I could get in just now.'

His eyes were large and shining and he smiled. 'That's because I wanted you to find me,' he said.

'To see the room? Oh, Angel, that's sweet of you.'

'It can be our secret, can't it?'

'It's not completely a secret, though, is it, because Arlo knows about it.'

'I did a spell,' he said, raising his chin in a defiant fashion.

'A spell? What kind of spell?'

'Yes. To keep him away.'

'I hope it's not a horrible spell,' she said, thinking this child was most peculiar, but she'd play along with him. 'It won't hurt him, will it?'

'No.'

'That's all right then.'

While Angel returned to his fairy tales she took out a volume from the box and was surprised to see that it was an old nursing textbook, musty-smelling and covered in sticky dust. She lifted it by a corner with a moue of distaste. The contents page listed 'Anatomy, Physiology, Hygiene ...' She laid it aside and picked out several novels one by one. Three had titles she knew – *Rebecca*, *Gone with the Wind*, *The ABC Murders* – and there was one she didn't, but whose author,

Nora Gentles, rang a faint bell. There were more books underneath but she didn't bother with them. Tucked down the
side of the box, however, were some dog-earred papers and
several old pocket books tied together. She eased these out
and unpicked the ribbon. Engagement diaries, four of them.
She read the name on the first page of one and drew a sharp
breath: 'Imogen Lockhart'. What an almighty coincidence. Of
course, Imogen had been under-matron here for a while, but
still, what were her books doing here?

She picked out pages of the papers and found them to
be medical lecture notes so she left them. Then she piled
everything back in the box, except the diaries. Arlo wouldn't
be interested. Mrs Kitto definitely would be. She'd accidentally torn one of the box flaps and it wouldn't close down
now. Never mind.

'Angel, dear,' she said, rising to her feet, 'we're late for
lunch. Come on.'

'I am SO hungry I could eat … a DRAGON!' he said with
a grin. He closed his book and tucked it under his arm, then
she followed him out, ducking to get through the little doorway. He swung the door shut behind them with a click and
showed her where the catch was, hidden behind the books,
then they went off companionably to the kitchen.

Later, when she was alone upstairs, Belle glanced through
the diaries. They covered the early war years, but Imogen
had simply recorded appointments in them – 'Dentist,
4 p.m.' or 'Mother's birthday' – and often these were in an
illegible scrawl. Still, it was wonderful to hold them in her
hands as Imogen had once done. It made Belle feel closer to

her. She looked round their bare bedroom and wondered whether it might, just might, have been Imogen's when she'd lived there. A possibility, she thought. Maybe Mrs Kitto would know.

Sixteen

The following day, a Tuesday, Belle slipped down to the cottage soon after breakfast. She'd been at Silverwood for eleven days now and every day the weather seemed different. It must have rained last night. The sky was cloudy and a mist still hung in the air, but it was lifting and the air felt warm. She arrived to find Mrs Kitto in the garden plucking dead blooms from the petunias. She was cheerful and immediately invited Belle inside.

Belle took off her sandals. 'They're soaked. The grass is so wet.'

'The weather is very changeable here,' Mrs Kitto said. 'It was quite a storm last night. Did you hear it?'

Belle hadn't. 'I sleep so well here.' She followed Mrs Kitto into the kitchen. 'Do you know which bedroom Imogen had here, by the way?

'I couldn't say,' Mrs Kitto replied without meeting Belle's eye, which puzzled her, but then why should the woman know the answer?

As they sat at the kitchen table to drink their tea, Belle brought out the diaries and explained where she'd found them.

'I didn't know about that secret room, but I did know that Imogen left some things here once,' Mrs Kitto said, flicking through one of the diaries. 'How marvellous to recover these. I don't suppose you found any photographs, did you?'

'A nursing textbook, a few novels, some papers. Were there photographs? I should have looked properly. I'll go back. I wonder how the box got into the room.'

Mrs Kitto fixed her eyes on her. 'I wonder too,' she said and again Belle got the sense that she was hiding something.

The old lady put on her spectacles and flicked through the diary for 1942, occasionally frowning to herself. Finally, she looked up and said gravely, 'There's nothing recorded for the sixth of August, when the hospital was bombed. But then I suppose these diaries are not meant to be records of what happened.'

She continued to browse, then nodded. 'It's interesting,' she said, 'that the rest of the year contains the odd reference to meeting "D". Look,' she said, showing Belle. '"D, nine p.m.", and further on, here, "Day off, D ten thirty a.m." She picked up the diary for the next year, 1943. 'After that there's no more.' She sighed.

'Is D for Dalton?' Belle asked, her eyes wide.

'Probably,' Mrs Kitto said, so hesitantly that Belle again felt she was hiding something. 'I suppose she might have thought of him as that because of the habit of calling men and boys by their surnames at school. What I definitely know is that this was a particularly happy time for Imogen. If you're interested I'll tell you about it.'

'Yes, please,' Belle said with enthusiasm and Mrs Kitto began.

Seventeen

August 1942

The aftermath of the air raid was a strange time, but as Oliver implied, Imogen had to stiffen her resolve and get on with her work alongside everyone else. The brave determination of those in charge set the tone and anyone who moaned got short shrift. She found it hard, though, to go about her daily tasks with the children in a temporary ward without being brought up short by an unbidden memory of that dreadful night and the staff and patients who'd been lost. She was much happier when, as part of her training, she was transferred to the men's medical ward towards the end of the month.

The first time she was able to meet Oliver was one Tuesday evening a fortnight after the air raid. It was only for an hour or two, but this was enough time to walk together by the river in the fading light. Although she had rushed off to eat supper at the end of her shift in order to be on time, she had taken care to apply a little powder to her tired face and a slick of lipstick and brush her hair before she dashed out.

He was waiting for her on New Bridge Street, leaning on the parapet of the bridge to gaze downriver, smart in his crisp uniform. She called his name and he looked up and smiled. 'Hello, you look nice.'

'A jolly sight better than when we last met,' she said ruefully. 'I hope I haven't kept you waiting long.'

'My pal dropped me off on his way a few minutes ago, so no. Shall we walk? There's a decent enough place down this way where we can go for a drink later.'

'I think I know it. When will your pal be going back?'

'I promised to meet him at eleven.'

He offered his arm and they joined a path that ran south along the riverbank past a line of moored boats. Their talk was awkward at first. Neither could forget the tragic circumstances in which they'd last met.

'It's odd,' Imogen said, 'that there was nothing in the papers for days about what happened, then someone showed me a report in the *Gazette*.'

'I missed that. What did it say?'

'It didn't mention that it was Truro for a start. It made me feel funny knowing more than the reporter appeared to. Once again you realize how little we're being told by the authorities.'

'That's understandable, though, isn't it – the need to keep mum?'

'Yes, of course, but what I mean is that some of the

secretiveness seems unnecessary. Maybe if the Germans knew they'd hit a hospital they'd feel sorry.'

'I agree, it's maddening for us' – Oliver paused to light a cigarette – 'but I worry that the nastier sort of German might actually be pleased.'

'How horrid of them. I hope our lot aren't doing anything like that – shelling hospitals, I mean.'

'I hope we're not,' he said quietly. 'At least, not deliberately.'

'Nothing's black and white, is it?' she sighed, remembering a conversation she'd once had with Ned about the frustrations of obtaining reports of the war, yet before the air raid she'd never thought to question their truth. She certainly obeyed government instructions published in the papers. Most people did, though there were exceptions. People publicly disapproved of black marketeers as unpatriotic, but one of the student nurses had a boyfriend who kept her illicitly supplied with nylons and Swiss chocolate and didn't think anything wrong with it. Imogen had eagerly partaken when the girl had passed the sweets round. But these were small rebellions.

Imogen remembered the men she and Oliver had helped at Falmouth two years before, their complaints about the cack-handed evacuation from the doomed ship *Lancastria*. She'd not seen that debacle mentioned in the newspapers she'd read in the staff common room. Oh, what was the point of worrying about these things? It wouldn't help them win the war.

'Still, I wish we knew more,' she sighed. 'I'm usually too busy to think about anything except my job, but if I do stop to brood I feel unsettled. Knowing the truth might help.'

'I know what it's like having time to brood. Keep calm

and carry on, they tell us. Actually doing so day after day is pretty hard.'

'The patients help most. Some are always so cheerful despite what's happened to them. There's a young man of eighteen with advanced cancer. Doctors say he's unlikely to make it, but I'm helping him write a list of places he wants to go that he's read about. "When I'm out of here and the war's over," he says. He's got Timbuktu on the list and China and America . . .'

'That's very sad,' Oliver murmured.

'And then there's a sergeant who's lost his leg. He calls it Fred the Phantom. Says, "Fred's playing up today, Nurse, he needs his sock on" so I have to pretend to put a sock on the missing leg and we have a good laugh. He tells the most unsuitable jokes when Sister's not about. Worse than anything the boys used to say.'

'They're very well brought up little boys at St Mary's.'

'No, I mean my cousins. I told you about them, I think. Oh, Oliver, I haven't asked anything about you.'

'There isn't much to say. I can't pretend that what I'm doing is more interesting than schoolmastering, but that's hardly the point of it. Still, I wish I wasn't stuck here in Cornwall waiting for something to happen. From time to time there are rumours that we'll be on the move, then someone higher up must decide we're best off guarding these shores. Last week's invasion exercise has been the nearest we've got.'

'It's a valuable job, Oliver. I feel comforted knowing that you're nearby.'

'I'm not saying it isn't useful, just that the threat of invasion isn't as great as it was and the action seems to be going on elsewhere. Oh, we shouldn't be talking like this really. It's defeatist.'

'No one can hear except me.'

'And these lads!'

They'd come to a point where the riverbank had dropped and a muddy beach formed. Here half a dozen boys were swimming in the murky water, calling out and splashing one another. Imogen and Oliver stopped to watch for a bit, smiling at their antics, before walking on.

The twilight began to thicken and shoulders of violet cloud were gathering under the trees so they turned round and visited the pub Oliver had mentioned. The bartender was welcoming and respectful of Oliver's uniform. It was a quiet place with a sheltered garden and they sat outside with their drinks for a while before the darkness and the midges drove them in. At a table inside they fell into conversation with a middle-aged couple, Dick Varcoe, a local journalist, and Doreen, his wife, and Imogen noticed Oliver's pleasure in good company, for he laughed as he listened to the man's stories and asked shrewd questions about his work. The journalist confirmed their earlier conclusions, that every aspect of wartime reporting was heavily monitored. 'I like the challenge it offers, though,' he said. 'We can set a tone, cheer people up, give them local information that they can't get on the wireless, promote the war effort. We love a nice "Lend to the Navy's Sinking Fund" parade. Gets everyone buying papers and shows Hitler we won't be beaten.'

Dick was a cheerful sort himself, a small wiry man; the tools of his trade, a notebook and pencil, causing the pockets of his jacket to sag, Imogen noticed, when he went to bar to refresh their drinks. While he was gone his wife Doreen fixed earnest eyes on Imogen and said, 'We're so appreciative of you nurses. Dick's mother was in for an operation at the time of the blast and says you were all splendid. She was carried out on a mattress down a fire escape and taken by ambulance to Redruth. Hasn't stopped talking about it since – I'm sure it's the most exciting thing that's ever happened to her! Dick's been doing all he can to raise money for the hospital, you know.'

'I'm so glad to hear it,' Imogen replied. 'And thank you for the compliment, but we nurses are just doing our job.' She asked politely after her mother-in-law's health and was assured that she was recovering well.

The Varcoes left shortly before Imogen and Oliver, who sat over their drinks until the time for Oliver's lift back to barracks came near.

'This is the most enjoyable evening I've spent for ages, you know,' Oliver said, his eyes glowing. 'They're good lads in my platoon, but they're not my type if you take my meaning. I'm a fish out of water.'

'And I am your type?' Imogen said lightly.

'Of course you are!'

'I'm afraid I'm ill educated compared to you, though at least I read books.'

'Don't be silly, Imogen, I beg you. We're cut from the same cloth, you and I.'

'Are we really?' she wondered, thinking of the eccentric nature of her upbringing.

'Our fathers were both academics.' Oliver described how his had been an Oxford professor, though his childhood in leafy North Oxford sounded a more formal affair than Imogen's more ramshackle upbringing. His was too rigid, possibly, she thought, recognizing that he was highly strung. Strangely, that was part of what drew her to him, that sense of coiled-up energy. And she loved the admiring way he looked at her. As though she was special.

It was approaching eleven when they walked reluctantly to Oliver's meeting place, arms linked, through the darkness of the quiet streets, their dimmed torches picking out the white-daubed kerbs and lampposts, she sharply aware of Oliver's closeness. She felt the warmth of his arm through the coarse cloth of his uniform, breathed in the scent of him, and it quickened her blood.

'This is Boscawen Street,' she said. 'And here's the hotel. I'll wait with you till your pal comes.'

'You won't get into trouble yourself?'

'No, I'll sneak in. House Sister sleeps soundly – or pretends to.'

'Here he comes now,' Oliver said as faint headlights appeared and a jeep pulled up alongside. Pale faces gleamed from the back. There was laughter and a strong smell of beer. A door swung open and a voice cried, 'Give 'er a kiss and 'op in, Byron!'

He turned to her with a sigh. 'Sorry about the lads. And sorry, too, that we didn't have longer.'

'It's nobody's fault.'

'Can we do this again? Say you will, dear Imogen.'

'I don't see why not.'

'Good. I'll write.' He touched her cheek lightly and there were catcalls from the jeep. 'Take care of yourself.' He climbed into the vehicle and she watched it pull away then walked up the hill to the nurses' hostel deep in thought. Something had changed between her and Oliver that evening, but she felt a certain wariness. Oliver was a highly strung man marked by grief. He felt things strongly and took life seriously. She felt deeply attracted to him but knew there to be a risk. A relationship with him would involve heading into the unknown. Her head told her to be careful. Her heart didn't care.

Eighteen

'She met him several times more,' Mrs Kitto said. 'Late September, October and December. Look, she recorded the dates.'

Belle studied the entries and Mrs Kitto continued.

~

September 1942

For several weeks every post was a disappointment for she heard nothing from Oliver and her feelings banked up. Then in the middle of September she drew a sharp breath when she hungrily glimpsed his familiar scrawl. The note he'd sent informed her of a weekend's leave in ten days' time. Did she happen to be free? A moment's hesitation before she plunged in, writing back, 'Yes. I am on the Saturday,' and then ten beastly days passed waiting for him to reply. Finally, on the eve of the day in question, he telephoned the nurses' hostel just as she was eating supper. She swallowed her mouthful and hurried to the phone.

'Oliver? Hello?'

'Imogen? I wonder if you received my letter?'

'I had one from you over a week ago and replied.'

'Oh, I didn't get it. What did it say?'

'Yes, Oliver,' she cried with relief and impatience. 'It said yes, I can see you tomorrow.' In truth, she'd made other plans now and would have to put off her pal Summers, but she was sure Summers would understand. She'd told her about Oliver because Summers was always talking about her fiancé who was still missing and it seemed right to confide in her in the same way.

'That's wonderful.' The happiness in his voice was palpable and now she felt thrilled at the prospect. 'I can get a bus into Truro for late morning. Shall we say eleven? Meet you by the Red Lion and then ... Oh, blast, the pips already. Eleven at the Red Li—' And the line went dead.

The following morning, a light but constant drizzle was falling and the road down to the town was slippery with wet fallen leaves. Imogen borrowed Summers' umbrella and waited outside the Red Lion Hotel for twenty minutes, watching the efforts of a troop of Sea Scouts who were guarding a small rowing dinghy on a trailer to which passers-by were adding metal items such as old saucepans and broken bicycle wheels. 'Any old iron for the war?' one of the boys was shouting.

Bus after bus dropped passengers but there was no sign of Oliver and her anxiety grew.

Then, 'Imogen.' He appeared beside her, out of breath. Raindrops beaded the epaulettes of his coat.

'Oh, you made me jump!'

'Sorry, there was no bus after all, but I managed to get a lift as far as the railway station.'

He was looking her up and down in open admiration and she blushed, self-conscious. She'd chosen to wear a summer dress on this occasion, with a cardigan for warmth, having torn her mackintosh.

He took her for coffee in the snug of the handsome old coaching inn, which she hadn't visited before. She admired its fine moulded ceilings and oak staircase and in the quiet they swapped news, though there wasn't much. She told him with a sigh that she was swotting for the next lot of exams and trying not to fall asleep as she did so. Also that she had got into trouble again, this time for riding a trolley down a ramp and accidentally crashing into one of the consultants. The man had not been hurt and found the episode hugely amusing, but a Sister had seen everything and Imogen had been sent to Matron's den in disgrace.

'I fully expected to be asked to leave,' she told him, 'but Matron was in an unusually good mood and barely gave me a glance. She said she'd had good news, that her nephew, who'd been feared killed, had been found alive. Honestly, it felt like when kings of old freed prisoners to celebrate victory.'

Oliver laughed. 'What should we do now?'

'I suppose it's raining still. Something indoors, I imagine.'

'Isn't there a museum?'

'Is there?' she said in astonishment. 'I've never had the time to notice.'

'Yes. In River Street, I think. My FIC's a local and he told me. Says it has some rather good paintings unless they've been taken away for safekeeping.'

'Mother says that's what they've done at the National Gallery, but they bring back one painting to show at a time and it's proving very popular. You really have a chance to study it when there's only one, she says.'

'My FIC reckons the authorities didn't expect Truro to be a target for air raids so maybe we'll be lucky and everything is still there.'

'The authorities were wrong about the air raids,' she said with a sigh, remembering.

They were lucky. The museum was open and they spent a pleasant couple of hours in the airy galleries of the gracious old granite building studying ammonites and lumps of sparkling quartz, old timepieces, gloomy portraits of grave dignitaries and newer landscapes, brightly painted.

'It's the most beautiful place, isn't it?' Imogen declared as they climbed the stone steps towards the exit.

'Takes one away from one's troubles for a while,' Oliver agreed. 'Oh well, back to sordid reality.'

And then they were out in the rainswept streets, where water was rushing through the gutters and people on the narrow pavements shouted angrily at careless cyclists spraying mud.

Imogen and Oliver huddled together under the umbrella, dodging the puddles, and eventually found a small café near the cathedral for lunch. It was filled with families and servicemen, but they secured the last table, tucked away in a corner and so small that their heads almost touched when they sat down opposite each other. They had to wait some time to be served, but eventually food came and while they ate they discussed what they'd seen.

'Delicious,' Oliver said at last, sitting back. 'Better than the grub we're getting in the mess. The new cook is a tricky beggar, throws tantrums like a French chef but can't cook like one. The consequence is that half the meals are burned and the other half underdone. We place bets as to which. There'll be a revolt soon, I reckon.'

Imogen laughed, but said, 'That's a shame. We do rather well. The hospital cook's very good considering, but there's never enough food and I always seem to feel hungry.' She glanced at her watch. 'I'm going to have to get back soon. If I don't write up my Physiology lecture notes I'm going to be even further behind.'

'It's a shame time has been so short. Maybe we can meet on another evening, Imogen. I noticed when we passed it just now that there's a dance at the City Hall next Friday. Of course, if I were an officer I would invite you to one out at base, but I fear you'd find mixing with the ordinary men a little rough.'

'Oh, I'm used to all sorts, don't worry about me. But the City Hall is nearer. Of course I'll come. It won't be until nine, I'm afraid, if then, as it's hard to get away on time. Do you mind?'

'I'll try not to!'

'How will you travel here?'

'I'll find a way, don't you trouble yourself.'

Remarkably, the following week Imogen arrived promptly at
the dance at nine. She wore a pretty blue dress that flattered
her figure and felt at a high pitch of excitement. They'd never
been to a dance together and she was already looking forward to feeling Oliver's arms around her.

Oliver was standing at the bar as arranged, lean and
handsome in uniform, a glass of whisky in his hand. She
was initially disconcerted to see he was in conversation with
another soldier, a burly man with a broad friendly face, whom
he introduced as Larry Higgins. Private Higgins bought her a
lemonade then took his own drinks across to a brassy-looking
woman she glimpsed through the foxtrotting dancers who
was fanning herself on a chair at the side of the hall. Finally
Oliver could give her all his attention.

'Sorry. Higgins gave me a lift on his motorcycle this
evening,' Oliver said. 'Don't know where he gets the petrol,
better not to ask. I have to meet him at half-past eleven if I
want him to take me back.'

'I'm very grateful to Private Higgins for bringing you, but
not for taking you away again.'

He laughed.

The foxtrot ended and the band struck up a quickstep that
Imogen vaguely recognized. 'Shall we?' Oliver said and they
left their drinks on a ledge while he led her onto the dance
floor. Initially they danced awkwardly, Oliver seeming to
have little appreciation of rhythm and frequently treading on

her toes, but after a bit he seemed to get the hang of it. 'You can tell I'm out of practice,' he said, grinning.

'Me, too,' she lied, for she'd danced frequently on her covert outings with the other nurses and enjoyed it more than she'd imagined she would. Both were glad of the slow dance that came next.

'The Anniversary Waltz!' she cried as he took her in his arms. It was a current Vera Lynn favourite and round the hall people took up the tune and crooned along. It was about hope for the future and undying love.

For some reason as she danced, Imogen felt her eyes swim with tears. When she looked up she saw that Oliver was watching her with alarm and she blinked them away.

'What's the matter?' he asked softly, his brow furrowed.

'Nothing.'

Later, as he walked her up the hill to the nurses' hostel, he felt for her hand and asked, 'Why were you crying earlier?'

'Oh, I was being soppy. It was the words of the song. I find thinking about the future difficult to bear when our lives are about now and simply plodding on.'

'That's unlike you. You're usually cheerful.'

'I must be tired, that's all.' She squeezed his hand in the darkness. 'I'm dreary company tonight, I'm so sorry.'

'Not dreary at all,' he murmured. 'Quite the opposite in fact.' He stopped and steered her to face him. His eyes glinted in the faint moonlight. 'You always cheer me up. I'm sorry, I'm a melancholy sort. A bit serious, I'm afraid.'

'I like serious,' she whispered and knew it to be true. Their faces were close and she could hear the beat of his pulse in the silence of the evening. His arms slid round her waist and after a moment's hesitation he leaned and gently kissed her mouth. His lips were soft and when she did not pull away, he cupped her face with his hands and kissed her again, more passionately this time and she kissed him back in wonder and surprise. The sound of voices came and approaching footsteps, faint torchlight and he drew her off the pavement into the shelter of some trees. There was a low wall nearby which they sat on and continued their embrace.

When they broke free, panting for breath, he laughed. 'I've been wanting to do this for ages but never had the courage. Now I wish I'd done it before. I've wasted so much time.'

She smiled and stroked his hair, finding it smooth and soft. 'There has to be a right moment and maybe I wasn't ready.'

'You are now.' He bent and kissed her again then they rested together, talking about nothing much. Then she shivered at the cold of the stone wall seeping through her clothes and snuggled into him closer.

'It is cold, isn't it? It's damnable that there's nowhere to go and we have to be so hole-in-corner.'

'But all the more fun for that,' she laughed. 'Oh, Oliver, what's the time? Won't you miss your lift?'

He pushed up his sleeve, shone the torch on his watchface and cursed. 'You're right, I must go or I'll be walking back to barracks. Come on, I'll see you safely home first.'

'I'll be perfectly all right. It's only round the corner.'

'If you're sure. I should rush. But we must meet again very soon.'

'Yes,' she breathed, lost in the moment, and they kissed

once more before returning to the road where they parted, she letting him stride away down the hill into the chilly darkness.

She continued uphill quickly, slipping inside the nurses' hostel as quiet as a mouse. In her room she changed quickly and climbed into bed without disturbing Summers. There she lay awake, reliving the evening and the memory of Oliver's lips against hers, the way her body thrilled to his, as the gentle rhythm of her roommate's breath sighed in the darkness. She wasn't sure where this love would take her. She'd spoken the truth, that she could not think about the future, but for now he filled her mind and the thought of him made her body tremble.

How long before she would see him again, she wondered, as she turned over sleepily. Soon, she hoped.

But Fate had other plans.

The following week Imogen was moved onto night duty on the women's medical ward. It wasn't the first time she'd been on nights and although it made her constantly exhausted and disrupted her social life, there were aspects of it that she liked. Life on the wards was not as busy. There was something satisfying, too, about helping patients in the dark reaches of the night when they were at their most low and anxious and appreciative of a nurse's company. She cherished such moments, particularly a conversation she had with Angela Boswell, a frail young woman with a heart condition who was in hospital for observation and so frightened of death that she dare not fall asleep in case she didn't wake up. Imogen, who'd brought in a novel to pass the long, silent hours, read some to her by the light of a torch, her low voice whispering in the darkness. It was *Three Men in a Boat* and Angela's giggle at the funniest bits was delightful to hear. After a few pages of this Angela sank into restful sleep, a smile on her lips.

It was a long time before she and Oliver could meet. They made plans for snatched meetings, but at the last moment something would happen to spoil them. Then, at the end of October, Imogen received a note from him to say that his garrison was being moved elsewhere in the county – he wasn't allowed to say where. After that they met once more, in mid-December, when he was given twenty-four hours leave and she almost ran to meet him at the station, eager to savour every minute with him.

It was a cold, crisp day and the temperature had woken her up, though normally she'd have been asleep at this hour. She'd pinched her cheeks to put colour in them, but in the mirror in the waiting room saw they were rosy from the chilly air. The train was late and packed with cheerful Christmas shoppers coming in from the country, though there was little to buy and no festive lights. This year traditional Christmas fare was harder than ever to come by. 'I bet it'll be sardines and Yellow Peril for us again,' Summers predicted gloomily, referring to the glutinous, sugarless custard that was a staple for the nurses.

'Or rabbit,' Imogen replied.

'Poor rabbits,' Summers sighed. She had once had one as a pet.

Imogen waited on the platform, clutching her bag tightly as she scanned the crowds.

'Oliver, here!' She waved and he hurried to meet her with an eager gaze. He kissed her cheek quickly then took her arm.

'It's so good to see you,' he said as they queued at the barrier. 'Shall we go to the Red Lion again? I rather liked it.'

Over coffee he said, 'You haven't noticed, have you?' His eyes were dancing.

'What?' She studied him and eventually noticed the chevron sewn onto each arm. 'Oh, Oliver! You've been promoted.'

'Lance Corporal Dalton! My FIC encouraged me to apply. Said if I was doing all that administration I ought to have a handle.'

'That's splendid!'

'Here, I brought you some chocolate I saved from the ration.'

'Oh, Oliver, you shouldn't have done that. You'll want it yourself.'

'It gives me pleasure, Imogen. Do allow me that.'

'All right then,' she said, slipping the packet into her handbag. 'I'm afraid all I have for you is this.' She brought out a small photograph of herself set in a cardboard mount and passed it across the table, a little nervous of his reaction.

She had no cause to worry. His face lit up.

'You couldn't have given me anything nicer,' he said with one of his twisted smiles.

'It was taken ages ago, when I started my training, before I became haggard with trouble and lack of sleep.' Her eyes sparkled.

'Nonsense. You've hardly changed at all.'

'I've only had two hours' sleep,' she said and clapped her hand over her mouth to stifle a sudden yawn.

'It's good of you to meet me,' he said in a low, serious voice. 'I couldn't miss wishing you a happy Christmas.'

'There's still a couple of weeks to go.'

'I shouldn't be telling you this, but there's rumours we'll go abroad soon.'

'Oh, Oliver,' she whispered and reached for his hand.

'So you see this photograph will be very precious to me. Thank you.' He tucked it carefully into his top pocket.

'Don't be sad,' he said, seeing her face. And she was alarmed to see a fierce joy in his. 'You knew I wanted to do something useful. Properly useful, I mean, not building sheds or typing up minutes. Yes, I know they're jobs that have to be done, but they're not why I joined up.'

She felt a flare of anger. 'You should be careful what you wish for, Oliver. There are plenty who would have changed places with you. I've nursed some of them.'

'Now I've offended you. I'm sorry. But I don't have any family to grieve for me and I still want to do something to make up for Andrew's death. To prove that I'm as brave as he was.'

'You may not have family but you must have friends, and you have me.'

'I'm glad to know that, Imogen. You know I'm fond of you, don't you?'

'Yes, I do. I don't hand out my photograph to anyone, you know. But it's not about me. I believe it's wrong to throw your life away. No greater love there may be when there's a reason, but to long to put yourself in the firing line, that's crazy.'

Oliver was silent for a moment. He gazed out of the window, his face cast in a frown. 'I would never do that, exactly. I'm not one for heroics.'

'Anyway, wherever you go they might still give you a desk job, Mr Poet.'

He grinned. 'There is always that possibility.'

'So, I suppose this might be the last time we meet for a long while. I'll be sorry if it is, Oliver.'

'Not as sorry as I am.' His expression was grave.

'You'll write, though? Promise me you'll write. I'll hate to hear nothing from you. I'd fear the worst.'

'I promise. Now, do we squeeze another cup of coffee out of this pot or are we ready to go? It's chilly out, but shall we walk a bit?'

'Yes, let's. There's a rather pretty park nearby.'

Victoria Gardens, on the side of a gentle slope, gave a view over the city. Some of the lawns had been dug up to grow vegetables and the railings had largely gone for scrap, but the bandstand remained, alongside a pond with an iced-up fountain, and Imogen liked the railway viaduct towering in the background. A chill wind blew, which might have been why there were few people about, for which they were grateful; just an elderly man walking an equally elderly fox terrier and a couple of gleeful young lads bouncing stones on the ice.

They found a bench to sit on, shielded by trees, and she cuddled close into the shelter of his arm. They sat in silence for a while, then Oliver bent towards her and she shut her eyes and lost herself in his kisses.

'I will miss doing this,' he whispered after they came up for air and she smiled.

'So will I.' She could hardly keep her voice steady. 'I wish you weren't going.'

'And I wish there wasn't a war,' he said, 'but there is, and I must do my bit. I'm sorry, dear.' He reached in his pockets and lit a cigarette and for a moment the ground beneath her felt uncertain. There was something he wanted to do more than to be with her, she thought, and the idea made her miserable. But she must try and put herself in his shoes. Perhaps he was simply bracing himself for what was to come. She could already feel him cutting himself off, distancing himself from her and if that was a survival technique, she understood that. But still, it hurt.

They kissed again, but his mood had grown darker and the strength of his passion frightened her. Who was this man? After all, she hardly knew him.

Half an hour had gone by and the cold was seeping through her clothes, making her shiver, which he noticed with some dismay. 'You must think me a real cad. Come on, let's find something hot to eat.' He held her hand tightly as they walked back down the hill into the town, and when she glanced at him his dark eyes were soft and sad, sending her heart into freefall.

They ate at the café they'd visited before, but although she'd felt hungry earlier, now she only picked at the greasy fish and chips on her plate and Oliver finished them for her. He was more cheerful now and apologized for his earlier bad mood. 'It's not you,' he explained, 'it's the situation. I hate the waiting, the uncertainty. I'm not cut out for it.'

'Nobody is. Though maybe that's why you were a good deputy head. You understood that the boys needed certainty. They knew what the rules were and what would happen if they broke them. But you would also be kindly. Don't forget that. And don't be so hard on yourself.'

'You are good for me, Imogen.' His eyes crinkled as he smiled. 'I bet you're a marvellous nurse.'

Imogen laughed. 'I'm not sure that Matron thinks so. I'm really worried about this next set of exams, though so far I've muddled through. And I like what I do on the whole. It feels a privilege to look after people.'

'They're lucky to have you. Now I'm afraid I really must go, dear Imogen, the trains being as they are.' He paid the bill and left a few coins for the waitress then helped Imogen with her coat.

Outside it had started to sleet and the pavements were slushy. 'I'll come and see you off,' she offered, but he shook his head.

'No need, the hill up to the station will be slippery and I'll worry about you going back down alone.'

'Just to the bottom of the hill then,' she sighed.

They walked together slowly as though to savour every moment, and when they arrived at the foot of Richmond Hill, he drew her to him and kissed her.

'You'd better bloody well come home again,' she cried through gritted teeth.

He smiled. 'Oh, dear girl, I certainly plan to.'

'And promise me you'll write.'

'I will.'

She watched him walk away, wrapping the collar of his greatcoat more tightly against the weather, the sleet lightly coating his shoulders. He turned briefly, saluted her, and she raised her hand in farewell. Then she watched his receding figure grow smaller until he passed beyond sight.

For a moment she stood feeling bereft. Then with a sigh, she squared her shoulders and set off back to the hospital.

Two days later a note from him arrived. When she unfolded it, a small photograph fell out. 'Fearful chaos here,' he'd written. 'Just quickly, before we leave, here is one of me. Take care, my darling. Yours ever, O.' Imogen picked up the photo and examined it. It was a head-and-shoulders shot in uniform such as he'd use for a passport or identity card. He was unsmiling, his dark-eyed gaze piercing. It was precious. Imogen slipped it into her purse and added the note to a stash of letters in her top drawer. There were only a few from him, but from time to time she would pull them out and read them until she knew them by heart.

There had been no promises between them, no talk of the future, and Imogen did not know what she'd have said if he'd asked. Each of them had important things to prove and, anyway he was right, beating the Germans must surely come first.

Nineteen

June 1966

'I have a new plan,' Rain announced that evening as they all sat round the table after dinner. They had just finished recounting their activities of the day. Belle had mentioned visiting Mrs Kitto but had not revealed the nature of their conversation. Arlo stared at her hard, though, and she wondered what was going through his mind. She ought to rescue Imogen's box but that would have to be tomorrow now.

'There are too few of us here,' Rain went on. 'We need to grow. Then we can do more. We must spread our ideas.' Angel, who'd been sitting next to her swinging his legs, yawned, hopped down from his chair and wandered out into the garden, closely followed by Figgy.

'You mean your ideas,' Sirius put in with a supercilious smile. 'I think doing that would turn us into something different. Frankly, I can't work when there are too many people around.'

'We agreed, Sirius, did we not,' Rain said, fixing him with a stately glare, 'that we would work as a community free from the constrictions and manipulation of capitalist society. To do that successfully there must be more of us and with different skills. And we have to grow more of our own food. Janey can't do everything on her own, can you, Janey?'

'What are you suggesting, Rain?' Janey's expression was guarded.

Rain, Belle noticed, remained utterly unflustered by the resistance. Arlo looked perturbed, as well he might, the house being his uncle's. Chouli, playing with her hair, showed no emotion at all, and Gray listened with folded arms and a polite expression.

'We need people of vision,' Rain intoned, raising her hands like a Hindu deity and briefly closing her eyes. 'It has been shown to me.'

Sirius rolled his eyes. 'What we really need is someone who'll bring in a bit of cash.'

Rain glared at him again. 'If we run Silverwood properly we won't need money. Everyone will share their skills and work hard.'

Janey's heartfelt 'Hear hear' was the only response and Janey, Belle discerned, simply thought that Rain was asking for more help around the house and garden. This was certainly not all that Rain was proposing.

When she asked Gray later what he thought, he only shrugged. 'It'll work out,' he said vaguely. *He doesn't like conflict*, Belle realized. Perhaps that was because of his upbringing. It was funny learning about people and how to get on with them. She didn't like conflict either, but that didn't stop her feeling annoyed about injustice in the world or overbearing people like Rain.

'Rain comes out with these things sometimes,' Chouli told Belle the following morning, when Belle asked her. They were sitting on the grass in front of the house where Chouli had been plaiting strands of coloured embroidery cotton into Belle's hair. 'Especially after she's met up with that guru fellow. We love Rain, but it annoys Sirius a lot when she says this stuff because he's trying to be creative and it upsets him being bossed around. Especially as it's his money that helps keep things going here.'

Belle pursed her lips. Since Gray and herself were short-term visitors – weren't they? – she would be wise to keep her thoughts to herself. Gray clearly thought life here was perfect. Or, if he didn't, he would withdraw rather than complain. It occurred to her, though, that it was the men who were resistant to change. Even Chouli's opinion centred around Sirius's happiness. She wondered what Chouli herself believed and was about to ask when Rain came out and loomed over them, hands on hips and flexing her supple back.

'I would like to invite you both to join me for meditation.'

Belle and Chouli exchanged looks. 'Hang on.' Chouli calmly gathered up the spare bits of cotton, then they followed Rain's purposeful figure across the grass and up the brick steps into her wooden hut. They left their shoes in the little lobby, then Rain opened the inner door into a warm sunny room that smelled overpoweringly of incense. Smoke coiled from a burner on the shrine at the far end and Belle's eyes began to water. Rain didn't notice; she was bending to lay three long woven mats close to one another on the floor.

'A short meditation, I think,' she said, 'Just the breathing today. Belle, have you done this before?'

Belle shook her head.

'You probably won't manage the *padmasana* position at first, so just sit down and cross your legs normally, which is *svastikasana*.'

Belle wondered what on earth she was talking about but didn't dare ask.

Chouli sank readily onto her mat in a single lithe movement and folded her legs so that each foot rested on the opposite thigh. Her back was straight, and she laid her hands palm up on her knees. Belle copied this calm pose clumsily, trying and failing to force her feet into the strange position, and wondering what on earth was in store. She was both fearful and intrigued.

Across the room Rain fiddled with the controls of a tape recorder plugged into the wall and soon the soft sounds of Indian sitar music filled the air, taking Belle briefly back to the momentous gathering in Stu's flat where she and Gray first got together. Rain returned to the mats bearing a small shining metal bowl and a wooden stick, which she laid on the ground before her then gathered herself into an identical position to Chouli's. 'Are we ready?' she asked in her normal voice.

Belle nodded. 'Eyes closed,' Rain said and Belle obeyed. She heard Rain strike the bowl. It rang out with a long low mellifluous note that reminded her of her Aunt Avril's pretentious dinner gong, then Rain began to issue instructions in a quiet, sonorous tone. Belle breathed in deeply and out again slowly as she was told, in and out, in and out, until her head began to swim. The strange sound of the music and Rain's chanting voice mixed with the pungent aroma of the incense and after a while she experienced the strange sensation of sinking into a dream. In what felt like only a moment later, the soft vibrations of the bowl broke into her consciousness. At Rain's bidding she opened her eyes and blinked as her focus returned to the room and the music. The other two were both watching her, an expression of sternness on Rain's face and amusement on Chouli's.

'Are you all right?' Rain asked.

'I don't know,' Belle replied truthfully. 'Sleepy. Relaxed.'

'You're very pale,' Chouli offered, uncoiling herself and stretching her limbs.

'What happened? I stopped hearing you, Rain. I can't have been asleep, can I? Not sitting up like this.'

Rain rearranged herself into a kneeling position and studied Belle calmly. 'You're a natural, my dear. A pure spirit. Your soul became "like the flame of a candle, undisturbed by any breeze". That is from the *Gita* and that is what happened to you.'

'Really?' She was glad that Rain was pleased with her, but candles and flames, no, that wasn't what she'd experienced. There had been something, though. It had felt more like being underwater in a swimming pool and hearing sounds going on above.

Rain was talking again and she forced herself to listen. It was something about looking inward and something she called the Higher Self. There would be a mantra that sounded like 'aum'. They were going to return to the meditation position and Rain would speak it out loud over and over and she and Chouli must think it to themselves and dwell on it. Belle felt a little lost, but would have a go. Chouli was already making herself comfortable.

This time, when Rain struck the bowl and they began, Rain's intoned 'Aum ... Aum' initially sounded odd. Belle didn't know what 'aum' meant and why they were doing this, but very quickly she became used to it and this time when she sank beneath the surface of consciousness, she could hear the 'aums' in the far distance like a low hum, but it sounded as though many people were speaking them, not just one, and she was floating underwater like she used to in her local swimming pool. Then that other experience again, someone speaking, like a radio left on, voices, no, *a* voice, but she couldn't hear what it said. Yes she could, it was speaking her name. Now she pushed upwards, was swimming to the surface again and burst out into reality, gasping in air. 'Belle? Belle!' Rain was saying and she heard relief in the other woman's voice as she opened her eyes.

'Belle. Thank heavens. We couldn't wake you.' It was Chouli.

'You'd gone in deep.' Rain's voice was sharp with concern. 'What were you doing?'

'Nothing,' Belle replied. 'Dreaming, I suppose. But I wasn't asleep,' she added hastily in case Rain thought she wasn't treating the exercise seriously.

'Mmm. I think that's enough for today,' Rain muttered. 'We're on a ley line here, it might be channelling something.'

'What is a ley line?' Belle asked, her brow wrinkling. She remembered Arlo mentioning them.

'A druid I met in Wales told me about them. There's a network of paths – straight lines – across the country. Old sites – manmade mounds, sacred wells, ancient churches – are found on places where they intersect. Prehistoric man used them like a map, to get around England when it was forest. I'm sure one runs through the well here at Silverwood and maybe up to the standing stones in the nearby field. If so, it passes through this hut. Most modern people can't see them, my friend said.'

Belle frowned. 'Why would they affect me?'

'I don't know,' Rain shrugged, 'but they might.'

'It sounds . . . spooky,' Belle said with care. She had never heard of ley lines before. Duncan, the postgraduate chemist who led the Rambling Society, would know about that sort of thing and whether it was true or not. But she wasn't at college to ask him, she was here, and having to make sense of her situation using her own wits.

Still, the experience she'd just had didn't make sense on any reasonable level. She must have been half asleep and had a strange waking dream. The chanting and the thick aromatic smoke in the over-warm room must have been the cause. As she helped put away the mats and watched Rain snuff out the burning incense, Belle pondered what she'd dreamed. She remembered it clearly. It hadn't been frightening exactly, but it left her feeling dissatisfied, intrigued.

'Thank you,' she said to Rain, smiling as they went out into the sunshine. 'That was extraordinary. I'd like to try it again.'

Rain face brightened. 'I'm glad you thought so. You have a gift, I think. I had to practise many times before I achieved what you did today. Chouli, too, has the gift,' she added hastily.

Chouli gave one of her small, serene smiles. Perhaps it was the incense, but her gaze was unfocused as though her attention was somewhere far away.

In the kitchen Janey was at the sink peeling potatoes for the evening meal. Chouli and Belle sat down at the table to shell peas while Rain wandered off to look for Angel, murmuring something about a nature walk.

Janey was irritable this morning, clearly disturbed by Rain's speech the evening before now that she'd had the chance to reflect. 'These grand ideas are worrying,' she said. 'We're already stretched to run this place as it is. Having more animals and a bigger artistic community is all very well, but who does the hard graft and where does the money come from, that's what I want to know.'

Secretly Belle sided with Janey. Rain herself appeared to do little of the hard graft and Belle wondered how much money Sirius really provided. Once again he had shut himself in his studio for the morning.

Janey started chopping the potatoes into a big pan. 'After this, girls, housework.'

'I'll see where Gray is,' Belle said grimly and went upstairs, but he was nowhere to be found and she returned infuriated. She was happy to help Janey. After all, apart from the pittance that Gray had said was her portion for singing at The Ship, she wasn't contributing financially towards her keep.

'It'll just be us again then,' said Chouli with a sigh. It was Arlo's birthday so there was no attempt to look for him before Janey handed out the brooms, dustpans and cloths with orders to tackle the kitchen, bathrooms, stairs and hallway. As they were finishing, Rain and Angel returned from their walk with their arms full of wildflowers, which they arranged in jars on the kitchen table, shedding grass seed across the flagged floor the women had just brushed. Belle rolled her eyes at Chouli, but Chouli appeared lost in thought once more and didn't notice.

At one o'clock a delicious buttery aroma wafted through the house, drawing everyone except Arlo to the kitchen. 'Bad luck,' Janey said to them all. 'We're not having the cake until tea time.'

Instead she set mushroom pâté, goat's cheese, homemade bread and salad on the table and a jug of ice-cold water. Everyone helped themselves to lunch and disappeared off to their own private corners to eat: Rain and Angel in the kitchen with Janey, Chouli and Belle in the back courtyard, now drenched in sunshine; Gray upstairs and Sirius back in his studio. There was no sign of the birthday boy. After lunch Belle helped Angel make a birthday card with pictures cut out of old catalogues, then they went looking for Arlo to give it to him.

There was no answer when they knocked on Arlo's bedroom door. Belle inched open the door and peeped round to find it in near darkness, the curtains drawn across, the unmade bed empty and a collection of dirty crockery spread across the floor.

'Shall we try the library?' she asked Angel, whose lower lip was quivering with disappointment at not being able to present his card. He cheered up at once. The door to the secret room, however, was firmly in place.

'Perhaps your spell worked,' Belle smiled. 'To keep him away.'

'Can we see inside?' Angel begged stubbornly, so Belle moved several books to one side and pulled the catch so that the door swung towards them. They peered round, but there was no one in the warm, sunny space.

Angel ran in and fell onto his knees on the cushion by the window. 'Oh, where is he?' he sighed. He leaned on the sill to look through the glass as though he might catch sight of Arlo in the grounds below.

Belle didn't reply. Her attention had been caught by the collection of possessions in the corner. The mattress looked too tidy. Something else was wrong. Where was Imogen's box? She stepped across and flicked back the blanket in a useless gesture. The exercise book had gone, so had the other things. It was then that the distant low throbbing noise of a motorbike engine caused her to look up.

'Maybe it's Arlo,' Angel said excitedly. He jumped up and scrambled his way out of the door.

Belle dropped the blanket, picked up the birthday card

that Angel had forgotten in his hurry and followed, stopping only to fasten the door behind her, then to rearrange the books on the library shelf to cover their tracks. It must have been Arlo who'd taken Imogen's box; but why, and where had he put it? She glanced around the library and the study next door but there was no sign.

Outside she found Angel jumping up and down on the front steps in excitement as Arlo circled the concourse on his motorbike in a lap of triumph. A lingering trail of black smoke marked his journey down the drive. He wore a T-shirt and shorts, a red band tied round his head and a smile of delight on his face. Seeing Belle appear he drew to a halt beside her and killed the engine. He smelled of beer and engine oil.

'Wow!' Angel said, jumping up and down beside her. 'You made it go.'

'I certainly did.' He looked joyful.

'Happy birthday,' Belle said, coughing at the smoke.

'Thank you.'

'Where've you been?' Angel said. 'We've been looking *everywhere*.'

'Everywhere?' He regarded Angel coolly and Belle felt a prickle of unease. *He knows.*

'I've been into Falmouth to see some mates,' he addressed Belle. 'And give something to Francis.'

'What?'

'Wouldn't you like to know?'

She shrugged and pressed the birthday card into Angel's hand for him to present proudly to Arlo.

'What's this?'

'I made it.'

'I can see. It's great. I've got some others.' Arlo opened one of a pair of panniers at the back of his bike and withdrew several cards and, still wrapped in torn wrapping paper, an album by a band Belle didn't recognize.

'Happy birthday! Happy birthday!' came a chorus of voices and Belle saw that the others had gathered.

'You got it going.' Sirius eyed the motorbike in grudging admiration. 'I never thought you would.'

'In the end it just needed a good clean.' Together they examined the machine, Sirius asking questions and Arlo explaining technicalities while Belle and Gray looked on, Chouli and Rain sat on the step and Janey smoothed the kicked-up gravel with her shoe.

'There's a cake!' Angel interrupted, looking eagerly from one adult to another. 'With candles!'

Arlo broke off and beamed round at Angel. 'Cake? I don't remember when I last had a birthday cake.'

Angel grabbed his hand and everyone ambled off talking towards the kitchen.

Everyone except Belle. She was still staring at the bike. The panniers were large, large enough, she thought, to carry the cardboard box of books. Glancing up to check that the others were out of sight, she quickly looked inside first one, then the other. Both were empty apart from a scrap of cardboard in the second one. It had something scribbled on it in black marker. A capital B for Bandages. It was obvious that Arlo had taken Imogen's box with him. And presumably given it to his uncle. But why?

She stuffed the cardboard scrap into her pocket as evidence and closed the pannier.

'Belle, are you coming?' Gray appeared from round the corner.

'Yes, sorry, just daydreaming.' And she followed him inside.

Belle lay awake that night trying to puzzle out what had happened and what to do about it. Her first thought was to come straight out and admit to Arlo that she and Angel knew about the secret room and to ask why he'd taken the box of Imogen's possessions, but this approach worried her. By his sneering comment about giving something to Francis, Arlo had already indicated he was ahead of her. He knew his space had been invaded and resented it. She flushed as she remembered deleting her name in his stupid exercise book. She imagined he'd noticed that the box had been opened and had probably searched it himself. But why would he have taken it away? Was it some sort of revenge on her? It was all so petty.

She pondered what she knew of him. He was part of Silverwood, being Francis's nephew and heir apparent. His role in the house was therefore different from everyone else's and for all she knew he might be reporting back to Francis about any transgressions. He also had more of a right to be there than anyone else and maybe felt less inclined to follow the rules. Yet she hadn't noticed any of the others worrying about this and in most respects, Arlo was a perfectly compliant and enthusiastic part of the household, not a rule-breaker. It was only his behaviour to her, Belle, that was often so odd.

Lying next to the sleeping Gray, Belle tossed and turned. There was a definite undercurrent to her relationship with Arlo. She would look up sometimes and find him watching her, not in a nice way. He spied on her, saw her as a threat. It ate at her confidence, made her worry that she didn't really know any of these people or feel properly at home with their lifestyle, despite trying hard and wanting to fit in. Her own values were so different, though. Perhaps Gray was right – she was too 'buttoned-up'.

And then there was Mrs Kitto. Sirius, particularly, was sneery about her. What did the others think of her and did they mind Belle spending time with her? With this her thoughts rolled back to Imogen's box … why was it so important? She wished she'd looked through it thoroughly. Mrs Kitto had mentioned photographs, but hadn't explained properly. What was she not telling Belle and why? Oh, who could Belle trust?

Twenty

The next morning she felt weary, but went with Gray into Falmouth. Belle needed to go to the bank and the post office for stationery and stamps, then to buy toiletries. Gray had to sign on and try to buy spare guitar strings. He also intended to enquire at The Ship when they opened at lunchtime as to whether they'd like to book The Witchers again. 'Meaning you too,' he said with a twinkle, 'though it's only fair to let Stu know the date as well.'

Knowing she had only a few pounds left in her account, Belle just withdrew the amount she immediately required. She'd spent all her grant and supposed she too would have to sign on, although that meant being available for work and travelling to a job would be difficult from Silverwood. Gray, so far, had not been offered anything, but it was surely only a matter of time. She didn't know what the others' financial arrangements were. Everyone kept quiet about their individual circumstances. Sirius broadcast it loudly when he sold the odd painting, but only Arlo had occasional work, behind the bar of a local pub.

They were the first customers when The Ship opened. The landlord was delighted to see them. He'd had a cancellation on Friday week and wrote down the booking in a large beer-stained diary.

They bought bread and cheese and oranges and walked to the end of a quay where they sat on the edge, dangling their legs, and ate their lunch with the unwanted attention of several gulls.

'You know I told you about that room in the library,' Belle said carefully.

'Yeah.' Gray had been interested to hear about it, but worried about Angel becoming locked inside.

'I'm not sure what to do.' She explained what had happened, but Gray was merely puzzled and then, unusually, annoyed when she admitted to searching the panniers on Arlo's motorbike.

'That's wasn't a good thing to do. Do you want us thrown out?'

She lowered her eyes. 'No, of course not.' Her voice quavered.

He sighed. 'Do you think you're getting a bit obsessed about this Imogen?'

'I don't know. I think there's some particular reason Mrs Kitto is telling me about her.'

'Sirius says Mrs Kitto is odd and best avoided.'

'She's not odd. Well, not crazy odd. She lives on her own and welcomes a bit of company, that's all. And she knows all about Silverwood and its history.'

Gray shrugged. 'It's probably best not to interfere any further about the box.' He screwed up his sandwich bag, aimed it at a nearby rubbish bin and missed. It skittered across the quay in the breeze and dropped into the sea. Belle pressed her lips together but said nothing. It was their first row and she felt shaken by it.

He sat staring out over the sea and, with a lump in her throat, she snatched glances at his handsome hawkish profile, his blond hair lifting in the breeze. She was beginning to realize that she loved him. And what did he think about her? She remembered the looks he often gave her when he sang to her, the tenderness of his lovemaking. It was still hard to get to know him, though. He said so little about himself, his thoughts and feelings. What he stood for.

It occurred to her with a flash of insight that he poured his feelings into his songs. That was his way of telling people about his love of nature, of women, of life itself. Perhaps she was getting to know him after all. She puzzled now about how to end the quarrel, then remembered what her mother often quoted. *A soft answer turneth away wrath.* So she touched his hand gently and whispered, 'I'm sorry. I didn't mean to upset you,' and he turned his head and smiled at her, narrowing his clear blue eyes.

'It's fine, Belle. Shall we go home?'

'Silverwood.' It was her turn to smile. 'Do you think of it as home?'

He paused. 'No, not long term. I haven't got a home, though Darbyfield's where I go back to. I suppose you think of Surrey because of your family.'

'Yes, my family are where my home is.' Despite everything, she felt this to be true. 'Gray ...' She halted, not knowing how to say what she wanted to tell him. 'How long do you think you'll be staying at Silverwood?'

He pushed back his hair as he studied her, his brow creasing. 'I'm not sure. I've written several songs, good ones. It's going well so I intend to stay longer, but you, I worry whether you're happy. Are you, Belle?'

She breathed deeply and stared out to sea. 'I don't know. I mean ...' She looked at him. 'I love being with you and I love Silverwood, the place itself, and I'm finding out things about myself, but it only works if I live a day at a time. Whenever I think about the future I feel panicky. I don't really belong with this group of people, you see. I can stay a bit longer because of you, but not for ever.'

'Nothing's for ever.' He touched her cheek with his fingers. 'Poor Belle. I shouldn't have brought you.'

'Oh yes, you should.' She spoke forcefully. 'I said I'm finding out things. There's a reason I'm here. It's just ... painful if I think too much.'

Gray looked at her curiously, then shrugged. 'Living in the present is what I do. Just try to fit in, love. Don't annoy Arlo any more than you can help. That's my advice.'

'Don't you think about where you're going with your music, Gray? Are you ambitious?'

He fixed her with his clear blue gaze. 'Of course I am,' he said. 'But I won't get anywhere by worrying about it, will I?'

*

They were silent on the return journey, with Belle reflecting on what Gray had said. Despite everything, her family and where she'd been brought up were indeed home. *They'll be missing me,* she thought, the guilt flooding in. *I must write again.* She would also write to her friend Carrie. And Duncan, too, of the Ramblers Club. She'd paid him a small deposit for the club's summer holiday that she wouldn't be going on. She'd write to him and ask for her deposit back. She was sure he'd understand if she pleaded poverty.

After lunch she sat at the old desk next to the library to write her letters. The hardest one was to her parents and sister because she had to leave so much out in case she upset them. Such as her visit to Kynance.

> *Dear Mum and Dad and Jackie,*
>
>   *I'm just writing to tell you that I'm perfectly fine. I'm still in Cornwall staying at this great house with a group of new friends and learning all sorts of things. I can milk goats now – imagine! And we've made jam and I'm writing songs and performing them. Everything's super! I'll write again soon.*
>
>   *Miss you.*
>
>   *Your Belle*

While writing to Carrie she realized that she didn't have her friend's home address with her. Instead she addressed the envelope to the university and wrote 'Please Forward' across the top. Duncan, being a graduate student, who didn't follow the pattern of terms, was probably still on campus, so she sent his letter there, too.

Licking the stamps, she tasted their bitterness, but going to the postbox along the lane gave her a feeling of achievement. For a moment she paused, wishing that she'd given Carrie her return address so that she could hear from her, but the last thing she wanted was for Carrie to turn up unannounced to 'rescue' her so she pushed the letters into the slot. She didn't honestly believe that Carrie would do such a thing, but couldn't take the risk.

Belle ambled back down the lane in the dreamy late afternoon sunshine to find Silverwood apparently deserted. She'd already noticed on her way out that Arlo's motorbike and Sirius's van were gone from the drive. In the kitchen two large dishes covered by tea cloths lay on the stove. She peeped in at them. Cheese and potato pies, waiting to go into the oven. Lovely. A saucepan of sliced carrots in water stood beside them. Supper was obviously under control, but Janey was elsewhere.

She thought about doing some laundry, but that seemed a waste of a lovely day. She'd walk down to the cottage to see if Mrs Kitto was in.

Twenty-One

'I'm sure that Arlo took the box and gave it to Francis, but I don't understand why and Gray said I should stop annoying him.'

Mrs Kitto had been gardening, but immediately invited Belle into the kitchen where she put the kettle on. While she made tea Belle told her about the mysterious disappearance of Imogen's books.

Mrs Kitto's hand stilled as she spooned leaves into the teapot. 'He's a strange one, that boy. What else could have been in the box? Apart from the books and the diaries?'

Belle thought. 'You said something about photographs. I should have had a good look, shouldn't I?'

She followed Mrs Kitto into the sitting room, and when they were comfortable, she begged Mrs Kitto to tell her the next part of Imogen's story. 'I have to know what happened next. It's like a compulsion,' she said smiling.

'You don't know how pleased I am to hear that,' Mrs Kitto

said with a smile. 'I hope it's not long before you realize why the tale's so important.'

~

August 1943

Eight months had passed since Oliver's unit had left Cornwall and during that time he and Imogen had corresponded only sporadically. Although he didn't specifically say where he was, she sensed disappointment that he hadn't left English shores. Possibly, from his hints, he was in Plymouth. Poor Oliver. Action was denied him still. Privately she was glad to know that he was safe, or as safe as one could be with the heavy air raids. Meeting, however, proved impossible. Their schedules did not allow it. When a weekend finally approached during which they might manage it, Oliver's leave was rescinded at the last moment.

Towards the end of August she and her roommate Sarah Summers found that they'd both been granted the same weekend off, two days and two nights. Imogen had written to her mother to suggest coming home, but the letter crossed with one from Mrs Lockhart, saying that she was going to stay with an elderly cousin in Norfolk who was recovering from an operation.

From time to time she'd met with Ned and was wondering now whether to write to him to propose a day out. Then, Summers suggested that Imogen go home with her to Falmouth. Her mother would be pleased to meet her, she said, and Imogen could always arrange to meet Ned there. It seemed a wonderful idea, especially since Summers needed cheering up. She had just heard with horror from her fiancé Sam's parents that he'd been taken prisoner by the Japanese.

The Summers' house was part of a white-painted terrace on the hillside above the town with fine views of the sea. Its balcony and Dracaena palm trees growing in the front garden gave it a feel of the Mediterranean. A long flight of steep stone steps led down to the town, which meant quite a climb down and back up again. The beach was, however, only a short walk away and the girls were more than willing to sneak past the defensive coils of barbed wire to swim. It was an almost perfect weekend. Long nights in soft beds and the bracing breeze off the sea restored Imogen after the long haul of the previous months. And on the Sunday afternoon whilst Summers accompanied her mother to visit relations, she met up with Ned.

She'd arranged to meet him at the Princess Pavilion Gardens where – was it as much as three years ago? – she and Oliver had helped the oil-covered wretches from the stricken RMS *Lancastria*. Today it felt a different place, with a brass band playing in the bandstand; British servicemen and some of the Dutchmen billeted in the area, a couple of Wrens and some local families, all taking tea and enjoying the sunshine. Imogen nabbed a spare table under the colonnade, a good distance from the band.

'Imogen. I hope I'm not terribly late.' Ned was out of breath, his face flushed with effort, but this time he'd remembered to remove the cycle clips from his crumpled linen trousers. Imogen smiled at the memory.

'Honestly, Ned, do sit down, I've only just got here myself.' They briefly clasped hands. 'A hot day to cycle, I imagine?'

'It certainly is.' He sat down opposite, mopped his brow and smoothed his hair. 'Phew,' he said, then, 'You, on the other hand, look beautifully cool and rested.'

'It's nice to be able to wear a summer dress instead of uniform.'

'Well, it's very *charmant*. Have you ordered?'

She shook her head, so he flagged down a passing waitress and ordered tea and cakes.

'It's good to see you, Ned. I'm sorry it's been so long.'

'Don't feel guilty. We're all in the same boat. It's not getting easier, is it?'

'It's been simply non-stop at the hospital. We're short of staff and rushed off our feet. And I've had exams, of course.'

'How have you got on? Do you know yet?'

'I passed by a whisper. No idea how. So I'm a fully fledged nurse, Ned! I have to pinch myself. It feels such an achievement.'

'Congratulations. You've worked hard for it.'

After tea, Ned's natural colour returned and he began to relax. Soon they were swapping news of families and work. Ned's mother had received a pre-printed card from his brother in an officers' prison camp that indicated that he was in good spirits. 'Though, of course, he couldn't say otherwise.' His sister and her children were managing while her husband was away as an army chaplain, but only just, if her letters were to be believed. Imogen told him about Summers, whom Ned had met once when he'd visited Imogen in Truro and they'd all had lunch out together.

'Her father is away, so her mother is glad to have us visit.

She has family around and has taken a lodger, but she misses Sarah dreadfully.'

'I liked your friend. It must be hard for her not knowing where her fiancé has been taken. Has anyone said?'

Imogen shook her head. 'The best we can hope for is that the Japanese are not treating him too badly.' She was touched by Ned's concern. He was such a lovely man. 'I could weep for her. She's so patient. I could never be like her.'

'We don't know how we would be until the moment arrives,' he said softly. 'Don't do yourself down.'

'It's just I see so many people ... patients, other nurses ... having to put up with all kinds of difficulties. I honestly don't know how they manage. There was a mother admitted to the medical ward with advanced leukaemia. There's nothing anyone can do. Her son, her only child, never returned from Dunkirk. No one knows what's happened to him, but she's so bloomin' accepting. Puts the rest of us to shame. Will you have the last piece of cake? Go on, I don't need it.'

'I'm hungry all the time. Cook does her best but I have fantasies about steak and kidney pudding in rich gravy with a thick layer of suet.'

'Oh, don't,' Imogen groaned. 'I could murder for lemon meringue pie.'

'Roast lamb with all the trimmings.'

'You're torturing me. How is Cook? And Kezia?'

'Cook's gone to her mother's in St Ives for a fortnight, and Kezia's standing in. Nobody dares complain.'

'Does that mean there's something to complain about?' Imogen laughed, remembering Kezia's feisty temper if roused.

'Let's just say that if something can go wrong with the grub then it will. She burned the breakfast bacon yesterday.'

'Bacon? You get bacon for breakfast?'

'And eggs. Courtesy of her mother's hens. There aren't many of us to cater for in the summer so we do very nicely with what there is.'

Imogen laughed. 'Well, count your blessings. We get standard loaves and ersatz jam. Oh, and fish roe. Call me fussy, but there's nothing more disgusting than fish roe in my opinion.'

'You're fussy! Oh, your face, Imogen! I mean it's a very beautiful face, but you look so funny when you screw it up like that!'

Imogen turned serious. 'Ned, do you think all of this – the war – will ever end? I was remembering being here in this exact spot more than three years ago after the *Lancastria* was bombed. Three years!'

'They never admitted to the *Lancastria*, you know. The authorities, I mean. But, yes, it will end. I believe there's plenty of cause for optimism now.' Ned looked about him as though someone might overhear, then leaned forward. 'We can't go down to the beach by Silverwood now. It's forbidden. And the place is swarming with activity. Something big is planned, I'm sure.'

'Ned, you shouldn't be saying anything, but, yes, with all the Americans coming into Cornwall . . .'

For a moment they were silent. Imogen occupied herself sharing the last of the tea between them.

She knew what he would ask next before he asked it.

'Have you heard from Oliver at all?' His voice was light,

as though he'd asked something trivial. 'We never do at the school.'

Imogen explained that she had and tried not to notice that Ned's eyes hardened. 'I think he's in Plymouth. The bombing's been dreadful there so I imagine his unit's been helping out. Poor Oliver. No real action for him.'

'Lucky bloke.'

'Action is what he left school-teaching for.'

'Imogen ...' Ned started to say and she saw the pleading in his face and couldn't bear it.

'Shall we go, Ned? We could walk down on the beach for a bit.'

'Can we?'

'Summers and I do. Anyway, someone will tell us soon enough if we're trespassing.'

'All right then.' The waitress arrived and began to stack crockery, then hovered as Ned felt in his pocket and laid some change on the table.

She took off her shoes to walk along the shore past giant concrete blocks placed to ward off an enemy landing, but Ned kept his brogues on. Imogen enjoyed the feel of the warm dry sand under her feet, but there were gobbets of tar to avoid, and ugly scraps of flotsam, and soon they turned inland and continued along the pavement until they left the town and the crowds behind.

Reaching a small headland, they stood silently together looking out to sea with the breeze gusting about. Imogen let him take her hand, sensing that he had something important to say, but dreading to hear it. He led her to a bench in the shelter of a rock, out of the wind, and he turned towards her.

'Imogen,' he said hoarsely and she bit her lip.

'I wish you wouldn't,' she sighed.

'I have to. You must know how I feel about you. No, please listen. If I don't say it now then I never will. I'm awfully fond of you. No, it's more than that. I'm in love with you.' She heard the crack in his voice. 'Is there any hope at all?'

'Ned.' She met his eye and saw his pain. 'You know I'm fond of you, simply not in that way. I can't help it. I don't want to hurt you. Can we just go on being good friends? I would value that so much.'

'I suppose it's Dalton.' He stared gloomily at the ground.

'That's not the reason, Ned,' she said. 'I'll be honest with you, though Oliver and I are not your business. I don't want to be serious about anyone at present.'

'You're right, of course, it's not my business.' He squared his shoulders against his disappointment then smiled at her warmly, his fine hair blowing in the breeze.

'Oh, Ned,' she sighed.

'We'll carry on being friends, Imogen. I'd like that very much, but I'd like you to promise that you'll call on me if you ever need help of any kind. Will you promise that?'

'I promise,' she said, her voice trembling at his generous response.

After a while they walked on to the tip of the headland and looked out over the water. It was breathtakingly beautiful, Imogen thought. They watched the boats go to and fro, listening to the metallic clanks and scrapes that reached them from the docks, a bravely thrilling sound.

'It will end,' Ned said. 'Maybe sooner than we know, but I can't think we'll go back to how we were. Everything will have changed profoundly.'

'Let's hope for the better,' Imogen remarked.

'What will you do after the war ends?'

'I don't know. I simply don't know. Maybe I'll travel. With a nursing qualification I could earn my passage, I suppose. Or join the forces, maybe.'

He regarded her seriously. 'Not marry or have children?'

'Perhaps,' she said vaguely, thinking of Oliver. 'Just not yet.'

When they arrived back at the Pavilion, they said goodbye. Ned rescued his bicycle from where he'd hidden it behind some bushes and she watched him wrap the clips around his trouser legs and set off, a slightly comic figure, she thought tenderly, wobbling as he waved farewell. Then she turned and walked thoughtfully back into the town.

Summer turned to autumn and everything started to drag. The war would go on for ever, Imogen thought at low moments. The best and worst part of each day was looking eagerly through the incoming post for a letter from Oliver, only for hope almost always to be dashed. She'd been wrong about him, she thought sadly, one such morning. He didn't need her after all. None of the men she came across at the dances or group visits to the cinema made much impression on her. Not compared to Oliver. She smiled to read a letter from Kezia saying that her Will, the farmer's son, had joined the Navy and they were getting married straight away!

~

June 1966

Mrs Kitto's soft voice faded and Belle, who'd sat with eyes closed as if in a dream, opened them. When she glanced at the older lady she was surprised to see a sadness in her gaze, but this was quickly replaced by a smile. She wished Mrs Kitto would explain exactly how she knew Imogen, to be so moved by the story she told. Mrs Kitto always deflected such questions. Instead Belle asked,'Was it long before Imogen saw Ned or Oliver again?', hoping that she'd continue.

'We'll save that for another day.' Mrs Kitto rose from her chair and began to clear the table. 'The next part of the story becomes complicated and I need to think about the order in which to tell it.'

Though disappointed, Belle nodded. 'I understand.'

'Now, how are things at the house? Has Rain cooked up any new schemes?'

'She's being mysterious. Something about it being the Summer Solstice tomorrow.' Arlo had once mentioned a ceremony and Belle remembered not liking the sound of it.

'Ah,' Mrs Kitto said, her expression turning stormy. 'In which case I think I'll go and stay with a friend.'

'Why, what will happen?'

'I don't really know, but last year there were a lot of strange lights and loud music on the upper field.'

Belle sighed. 'I suppose we'll all have to join in.'

'I imagine so, if Rain has anything to do with it.'

Twenty-Two

Mrs Kitto's prediction was correct. That night Rain explained arrangements for a Midsummer's Eve feast, a bonfire and dancing at the standing stones. Everyone was to come and everyone was to help.

The inhabitants of Silverwood were up early the following morning. There was an air of activity when Belle entered the kitchen, yawning, to make tea. The table was covered with tins of meat and boxes of vegetables and Janey had her head in the fridge. Sirius wandered about in a tattered dressing gown assembling bottles of drink, Rain was scraping porridge into a bowl for Angel. The boy was sitting at the table swinging his legs and talking to Figgy, who watched him expectantly for scraps. 'There's lots to do today,' Rain called when she saw Belle, 'and Janey will need your help later. And we're reliant on Gray for some music.'

Belle nodded, thinking that so far it sounded fun rather than something to worry about. As she waited for the kettle to boil, Chouli came in and Belle eyed her with concern, for her narrow shoulders were hunched above folded arms and the white of her dress emphasized that her eyes were red-rimmed from crying and her face blotchy. Sirius ignored her and the others seemed too preoccupied to notice.

'I wonder what's wrong,' Belle commented to Gray a few minutes later. She was sipping her tea by the open window upstairs, watching him pull on his jeans. 'I took a mug out-side to her and she spoke in a small voice, but wouldn't look at me. She seemed awfully miserable, poor thing. She and Sirius have obviously had a row.'

'None of our business, then,' Gray said, scrabbling in a drawer. 'Are there any clean shirts?'

'Only the one you haven't had time to iron,' she snapped, pointing to a different drawer. 'Why isn't it our business when she's obviously upset?'

'I'm sure she'd tell someone if she wants to.'

Belle gave up and straightened. 'I'd better go down. Rain's fitting in a meditation class.'

Just then came scraping and trundling noises from below and she leaned from the window to look. Arlo in clogs and wearing thick gloves was bumping a wheelbarrow piled high with brushwood across the courtyard in the direc-tion of the upper field. As she watched, a branch fell off. He cursed and stopped to pick it up, rebalanced the load, then set off again. 'Is he in charge of the fire?' she asked Gray, who joined her at the window, buttoning the crum-pled shirt.

'What makes you suspect that?' He rolled his eyes in a clownish fashion and she gave him a light slap.

He leaned over to give Belle a quick kiss then headed for the stairs. Sighing, she bent to the task of making the bed, before sliding her feet into her sandals and following, eager for the meditation.

Once again the wooden hut was filled with peace and sunshine, a welcome antidote to the manic activity in the house. As Rain was lighting the incense burner, Chouli arrived, wearing an expression of abject resignation. Rain threw her an anxious frown, but seeing the girl assume the lotus position, her swollen eyes closed, said nothing. She began the meditation, bidding her two acolytes to focus on their breath.

Belle's breathing became long and rhythmic. She sank quickly into the feeling of deep calm, like suspension in warm water, all her worries falling away. She was aware of the low sound of Rain's voice coming from somewhere far, far away, but it didn't seem long at all before it grew closer and louder again. She was calling Belle back. Belle swam to the surface of consciousness and opened her eyes, blinking in the smoky light. Next to her Rain was reaching up to retie her ponytail. Between them, Chouli opened her eyes and sighed a long, quavering sigh.

'That was wonderful,' Belle said, raising her arms and stretching. 'Honestly, I felt like a baby in the womb.'

Beside her, Chouli froze, then a sob escaped her and she pressed her palms to her face.

'Chouli, dear?' Rain said. She reached out and squeezed Chouli's slender forearm. 'What on earth's the matter?'

'Nothing,' the girl choked. Then, 'Baby. I'm having a baby.'

Rain and Belle stared at each other. Neither knew what to say.

'Sirius is mad at me,' Chouli sobbed to Belle. They had found a secluded part of the grounds to sit, a field of long grass full of the scents of summer and great bumbling bees visiting the wildflowers. 'He thinks it's my fault. Well, I don't really see how he can believe that, but that doesn't stop him blaming me.'

'Didn't you, um, use anything?'

'Of course, we're not stupid, but ... he was responsible for that.'

Belle nodded. It was the same for her and Gray. She felt a sudden rush of dismay. If it had not worked for Chouli then maybe ... She dismissed the thought and concentrated on Chouli's misery.

'Is it really a disaster? I mean, if you're together and ...'

Chouli's expression darkened further. 'Sirius is *married*, Belle.'

'Oh.'

'He has three children already and he doesn't want any more. He says it's bad enough paying for the ones he has already. That's why he's so eager to sell his pictures. He ... he wants me to ... to get rid of it, Belle. He says Rain would help. And Janey knows about herbs.'

'Get rid of it? Would you really do that?'

'I don't know. I've only just found out. I can't think straight.'

'What about your family? Would they help?'

'My parents would be furious. They're very churchy and they know all these stuck-up people who would be shocked. It's bad enough for them that I'm here with Sirius.'

'They'd look after you, though, wouldn't they? If you chose to have it and Sirius wouldn't help.'

'I think so. They'd send me money, anyway. But they'd be so disappointed in me. They are disappointed, now.'

'Perhaps Sirius would come round.'

She nodded. 'Perhaps. It's not just that. Belle, I don't want a baby. Well, one day maybe, but not for years.' She looked frightened. 'I wanted to make something of my life.'

'I see.' *Then what are you doing here with a much older man who treats you like a child*? Belle wanted to ask but didn't. She could hardly judge Chouli without pointing an accusing finger at herself. She plucked a blade of grass and tickled a ladybird with it, deep in thought. She herself had jeopardized her education and disappeared from her family's life. For what? For love? To find herself? What happened if she started a baby, too? That really would change everything. Despite her reservations about its occupants, she was content to live at Silverwood for the moment, happy to delve into the past, but finding it impossible to think of the future. And this worked if she lived a day at a time. Chouli's situation had brought her up short.

There was an air of excitement in the house that could not be overshadowed by Chouli's distress and Sirius's anger and was amply expressed by Angel, who capered about getting in everyone's way. Sirius removed himself from proceedings by shutting himself in his drawing room studio. At the slam of the door everyone looked at each other with relief.

Janey set Chouli to work hulling strawberries, while Belle was put in charge of a stew that consisted mainly of different kinds of bean that Janey had left soaking in a pan overnight plus a giant canful of tomatoes. Janey kneaded a great quantity of dough that she wrapped in a cloth and left on the stove to rise. Rain, too, was busy on mysterious errands about the sheds and garden. She passed through the kitchen once with her arms full of sweet-smelling herbs, then carrying an old blue silk bedspread and a bag of Christmas tinsel.

Later, Gray helped Arlo clean a grimy trestle table which they carried up to the field, Angel following with a tarpaulin to lay over the brushwood. Grey clouds were gathering and the mood turned anxious. At four o'clock they watched from the kitchen as a light shower fell. Angel started crying with disappointment, but soon the sky cleared and everyone cheered up again. Near six Janey declared everything finished and took off her apron. People drifted off one by one to get changed.

'What are we supposed to wear for a solstice party?' Belle asked Gray in the privacy of their room.

'The less the better,' Gray said, amused.

'I'm not doing that,' Belle said grimly, reaching for the long white dress that Chouli had lent her. It was grass-stained at the hem, but she reckoned no one would notice. Gray dug out a black top with a drawstring neck and tied a narrow black tie around his head, which gave him a piratical air.

Outside dark clouds were gathering once more. A cool

wind blew in the scent of damp earth. 'Will it rain again?' Belle said anxiously.

'Only a shower, I should think.' He waited for Belle to draw a brush through her hair, then looked up at a rumble of thunder.

'Wait.' She ran back and raised her arm to close the window. As she looked out, lightning zigzagged above the horizon and great drops of rain began to fall. She pulled the window sash down. Outside, the rain intensified. 'It's more than a shower,' she said.

'I expect it'll pass,' Gray called back from the top of the stairs.

In their half-hour's absence the atmosphere in the kitchen had changed, become charged. It was, Belle thought, as though everyone was under a spell, or they'd taken something. Perhaps it was the storm, which must have raised everyone's hackles.

Sirius, in his usual clothes, spattered with paint, was smoking a roll-up and opening the bottles that he'd set out earlier. Arlo, wearing a short white toga that hung over one shoulder, poured wine into the assortment of glasses belonging to the house: old cut-glass, cheap petrol station and a couple of odd tumblers. Gray passed Belle a brimming crystal goblet and she swallowed a large mouthful, wincing at the sharpness then relaxing as the warmth travelled down her throat. One by one the other members of the household assembled. Belle was amazed at their assortment of outfits and make-up. Each costume, she thought, somehow suited its wearer.

With his dark wavy hair and muscular arms, Arlo's tunic
made him a perfect satyr. Angel, in a belted silver tunic and
scallop-topped bootees, was a slender wood-elf. His mother,
in a long gold pillar dress that pooled about her feet, was a
magnificent Greek goddess, her heavy hair plaited and piled
up on her head, her pointed silver pendant glinting at her
breast. Chouli, in pale green, looked nauseous, a lost expression on her face. *Like Andromeda*, thought Belle, who'd avidly
read Greek myths as a child, *chained to a rock and abandoned*.
Chouli's pupils were large in her guileless blue eyes and she
drank too eagerly of the tumbler of wine Arlo gave her. And
Gray, what of Gray. Gray the musician, not mythical at all, but
exotic all the same. Belle smiled at her pirate, already feeling
woozy from the wine.

'Where's Janey?' someone said and at that moment the
door to the garden opened and a figure stepped inside. It was
Janey, struggling with a large umbrella.

There was a silence, then, 'Good Lord,' Sirius whispered.
Janey's smile was uncertain. She wore a blue toga dress gathered around the hips and Belle recognized the silk bedspread
she'd seen Rain with earlier, now knotted and fastened into
place with safety pins. On her thin brown hair was set a
garland of trailing ivy, woven with roses from the garden.
It would have suited a young woman like Chouli, but above
Janey's weathered face appeared faintly comic. Poor Janey,
Belle thought. Janey adored Rain and did anything she was
asked, but Rain had not been kind in dressing her friend.

No matter. Someone put a drink into Janey's hand and
soon everyone was laughing and talking together, any

embarrassment over costumes forgotten. The room, already warm from the range, grew warmer and Belle's eyes watered from smoke and her head swam. What was in the wine, she wondered briefly, holding out her glass for a refill. She'd got used to the sharpness of it and it slipped down like syrup. Listening to Sirius and Gray discussing cars, about which she knew little and cared less, her attention faded in and out. Janey's garland was awry, her face flushed. Chouli was sitting on a kitchen chair, out of the way, watching Angel play with the dog. Belle slipped across to ask how she was, but she barely replied, so Belle put her arm round her narrow shoulders and gave her a hug, feeling a sob escape her.

'Arlo!' Belle looked up in time to see him at the potato salad, his finger in his mouth. Janey slapped his arm.

'We need to eat now,' Rain said, craning to look at the sky through the window. There followed an argument about whether to take the food outside, with the risk of show-ers, which Rain settled by seizing two bowls of salad and marching to the door, Figgy and Angel bounding ahead. The household followed in dribs and drabs with trays piled high. Belle carried a stack of plates and cutlery, Gray a crate of bottles, and Sirius and Arlo hauled the pan of stew between them. They wove an unsteady path across the wet courtyard towards the fields, Belle falling back to encourage Chouli who trailed behind carrying a blanket and a hessian bag contain-ing the loaves banging against her legs.

The clouds were clearing as they passed onto the upper field, and a veiled sun cast a slanted light that picked out raindrops on every leaf and blade of grass, making them sparkle like magic. It might just turn into a perfect evening full of birdsong. Belle followed the others up a gentle slope and gasped as she reached the brow of the hill. For there, circling a shallow dip, stood the ring of boulders, tall and narrow, some twisted, others bent, like dancers frozen to the spot by some curse or catastrophe. She'd seen them before, but in this magical light they seemed alive.

Beside her, Arlo grinned, his eyes lacking focus, flicking over her.

'Good, isn't it?' he said. They approached the trestle table, set up near the stones. Beyond the circle was a rocky hillock where the bonfire lay under its tarpaulin, ready to be lit. Belle laid down the plates and scrambled to the top where she drew a deep breath to see the view. It stretched across the fields down to the estuary, with the expanse of the sea beyond. She felt someone's presence close behind her, warm breath on her neck. Imagining it to be Gray, she turned her head to see Arlo again. Was he haunting her?

She inched away. He didn't appear to notice.

'Brilliant,' he breathed, nodding at the view.

'Yeah!'

He walked to the edge, past the bonfire, and stretched his arms up and outwards, tipping his face to the heavens, like some ruler presenting himself to the people. 'Lord of all I survey,' he said and laughed. Belle, standing behind with the breeze in her hair and the magnificence of the sight before her, caught his exhilaration. Figgy galloped up behind them, barking. Arlo ignored him.

After a moment he turned to the bonfire. 'This is an old

place for beacons,' he told her conversationally, kicking a stray piece of wood into place. 'Look over there. See that hill-top, high above the others? That's the next one in line. They used to light them to warn of invasion.'

'What will happen when we light ours – won't it be like a false alarm?'

'That would be fun, wouldn't it, if they call the army out.' She smiled uncertainly.

'Come on,' he said, starting back. 'Let's eat. Then when it gets dark the ceremony will begin.'

'What is this ceremony, Arlo?' she asked, but he appeared not to hear. She followed, with Figgy in tow.

By the table Janey handed round plates of bean stew, hunks of bread and salad. Sirius poured wine and they sat on blankets and ate hungrily. All except Chouli, who refused the stew and merely nibbled crumbs from a slice of bread. All of a sudden, she dropped the bread, rose, stumbled down the hill and fell to her knees, retching. Everyone stopped talking, then Janey hurried to her side. After helping the girl to her feet, she called up, 'I'm taking her back to the house.' They limped off together, Janey's arm round her shoulders. Figgy seized the bit of bread and chowed it down.

'She'll be all right,' Rain said through a mouthful of salad.

'Do you think so?' Sirius, shovelling stew in his mouth, stared at her and wiped his lips with the back of his hand.

'It's women's work. Leave her,' Rain growled.

Sirius's eyes fixed on Rain's face for a moment, then he shrugged, reached for a bottle of wine and took a long swig from it.

Belle looked from one to the other and for the second time felt a pang of real unease. Something wasn't right here. It wasn't just the wine – which wasn't, she suspected, ordinary wine – there was something else going on. Her eyes fell on Angel and she wondered if he ought to be here, this young innocent exposed to adult pleasures.

Everyone finished their food in silence, then the plates were piled up and the bottles of wine passed round again. The group lay around talking casually about not very much. There was a sense building that something was going to happen. Rain rose, her gown blowing against her legs in the mounting wind. As Arlo had done, she walked in long strides to the beacon and stood looking out over the landscape, then secured a fallen plait of hair and returned to the group.

'It'll rain again later, I think. It won't be dark for a while but we must start the celebrations.'

At this, people clambered to their feet. Sirius lurched to the table and uncorked another bottle. Angel jumped up and down, but his expression was uncertain. The wind blew stronger. Far away on the horizon a line of grey cloud was gathering.

'Wait!' Janey's voice, a thin call, came from below. They watched her scale the slope and reach them, breathless.

'Is all well?' Rain asked in a low voice.

'I think so,' Janey panted.

'Is Chouli all right?' Belle wondered.

The women both turned, surprised that she'd spoken. 'Of course,' Rain said.

'She's just sick. She'll sleep now.' Janey sounded firm.

'A pity she's missing the ceremony,' Rain remarked with a sigh. 'But perhaps it's for the best. The vibes would be wrong.'

Belle felt her blood freeze. 'Should I go and sit with her?'

'No,' both women said at once. 'Your place is here.' It sounded at once corny and frightening, but she obeyed.

'Arlo and Gray – the music,' Rain ordered and Arlo rummaged under the table and brought a drum and his wooden flute out of a bag.

'Come!' Rain intoned, her sweeping arm inviting all present, and they staggered over to the circle of stones.

Arlo handed Gray the drum, then blew into the flute and inexpertly began to play an eerie tune. Gray secured the drum in the crook of his arm and joined in, tentatively at first, then with more confidence. It was Angel who danced first, running into the centre of the circle and twirling, supple and laughing. Figgy ran to him, barking and tugging on his clothes with his teeth and growling as though it was a great game. Rain entered the ring and caught her son's hand, drawing him round in a circle. Figgy retired from the dance to sit and watch from the sidelines. One by one the others joined in.

At first Belle found dancing on the soft ground in her bare feet fun, the blood pounding in her veins, her spirits soaring, the whole scene cast in golden light as the sun sank towards a line of hills to the west. The rhythmic beat of Gray's drum and the wild squeal of Arlo's flute stirred the blood and now everyone was capering about, Sirius waving a bottle and cavorting in an ungainly manner, Rain weaving in and out of the stones with supple fluidity, Janey skipping about with

little idea of rhythm, clutching at her dress where it was slipping from her shoulder.

Time passed and the sun sank below the hills, the detail of
the dancing figures fading to silhouettes as the light drained
from the sky. Then Rain shouted for a break. It went quiet
and everyone collapsed on the grass while Arlo went to light
the beacon, removing the tarpaulin with a flourish, Sirius
holding it like a windshield as Arlo lit matches and touched
the newspaper at the base. Everyone held their breath as the
flames licked the kindling, smoke rose, and finally cheered as
the branches caught. Then a bottle or two was passed round
again and the music and the dancing recommenced.

The sky grew dark and soon the dancers were lit only by
the flames of the fire. In the shadows cast by the flickering
light, Belle imagined that the stones themselves were moving
in their places, twisting and bending like saplings in a gale.
Sirius tripped and fell, stumbled to his feet and shambled
away into the darkness, Janey stood alone as if in a trance in
the centre of the ring, her hands folded in prayer, the knotted
sheet of her dress coming undone, revealing her bare breast.
Rain left the stones and climbed to the beacon. Belle stopped
to watch and saw her throw a handful of something into
the flames, making the fire spark with a dozen colours and
crackle. Soon a strange heavy smoke drifted down to them
enveloping them all in a lurid green light. The smoke smelled
pungent, mysterious, a bit like the incense Rain burned in her
hut, but it stung Belle's eyes and when she breathed it in, she
began to cough.

'Gray.' Her voice was hoarse. 'Gray.' But he mustn't have

heard her for the drumbeat continued, erratically now. Belle edged blindly to the table in search of a drink, and as she fumbled the bottles, her foot touched something warm and soft and she withdrew it with a little squeal of surprise. It was Figgy, curled up in a ball, asleep. Where was Angel, Belle wondered. She put down the bottle she was holding and gazed around. There was no sign of him. *Actually, he ought to be snug in bed*, she thought, *not out on a chilly hillside late at night with a lot of ridiculous, feckless adults*. Was that where he'd gone?

Rain was absorbed in tending the fire so Belle set off down the hillock on her own, her eyes raking the gloom for the figure of the small boy, her eyes gradually getting used to the darkness. There was still no sign. She widened the circle of her search, wondering again if he'd gone back to the house. Eventually, she heard a splash, then sobbing and followed the sounds towards a dark mass of trees in the corner of the field. Suddenly she saw movement. A great muddy puddle stretched away glistening at her feet and from it the child emerged, staggering towards her. 'You poor old thing,' she said as she gripped his hand and led him back shivering towards the light of the bonfire and the dancing figures. Halfway up the slope she found the blanket that Chouli had dropped and wrapping him in it, persuaded him to join Figgy under the table.

The smoke was overwhelming and her mouth felt dry and tasted acrid. She sank down beside the shuddering child and waited for the faintness to pass, counting the dancers and wondering where Sirius had gone. Hopefully back to the house to see how Chouli was. She badly wanted to go too, to crawl into her bed and sleep, but it wasn't right to leave Angel. Certainly not without alerting Rain.

The weird smoke from the fire was clearing and the music faltering when a few minutes later Belle felt recovered enough to climb to her feet. The women had given up dancing, she saw, by the light of the dying flames. Janey lay on her back with her eyes closed, making moaning noises. Rain leaned against one of the stones, holding her side as though she had a stitch. Gray had vanished, Belle thought with surprise, but then she realized that he was sitting with his back against one of the stones, the drum on his lap, and holding a bottle. He looked completely worn out and his eyes wouldn't focus.

'Gray,' she said, touching his shoulder, and he glanced up, his eyes bleary and sad. 'Can we go back now? Poor Angel's had enough and so have I.'

He nodded and heaved himself to his feet, staggered and would have fallen had Belle not shot out her hand. 'We've got to take Angel,' she murmured and he stared at her, puzzled, then saw where she pointed, at the pathetic bundle under the table.

'Let's tell Rain.'

'We haven't performed the ceremony,' Rain was saying to Arlo, hands on elegant hips. 'You can do what you like, but I'm staying.'

'So am I,' Janey said woozily.

'Arlo?'

'I suppose.'

Rain glanced up at Belle and Gray. 'What about you two?'

'No, we're going in,' Gray said, shuffling his feet. 'Belle's not very feeling very bright.'

'We're taking Angel,' Belle announced.

'Angel. Where is he?' She peered into the gloom, following Belle's pointing finger. 'Poor mite. Yes, please.'

'I'll carry him,' Gray offered. He knelt and gathered up the sleeping child. 'Goodnight, folks,' he said. 'Sorry to miss the rest. See you tomorrow.'

'It's already tomorrow,' Arlo replied with a snigger.

'And soon we will perform the sacrifice to the goddess of the dawn,' Rain cried in theatrical tones, her arms spread wide. Something glinted in the darkness in her hand – a knife. Angel's knife.

Belle edged away nervously. 'C'mon, Gray, let's go.'

They felt their way carefully down the slope, Figgy loping ahead. Away from the firelight they grew used to the grades of darkness, the black shadows of rabbit holes, the whispering shapes of trees, the sighing wings of a night bird crossing their path. Overhead, gathering clouds were muffling the stars. 'It's going to rain,' Gray said. As they rounded the ruins, the vast presence of the house filled Belle's vision. No light was on, but reflected light glinted on glass. Belle turned to look, expecting a moon or the light of the fire, but, no, Mrs Kitto must have left the landing light on when she'd gone to stay with her friend.

Just then they heard a loud scream from behind in the distance, a terrible sound that went on and on. They glanced at one another, eyes wide.

'What was that?' Belle whispered.

'It'll just be the ceremony. Let's go inside.' It was starting to rain.

She pressed on, heading for the passage under the surviving wing. The rain was becoming a heavy, relentless downpour. The short dash round the side of the house to the kitchen door was enough to leave them soaked.

Angel stirred, shuddering in Gray's arms. Under the kitchen light he struggled to full wakefulness and cried out in surprise. While Gray reassured him, Belle ran upstairs, seized a flannel and a towel from a bathroom and fresh nightclothes from the boy's room. Once Angel was clean and dry, he sat by the range wrapped in the blanket with a cup of warm milk. Figgy, nearby, watched with anxious eyes. Gray sent Belle off to change her own damp clothes and to bring some dry ones for himself.

Halfway down the stairs again, she remembered Chouli and Sirius and prowled along the shadowy corridor to check that they were safe. Their door was closed, but not quite, she discovered when she knocked gently. There was no reply, so she poked her head round, peering into the darkness. The room smelled pungently of alcohol and she heard soft snoring.

'Who's that?' A whisper and a restless movement. Chouli. The snoring continued uninterrupted.

'Me, Belle. Are you all right?'

A silence, then a sob. 'No. Yes.'

'Is there anything I can do?'

'No.'

'Goodnight then.'

"Night.'

Belle retreated, drawing the door to, then paused, wondering if there was anything she should be doing to help Chouli. Probably not, she decided. Sirius had clearly returned and passed out in a drunken state, but presumably Chouli could rouse him if necessary. She continued on her way.

It wasn't long before she and Gray got Angel safely into bed and sweetly sleeping. Too anxious to go to bed themselves, they sat together in the kitchen for half an hour, drinking coffee and waiting for the others to appear, but there was no sign of them. Outside, the rain had stopped, so perhaps they'd carried on with whatever they were doing.

'What is this ceremony?' Belle wanted to know.

Gray swallowed the dregs of his tea and shrugged. 'As I said, I wasn't there for last year's.'

'But aren't you curious? I didn't like the look of that knife,' Belle snapped. 'And the scream ...' She yawned suddenly. 'I don't know. Let's go to bed.'

When Gray turned off the kitchen light, they realized the sky was getting lighter. They looked at each other. 'It's dawn,' he said. 'Whatever was to happen will have happened.'

~

Belle blinked against dazzling daylight to realize they'd been too tired to draw the bedroom curtains. A bird was scrabbling somewhere and the room was already warming up. Gray slept on, snoring lightly, so she tiptoed out of the room and downstairs, checking on Angel on the way. He was cuddling his ragdoll and deeply asleep.

In the kitchen she found Figgy leaping about, desperate to go outside. She opened the back door, which had been left unlocked, and he shot out, and a moment later ambled back in again.

She heard a sound from the hall and glanced up to see Chouli sidle in wearing a dressing gown. Her arms were folded tightly across her chest and she looked ghastly, with trails of dried tears on her cheeks.

'You look as if you need some tea.'

Chouli made a face. 'Hot water. Tea smells like fish.' She plonked herself down at the table and bowed her head.

Belle placed a steaming mug before her and sat down with hers. 'I'd ask if you were all right, but that's a stupid question. Can I get you anything to eat? Toast, perhaps. Or will that smell of fish, too?'

'Toast should be all right.' She managed a smile.

Belle got up again, cut the remnants of last night's bread, grilled it on a fork over a hotplate, checking with Chouli before slathering it with margarine and strawberry jam.

'What happened last night, Chouli? You seemed awful. Are you feeling any better?'

Chouli bit into a crust and chewed thoughtfully, staring at nothing though her colour, Belle noticed, was beginning to return. Then she began to speak.

'Janey and Rain gave me something to drink before supper. Boiled herbs of some kind.'

Belle remembered Rain passing through the kitchen earlier in the afternoon, carrying a bunch of leaves. What were they, she wondered, not having thought anything of it at the time.

'I drank a few mouthfuls,' Chouli continued, 'but it tasted disgusting so while they weren't looking I poured the rest down the basin.'

'Were they to—'

'Get rid of the baby, yes. It's my fault, I kept telling Rain I didn't want it so she did something about it. She said it would take a while to work, but she didn't tell me how ill I'd feel.'

Belle stared at her in horror. 'So . . .' she prompted.

'So nothing's happened. I threw up, didn't I, so got anything I did drink out of my system.'

'It hasn't worked?' Belle said, relieved. The whole thing sounded wretched.

Chouli shook her head. Then she said forcefully, 'I'm glad. I don't want this baby, but I don't want to lose it like that either. Does that sound stupid?'

'I don't know.' Belle felt helpless.

'I'm fed up with doing things because other people tell me to.'

'By other people you mean . . . Sirius?'

'Sirius, Rain, my parents. I thought it would be different coming here, that I could be myself. I'd flunked everything at school, hated going home to stupid tennis parties and dances. And the boys, God, the boys, braying nobs, all of them. I went to stay with a schoolfriend in London and she took me to an opening at an art gallery in Soho and that's where I met Sirius. A proper grown-up man. I was besotted.'

'Is Sirius really his name?' Belle wondered.

'Yes, it is. Chouli isn't mine, though. I'm Julia really. It was Sirius who started calling me Patchouli to tease me and

I thought it was funny at first, but now I hate it.' Her voice was stronger now, and she sat up, squaring her shoulders as though she was coming back to life. She swallowed an extra big mouthful of toast. 'Gosh, I'm hungry, Belle. I couldn't eat anything last night, I was feeling so ill. I don't know if it was the baby or the herbs. I hadn't felt sick in the mornings, only later in the day, but I'd never actually thrown up before so it was probably the herbs.'

Belle didn't know what to say. Chouli or Julia must only be a year or two older than herself, yet all this was beyond her experience. Gray was right, she realized: she was very innocent. *What had happened to Chouli could happen to her!* That would be disastrous.

'I'll make more toast,' she mumbled and set about doing so and soon they were sitting together more cheerfully, chatting about whether Rain would be up to meditation this morning. They were laughing at Figgy, who was snapping at a bluebottle when Arlo came in. He must have dragged on the nearest clothes he could find, his hair was ruffled and his face puffy.

'You look like death,' Chouli remarked.

'Hello to you, too. Has the kettle just boiled?' He picked it up, found it empty and groaned.

'I'll do it,' Belle said, taking it from him.

'Oh, okay. I'll be outside.'

She found him sitting at the courtyard table in the sun, smoking a cigarette and he muttered his thanks when she placed the tea in front of him. She stood with arms folded, trying to look stern, determined to say what was on her mind. 'That was awful last night. So many bad things happened.'

'Angel, yeah?' he mumbled.

'That was the worst. How could Rain do that? Forget about her son. Leave Gray and me to put him to bed.'

'It was bad, but he's all right, isn't he?'

'I checked just now. He's still asleep. What happened after we went?'

'Ah, I don't remember very clearly.'

'The ceremony, Arlo. What was it? Why did Rain have Angel's knife?

'Oh that. Nothing dramatic. She just waved it around a bit, cut herself and shouted.'

'Cut herself?' Belle was shocked. 'Accidentally?'

Arlo shrugged and drew on his cigarette. Belle slumped down on a chair opposite, suddenly very weary. Arlo watched her warily. 'Everything's fine,' he ventured. 'You should relax a bit more.'

She stared at him then looked away, disgusted.

'You're annoyed with me, aren't you,' Arlo said with an unpleasant sneer. 'Not just about last night. Before then. What?'

Belle looked at him, biting her lip, wondering how much to say about Imogen's box and the secret room, and what he thought she knew about her, Belle, but he volunteered nothing.

'I don't understand how things work here,' she ended up saying. 'When Gray brought me here, he said what good people you all are, how you're working together to make life better. At first I thought that must be true, but now I'm wondering . . .' She stopped.

'What do you wonder, Belle?' Arlo's voice was even, dangerous.

'Well, you don't always get on, all of you, and . . .' She flailed for the right words. Did he know about Chouli's pregnancy and what Rain and Janey had done? 'There are bad things. The ceremony, that sounds weird. And secrets. And odd things, horrible things, like Rain scraping someone's car with her pendant and people snooping.'

There was a sound from above, a window opening. They both glanced up. It was her and Gray's room. Gray looked out and waved, then withdrew. Soon after, the music of his guitar began, distant, ethereal. Arlo grinned. 'He's good, isn't he?'

'I think so.' She was astonished at his sudden change of mood.

'You are, too. You sing beautifully. When are you performing at The Ship again? Gray told me, but I've forgotten.'

'Next Friday.'

'I'll definitely come. And I'll tell Uncle Francis, too.'

Thinking of Francis brought her back to the subject of the box. She might as well have it out with Arlo.

She drew a deep breath. 'You must have guessed by now that we – Angel and I – have discovered your secret room.'

'My secret room,' he repeated. 'That does sound spooky. But yes, I had guessed, as you put it.' He drained his cup. 'Francis first showed it to me when I was Angel's age. He'd been shown it by his father. I knew Angel had found it. He left a book behind and a plate of breadcrumbs once. I took him aside as soon as I could. No point me forbidding him to go there – he does what he chooses. I made sure he knew how to get out.'

'He told me that you didn't know he'd been in there,' she said with surprise. 'The little monkey.'

'I expect it suited him to believe that. He makes things up. It's not lying exactly, but he lives in a storybook world.'

'Do you sleep there? The mattress ...'

'I used to – when I was younger. I still like to go to lie and think. No one knows you're there. Except now Angel and you do. And you messed with my things. That wasn't nice.'

'I'm sorry, I shouldn't have. But the box with old books in it,' Belle plunged on. 'Why ...?'

'Yes. It's been there for years. But it interested you, didn't it? You took something from it.'

'Borrowed.' She felt herself blush. 'Some old engagement diaries. I was going to put them back. I didn't look at the rest of the contents properly, just some of the books.'

'You didn't see the photographs then?' He gave a taunting smile.

'No. What were they of?'

'Oh, this and that. I've given them to Francis. He was delighted. Says he remembers the woman whose box it was.'

'Imogen? I suppose he would have known her,' Belle said glumly.

'So you know about her?' Arlo said with interest. 'I hadn't heard of her before.'

Belle sighed. 'She was under-matron here at the beginning of the war. Then she went off to be a nurse. Mrs Kitto's been telling me about her.'

'Mrs Kitto,' Arlo said in a tone of disdain.

'Don't be like that.'

Arlo raised his eyebrows. 'The two of you are pally, aren't you?'

'I like her.' A heartbeat, then Belle plucked up courage. 'Why do you follow me sometimes, Arlo?'

An embarrassed laugh.

'You do. Down by the beach. I saw you. And there have been other times.'

'You're imagining things,' he sneered. 'If anyone's snooping, it's you. If you disapprove of us so much, why d'you stay?'

'That's not fair,' she snapped and stalked off, furious, to the kitchen.

Sometimes it seemed that, apart from Gray, Mrs Kitto was her only real friend at Silverwood.

Twenty-Three

Gray was playing his guitar again. Desperate to get away, Belle walked Figgy down to the beach. When she passed the cottage it still looked shut up, though the cat was lying on the doorstep and eyed Figgy with alarm when he poked his nose between the palings of the gate. Belle called the dog away, disappointed because she'd half hoped to see Mrs Kitto. But a walk was what she needed most and she cheered up as she followed Figgy down the hill, past the copse and between sun-bathed pastures towards the shore.

It had been a difficult day so far. First her conversation with Arlo, then Janey had come downstairs looking much the worse for wear and in a terrible temper. She'd snarled at Belle and Arlo to help her clear up the kitchen and they did so in awkward silence. Chouli had vanished, but it wasn't long before Rain and Angel appeared. Rain had bandaged her forearm but was looking brighter than she had a right to. She had a forlorn and tearful Angel in tow, who wanted breakfast. Sirius trudged in, stooped and cross, made himself black coffee and departed to his studio, all without a word. 'Good riddance,' Rain murmured under her breath; then, 'Come on, let's get out of everyone's way,' and ushered Angel outside. 'No meditation this morning,' she called over her shoulder. Belle was relieved. She was sure she would have fallen asleep in that warm hut.

'She could come and help,' Arlo muttered, flicking a tea towel at a fly.

'I'm sure she will shortly,' Janey snapped, loyal as ever.

'I bet she doesn't.'

'She has Angel to look after.'

'She didn't last night,' Arlo observed. 'Why d'you defend her, Janey?'

Janey turned from the sink where she was doing the washing-up. 'I don't.'

'You do. There's always an excuse.'

Janey was silent for a moment. 'You wouldn't understand,' she muttered.

'Try me.'

She turned to face Arlo and wiped her hands on her apron. 'All right. I wouldn't be alive today if Rain hadn't helped me.'

Arlo stared at her, open-mouthed, as she continued.

'My husband would have beaten me to death if I'd stayed with him, but she helped me escape and took me in and when he turned up drunk to find me, she was magnificent: she terrified him, sent him packing. Then she said I could stay with her. I couldn't work, I was too traumatized, but she looked after me. Later she paid the legal fees for my divorce.'

Another silence in the kitchen. Janey turned back to the sink and continued with her task.

The atmosphere in the house remained tense. Chouli stayed in her room most of the day. Rain asked after her and Belle explained that she was tired. No further mention was made of the baby. Rain suggested a meditation session in the afternoon, but Belle couldn't stand the idea of being alone with her today and when Gray and Sirius went off together said she'd prefer to go on a walk by herself.

On the beach, the tide was in but starting to turn. Belle walked along the narrow strip of shore, throwing sticks into the water for Figgy and laughing, despite herself, as he leaped over the little waves to fetch them. She didn't swim, remembering how Arlo had watched her last time, even though she'd probably frightened him off now.

It was good to be here alone, away from the tension in the house. After a while she climbed up a rabbit path between trees to the prow of the low headland to examine the pill-box, ducking in through the doorway. The muddy floor and moss-covered walls smelled stagnant and Figgy refused to follow her inside, but it was intriguing to imagine being on sentry duty here. She crouched to stare through the apertures out across the water as the sentries might have, searching for signs of enemy activity. She felt as cramped and uncomfortable as they probably had, and she was glad to emerge into the fresh air. As she and Figgy scrambled back down to the beach the lonely cries of gulls were the only signs of life.

*

When they passed the cottage on the way back to Silverwood, Belle saw that Mrs Kitto had returned, for the door was ajar. She let herself into the garden, leaving Figgy to wait on the path outside, and knocked.

'The cat's safely upstairs on my bed,' Mrs Kitto said when she appeared, seeing Figgy's pleading eyes beyond the gate. 'So go on, let him in.'

'If you're sure.' Figgy settled the question by leaping over a low bit of fence. Once inside he sniffed his way round every downstairs room before licking the last scraps from the cat's dish in the kitchen and settling at Belle's feet.

While Mrs Kitto made tea, Belle poured out the story of last night's activities, becoming quite tearful as she described what had happened to Chouli. 'I shouldn't be telling you about it. Poor Chouli. But there's no one else who understands. I'm sorry, you're probably really shocked.'

'Not much shocks me now, Belle.' Mrs Kitto smiled sadly and poured the tea. 'How far along is she?'

'Oh, very early. Nothing's showing and she's only recently been feeling sick. When does that start, do you know?'

'At about six weeks. If she visited a doctor he'd be able to pinpoint it. She should go.'

'I . . . think she's hoping the problem will go away by itself.'

'Sometimes that does happen,' Mrs Kitto said gravely. 'It's dreadfully sad, but it's nature's way when a pregnancy is not going well.'

'Have you had children?' Belle asked, as Mrs Kitto appeared to know all about it.

'I married too late for that, but I was a nurse early in

my career and I attended a good few deliveries.' Her eyes twinkled.

'Were you at the same hospital as Imogen?'

Mrs Kitto shook her head. 'Shall I tell you more of the story?' she said.

Belle took another biscuit and nodded.

'At the beginning of 1944,' Mrs Kitto said, 'once again, Imogen's life changed.'

Twenty-Four

January 1944

Imogen emerged from the private hospital room carrying a bedpan, shut the door behind her and leaned against it, briefly closing her eyes. Though back on day shift she felt completely exhausted this morning.

'How's him in there doing today, Nurse?' an old man called out in a reedy voice as she set off down the ward. 'You're a bloody marvel, you are, looking after the likes of him given what he's done.'

'Nothing marvellous about it, Mr Bruce,' she shot back, aware that other patients were listening avidly. 'It's our duty. Anyway, he can't help what's going on any more than our boys can. He's got a wife and two little daughters back home in Hamburg, if you want to know, and he's worried sick about them.'

'We've made a mess of Hamburg all right,' the officer

in the next bed muttered. 'Poor blighter, he's right to be worried.'

'I still say they shouldn't bring 'em in here.' Old Mr Bruce was not to be put off. 'They're the enemy. Deal with 'em at the camps if they have to.'

'You wouldn't say that if this was Germany, Bruce, and he was your lad,' the officer rasped.

Imogen, who had no time to stay and argue, hurried away, eager to dispose of her burden. There were beds to change and much else to get done. She felt sorry for the German prisoner-of-war who'd been admitted with lockjaw, to the chagrin of some of the patients and staff. Now that his symptoms had abated she'd chatted with him as she helped him wash. His English was basic, but she could tell he was a decent sort and grateful for all that was being done. Still, it was sensible of the powers-that-be not to have put him on the open ward. Men like Bruce would have made their displeasure felt in no uncertain terms, but then Bruce probably had his own reasons. War was, as Bruce himself liked to say, 'a bugger's muddle'.

She finished washing up and stretched her aching back. She'd been fighting a sore throat for days. She'd beg Summers for a spoonful of her mother's iron tonic later. She did feel run down, she thought, blinking – her eyes felt dry. The weather was miserable without being properly cold and she'd got soaked the other night when she'd been caught out in the rain without her coat. Such a nuisance if she'd caught a cold. She fumbled the buttons on her cuffs and swallowed. Her throat was definitely worse. Blow. Now she'd give it to the whole ward. Perhaps if she told Sister she'd be sent home to bed with a hot water bottle. Or perhaps she'd merely scold her for shirking. You could never tell what was right. Imogen shivered. The sluice room was even colder than usual.

In the end the decision was made for her. At lunchtime she was spooning custard and crumble into dishes with shaking hands when she fainted, dropping the custard ladle as she fell. Summers told her later with a giggle how the glutinous yellow sauce had splashed over Sister's sensible shoes.

It was a very bad case of flu. Summers caught it soon after, though more lightly. Someone thought it amusing to leave a sign saying 'Plague' with the mark of a cross on their bedroom door. This didn't stop the house sister from seeing to their needs, but the point was well made. It would be disastrous for the virus to spread amongst the nurses.

Imogen was hardly aware of any of this. For days she lay delirious, unable to eat or drink much, her body alternately shivering with cold or sweating with fever. At times she was dimly conscious of a soft voice soothing her, a strong arm lifting her to sip water through parched lips, a cool flannel wiping her aching temples. As the illness progressed, coughs racked her aching body and her mind wandered off into dark places.

From far away she heard a man's voice. She sensed the cold metal bell of a stethoscope pressed against her chest, the word 'pneumonia' whispered, then, 'We have to move you, Nurse Lockhart. Nurse? Can you hear me?' She groaned. They wrapped her in blankets and transferred her to a trolley.

As she was bumped along the short distance to the hospital, she felt the cold on her face, opened her eyes and was puzzled to see the white pinpricks of stars above in the night sky.

In the hospital she lay for days, propped high on the pillows in a small hot room where the radiator drove her mad with its clanks and burbles and despite the machines and the oxygen, she struggled to breathe. One afternoon she awoke to the familiar scent of eau-de-Cologne and saw an elegant figure in a fur stole sitting by the bed, scribbling in a notebook.

'Mother ...'

'Just passing the time,' Mrs Lockhart mumbled, putting her writing aside to look at her. 'How are you, darling? Aunt Verity sends her love. Everybody does.' She brought a box of chocolates from her bag and set them carefully on the bed-side cabinet. Imogen smiled weakly. She felt better seeing her mother and was touched that she'd come all the way from Hertfordshire. Mrs Lockhart was staying in a hotel and came in every afternoon, Sister turning a blind eye to her disregard for visiting hours. She was happy to sit out of the way writing if her daughter was asleep or undergoing treatment.

After ten days Imogen was over the worst and able to engage in limited conversation. Mrs Lockhart did most of the talking. Her life was centred on her work and she chatted about gushing fan letters and arguments over book jackets with her publisher. More interesting to Imogen, she had news of family. Aunt Verity was well, but worried about her eldest, who was somewhere at sea. The middle brother was safely in a desk job at the Portsmouth Naval Base and hopefully the war would be over before the youngest was sent anywhere after his military training. Remembering the rough and tumble with the lively boys she had grown up with filled Imogen with tenderness. Tears came easily at present, but her sniffling made her mother fluttery and anxious. Imogen had never seen her mother cry, not even when her husband died. She'd simply looked pale and pained and retreated into her writing. Imogen, who'd been wild with grief, couldn't understand it.

By the time ten days became a fortnight, they'd had enough of each other. Imogen was clearly on the road to recovery and Mrs Lockhart was fed up with the lumpy hotel bed and ill-cooked food and longed for the peace of her study. 'If you need to come home for a while, you must, dear,' she said, patting her daughter's hand with her gloved one. Then her face brightened. 'Or stay with Verity. I'm sure she'd have you. She doesn't have enough to do with the boys away.'

'Don't go,' Imogen begged, seizing the hand, suddenly overwhelmed, but seeing the sudden panic in her mother's eyes, let her go. She knew her mother loved her in her funny way, and she was immensely grateful that she'd come, but it would be no good for either of them for her to stay longer. She felt guilty because she didn't miss her for long. In fact it was rather a relief.

Halfway through the third week, the infection gone, Imogen was lying back on the pillows with her eyes closed, wishing that her energy would return, when a small delegation headed by Matron came to see her. She tried to sit up, but Matron motioned for her to lie back, then lowered herself into the chair at her bedside and watched as a nurse took her temperature.

'It's normal,' the nurse pronounced with satisfaction. Matron nodded and a young doctor marked the chart that hung at the end of the bed.

'You must stay in bed for a few days more,' he pronounced, 'and there's no thinking you'll come straight back to work.'

'I don't think I could,' Imogen said, her voice still hoarse. 'I feel so weak.'

'I'm not surprised. You've been dangerously ill. Now, you need to convalesce. Where can you go?'

'I'd like to send you home to your mother,' Matron said, 'but I gather she lives some way away.'

'Hertfordshire. I'm not sure I could manage the journey.' That also ruled out Aunt Verity. She squeezed her eyes tight shut and thought.

'Some sea air perhaps?' Matron pondered.

A picture of Ned came into Imogen's mind and she remembered his words the last time they'd met. *I'd like you to promise that you'll call on me if you ever need help of any kind.*

She opened her eyes and smiled at Matron. 'I think I know where,' she said. 'If they'll have me.'

Letters were exchanged and arrangements made. By a happy coincidence, Matron's engineer cousin, a Mr Percy Bland, was to drive from Truro to Falmouth on business. Matron asked him to convey Imogen the few extra miles to Silverwood. 'You must take all your things, Nurse Lockwood,' said the sister in charge at the nurses' hostel, 'as we may need the bed in your absence.' It was almost as though they assumed she wasn't coming back.

Sarah Summers packed her cases for her and found an old cardboard box that had once held bandages for Imogen's small collection of books, grumbling cheerfully at what she called her roommate's 'desertion', while Imogen sat on the bed, too weak to do more than watch. At the last, Summers fastened Imogen's coat around her thin shoulders, helped her into the passenger seat of Mr Bland's car and hugged her goodbye before hurrying off to her morning shift.

Everybody had been exceptionally kind, Imogen thought, her eyes filling with tears, as she waited for the lugubrious Mr Bland to stow her luggage in the boot. Despite the coat, she shivered in the cold February weather and was glad of the travel blanket he passed her.

Silverwood! How she'd missed it, she sighed as they pulled into the drive an hour later. The house was as she remembered it, a gracious silver-grey lady, today wreathed in mist, the passing clouds reflected in its windows, serene amidst the ugly tumble of prefab classrooms. When she stepped out of the car she smiled to hear the hum of human activity that filled the air.

She thanked Mr Bland, who set her luggage down, wished her well and drove away in a hurry for his appointment.

She waited alone for a moment, getting her bearings. From somewhere in the house a handbell rang, and after a moment the double doors swung inwards and a score of older boys in games kit and waving hockey sticks swarmed out in their socks and set about shuffling their muddy boots on. Behind them came a teacher whom Imogen remembered, Saul Hogarth, a brawny, square-chinned chap with a stiff left leg, carrying a basket of wooden balls. He limped over to greet her.

'Miss Lockhart, it's a pleasure to see you again. Fanshawe-Hicks . . .' He addressed the sturdy, ruddy-faced lad who was hovering nearby, and Imogen realized with a jolt that the boy wasn't Nicholas, but the younger of the two brothers whom she'd brought down to Cornwall more than four years before. How confident he looked. What was his name?

It came to her. 'Michael. Goodness, you've grown. I thought you were Nicholas for a moment. How are you?'

The lad beamed at her. 'Very well, thank you, Miss Lockhart. I'm not Fanshawe-Hicks *Minor* any more. Nicholas is at Wellington now. Our father's school. That's where I'll go, too, next year.' He straightened with pride.

'If you work hard, boy,' Mr Hogarth said tetchily. 'Now, nip off and find Mr Thorpe, will you? Inform him that our guest has arrived.' And as Michael hurried away he shouted after him, 'Remove your dirty boots first!'

Hogarth dispatched the rest of the boys in the direction of a field where the white frame of a hockey goal was just visible through a gap in the hedge.

Imogen said, 'Don't let me hold you up. I'm expect Ned will be along shortly.'

'If you're sure. I'd better go and supervise the brutes. You never know what they'll do with those sticks! Good to have you back, Miss Lockhart.' Imogen watching him stump off, feeling a twinge of pity for her expert eye saw that he was in pain. Too young to have fought in the last war, it had been something more mundane that had ruined a promising military career in his late twenties – a severe knee injury sustained in a fall from a horse.

A sharp gust of wind blew and she pulled her coat more tightly around her, feeling suddenly weak. The journey had exhausted her and she hadn't the strength to move her luggage. Michael ran back past her, waving, to join the others, the laces of his boots flying.

'Imogen!'

A dear familiar figure in brown tweeds was hurrying towards her across the gravel,. 'Oh, Ned,' she breathed. Weary, she trembled and almost fell into his arms.

~

Early March, still chilly, but the sun rose higher in the sky each day and in the shelter of the trees, delicate snowdrops and aconites had given way to lusty nodding daffodils. Each day, in her old bedroom at the back next to Miss Edgecumbe's, Imogen woke to cheerful birdsong and each day fingers of daylight played over her bed through a gap in the blackout curtains.

After two weeks she was beginning to feel stronger. Mr Forbes, the headmaster, had been kindly, welcoming, but it quickly became apparent that once she felt better he expected her to work for her keep. She didn't mind the prospect, but was a little annoyed that Ned had allowed him to think that way when persuading him to let her visit. Fortunately Miss Edgecumbe was her guardian, standing firm against all comers.

'Miss Lockhart must rest,' she told the head, her eyes glittering, and all she would let Imogen do was read to the little patients and play board games with them.

She often found herself in the library next to Mr Forbes's study listening to the low burr of his voice through the interconnecting door as she chose suitable books to read to her charges. Even this tired her, and she often crept off for an hour to sleep or simply to sit in the comfy chair by her window and daydream. She missed her work at the hospital, but knew she wouldn't have been able to cope if she'd stayed. She'd recently written to Summers, but hadn't heard back. Probably too busy to write. Someone, the sister at the hostel most likely, was forwarding her post to Silverwood so there was no relief from the constant, dragging hope that a letter would arrive from Oliver. Imogen missed his presence at the school too. The current deputy head was a mild-mannered grey-haired man who lacked the authority that Oliver had brought to the role.

Regular hours, stodgy but filling school food, and large spoonfuls of a special tonic from a large brown bottle that Miss Edgecumbe kept in the medicine cabinet combined to restore Imogen to health. Ned helped, of course. Every now and then his good-natured face would appear at the door of the sickbay. He'd ask her how she was and exchange banter with the patients and now that she was a little stronger, walked with her in the grounds during a spare half-hour if the weather was fine. Ned no longer seemed to care whether the boys would tease him about their friendship and if they did, it wasn't to his face. He no longer hankered after active wartime service either, but seemed more at peace with himself. A new hobby helped. He'd acquired an old Box Brownie camera from a departing colleague, and had started taking pictures as a record of the school's time at Silverwood.

Imogen had other pals among the staff; Saul Hogarth, for instance, and his sweet wife Laura and their baby girl. And of course there was Kezia. Kezia was as kind a friend as ever, but she had a deep sadness. Her young husband had been killed when the ship he'd been on had been torpedoed in the Bay of Biscay on its way to North Africa. 'Never had a chance to be a married couple, did we?' So here she was, a widow at twenty, carrying on with her job. 'What else is there?'

Kezia was still jocular with the 'pesky boys', as she fondly called them, but Imogen caught evidence of a more sober side. The girl rarely mentioned her troubles but sometimes, as she dusted or changed the bed sheets, she sighed and an expression of weariness crossed her face, and Imogen sensed that her thoughts were miles away, brooding over the dark depths of the ocean where Will's body lay.

This particular Saturday morning, Imogen suggested to Ned that they walk further afield. It was his day off and Kezia packed some sandwiches for them and a vacuum flask of tea. 'I can't manage a long walk,' Imogen said anxiously, 'but it's such a beautiful day and I'd love to go down to the estuary.'

'You'll find it changed,' Ned said sadly. 'They've cut a road across the fields near Trebah to the beach. We may be turned back. We'll have to see.'

This warning could not prevent Imogen's feelings of dismay when they reached the cottage and saw below a scar like a long white ribbon carved into the green countryside she loved. 'This war,' she whispered, stopping to take it in. 'It ruins everything.'

'I know,' Ned murmured in return, 'but we mustn't be sentimental. The Allies are on the front foot now, that's what the rumours say. Whatever the Americans are up to here, it'll bring the end of the war nearer, I'm sure.'

There were a few American servicemen working there, loading crates onto a truck, and a steamroller was driving up and down the road to flatten the surface. Ned and Imogen made their way down the hill, taking care to follow a little-used track well out of the way of the soldiers. It took them away from the beach and along paths where tangled trees hiding views of the river gave way briefly to fishing hamlets until they came to a larger village with a pub and a post office. Here the river was busy with sailing boats and a patient ferry carried passengers back and forth to the other side. Pretty, white-painted houses could be glimpsed on far tree-lined banks. 'It's so picturesque,' Imogen sighed. 'It's a pity you're not allowed to take photographs of the boats.'

'I'd probably get arrested as a spy!' Ned said wanly.

The fresh breeze and the light sparkling on the water raised Imogen's spirits. Inside the pub Ned brought glasses of amber cider to a table by the window and said that the landlord didn't mind if they ate their sandwiches inside.

'I feel happier than I've any right to.' She smiled at Ned, unpacking the sandwiches. 'D'you mind if I have the corned beef? I think you asked for cheese.'

'You've every right to be happy.' He sounded wistful

and Imogen suddenly felt the ghost of Oliver standing between them.

'Do I? Really, I feel guilty. So many people have suffered terribly.'

'We'll need happy people. To remind the rest of us of how life should be. To inspire us.'

'That sounds as though you're not happy, Ned.'

'Oh, I didn't mean myself specifically. I've nothing to complain about. I wonder where poor old Oliver is. There's a man who was only going to be happy if he put himself into danger.'

'That's true,' Imogen said with a sigh. If Ned hoped she'd reveal the true nature of her feelings about Oliver, he'd be disappointed. She kept those to herself. 'I wonder where he is now?' was all she said and gave Ned her warmest smile.

They sat together in silence for a while. Through the window they could see the tiny ferryboat come in. Two youngish dark-haired men in fisherman's jerseys stepped out onto the jetty; locals, Imogen thought vaguely, and after a moment the door of the pub opened with a draught of fresh air and they came in. The taller one ordered beer in a voice that carried and Imogen's attention was caught by his clipped accent. Not English at all, and certainly not the Cornish burr she was used to and loved. A bit like German but not really. She watched them covertly as they carried their brimming glasses over to a table by the fire. There was something about the lightness of their gait, the unusual way the shorter one held his cigarette when he lit it that marked them out as different. The publican clearly thought so too, for he kept glancing at them, though his expression was unreadable.

What were these strangers doing here, she wondered and, crucially, which side were they on? The men were still there, playing dominoes, when she and Ned got up to leave. Entirely innocent behaviour.

'Are we supposed to report them?' she asked Ned. 'Or simply forget about them?'

'I've no idea.' Ned's brow crinkled. After a moment he said, 'I'd leave it to the proprietor, you know. He sees all the comings and goings.'

'Everything's particularly strange at the moment,' she said, with a crack in her voice. 'There's a tension in the air. Can't you feel it?'

'The Americans moving in, d'you mean? There's certainly a lot more going on round here that we're supposed to ignore.' Ned looked so serious.

'We shouldn't even be talking about it really.' She giggled.

'We shouldn't.'

'Even the trees have ears!' Imogen snorted, stepping over the root of a large hollow oak. 'Maybe a German is hiding in this one.'

'Im, we shouldn't joke.'

'No, that's very naughty of me.' They walked on, but turning uphill, Imogen's feet began to drag and she found it laborious to breathe. Ned took her hand, waited for her to recover, then guided her slowly up the slope.

'I'm sorry,' she said with a sob when they reached the top and she sat on a boulder to rest. 'I was out of puff.'

'I'm not surprised. I shouldn't have taken you so far.'

'No, it's my fault. Oh, Ned, will I ever be my old self again?'

'Think of how weak you were when you arrived and what you can do now. You just have to give it time.'

'I suppose so. Thank you for putting up with me. I must be an awful bore.'

'You're never that.'

They took the last quarter-mile gently, Ned helping her over the stiles, and she was glad of his closeness and his warm strong hand to keep her from falling.

Imogen's health continued to improve and soon she was able to partake more fully in the life of the school, avoiding anything physically arduous for she feared the occasional attacks of breathlessness. Miss Edgecumbe was glad of her taking her turn in the sickbay, though the coughs and colds of the winter months were subsiding. Then a lad who returned from a weekend away with a face looking like a hamster's was diagnosed with mumps and quickly put to bed in isolation so that it did not spread. Imogen, who'd had the illness as a child and was therefore judged immune, volunteered to nurse him. This she did tenderly, though he was more upset at being separated from his pals than by the pain of his swollen glands. After a week it was impossible to keep him in bed and he was sent back to the classroom.

Miss Edgecumbe still kept a firm eye on her and sent her out to exercise every day. Wrapped up well against the wind, Imogen was glad to enjoy the sharp spring air, banks of pale yellow primroses, the scents of sap and the warming earth, but on the occasions that she ventured beyond the gates she almost wished she hadn't.

The road that passed Silverwood, usually quiet, had become busy with military vehicles bearing United States markings. They were jeeps and motorbikes mostly, small enough to negotiate the narrow winding lanes without getting stuck. She had to press herself against the hedges to avoid being run over. If she stepped into the woods away from the road, she heard strange rustlings and found herself looking over her shoulder. If she walked past the cottage at the back of the house, she'd see signs of activity down near the river, huge trucks travelling the new white road, loaded with who knew what.

One morning, in breaktime, she was out at the front of the house supervising a score of older boys, when they all turned to watch the progress of a jeep approaching up the drive. It came to a halt near Imogen and two American officers stepped out.

'Can I help you?' she asked the more senior of the pair.

'Good morning, ma'am,' he said, politely touching his cap. 'We'd like to meet with whoever's in charge here.'

'That's Mr Forbes, the headmaster. If you'll wait there, I'll fetch him for you.'

Mr Forbes came out at once and invited the visitors into his study. The boys all watched in amazement as they went in, then crowded round to inspect the jeep. One brave lad would have climbed in had not Imogen intervened. When the officers emerged a few minutes later, they handed round bars of American chocolate, smiled at Imogen, jumped into the jeep and drove off. The boys could speak of nothing else for the rest of the day.

Mr Forbes did not say what the men wanted, merely that they were collecting information. But his eyes shone with pride and an air of excitement filled the school at the changes that were happening all around them. Something was 'up' and they were in the middle of it!

At lunchtime the following Wednesday, Imogen entered the staff common room to look for Ned and saw that a group of the staff had gathered around him as he brandished a local newspaper. 'It says here, "Cornwall is to become a protected area for operational reasons."' In just over a week's time, on 1 April, Silverwood would be part of a Prohibited Zone. Little explanation was given.

'What do you think it means?' Imogen asked him later. The boys had gone to bed, and they were sitting by the fire in the almost deserted common room. Imogen was mending a pair of shorts that its owner had ripped while forcing his way through a prickly hedge, and Ned was marking exercise books, muttering to himself every now and then at a particularly inept offering.

'You mean why is it becoming a protected area?' Ned glanced at her over the spectacles he'd recently acquired for reading. 'Oh really, Blenkinsop,' he groaned, making a mark with his pen, 'you should be able to spell "ocean" by now.'

'Something important, that's what's happening.' Saul Hogarth was sitting at the big table in the window winding canvas tape round a cricket bat handle. 'They wouldn't do this for the purpose of exercises. No, this is the big push.'

The big push, Imogen mulled as she finished the shorts and moved on to darning socks, an endless task which she hated. She knew what Hogarth meant. It was what everyone was waiting for, what the Allies were working towards. To win the war, Hitler must be driven out of France. Had that moment finally arrived?

Slowly, slowly, the course of the war was turning. Germany had been defeated in Africa and was being forced out of Russia and Italy. Perhaps, the time had come. Imogen's heart leaped at the thought. But what would it take? What would the human cost be? She thought of the people she cared for and which of them might be involved and her heart sank again. Her cousins. Oliver. It had been such a long time since she'd heard from him, she was starting to give up hope. She tried to recall his face, the dark eyes, the crisp turn of his collar, his soft voice in her ear, but couldn't clearly. Where was he? Perhaps he'd been caught up in these latest preparations. If he went to France, even as an administrator, he'd finally be meeting the danger he craved.

She tried to put him from her mind. She hadn't heard from him for so long. Perhaps whatever feelings had flared up between them had been short-lived on his part, kindled and fed by the intensity of wartime. She'd seen these fleeting passions happen to others around her. Dancehall romances, the odd hasty marriage. She smiled sadly to herself as she balled a pair of mended socks. After her illness, anyway, it was more tranquil pastures that appealed. Which made her think fondly of Ned.

Twenty-Five

June 1966

Belle went upstairs when she returned from the cottage. She found Gray fixing a new string to his guitar in their bedroom and plumped down beside him on the unmade bed on the floor.

'Where've you been?' he asked and listened as she told him, tightening the string with deft fingers.

'What about you?'

He began to tune his instrument, an expression of concentration on his face. 'Here. Practising for next Friday.' The gig was a week away. 'Stu's coming, by the way. I rang him. He's going to hitch down. Don't worry, you're still needed.'

'What about his girlfriend Chrissie?'

'Ah, no.'

'Doesn't she sing or play?'

'No, she's got a proper job. Managing director's secretary. Pays their rent!'

'A good thing someone does,' Belle murmured and he grinned.

He strummed a couple of chords, then laid the instrument down, satisfied, before picking up the bits of broken string, coiling them round and slipping them inside a discarded envelope. He was tidier, more careful with his beloved guitar than with anything else, Belle had noticed.

'You've kept out of the way today,' she said grimly.

He gave a sheepish smile and she knew she was right.

'I don't blame you,' she said. 'No one's exactly cheerful.' She related her conversations with Chouli and Arlo, explained how she'd hardly seen Rain and Angel and that Janey had risen late and gone about her tasks with shadows under her eyes and scarcely a kind word. 'As for Sirius, he's shut himself away to paint as usual.'

'I saw him earlier. He looked bad, hardly spoke.' Gray pulled down his lower eyelids to mimic a hangover. 'A bear with a sore head.'

'I'm not surprised after what he put into himself last night.'

Gray looked at her and laughed. 'You do sound prim!' he said, eyes twinkling.

'I don't.'

'You do. Miss Prissy!'

There was a brief scuffle ending with him pinning her to the mattress and kissing her. One thing led to another. When they lay sated and breathless in one another's arms, Belle thought once again, *He always manages to avoid difficult situations. Perhaps it's his way of dealing with the world after what's happened to him. It's different from me.* Then it struck her that this wasn't completely true. She'd never wanted to investigate her family's secrets.

'Tell you what,' Gray said, sitting up and stretching. 'We need to practise the songs we do together.' She watched as he quickly dressed then she knelt on the bed with the eiderdown wrapped round her shoulders and when he strummed a few chords, joined in with the song. They went through it several times until he was happy.

'Can I try something?' She reached for her guitar.

She tried a chord, stopped to tighten a peg, then began to play. It was a song she'd written, the one that drifted through her mind, over and over. The harmony wasn't quite right yet, but she wanted him to hear it. The eiderdown slipped from her shoulders, but she hardly noticed. When she'd finished, Gray was silent for a moment, then said quietly, 'That was beautiful.'

'What do you think of the bit I got wrong?'

'Try it again.'

She fumbled her way through the tricky chord change. 'Try this,' he suggested, picking up his own guitar. He repeated the sequence of chords she'd played twice, then again, slightly differently. She frowned, tried them herself, didn't like them, and suddenly it clicked. A certain shift. She played again with more confidence and knew she'd done it. By Gray's slow nod and the light in his eyes she saw he knew it too.

'Can I sing it on Friday?' she asked, feeling brave. 'Please?' and a shadow passed over his face. For a moment she held her breath and then he said levelly, 'I don't see why not.' Relief filled her. It was, after all, his show, and she hardly dared to believe that he'd say yes. But he had and she loved him for it.

Twenty-Six

The next few days passed without incident, everyone subdued. Early on Sunday evening, the scent of Indian spices wended up the stairs. Dinner was on. Belle had been sleeping but got up groggily. 'We ought to help, Gray,' and they went down to the kitchen to find Janey and Chouli making supper in silence. Janey was stirring a bubbling golden curry, Chouli weighing dried rice on an old-fashioned pair of scales.

'Shall we lay the table?' Belle asked tentatively.

'If you want,' Chouli said with a glance at Janey, who said nothing, so Belle started picking cutlery out of the drawer and instructed Gray to fetch plates and glasses.

'Where's everyone else?' she enquired, but Chouli shrugged. She looked less downright miserable this evening, more simply resigned.

'Angel's not well,' Chouli said after a moment. 'Rain's with him.'

'What kind of not well?'

'A temperature. He's been in bed all day. That's why Rain didn't call us for meditation.'

'I've been asleep so I didn't notice. Poor Angel.'

They were a quiet gathering that evening. Sirius slunk in and hardly exchanged a word with Chouli. Rain stole in late, filled a bowl with curry and ate it standing up, then disappeared upstairs again. Janey assumed the expression of a martyr, eyes turned heavenward, though Belle was puzzled as to who the look was meant for and why. Arlo tried being cheerful until the atmosphere doused it and he was sensitive enough to help with the washing-up. Janey suggested their usual circle time in a half-hearted way, but no one was interested. She wiped the stove and said, somewhat mournfully, that she was looking in on Angel and Rain then going off to bed. She was closely followed up the stairs by Chouli. Now the only ones left in the kitchen were Belle, Gray and Arlo.

Though Belle had avoided Arlo since their argument, he and Gray got on superficially these days and the two men sat at the table, smoking and talking quietly about music and motorbikes, but Belle felt restless and wandered outside to walk in the failing light. The atmosphere in the house was tense and she was concerned about Angel. The hens had been shut up for the night, but the goats came up to greet her in the gloaming when she approached their pen. She loved the way they nibbled at her fingers. A light snapped on in an upstairs window and she looked up. It was Angel's room, she was sure. She wondered how he was, thought of going up to find out, but hesitated, not knowing whether Rain would appreciate it. She'd looked so preoccupied on her last sojourn downstairs. Perhaps, Belle thought, it was a fluey cold, the result of his soaking on Midsummer's Eve.

The next morning's post brought Belle a letter. She stared at the handwriting, thinking it familiar. *Of course!* She opened the envelope to find a sympathetic note from Duncan under an ink-stamped logo for the Ramblers Club. A postal order fluttered to the floor and she picked it up, relieved to see that it was for the full amount, her deposit on the summer walking holiday returned. She felt a twinge of regret. She'd have enjoyed that holiday in Wales, but she'd made her choice.

In the kitchen she discovered Rain, but a Rain she'd not seen before. She was pouring boiling water over a handful of leaves in a bowl and looked up when Belle entered. Her hair was a mess and she was still in last night's dress, now crumpled, and barefoot. Her normally strong, serene look was replaced by confusion and there were purple bruises beneath her eyes. Belle viewed her with concern.

'How is Angel?' she asked tentatively.

'The crisis is coming. I sense it. This feverfew will help him . . .' She prodded the brew with a spoon.

'What is wrong with him?'

'I don't know, but I have to bring his temperature down.'

'How high is it?'

She shook her head. 'I don't have a thermometer.'

'Gray and I could go into Falmouth, buy a thermometer and find a doctor. We could take him to a doctor. Or call one to the house.'

Her face hardened. 'What would I need with a doctor? It's simply a high temperature. I have all I need here.'

Belle nodded, but she felt anxious. She scratched at a stain on the worktop. 'Can I help in any way?'

'No, thank you. I'll manage.' But Rain would not meet her eye. Belle quickly made a pot of tea, poured out three mugs, leaving one for Rain, and started back upstairs with the other two.

When she reached the first floor where Angel's room was, she heard a sound, a strange high-pitched cry, and paused to listen. It came again. Quickly she laid the mugs down by the skirting board and crept along the landing to listen. There came a moan. She pushed the door open and put her head round. It was gloomy in the room for the curtains were still drawn, and it smelled rank, of sickness. 'Angel?' she whispered. She could make out the bulk of the bed and the slight figure of the boy lying curled upon it, the bedclothes thrown off. His eyes were closed and as she watched he shuddered. She stepped across the room and sank down on her knees beside the bed. Touching his shoulder, she murmured, 'It's Belle,' but his only response was another groan. His forehead was burning to the touch. Belle stood and tweaked the curtain so that the morning light fell on him. His eyes were open now, but sightless.

'Belle.' Rain's tall figure filled the doorway and Belle let go of the curtain. 'I'll take over now.' She held a mug in one hand, a bowl of water and an old flannel in the other.

'I'm sorry,' Belle whispered, feeling as if she'd trespassed. 'I heard him cry out.'

'I know, dear, but I'm here now and I'm his mother. Perhaps, though, since you're here, you'll hold him up so he can drink.'

'The herbs?' A pungent smell from the mug was filling the little room.

Belle did her best, supporting Angel's small body so Rain could put the mug to his lips, but he would not take much. 'Angel, love, please, it'll make you better,' Rain pleaded, but although he heard her, turning unfocused eyes on her, he was too limp and weak to drink and Belle laid him down on the pillow.

Rain put the mug down and dipped the flannel in the bowl, squeezed it out, then began to wipe her son's face in slow, calm movements, murmuring soft words to him.

'It would be easy to ask Mrs Kitto for the number of a doctor,' Belle said again.

'No,' Rain said in a level voice. 'He will get better without their meddling.' Belle thought she saw fear in her eyes.

'They'll have proper medicines.'

She shook her head. 'We've always managed without doctors here. Leave me with him.'

There was nothing Belle could do but withdraw with a heavy heart.

Back down in the kitchen she found Janey washing up after breakfast and took up a towel to help. She recounted the conversation she'd had with Rain and Janey glanced at her gravely. 'That's what she would say. Rain's mother died of an infection that she'd caught in hospital after an operation and it put her off doctors. That and her spiritual beliefs and knowledge of herbs. Her approach has worked so far. She says that Angel is much healthier not having had any vaccinations.'

'No vaccinations?' Belle was surprised. 'You mean against polio and diphtheria and the others?' She remembered how insistent her mother had been that Belle and her sister be given any vaccination going, had told them that Aunt Avril had nearly died of diphtheria at the age of seven. Belle had never questioned this, nor had she heard before of anyone else who had, and it puzzled her.

'Rain says that they weaken children, that we shouldn't pump them full of deadly germs.' Janey bit her lip. 'I don't agree with her, to tell the truth, but then I'm not medical. I don't know the arguments. And Angel's her child, after all.'

'But what about now? Surely he should see a doctor.'

'Perhaps, but she and I had this argument before. Angel was ill a couple of years ago. Something bronchial, but she nursed him and he got over it.'

'What if it's something really serious? I'm worried, Janey.'

'I'll speak to her if you like,' Janey said uncertainly. She dried her hands and left the kitchen with reluctant steps and Belle's hopes rose. They fell again when Janey returned a few minutes later, her face telling the story.

'He doesn't look good, does he? But she won't call a doctor, says she'll manage. I can't interfere, Belle.'

Upstairs, she consulted Gray, who was writing lyrics in the notebook, but he said the same thing.

*

The morning passed slowly. Belle sat out on the terrace trying to read a book about goat husbandry that Janey had lent her, but her eyes skated over the page. All the time she was worrying about Angel, whether he was getting worse. She put down the book and prowled about, unable to settle to anything. It struck her now how purposeless she was here. Although she did her best to be helpful, she was only assisting other people's endeavours. There was nothing that was truly hers. Even the music, she was finding, did not consume her in the way it did Gray.

Where was everybody? Arlo, she knew, had gone to his job at the local pub. Janey was digging in the garden. Sirius was probably painting. She didn't know where Chouli was – someone else she was worried about.

At lunchtime, Janey laid out dishes of houmous, salad from the garden and fresh bread and butter. The others drifted down to help themselves.

'Shall I take some up to Rain?' she asked Janey, who nodded through a mouthful.

Belle loaded a plate, made the camomile tea that was Rain's favourite and set off upstairs with a feeling of trepidation.

Rain was kneeling by the bed, looking wretched. Angel appeared to be no better. 'He won't drink. If only I could get him to drink,' she muttered.

Belle set down the plate and mug on an upturned crate and came closer to the bed, peering through the gloom at the fragile figure on the bed. The boy's chest rose and fell in quick shallow breaths and his skin was blotched with reddish patches. He didn't look right at all. Surely the child should be in hospital.

'Can I fetch him anything?' she murmured, but Rain gave no appearance of having heard. She was stroking her son's forehead with the damp flannel.

Belle retreated, closing the door quietly, then hesitated on the landing, her fists clenched. She couldn't stand this. Was she the only one who cared? No, Janey cared. The others must do too. It was just that no one liked to cross Rain. If Rain said she'd manage, then they believed her. Well, Rain wasn't managing. Belle had seen that for herself. And now she knew what to do. She must telephone. There was a public phone half a mile away, but Mrs Kitto had a telephone and she was nearer. She ran upstairs and said breathlessly to Gray, 'I'm going to call an ambulance. I don't care what anyone says.' She glanced out of the open window and a movement caught her eye. The distant figure of Mrs Kitto in her garden. That's where she'd go.

Gray stared at her for a moment. 'I'll come with you,' he said and her heart swelled with gratitude.

She hugged him. 'I knew you'd help.'

'If you think it's right, then I'm with you,' he said. 'Come on,' and he followed her out of the door.

Mrs Kitto was eager to assist. Belle's voice wobbled with nerves as she explained the situation to the woman on the emergency switchboard.

'Shouldn't we tell Rain what we've done?' Gray said, faltering as they passed the side entrance to wait for the ambulance.

Belle paused, her brow furrowing. 'Do we have to? What if she's angry?'

He gave a dry laugh. 'It's too late to worry about that.'

'I suppose we should warn her.' She squared her shoulders. 'I'll do it. You go to the gate to guide the ambulance.' And she headed into the house.

Upstairs she knocked lightly on Angel's bedroom door and pushed it open. Rain was slumped by the bed, but turned her head to glance blearily at Belle. She looked a picture of dejection.

When Belle told her what she'd done her eyes blazed fiercely for a moment, but then she nodded. Belle sat on the end of the bed and laid her hand on Rain's arm. 'It'll be all right,' she whispered. 'Why don't you pack a few things for yourself and Angel and I'll keep an eye on him.'

After Rain returned they sat with Angel until flashes of blue lit up the room. Belle rose and went to the window to see the ambulance pull up outside. She sighed with relief then ran down to the hall to admit the crew, unbolting the double doors for ease of access and dragging them open.

They bore Angel down on a stretcher with Rain close behind and Belle carrying Rain's holdall. The others gathered in the hall. They stood without a word as the party went past.

Twenty-Seven

'I've never seen Rain like that,' Chouli whispered, shaking her head. 'As if she's . . . broken.'

Chouli was right. Broken was exactly the word. All the light had gone out of her.

No one felt like returning to whatever they had been doing before the ambulance came. Instead they assembled in the kitchen. Sirius opened a bottle of wine and they sat round the table, drinking in silence. Each seemed lost in a private reverie.

Janey said, 'Poor little mite. He didn't look good.'

'No,' Sirius muttered. 'Let's hope he pulls through.'

'What do you reckon is wrong with him?' Arlo put in, but nobody knew exactly.

Janey, sitting next to Belle, put her hand over hers. 'You did right, dear. If Angel pulls through it'll be down to you.'

'That's true,' Sirius said gruffly.

Belle flushed but she felt no triumph. Only shame that

she'd been late plucking up the courage to do something. That she hadn't persuaded the others earlier. If Angel didn't make it, it would be the fault of all of them. They should have stood up to Rain, but no one ever had, all the time she'd been here. They'd let Rain run the show, gone along with whatever she'd demanded, looked up to her, dazzled by her strength and charisma. It wasn't fair that it had been left to Belle, a newcomer and the youngest, to take the lead. Everyone was smiling at her now and nodding their agreement, and she almost despised them. She withdrew her hand from under Janey's and lifted her glass, briefly hiding her face, to drink.

'How do we find out how they are?' Arlo wanted to know.

Janey fetched a dog-eared booklet from a drawer and flicked through it. 'You're local. Which hospital will they have taken them to?' she asked him.

'Truro, I reckon. But they won't have got there yet.'

Janey pushed the open booklet in front of Belle. 'Maybe in a bit you could go and ring from the cottage. Find out how Angel is.'

Belle nodded. 'Mrs Kitto will want to know they've got off safely. She'll be worrying.'

'Always worrying, that woman,' Sirius muttered. 'Sticking her nose in.'

Belle clenched her fists. 'She doesn't stick her nose in,' she said hotly. 'She cares, that's all. She cares about Silverwood and she cares about us. And I don't blame her if she complains sometimes because sometimes we're stupid.'

Everyone was staring at her. 'It's like we're pretending

here. Living the good life and stuff. Saying we don't need the outside world.' Her voice was shaky at first, but then it strengthened. 'But we do. We're living off other people. Arlo, this is your uncle's house and we're here through the kindness of his heart, as far as I can see. And most of us scrounge money from the government. That's paid for by working people's taxes. What are we giving back?'

'My art, that's what I'm giving,' Sirius muttered. 'If more people bought it, then ...'

'Why should they?' Chouli put in. 'I mean, even if it's good, and I'm not saying it's not, Sirius, there's no obligation for anyone to buy it. You have to paint things that people want and you're obviously not.'

'So you know all about art now, do you?' he snapped. Chouli flinched and laid a protective hand on her belly.

'No, I don't,' she said bravely, her voice shaking. 'I don't at all. And I know I don't do much. I mean I like making clothes, but I've never tried to sell them.'

'Perhaps you ought to,' Belle said. 'Your embroidery is beautiful.'

'Do you think so? That's kind.' They smiled warmly at one another.

'Going back to the question of my art ...' Sirius growled.

'Your painting's good,' Janey said in a breathless voice. 'I'm sure everyone agrees.'

Sirius ignored her. 'Rain and I always envisaged this being a creative community and if we take a little from the taxpayer that's because we believe that art should be publicly funded.'

'I agree.' It was unusual for Gray to enter an argument.

'But there are more formal ways of doing it,' Belle added. 'Why don't you apply for grants?'

'I have, but I've been passed over. Those pen-pushers at the Arts Council. No idea what they're doing. Anyway, they'd want me to become an artist-in-residence, perform antics, that kind of nonsense. No, what I do is purer than that. I'm happy here.'

There was silence for a bit, then one by one people made their excuses and left the kitchen. Soon only Belle and Gray were left. And Figgy, lying mournfully by the range.

'I'd better go down and see Mrs Kitto,' Belle said. She stood up, then paused. 'I suppose I've upset everyone now.'

'I suppose you have,' Gray said with a wistful smile. 'But you spoke the truth. And that's good.'

She shot him a grateful smile and set off. As she walked across the courtyard her mind was awhirl. She sensed that a kind of crisis had been reached, not just with life at Silverwood but in herself. She was never going to have belonged. Being here was just a kind of interlude, a place to take a breather before she decided what to do next.

She heard her name called from ahead. Mrs Kitto was hurrying to meet her. 'I was coming to find out what happened.'

'And I was coming to tell you. Oh, it's been awful.' And suddenly everything was too much and Belle's eyes filled with tears. She felt Mrs Kitto's arms around her.

'Belle, don't, please don't. What's the matter?' she murmured, her cheek against Belle's hair, holding her tight and rocking her, just like her mother used to do. Oh, how Belle missed home. For a while they stood there in close embrace, then she managed to explain about Angel. 'It'll be all right,' Mrs Kitto said a touch too cheerfully. 'Come back to the cottage and we'll telephone the hospital.'

Everything wasn't all right, of course. The receptionist Belle spoke to at the hospital said that Angel hadn't arrived yet and she was advised to wait and ring again. So Mrs Kitto sat Belle down and got out of her everything that had happened. Belle was much reassured by Mrs Kitto's reaction.

'It's about time someone took them to task. Especially that wretched man Sirius,' she said. 'I'm glad that Chouli stood up to him. I only wonder what took her so long.'

'She was overawed by him, I think,' Belle said. 'It is fascinating, isn't it, why people fall for each other.'

'Yes,' replied Mrs Kitto wearily. 'And why they break up as well.'

'What happened to Imogen?' Belle asked, wondering who she was referring to. 'Did she fall in love with Ned in the end?'

'I'll tell you. Then we'll try the hospital again.'

Twenty-Eight

1944

The air of excitement at the school turned to frustration as March became April and, with the Easter holidays, April became May. It was difficult to leave Silverwood in any direction without meeting clusters of American troops or being turned back by sentries or roadblocks. Access to the sea was completely cut off. The newspapers had warned this would happen and the reality of it was constricting. The very air hummed with activity and the loud noises of machinery reached Imogen's ears day and night, disturbing her sleep. Some of the boys, too, slept badly, and one or two had nightmares.

Mr Forbes revealed that he'd discussed the idea of moving the school with the visiting American officers, but in the end they'd been allowed to stay at Silverwood. The boys weren't believed to be in greater danger than before and, anyway, he wasn't entirely sure where they could go at such short notice. At the neighbouring Trebah estate, which was nearer the beach, Ned and Imogen, passing on one of their walks, noticed that trenches had been dug in the gardens. At least Silverwood had escaped that level of encroachment.

One morning at the end of May, Imogen woke before the rising bell, drew back the curtains and leaned on the sill of the open window, entranced by the view. The weather had been stormy for much of the past week, but today the air was still and filled with birdsong. A mist was rising from the grass, veiling a lemon-coloured sun. It would be a warm day, she thought. She dressed and padded quietly down to the kitchen to make tea. Cook and Kezia were preparing breakfast and she perched on a stool, nursing her cup and chatting about her plans for the day as Cook stirred the porridge and Kezia flew to and fro with bread and margarine and pots of ersatz jam.

'You're back to your normal self, are you?' Kezia said when Imogen moaned about the rising tide of mending. She was joking, but Imogen realized that it was true. She was better. She didn't want to leave here, but she really ought to think about returning to nursing. Then something happened that hastened her decision.

It was the last night of May; Imogen was awakened by the distant roar of planes and answering gunfire, followed by sickening crumps of exploding shells. Rising swiftly, she tied on her dressing gown and went to check the sickbay. The two small lads there were sitting up, awake and terrified.

Miss Edgecumbe arrived and comforted them while Imogen, aware of movement elsewhere in the house, set off downstairs to check how the other boys were faring.

'It's over at Falmouth,' Ned said when she joined him and a couple of the other staff in one of the dormitories where, ignoring orders to stand back, the boys were crowding at the windows to watch the terrible sight of fire and smoke filling the sky some miles to the east.

'Poor buggers,' another master murmured.

The raid went on for a while before the explosions ceased, the gunfire faded and the noise of the planes grew fainter. Then, to their surprise, they heard a droning sound coming from the direction of the estuary. This thickened to a terrifying roar as it grew nearer and nearer.

'Get under the beds, boys. Go!' Ned cried suddenly and everyone scrambled for cover. The plane slowed, hovering close overhead, so that the walls vibrated and Imogen, huddled under a dressing table, held her breath. Then it moved slowly inland and as they listened, frozen with terror, it drew a great ominous-sounding arc before accelerating away. As it sped back towards the sea, a ghastly explosion rocked the school, immediately followed by a crash of breaking glass. Then came a long expectant silence before a child under one of the beds emitted a tiny, heartbreaking whimper.

It was a relief to discover that the bomb hadn't hit the school, but had gone off in a nearby field. The blast had broken a number of windows in the house and left a huge crater and a few traumatized sheep, but apart from that the damage was minimal. The news from Falmouth was more sobering. Several people had been killed, Cook was told when she went in for supplies, and there were a number of injuries. She'd passed the site of a hotel that had been destroyed in the bombing.

The school had been remarkably fortunate, Imogen thought, hearing this and remembering with a shiver the terrible air-raid on the hospital almost two years before.

'I'm torn, you know that,' she confessed to Ned as they sat on the steps the following evening after the boys had gone to bed. 'I love being here, but I haven't done all that training for nothing. What's just happened, well, it's made me realize. The hospital is where I'm needed most and it's my duty to go.'

'I know.' Ned sighed. 'But I'll miss you like hell.'

She gave him a wistful smile. 'Oh, the school will get along without me, I'm sure.'

'You know that's not what I mean.' His eyes were pleading.

'I was only teasing.'

'Imogen.' He paused, took her hand in his, then rushed on. 'I've asked you before so forgive me, but we get on – so swell, as our Yankee friends would say – that I wondered whether you'd changed your mind? About us.'

Imogen closed her eyes, allowed a slight smile to play around her lips and rested her head on his shoulder. She was thinking that he was right, they did get on, he was the person she felt closest to, could imagine being with, having children by. It would be a gentle life with Ned, being part of the school, not always here in Silverwood, but back in Kent maybe after the war. It was time to put thoughts of Oliver behind her . . .

A blackbird's warning cry, a batter of wings, and she lifted her head, startled. It was too early to dream of the future. There was work to do and something big, important, was about to happen that Cornwall was a part of. They could all sense it. Something that would determine the course of the war.

Yet, perhaps it wasn't too early to hope . . .

Ned was waiting for her reply, the steady pressure of his warm hand an anchor, and at last she spoke.

'My feelings have changed, yes, dear Ned.' She watched, touched, as the anxious expression in his eyes turned slowly to wonder then delight. They stared at each other then, in a sudden awkward movement, he reached and hugged her to him so tightly that she felt his heart bumping against her chest. His lips landed inexpertly on her forehead, her jaw and finally her mouth, before he pressed her to him once more, his cheek against hers.

'Oh, Imogen, I didn't dare imagine . . . You can't guess how happy this makes me. I'd do anything for you, darling. I'm not much of a catch, a humble schoolmaster, but you know the life and it's not a bad one.'

'I don't mind about all that, Ned, I love the boys and . . . I take it you're asking me to marry you?' Her eyes twinkled.

'Of course, what an idiot I am! Imogen Lockhart, will you be my wife?'

'I think so, yes, but not yet.' She sat up and held him from her. 'Ned, we must be sensible. I do have to go back to the hospital, don't you see? I'm needed and what's more I want to go. And they won't let me if I'm married. At least I don't think they will. Even in a war they don't like married nurses. If I stay here it'll be like throwing in the towel.'

'I think I see.' Ned looked unhappy, but after a moment he perked up. 'Yes, you're right of course. I'm just selfish.'

'Not selfish at all.' She leaned over and kissed his cheek. 'Just very dear.'

There were footsteps on the gravel and they looked up to see the headmaster and his wife returning from an early evening stroll. They pushed themselves quickly to their feet. The head regarded them suspiciously, but his wife, a friendly woman, was smiling benignly.

'Mr Forbes, Mrs Forbes,' Ned said, straightening. He put his arm round Imogen and said proudly. 'You're the first people we can tell. Imogen has just agreed to become my wife!'

'Good Lord,' Mr Forbes said, his bushy eyebrows shooting up. 'Congratulations, man. I had begun to suspect that a romance was going on under my nose. I don't normally approve of this sort of thing, of course, but marriage. That's a different matter.'

'Many, many congratulations, both of you.' Mrs Forbes spoke warmly.

'Thank you,' Ned said. 'We won't be marrying for a while.' Mr Forbes nodded when he explained.

'We can't expect to keep you here when others need you, Imogen, but we look forward to you joining us again as Mrs Thorpe in due course. Had you thought of telling the boys?'

'Lord, not yet,' Ned said, terrified by the idea.

'I think it as well to inform the staff, at least,' Mr Forbes went on. 'Your, ah, friendship has been noticed by more than ourselves, you see, and it's as well to dispel rumour. Now everything's to become official and above board it'll clear the air.'

'Yes, sir.' Ned sounded annoyed, 'though I assure you that nothing untoward—'

'I should think not,' Mr Forbes said, flustered.

Despite the couple's request for confidentiality, the news of their engagement went through the school like a dose of salts. The following day they could hardly go anywhere without being shadowed by giggling small boys. The older ones were more respectful. 'Good luck, sir,' and 'Congratulations,' followed Ned wherever he went, but one precocious lad got the edge of Ned's tongue after he ventured the opinion that Ned had 'good taste'.

At the beginning of June, Imogen wrote to the hospital preparing them for her return in a few days' time, assuming that someone at the school was going into Falmouth and could give her a lift to the station with her luggage. The hospital matron replied immediately, her letter exuding an air of relief. *We're short-staffed at present so you'll be warmly welcomed back.* Imogen began to pack in anticipation.

Each moment with Ned became precious, for with the current restrictions on movement it would be difficult for them to meet, and who knew when these might be lifted? Over their last weekend together, as though to thwart their plans, the rain came down steadily, keeping them indoors with little opportunity for privacy and every need to amuse the boys. Imogen invented a game involving throwing bean bags at a series of buckets in the assembly hall, Silverwood's long drawing room, and it was here that Ned discovered her before supper on Sunday evening.

'Fanshawe-Hicks, take over, will you? Miss Lockhart is required elsewhere.'

'Yes, sir.'

Imogen followed him out, puzzled.

'Sorry about that,' Ned whispered as he closed the door. He took her hand. 'I didn't think I'd get to see you on your own otherwise. Cook found me just now. The groundsman is driving her into Falmouth tomorrow and there's a spare seat in the car.'

'Oh, I see. That's kind of him.' The expression on Ned's face was disguised by the gloom of the hall, but the sadness in his voice was undeniable.

She herself felt desolate. She wanted to go but she didn't. She reached for his hand and wordlessly, Ned led her away. The library door was open, the room deserted. He took the key from the lintel, drew her inside and locked the door. Then he pulled her into his arms. She laid her cheek against his chest and closed her eyes, breathing in the familiar smell of him, wool and chalk and soap, and began to feel calmer.

'You don't have to go,' he soothed her.

'I do, Ned. Don't worry, I'll be all right in a moment.'

He lifted her chin with his finger and kissed her mouth, gently at first then, as she responded, more passionately.

It was then that Imogen heard a sound. She looked up and was shocked to see a column of bookshelves moving towards her: no, it wasn't falling, it was a door opening. There came a giggle and two small boys emerged. She and Ned sprang apart.

'Dash it!' Ned growled. 'Mills and FitzPatrick. Where the hell have you come from?' He strode past them to look.

The boys, at first bashful, perked up. 'It's a secret room, sir,' Mills, the tall blond one, said. 'We found it yesterday, didn't we, Fitz?'

'Yes. We were sniffing about, sir, and—'

'I'm sure you were,' Ned interrupted, his voice disappearing as he ducked under the low doorway and stepped into the room beyond.

Imogen followed, straightened, brushed a cobweb from her face and looked round the room, gasping with surprise. 'It's like – stepping back in time,' she said, coughing at the dust.

Ned was prowling about, testing the floorboards with every step. He rubbed grime from the window with his handkerchief, peered out at the rain.

'It's a whizz place to build a den!' Mills piped up from the doorway.

Imogen shivered. 'What was it for, do you think?' The room felt forgotten, abandoned, not a whizz place for anything pleasant.

'No idea.' Ned shooed the boys away, drew the door to and tested the locking mechanism. 'Dangerous, I should think. Anyone could lock themselves in. Wait for me in the hall, you two.' He went to unlock the library door and Mills and Fitzpatrick scampered out.

Imogen was glad to leave the room to whatever secrets it

kept and to go upstairs to finish packing. Later Ned appeared at her bedroom door. 'How are you getting on?'

'Oh, fine,' she said with a sigh, folding the last frock into the case. 'What have you done about that wretched room?'

'I took the boys in to see the head and he's sworn them to secrecy. Hogarth and I have moved a heavy desk against the bookcase for the time being, but Mr Forbes is telephoning Francis Penmartin to see if he knows anything about it. Curious thing, isn't it?'

'You certainly wouldn't want any of the boys getting stuck in there.'

'I don't know. It would make life quieter.'

'Oh, Ned,' she laughed, flicking him with a headscarf she was packing. He grabbed the end of it, pulled and she spun into his arms, laughing. He kissed her and they held each other tightly against the sadness of the parting to come.

The following morning, when Imogen woke before the rising bell, pale sunshine was edging round the curtains. It wasn't just the weather or her troubled mood; something different was in the air. There was no need for hurry, there being no boys in the sickbay and her preparations were made. Ned had taken most of her luggage downstairs to the hall the night before. So she lay listening, her hearing suddenly acute. There were distant noises, the clank and grind of metal, the roar of vehicles, distinctive sounds she'd heard before, but this time they were louder, more urgent. The Americans, she realized, were on the move.

Her door opened to reveal Miss Edgecumbe already

dressed, bursting with news. 'Something's happening,' she gasped. 'I went out with a letter and they've sealed up the postbox. There are Yanks everywhere. One officer warned me to stay at home. Very politely – I love the way they call me ma'am – but all the same.'

'That's blown it for me then. You don't suppose it's just an exercise?' Imogen leaped out of bed and pulled back the curtains. The sky over the estuary was hazy with smoke.

'Something tells me it's the real thing. They're getting ready to go in.'

'The second front,' Imogen breathed. 'At last.'

The rising bell sounded.

'I'll tell Cook that her trip to town is off.' Miss Edgecumbe left, closing the door, and soon Imogen heard her sensible shoes on the stairs.

As she washed and dressed, Imogen felt alight with excitement. If Matron was right, if the Allies were going in, then this would be the moment everyone had been waiting for: the invasion of Nazi-occupied France. And, if they were successful, surely it would be the beginning of the end of the war. *If* . . .

She fumbled with the laces on her shoes and hurried downstairs. Ned was in the dining room supervising the first sitting for breakfast, thirty boys sitting around tables eating porridge and toast. 'I don't think I'm going today after all,' she murmured. 'Something big is happening. I'm going to see. I'll report back.' She stole a crust of toast and hurried to the kitchen where she found Cook, Kezia and the groundsman talking excitedly. 'Be right back.' She ran out across the back courtyard and when she came to the cottage where the path began its slope downhill, stopped dead and drew a deep breath of amazement at the panorama below.

Through the haze she saw that the estuary was alive with ships of all sizes, landing craft and huge floating platforms. All these bits and pieces were arranging themselves in an order, like a group of travellers preparing for a long journey. It was a curious, fascinating sight and she wanted to cry out encouragement, though of course no one would have heard except maybe the groundsman's wife in the cottage. Suppose the same thing was happening all along the coast? What an armada! But what danger might it be sailing into?

It proved impossible for the boys to concentrate on school-work that day so Mr Forbes cancelled afternoon lessons. Since no one could leave the grounds, games were organized on the grass beyond the back courtyard. Then Ned arranged the boys on benches for group photographs. He finished the film by taking a couple of snaps of Imogen and promised to give her the prints. She wanted to send one to her mother.

By early evening, the fleet on the estuary had formed itself into a broad column whose vanguard was already on the move, snaking out towards the horizon. It was an extraordinary sight.

When they listened to the news on the staffroom wireless that evening there was no mention of any of it. What was happening? It wasn't until the following morning that tidings came. Later that day the Prime Minister announced in the House of Commons: *'During the night and the early hours of this morning the first of the series of landings in force upon the European*

Continent has taken place. In this case the liberating assault fell upon the coast of France.' The long-awaited day the authorities were already calling D-Day had finally arrived.

By the end of the week the roads were clearer and Imogen got her lift but was worried the train would be busy. 'I can only manage the two cases,' she told Ned. 'I won't need my box of books right away, so I'll pick them up another time.'

Ned tucked the box into a cupboard in the library, out of the way. A few days later, after the camera film was developed, he slipped two prints into an envelope for Imogen and put this in with the books. From time to time he or Imogen remembered the box, but always at the wrong moment, and since no opportunity arrived for her to visit the school, it remained there, gathering dust.

Twenty-Nine

1945

Imogen was to marry Ned and she did her best to banish Oliver from her thoughts. Soon after VE Day in May 1945, however, she couldn't help wondering what had happened to him. She'd heard nothing for a year, not even a postcard. She had celebrated Victory in Europe along with everyone else. The main streets of Truro had been filled with people of all ages and backgrounds, waving flags and cheering to the bright brass of the Home Guard Band. She'd mingled with the jubilant crowds all afternoon, and again in the evening when many of the buildings were floodlit and she and her fellow nurses joined in the dancing.

Spirits were high in the hospital, too, relief palpable everywhere, though the war wasn't over in the Far East. The question on people's lips was when were their loved ones going to come home? The grumble was that there would be more waiting. There was still much to do to restore order in Europe, to rout pockets of the enemy, to relieve the suffering of displaced peoples and sort out the general chaos. The papers shocked everyone with news of terrible things the Nazis had done to Jews and to others in their camps. There were tales, too, of brutal retaliation and revenge by liberated populations on collaborators and on remnants of occupying forces.

Sarah Summers was as relieved at the end of hostilities as everyone else, but as the days passed she could no longer hide her deepest fears. Her fiancé Sam's fate was still unknown. Until he was safely back in Cornwall Summers wouldn't be happy. She worked as hard as ever, trying to keep cheerful, but one evening Imogen arrived back at their room to find her friend in tears. She did her best to comfort her, but she herself was worrying ever more seriously about Oliver.

Perhaps Oliver was a prisoner-of-war, or worse. Who would the authorities contact – the Scottish uncle he'd spoken of? And by what process might the information reach the school? Ned would tell her straight away because Ned was a decent person, so she tried hard to put Oliver out of her mind and to concentrate on Ned. Her time with Oliver was only a vivid memory. It didn't do to brood and she usually didn't. Her life was too busy.

'We must be strong, dearest,' she told Summers now. 'There is always hope.' These were platitudes, of course, and it was the warmth of her arms around her friend that gave poor Summers the reassurance she needed. After a while she dried her eyes, gave a tremulous smile and accepted the offer of a cup of sweet tea. Blow the sugar ration.

Imogen and Ned saw one another as often as they could, but Ned wasn't a good letter-writer and only when the school holidays began was he able to escape to see her on her days off. Sometimes he came to Truro and they'd have lunch out and go to the pictures.

One Saturday in late July, Imogen took an early train to Falmouth. She and Ned had planned a ferry ride across to St Mawes, a walk and a picnic. She smiled when she caught sight of Ned's purposeful figure striding towards her on the busy platform. His beaming face when he spotted her made her heart swell with tenderness. Dear Ned in his tweed jacket patched at the elbows, his plus-fours, walking boots and rucksack with the picnic, she was so very fond of him.

'Im, darling.' He kissed her briefly, interlaced his fingers with hers and examined the engagement ring on her finger. It was a band of gold inset with sapphires and had belonged to his grandmother. She'd been a woman of generous proportions and the ring was a little loose, but since Imogen couldn't wear it on duty anyway, she hadn't got round to having it altered so she only wore it when she and Ned met.

'All well?' he asked as he always did, a note of anxiety in his voice.

'All well,' she replied, as she always did. She took his arm and the pair of them fell into step, chatting easily as they left the station. There was always so much to talk about. The head, Mr Forbes, was hoping to move the school back to its old premises in Kent by the end of the summer holidays, though the Ministry of Defence hadn't confirmed that this was possible. More importantly, Ned and Imogen were planning their wedding. It would take place in Hertfordshire at the Lockhart family's parish church where she'd attended Sunday school as a little girl. Her mother had already met and purported to approve of Ned the previous Christmas and Imogen had visited his family in Sussex twice, and they had been most welcoming. She'd liked Ned's sister, and felt sorry for poor Vaughn, who was thin and anxious after his ordeal in the German prisoner-of-war camp.

Imogen would be sad to leave the hospital and move to Kent. She didn't feel quite ready yet to hand in her notice, but she'd have to do it soon. Something made her drag her feet, though, and they'd started to argue about it. She'd promised to do it the previous week and it was one of the first things Ned asked her now.

'There hasn't been the opportunity, Ned,' she said, but didn't meet his eye. They were waiting for the ferry to take them over the harbour to St Mawes.

'What is stopping you?'

'I don't know. I worked so hard to become a nurse and I love it. It's such a big step.'

'To become Mrs Thorpe?'

'No. I'm longing to marrying you, you know that.'

'Then I don't understand.'

'I can't marry and be a nurse, you know that, so I want to go on for as long as I can.'

'I'm sure Miss Edgecumbe will still need help at the school. I don't mind you working with her. Until we have children, of course. Then you won't have time.'

'I would like to have a child,' Imogen said solemnly.

'Me, too. I'm glad that's agreed. Look!' They watched as a ferry chugged close and prepared to moor. It was turning into a beautiful day and the waters danced with sunlight. When it was their turn to embark, Ned held Imogen's arm as she stepped into the boat. They found a bench near the bows and huddled together against the bracing breeze.

'Oh, this is exhilarating!' she said, adjusting her headscarf as the ferry cast off. 'I'll miss Cornwall when we leave.' She had to raise her voice above the wind and the noise of the engine.

'That reminds me. Here.' He reached in his knapsack for the guidebook he'd once given her. 'Rescued from the box in the library. We'll have to get the whole thing back to you sometime.'

'There's no hurry; I'll be coming to the school soon, I imagine. Now, we can look up where we're going. Oh, look at the colour of the sea, Ned! Isn't Cornwall the most beautiful place in the world?'

'We'll come back for holidays after we're married,' Ned went on. 'Parts of Kent are pretty, though. I've told you you'll like it, honestly. And don't forget London. We'll be able to pop up for the odd show.'

Imogen nodded. 'I'd love that.' She had enjoyed living in London before the war, but had been dismayed by the bomb damage and the abject mood of its inhabitants when she'd last passed through on her way back to Hertfordshire.

The day went almost perfectly. They enjoyed walking round the old fishing village of St Mawes, then out along the coastal road, finally properly open to the public though signs of war defences were still everywhere. The approach to the viewpoint at St Anthony Head was still guarded, however, the sentry at the entrance to the barracks civil but firm in denying them access. They contented themselves with sights of Falmouth from the cliff path. At lunchtime, Ned unfolded an old travelling rug and they sat and ate lunch just off the path, then lay down together, gazing into one another's eyes and talking, enjoying their closeness.

It was only later in the afternoon, on the ferry back to Falmouth, that Imogen gave a cry of dismay. She'd lost her engagement ring. They stared at each other in despair. 'I haven't got time to go back!' she said. She was on night duty later.

When they reached Falmouth, Ned remained on the ferry, returning to St Mawes to search, but without success. On Monday he came back, put up notices and placed an advertisement in the local paper offering a small reward. Despite this diligence Imogen thought him remarkably phlegmatic about the matter. It was she who was distressed, shooting herself with fiery arrows of blame. They returned to the spot the following weekend.

'I should have got it altered,' she wailed after another fruitless search. 'Oh, whyever did I wear it on a country walk? I'm stupid, stupid.' Later, over tea in a waterside café in St Mawes, she added, 'Your mother will be so angry with me. I'm a disappointment to you, Ned.'

'You're not,' Ned soothed, his eyes soft with concern. 'It's . . . it's only a thing. It's you and I who are most important.'

'It's not just a thing. It's a symbol.' On the ferry she became irrational in her distress, blaming him for not caring enough about the matter. He should have looked harder. Ned was affronted. 'To hell with the blasted ring,' he said. They walked back to the station together in aggrieved silence.

Imogen began to wonder why she was allowing the loss of the ring to become a wedge driven between them, but she couldn't stop herself dealing it further hammer strokes. Perhaps, as Ned said, it was simply wedding nerves. But perhaps something deeper, more dangerous, was wrong.

Thirty

1966

Two days later, Janey and Belle sat on plastic seats in the reception area of the Royal Cornwall Infirmary waiting for Rain to appear. Janey had insisted that Belle accompany her today, rather to Belle's surprise since no one had spoken to her much after her outburst two nights back. Janey made no reference to that on the journey up to Truro. Instead she'd reminisced about life in the condemned house in London where she'd lived with Rain and others for two years. Belle, hearing descriptions of the outrageous behaviour of various odd characters who had been part of the household and the periodic visits from the police, thought it sounded hair-raising. Certainly a strange place to bring up a child. When she ventured this opinion, Janey agreed. 'It's much better here,' she said.

Now they waited in silence, watching people go

purposefully to and fro. Janey had a bulging canvas shopping bag resting on her knees. In it were Angel's ragdoll Dandy, extra clothing for Rain, and a box of caraway-seed biscuits Janey had baked the evening before. They'd already sat there a long time, because despite various efforts, they had not been able to warn Rain when they were coming and it had taken a while for her to be tracked down. Once Janey had clarified that the family surname was Fisher and Rain's proper forename Lorraine, they had better luck.

The Rain who trailed down the stairs to meet them was a shadow of her former self. Her bowed figure and shuffling steps spoke misery and when they rose to greet her, Belle saw that her eyes were full of unshed tears.

'Rain, darling,' Janey breathed and gave her a hug. Rain laid her cheek on Janey's head and held her tightly for a moment.

They moved apart. Rain smiled shakily at Belle. 'How is he?' Belle whispered.

'He's on a drip with antibiotics. The doctors wondered if it was meningitis, but it's not thankfully, it's blood poisoning, though that's bad enough. They don't know how he got it. Said it's early days. Oh, Belle.' Rain gripped her arm. 'I should have done what you advised and called a doctor right away. I had no idea it was so serious. He's never been ill like this before.'

Now it was Belle's turn to feel tearful. 'I didn't do anything, not really. It seemed sensible, that's all.' There was no point in blaming Rain further when she was already making herself miserable.

'It was brave of you and I thank you from the bottom of my heart. If he pulls through . . .' Rain brushed her eyes with the heel of her hand.

'Of course he'll pull through.' Janey's voice was uncertain. 'You must believe it.'

'Yes,' Belle echoed.

Rain managed another shaky smile. 'Thank you,' she whispered. 'I know I must be strong for him. I'm sorry, I feel shattered. Hardly slept the last two nights. The nurses found me a bed, but it's downstairs and I don't want to leave him so I've sat in a chair next to him.'

'Of course,' Janey soothed.

'We should know more later today. Is that for me?' Rain took the bag Janey held out and glanced inside. 'Oh, wonderful. Angel will be glad to see Dandy when . . .' She swayed suddenly and Janey grabbed her and made her sit down.

'Sorry.' Rain's voice was hoarse. 'I'll feel better in a moment.' After a while some colour returned to her face. She rose and picked up the bag. 'I must go now. I don't like to leave him for long.'

'There's a purse with some money there,' Janey explained. 'So you can telephone and buy food. And here's Mrs Kitto's telephone number. You can ring her with news or if you need anything and she'll give us the message.'

'That's good of her,' Rain said humbly.

'She sends her best wishes. Everyone sends their love. Angel is very dear to us.'

Rain let out a sob and nodded, then she turned and shuffled back upstairs.

Belle and Janey hardly spoke for a while on the drive home, each lost in private thoughts. Belle couldn't stop thinking about Angel and, though she wouldn't call herself fervently religious, sent up a little prayer for him. She imagined him lying in the hospital bed, linked up to tubes and machines. Poor Angel. Poor Rain.

'How do people get blood poisoning?' she asked Janey.

'I don't know. An infected cut perhaps.'

'He got cut somehow on the night of the ceremony.'

Janey frowned, but said nothing and Belle saw with a little pang of victory that she'd struck home.

Angel had had blood on his lip when she found him, she was sure of it, though it hadn't looked much. How long did it take for an infection to set in? Not as quickly as this, surely.

'At least he's in the right place,' Janey said grimly, swerving to avoid a pheasant. She glanced at Belle. 'Rain's right, you know, I'm glad she could admit it. If it wasn't for you ... Well, as we said the other night, the rest of us never know what to do. She's always in charge, you see. There's hell to pay if anyone goes against her.'

'It was easier for me. I'm not part of Silverwood.'

'You made that clear the other night.' Janey gave her a guarded glance. 'It's a shame. I've always liked you, Belle. And you're good for Gray, too.'

Belle flushed. 'Yeah? Thanks.'

Janey laughed. 'Arlo always said you disapproved of us, but I thought he was wrong.'

'It's not you,' Belle said. 'I think you're amazing.'

'It started well at Silverwood.' Janey paused and slowed

to let a speeding car overtake, then continued. 'I thought we were doing something new and different. Rain's inspiration ...'

'I can see that.' Belle was fed up with hearing how inspiring Rain was.

'We were full of hope. Sirius was excited. His work was going well. He was sure Cornwall would invigorate him. He and Chouli were madly in love – it was so sweet to see. But it didn't keep up. I don't know why things go wrong.' Janey sighed. 'I wasn't meant to have the bulk of the work to do. There were rules at the beginning, but they went out of the window after a bit. People would forget or get wrapped up in whatever they were doing. It's hard to keep going. Sirius and Rain are still passionate about it all, but they're the only ones.'

'What about Gray?' Belle asked. 'He loves Silverwood.'

'Dear Gray. He's so talented and we do all love him, but he stays at arm's length. Sensible, I suppose, under the circumstances. He was so shy when he came last year. It's nice that he seems more confident now and more purposeful about his music. As I said, that's down to you.'

'Janey, do you think he's going to make it as a musician? He seems incredibly talented but I don't really know about these things.'

'Nor do I, but I hope so, love, I hope so.'

But what do I do, Belle asked herself, feeling crestfallen. *I wish I could see the future.*

They'd come to the outskirts of Falmouth now. Janey steered onto the road west and soon the countryside proper began. The Helford Estuary was to their left, but it was hidden by woodland and the lie of the land, though every now and then they would catch a dazzle of blue.

How Belle loved this place. She wouldn't live at Silverwood for much longer though, she knew this now. Her values were definitely different from theirs. She was beginning to recognize that Gray's were too, and was encouraged by Janey's observations. He did hold himself at a distance from the others. He inhabited his own world and she wished she felt more a part of it. It was lonely here at times. She bit a splinter off her fingernail. What should she do?

'I hope Chouli's done something about lunch,' Janey muttered as they turned off the main road, the van's gears grating, and began to negotiate the winding lane where the trees met overhead. 'Making soup's not hard, I told her.'

'I'm too churned up to eat.'

'Me too, but I bet the men aren't.'

The van slowed as they passed through a hamlet and rounded a sharp bend. They were nearing Silverwood now. There was the telephone box, then the post-box. A few hundred yards further Janey swung the van wide to take the entrance. Soon the vista of the house rose before them, everything as usual. And yet not quite.

Next to Gray's bright yellow car a dull green-coloured Ford was neatly parked. It looked familiar. Belle knew what it was, a Ford Popular, her father had one, but of course this was someone else's.

'We have a visitor.' Janey drove into the space next to it with a puzzled frown and now, with shock running through her, Belle recognized the number plate.

'It's my dad's,' she gasped. 'Oh, Janey, my dad's here.'

'My goodness,' she heard Janey say politely as she killed the engine, but then of course Janey wouldn't understand.

For a moment Belle couldn't move, trying to take it in, then with leaden limbs she opened the van door and stepped down. Shading her eyes, she peered through the car's front passenger window, saw a road atlas and driving gloves on the seat, a bag with a vacuum flask and a Tupperware box in the passenger well. She smiled grimly to herself. If her mother wasn't with him, she had at least sent her husband off well prepared.

How had he tracked her down and where was he now? She looked up, took in the sweep of the house, but there was no clue and Janey was waiting. 'Better face the music,' Belle muttered and trudged towards the kitchen door.

In the hall she stood and listened. She heard a scraping noise coming from behind the drawing room door. She knocked, opened it without waiting for a reply and stuck her head round. Sirius was there, working away at something on the easel. He didn't look up so she retreated quickly.

Back in the kitchen she found Janey with her nose in the fridge. 'I can't find him,' Belle called to her as she hurried out to the courtyard where Chouli was lying stretched out on one sunbed and Figgy curled up on another.

Chouli raised her head and lifted her sunglasses. 'How's Angel?'

This brought Belle up short. In her confusion she'd momentarily forgotten Angel. She composed herself. 'It's too early to tell,' she said. 'It's blood poisoning.'

'Belle, that's awful.' Chouli sat up, blinking. Then she said, 'Oh, someone's here for you,' bringing Belle back to the moment.

'It's my dad.' She looked around. 'Where is he?'

Chouli pointed towards the distant cottage.

Belle screwed up her eyes. She could make out the profiles of two figures standing together in the cottage garden. A tall, scholarly-looking man in a tweed jacket, with salt and pepper hair, hands clasped behind his back. He was speaking to a woman in a navy skirt and rose-coloured blouse who was gesturing animatedly. Belle could hear the urgent sound of their voices but not the words. What was her father talking about to Mrs Kitto, and what on earth was making them so worked up?

She drew a deep breath and started to walk towards them.

Thirty-One

'Belle.' Her father stepped forward briskly to greet her at the cottage gate, reaching for her hand, his dark eyes anxious but his smile bright, clearly making an effort to keep the mood light. Behind him, Mrs Kitto managed a watery smile. The cat sat sphinx-like on a garden chair watching with interest, its ears twitching.

'What are you doing here, Dad?' Belle asked in a level voice, her arms folded, and his smile faltered. 'Don't you have school?' It was a question he might have asked her, but now their roles were reversed.

'St Faith's has broken up for the summer, of course. I hoped you might be pleased to see me. Indeed, I was just telling this dear lady' – he threw Mrs Kitto a warning look – 'I was saying how worried your mother and I have been, my girl. You heading off like that.'

Now their respective roles were back to normal. Belle

hunched her shoulders and looked down, shuffling her feet. 'I wrote twice and told you I was all right.'

'I'll put the kettle on,' Mrs Kitto murmured. 'Come in when you're ready, both of you.' The cat leaped off the chair and followed her indoors. Belle's father waited until they were alone before saying in clipped tones, 'D'you really think a couple of letters without a return address was sufficient? Your mother's been sick with anxiety, physically sick, I tell you.'

'Dad, I'm sorry, but I've been okay,' she whined, yet her father appeared not to hear.

'It doesn't take much to imagine what bad lot you might have fallen in with, what might have happened to you. The university telephoned and we couldn't tell them where you were or how they could reach you. You missed an exam, they said. You've to go back and take it in August or you'll be out. Is that what we all worked so hard for, eh? What d'you have to say for yourself?' His eyes blazed and he squeezed her arm too tightly.

'Dad, don't!' He froze, and let her go. He'd frightened himself, she saw.

'I'm sorry,' he said quietly, his anger draining away. 'It's simply we've been so upset.'

'You didn't need to be,' she muttered, staring at the ground. He made her feel like a child. She bit her lip, then said, 'I knew you'd follow me and take me back, that's why I didn't tell you the address.' Her head snapped up. 'How did you find it out?' She hadn't given it to Carrie.

'I drove all the way to Darbyfield last weekend to speak to your tutor. He took me to the porter's lodge to see if you'd left a forwarding address and there was a student in the lobby, leafing through some post at the pigeonholes. He heard me mention your name and asked if I was your father. Turns out you'd written to him and given your address. When I explained how worried we were he fetched your letter from his room. Decent of him, though when I saw where you'd gone—'

'Duncan,' she interrupted, her heart sinking. Of course, he wasn't to know not to hand out her address.

'I believe that was his name. He seemed a very nice chap. Rather keen on you, I thought!' His eyes twinkled suddenly.

'He is nice ...' she said. She was trying to feel annoyed at Duncan, but actually she couldn't be. He, too, might have been worried about her. All this worry. People cared. It was rather warming. 'How is Mum?'

'Your mother sends her love. She wanted to come, but I said better not. I needed to talk to you first. But it seems that the talking's been done for me.'

'What do you mean?'

He paused to gather breath and narrowed his eyes as he studied the back view of Silverwood. He muttered something that sounded like 'Still much the same' and his expression grew more thoughtful. Belle saw with relief that his anger had ebbed. He'd been blowing off steam, that was all. He and Mum had been genuinely anxious about her.

'I'm sorry about everything, Dad.' She bit her lip.

'I never thought you'd find your way to Silverwood,' he murmured. 'How did you know?' and she glanced at him, puzzled and, seeing this, he took her arm again, this time gently. 'Look, we have things to talk about. Let's go and find Miss Edgecumbe, eh? I could do with that cup of tea.'

'Miss Edgecumbe?' The school matron here during the war was Miss Edgecumbe. He'd completely lost her now.

'Whatever she currently calls herself.'

Understanding suddenly dawned. 'Mrs Kitto? Do you mean Mrs Kitto?'

'That's it. I didn't know that she'd married.' He smiled. 'The Reverend Charles Kitto, she said just now, from a church in Falmouth. Dead a few years now, sadly. Then, when she was left with chronic health problems and nowhere to live, Francis let her take the lease here.'

Belle, stunned, tried to process all this information as they went inside. Mrs Kitto had been Miss Edgecumbe. And how did the woman know her father? Her mind whirled.

While he studied a map of the county hanging in the hall, Belle found Mrs Kitto in the kitchen spooning tea leaves into a silver teapot. She looked up, her eyes bright, but gave nothing away. 'Will you take this into the sitting room?' She handed Belle a tray with her best scallop-edged crockery, and a plate of homemade biscuits.

'Thank you,' Belle said. *'Miss Edgecumbe.'*

'Ah, so the game's up.' The woman gave her a cautious smile, but Belle didn't smile back.

'I think Dad's cross with you.'

'I know.'

'But why?'

'Because I've been relating a story which wasn't mine to tell. But then, it wasn't fair of him not to tell it to you himself a long time ago. Come on.'

*

In the sitting room, her father was standing by the window holding the photograph of Imogen in her nurse's uniform, tracing her features with a gentle finger. Belle was shocked to see his expression of devastation. Mrs Kitto went to him. She put out her hand for the photograph and he gave it to her without a word and she set it back in its place. Belle watched as her father sank onto the sofa and stared into the distance.

Mrs Kitto seemed perfectly tranquil as she poured tea. Her father took a cup from her and balanced a biscuit on the saucer, and stared, ashen-faced, into his tea. For a while there was silence apart from the clink of silver teaspoons on porcelain. Belle watched him, bewildered, waiting for some sign.

Eventually, Mrs Kitto cleared her throat. 'I think, David,' she said, 'it's time for explanations, don't you?'

Belle's father took a sip from his cup and the colour returned to his face. 'More explanations,' he echoed.

'As I said earlier, I've been telling Belle all about her mother.'

'My mother?' Belle said, not understanding.

'Yes, your real mother.'

Belle stared at her, utterly baffled.

'It was time she knew, David, you must agree. As soon as I saw Belle, I thought of Imogen. I will admit that photograph, though' – she nodded towards it – 'is misleading. The studio must have touched it up. You can't even see her pretty freckles.' She said to Belle, 'Imogen had a scattering of them across her cheeks and nose just like you do, but they weren't fashionable back then. Some girls used to bleach theirs with lemon juice but Imogen never bothered. It was one of the many things I liked about her.'

Belle stared mutely at Mrs Kitto. She was still trying to process everything. Fragments of that conversation from long ago swam to the surface of her mind. *'You mean you haven't told her?'* in Aunt Avril's high-pitched tones. What about the blurred photograph of herself as a baby at Kynance Cove? Was the woman who had been holding her actually Imogen? And where did her father fit in? Her thoughts ran on. Such anguish. She had a mother already. Jill Johnson. A mother who loved her dearly. Tears filled her eyes. She jumped up, then gasped as hot tea sloshed over her hand and set the cup down. Her father produced a handkerchief and Mrs Kitto mopped up, murmuring soothing words.

When all was calm, Mrs Kitto said gently, 'Belle, I've been trying to tell you the whole story first without connecting it to you. Or indeed to me. Imogen wrote to me from time to time, but there's a lot I don't know, and it's good that your father's here. The story is his to complete. Will you tell her?' she addressed him. 'I got as far as summer 1945.'

'Summer 1945.' Belle's father folded the damp handkerchief back into his pocket and sat silently for a moment. Then he slowly shook his head. 'I don't know what happened then. I was still abroad.'

Mrs Kitto regarded him with a steady gaze, then she rose without a word and left the room. Belle heard her light feet on the stairs, then movement overhead. When she returned she was holding two pages of a letter, which she passed to Belle's father. 'I didn't keep all Imogen's correspondence,' she said. 'I lived with my father in his last days and it must have gone in the clearout after his death, but I do have this.'

Belle's father read it quickly, then gave it to Belle without a word, only an expression of deep sadness.

'It feels the right moment for you to read it, Belle,' Mrs Kitto said.

Belle smoothed out the large cream-coloured page and stared in wonder at the confident black script she recognized from the engagement diaries. Imogen's handwriting. She felt a stab of tenderness. It was dated 13 September 1945 and began, *'Dear Miss Edgecumbe, I do hope you've recovered from your summer cold. There's a nasty one going round the nurses' hostel, but thankfully it's missed me so far (fingers crossed). I thought I'd respond quickly to your latest as I have interesting news and I can't be confident that Ned will have told you . . .'*

Belle read on, her brow creasing with surprise and confusion.

Thirty-Two

1945

It was an overcast Monday afternoon and a chill September wind was blowing leaves around as Imogen walked under the arch from the hospital to the nurses' hostel. She was eating a ripe pear that a patient had given her. It had looked so nice and she was so hungry that she couldn't wait, though if anyone in authority caught her eating 'in public' they'd have had her guts for garters. Ahead on the path she saw someone loitering outside the door of the hostel, a man dressed in a cheap, ill-fitting suit as though he'd recently been demobbed. Even standing in quarter-profile there was something about him that looked familiar and she frowned. Dark good looks. Cropped hair that accentuated a narrow face pared to the bone like a chip from a carpenter's bench. He drew on a cigarette with a sharp, nervous action. Her shoe scraped on the path and at the noise he turned towards her and straightened.

And with a mixture of shock and elation she saw that it was Oliver and time fell away. All her feelings for him rushed back. She gave a laugh of joy and rushed towards him, then paused, uncertain, seeing the suffering etched into his face.

'Imogen, thank God.' He threw the stub on the ground and came to greet her.

'What are you doing here?' she breathed, recovering herself. 'If Sister catches you . . .'

'Damn Sister.' His voice was gravelly and he cleared his throat. 'None of the nurses would tell me if you still worked here. Then one invited me to leave a message so I knew that you must.'

Imogen wasn't surprised at the hesitation of her colleagues. There was a desperate look about him. It wasn't simply that he'd become so thin; his eyes were haunted, his lips twisted with bitterness.

'Where can we go?' He glanced about.

'Not here. Listen, give me a moment to tidy up and I'll be with you.'

Inside she sat down on her bed to collect her feelings. Why had Oliver come? She could hardly believe the difference in him. After a moment she composed herself sufficiently to change and to pull on her coat. She hurried outside to find him.

'I can't believe you're here,' she said, taking his arm. 'It's so wonderful to see you.'

'And you, of course.' His dull tone disturbed her. A dozen questions rose in her mind, but she didn't know which to ask first so she simply clung onto him as though he might try to escape. They set off down the hill to the city. When she glanced at him he smiled, but he did not speak and her puzzlement grew.

She took him to a café in a side street that served simple filling meals but, more importantly, had a table upstairs where they could be alone.

'Does the school know you're back?' was her first question after they sat down. What she really meant was, did Ned know.

'I haven't told them, so probably not.'

She felt relief. For this short while then, it was just the two of them together, sharing a moment out of time.

'The school is still in Cornwall, but waiting to hear when they can return to Kent.' Wanting to avoid the subject of Ned, she told him how the county was emptying of incomers now. The Americans were gone, evacuated children returning home to the big cities.

'Everybody's exhausted,' she said and was able to bring the conversation round to him. 'You too, if you don't mind me saying. What happened to you, Oliver?'

'You remember I wanted to see action?' Again that bitter smile. 'Well, I saw more than I ever imagined. And by rights I should be dead with the rest of the poor buggers.'

She waited, but he didn't go on. A motherly waitress puffed up the stairs and took their order, then returned shortly afterwards with plates of savoury-smelling steak and kidney pudding. Perhaps sensing their mood, she quickly retreated.

Imogen tucked in hungrily enough, but from the way Oliver attacked his lunch she wondered when he'd last been fed.

He swallowed his last forkfuls, gulped his tea, then sank back in his chair looking, she thought, a little better.

'How long have you been back in England?' she asked, scraping up the last morsels.

'Two days. Picked up my papers, spent a night in an indescribably hideous hotel in Victoria then caught the early train down to find you.'

'How did you know I'd still be here?' She laid down her knife and fork. 'It's been years, Oliver. You scarcely wrote. There came a time when I had no way of knowing if you were alive or dead. Do you know how hard that was?'

'I'm sorry. Many times I tried.' His hand shook as he put down his cup. 'Many times,' he whispered. 'But there wasn't much I was allowed to say and what I could sounded bland. In the end it was easier not to try.'

Easier for you, she wanted to say, but held her tongue.

He looked her in the eye at last. 'The things I've seen, Imogen, you'd never believe. I'll be all right, it's simply that I need to rest. But I also need somewhere to live and in due course a job.'

'How long do you plan to be in Truro?'

Again he looked at her with those piercing dark eyes. 'That rather depends on you,' he said at last and her heart leaped into her throat.

'Oliver ...' she started, then looked away, unable to bear his searching look.

'I'm too late, am I?' He glanced at her bare left hand.

'We're not allowed to wear jewellery,' she said. It wasn't the time to explain about the loss of the ring.

'So you are married.'

'Engaged. Oh, Oliver, it's Ned.'

'I thought it might be. Old Steady Neddy. Well, good for him. It's my own fault. Should never have had such fatuous ambitions. Heroism is an overrated virtue, Imogen. I can't say I wish I'd never gone. Doubtless I played my part in our victory. But I expect we'd have won without me.'

'Oliver,' she cried. 'I can't bear this. What's happened to you?'

'"Depression, dear boy," the military doctor told me. "You've no idea of the numbers I've seen with your condition. I'm considering writing a book about it." I replied, "To hell with depression, it's a strong dose of cynicism I've caught. Can you give me something for that?"'

'I'm sorry. I don't know what to say.'

'There isn't anything.'

Neither had any appetite for the bread-and-butter pudding the waitress offered, so they finished their tea and squabbled over the bill, Imogen reminded how forceful Oliver could be. She would repay him by helping him find somewhere comfortable to stay for a few days.

After half an hour's exploration they were directed to a terrace of Edwardian houses with stained glass in the porches in a residential road close to the hospital where a pleasant widow took in paying guests. Mrs Quick took one approving glance at Imogen, heard that she was a nurse and promptly declared that of course she had a room for her gentleman friend if he didn't mind sharing a bathroom.

'I must dash or I'll be late for my shift,' Imogen told him, as Mrs Quick prepared to show him upstairs. 'Let's meet here tomorrow at three. Promise me.'

'I promise,' he said gravely. She turned to go but he called her back. 'Thank you,' he said, smiling, revealing a glimpse of the old Oliver, which cheered her.

Imogen saw Oliver several times more during the following couple of weeks and each time she thought he was stronger and more positive. He put on a little weight, which suited him, and his hair recovered its gloss. Each time she saw him he appeared more darkly handsome than ever and his glance stirred desire in her. She tried to keep things casual, to talk about practical things. He started scanning the press for teaching jobs straight away, though not at St Mary's, which he'd not mentioned again. Perhaps because Ned was there, she thought. Instead his application to Truro Cathedral School was successful – the head was delighted to employ a man of such experience. He would start in the autumn term, a couple of weeks away. Imogen was relieved for his sake but also for hers. The evening after Oliver's arrival she had written to Ned.

'You'll never guess who's turned up in Truro. Actually, yes, you probably will. Oliver. He's in a bad way, Ned, and I'm sure you won't mind me helping him.'

Ned's response was unusually swift. 'Of course you should help him. Just don't forget that it's me you're marrying!' She read this twice, wondering why it annoyed her. Perhaps because it implied that he didn't trust her.

Thirty-three

1966

'It was you, wasn't it?' Belle cried out when she'd finished reading the letter. 'You're Oliver Dalton. Though of course you're not. You're David Johnson.' She turned to Mrs Kitto. 'I don't understand.'

'You're right, Belle. I've been telling you about *both* your parents. "Oliver" is really David – your father. I disguised him because I wanted you to hear the whole story before you passed judgement ... Well, it seemed the best way to tell you. Forgive me, Belle, but you didn't guess from the photograph and the hints I dropped about Imogen's likeness to you. It was then I realized that you didn't know about Imogen and it seemed natural to tell you a bit about her, what sort of person she was. And then I couldn't stop.'

'How can you be Oliver, Dad? And what about Mum?' Belle whispered. Then the truth slammed into her and she could hardly breathe. It was a moment before she mastered herself. 'What about Mum? My mum, Jill? And where is Imogen now?' Then she realized something else. 'Was? You said, "*Was?*" What *happened* to her?'

'I—' her father stopped to clear his throat. 'It's another part of the story, Belle. If it's not told properly you won't fully understand.'

'So tell me!' Belle cried, '*Tell me!*'

Mrs Kitto and Belle's father exchanged looks.

'I think,' Belle's father said heavily, 'that I'll take over now.' For a moment he collected himself, then he began.

'It was a Sunday, not long after my return, and Imogen had a day off. She was supposed to see Ned, but the previous evening he telephoned to cancel. A sickness bug was going round the school and he'd caught it. He'd sounded awful, apparently, and ended the call suddenly without saying goodbye. His loss, I thought, my gain. I was in the bath when Mrs Quick called through the door to say Miss Lockhart was on the line and was there a message? I rather surprised the poor lady by rushing out dripping in my dressing gown to pick up the receiver. Was I free the next day? Imogen asked. I had promised my new headmaster that I'd attend morning prayer at the cathedral. However, when I pressed her she said she'd come too ...'

~

1945

After the beautiful service, Imogen hung about discreetly to one side pretending to study the stained glass while Oliver spoke to the cathedral school's headmaster and his wife, but on a wicked impulse he called her over and introduced her as my 'old friend'. Imogen flushed at the way the wife said, 'A nurse? How jolly useful for you.'

'You're annoyed with me, aren't you?' Oliver murmured, smiling, as they walked out and down the steps into the sunshine.

'Now she thinks I'm your intended! The look of approval on her face when I said I lived in the nurses' hostel. All very seemly.'

'They're just being nice. I'm sure she doesn't imagine anything.'

'Men can be so childlike. I'm engaged to Ned, Oliver.'

'You are cross. Don't be.' He gave her his arm as they ambled across the little square. 'What shall we do now? Is it too early for a drink and a bit of lunch? Church always sharpens my appetite.'

After a roast lunch at a hotel in the main street, they went for a stroll along the river and found a bench to sit on overlooking the water from which they watched small boats go to and fro. A dozen yards away a woman and two little boys were throwing bread for the ducks, the younger boy giving excited squeaks of pleasure at the darting birds. It was a warm afternoon.

'That second glass of sherry was a mistake,' Imogen yawned. She dozed off then woke abruptly at a particularly loud infant squeak to find her head was resting against his shoulder and that he'd sneaked his arm along the back of the bench. She must have felt comfortable for she stayed close for a while, then perhaps felt guilty for she straightened.

'A pity, I was enjoying that,' Oliver murmured, teasing her.

'I don't know why I'm so tired.' She yawned again.

'You work so hard,' he said, then couldn't resist asking, 'Have you told them yet? That you're getting married?'

'No.' She made a sulky moue.

'It's not long now, is it? Your wedding.'

'It's two months away. I told you.'

'You don't sound very excited about it.'

'I am. Of course I am.'

'Are you sure?' He leaned in and saw his teasing eyes reflected in hers.

'Stop it, Oliver,' she said, flustered, 'or I'll have to leave.'

'I'll stop.' He withdrew his arm disconsolately and sank back against the seat. Neither knew what to say for a while. A shadow passed briefly over the sun. Imogen picked at a loose thread on her skirt and looked unhappy. Talk of the wedding, perhaps, had annoyed her. He wondered whether she really wanted to marry Ned or if her reluctance was about giving up her work, leaving Cornwall and becoming simply one of the wives at the school. He sensed she felt at home in Truro. What was obvious was that he had lost his chance with her. After all that he'd suffered, there had been nothing worth coming home for.

His thoughts strayed miles away and weren't happy ones.

'Oliver?' He flinched with surprise when she touched his hand. 'Sorry.'

'Nothing to be sorry for.' He could not throw off his despair.

'What were you thinking about?'

'Nothing.' It would be too embarrassing to explain his self-pity.

'It didn't look like nothing.'

'Can't a man have his own thoughts?' He tried to say this gently.

She gave a shaky sigh. 'Of course, but ... it helps to share them sometimes.'

'Does it now?' he sighed. He hunched forward then reached in his pocket for a cigarette, lit it and inhaled deeply. 'I'm not used to doing that.'

'You should try.' She wouldn't let up. It was true, though. He didn't have close friends and only the survivors he'd fought beside could really understood his state of mind. He was touched, though, to realize that she sensed his loneliness and felt sorry for him.

'You've never told me anything about what you've been through.'

He glanced at her. 'No,' he said with a low laugh. 'Best not.'

'Can't you try, please? It might help. I'm used to listening. I've heard so many people's stories. Terrible things. So I won't be shocked.'

He studied her face, his own expression softer now, for this was probably true. Still he held back. 'Why on earth would you think it helps to tell someone?'

She shrugged. 'I've seen that it does. It's as though some people carry a bad experience around like a burden. And when they share it the burden falls off and rolls away.'

'A nice image. Don't you think it simply falls onto the listener and makes them despondent.'

'That has happened, too,' she admitted. 'One can't unsee, unhear things on the wards. But one learns how to manage it. And there are so many wonderful uplifting things that happen, too. People are cured or are helped to live with an injury.'

'Do you remember that night in 'forty-two,' he said suddenly. 'The bomb on the hospital.'

'Don't be silly. How could I forget it?'

'When I thought about the children who were killed, the fact that it was a hospital, that's when I really started to hate the Germans. That they could do that. It made me more determined to go and fight them.'

'You never said precisely that.'

'I suppose I thought it didn't make me sound a decent person.'

'You are a decent person, Oliver!' Her words sounded so certain, her expression was so full of love and trust in that moment that something in him shifted. All at once, he wanted to tell her everything so that she'd know him and understand.

He sighed and clasped her hand. 'All right. I'll try.' After a moment he said, 'Do you remember that I got that desk job in the army, Imogen?'

She nodded.

'And I was pleased because the alternative – square-bashing and digging trenches – was so tiresome? Well, when the time came for front-line duties, administration wasn't enough for me. I explained to my senior officer that I wanted to be part of the action. Thank Christ I didn't know what I was asking for at the time or I'd have kept my mouth shut. Stayed in my nice little office in Plymouth shifting papers from the in tray to the out tray. But no, you know about that chip on my shoulder. I had to prove myself.'

He was aware of her eyes on him, all her attention focused, but he had to look away in order to think. 'It was the end of May 'forty-four,' he went on. 'That's when the orders came through. Our unit was on the move. Portsmouth, we gathered, but no details. We'd been loading up for weeks and most of us guessed that we would soon be off to France. Some were scared; others, the battle-weary who'd fought in Africa and Sicily, felt resentful that they were being sent off yet again, but most of us were simply relieved that something was happening at last after all the training and the hanging around waiting. Many of the men were simple types, content to do whatever the sergeant ordered. Wouldn't know the name of their CO if you asked them. Didn't question anything.' He shook his head, remembering.

'No need to ask which type you were.'

He chuckled. 'As you've guessed, I was glad to be off finally.' He paused, briefly lost in memories, and when he came to, Imogen was still watching him with eyes full of sympathy. 'They packed us into trucks with our equipment and we joined a huge convoy thundering along the roads. Thousands and thousands of us on the move across southern England. Our lot were let out in a large field outside Portsmouth and camped cheek by jowl for a few days. I wrote you a postcard, but there was no means to send it so it went with me to Normandy. Anyway, on the fourth of June they started loading us onto ships. After that, there was more waiting. The rumour was we'd be on the move that night, but nothing happened.

'I remember sitting on my bunk in the dim depths of the boat, trying to read in the crowded cabin – one of your mother's books, in fact, rather a cracker – and not being able to concentrate. It was impossibly hot and noisy and every time anybody wanted to use the bathroom they'd trip over the heaps of luggage on their way. I'd used your postcard as a bookmark and I kept turning it over and wondering if I'd ever see you again. Cursed myself for having lacked the courage to write before it was too late. Then finally, in the early hours of the sixth, the engines started up and we were on our way.

'I tried to get a few hours' kip, but it wasn't to be. Sometime after daybreak we were summoned on deck. I was astonished to gauge the scale of the operation, the grey bulks of ships all around us, the churning of the water, the stink of fumes. And the noise. I hadn't slept a wink through the grinding of ships' engines and the roar of planes. Now our ship slowed and clanks and screams of metal on metal announced the launch of the landing craft. My head ached and my neck was stiff and the weight of my backpack dragged me down as we crept like snails down a ladder onto an open craft. I squeezed into a space on a bench and waited with dry mouth, my heart batting against my ribcage. Then the craft jolted forward into the early morning mist, its blunt bows sending up soaking fountains of spray. We shook with cold and from the monstrous noise of explosions. Where exactly we were off to, it was difficult to tell. There was no sign of land because of the billowing smoke. Flashes from gunfire ripped the skies.

'The craft rolled in the swell. I glanced at my companions, but none met my eye, too bilious or lost in terror. I swallowed against nausea and tried to remember what we'd all been told. *The landing craft will take you to the shore. As soon as the bows are lowered then go! Run straight up the beach towards the sea wall. Don't stop, don't go back, even for a chum, or you won't stand a chance. Your job is to take out the enemy defences. Good luck!*

'Good luck! We'd need it wading through water and over sand with our heavy backpacks. We'd tried it in training and things had gone wrong. If they went wrong now, in real life, then that would be it. And so it proved.

'They let some soldiers out of the craft ahead too far from the beach. Poor buggers, they never even made it to shore. Weighed down by their packs, they drowned in the surf or were sitting targets for the enemy, shot down in a spray of bullets. Our lot were all right at first. When they'd kicked open the ramp, we jumped out into three feet of water, holding our rifles above our heads as we'd practised. But we couldn't dodge the gunfire. Chap ahead of me was cut down and I trod over his body. I'm sorry, but I couldn't help it. It stays with me now. Then it was every man for himself as we stumbled across the sand, trampling barbed wire, our legs buckling. There wasn't time to be frightened any more or to process the terrible things we saw. British tanks on fire, the men in them screaming as they burned alive. And there were mines buried in the sand. It was a game of roulette, Imogen, and I was one of the lucky ones that day. No rhyme or reason to my survival, no skill or virtue of mine. So many good men felled by mines or bullets or blown to bits by shells. *I'm finally in the war,* I muttered, *I'm in the war.* And it was hell.

'Somehow I made it up the beach to the sea wall and

crouched there with a hundred others. There we waited like hunted animals, wondering what the hell to do next. A tank rolled towards us and I thought I'd bought it, but it was one of our own and it raised its cannon to fire shells at the enemy defences above our heads. Another tank joined it, letting off a volley of shots, then a huge explosion shook the wall and rubble rained down. The man next to me was crushed. The tanks swung away then and moved along the beach to continue their grisly work. When the chaos cleared I heard an officer cry in cut-glass tones, "That's settled the buggers. This way, chaps," and I joined the hordes scrambling up and over the ruins of the wall.

'In the sand dunes beyond I passed the blasted gun turret, averting my eyes from the blackened corpses, and bent to scuttle along a sandy causeway towards a village from which plumes of black smoke rose. We arrived to find it in ruins, the streets strewn with bodies. A British plane lay in flames. And the noise was deafening. Cracks of rifle fire, some of it mine, the stutter of machine guns and the crump of exploding shells. Hours passed before we got the better of the enemy and the last of their troops surrendered. We took many prisoners. Soon this pompous little chap, the village mayor, was wringing a senior officer's hand and the French flag was raised in the square, and I'm obliged to confess that I experienced a short burst of pride. One tiny part of the Normandy coast had been liberated and I'd done my bit for King and Country.

'But the cost, Imogen. The first time I killed a man, well, I didn't have time to think about it. It was just him or me and I was damned if it was going to be me. Afterwards I felt nothing. There were worse things that happened that kept me awake at night, constant fear, mostly, not to mention the state of my insides after badly cooked rations.'

Oliver lit another cigarette before going on. 'Anyway, weeks of tough fighting followed. The Normandy countryside is a bit like round here. Lots of little misshapen fields bordered by thick hedgerows. It was like a game of hide-and-seek. You didn't know what you'd meet round the next corner. A German sniper or a machine-gun crew, a pile of corpses or a bunch of our own lads who'd simply stopped for a brew. We forged on somehow. Sometimes it was hand-to-hand fighting with zealous Wehrmacht troops; sometimes we'd be met by a handful of foreign conscripts relieved simply to throw down their weapons and surrender. At night we'd dig foxholes and bed down in them or roll under hedges, our rifles ready in our hands. Lack of sleep came to be the worst thing of all. A whole month of vicious tank battles while we struggled to reach Caen, then a long and bitter onslaught to occupy the city. Do you know, I visited Caen once when I was twenty. It was an ancient and beautiful city then. We left it completely flattened with many of its inhabitants dead.' Oliver shook his head. 'Then the briefest of rests before we were made to push on.'

He fell silent for a moment then said, 'We were to be there for over a year. I can't bring myself to tell you any more about all the things I experienced. I'd prefer to forget, but they live with me still. That's all.'

Now that he'd finished, Imogen said nothing at all for a

minute. Then she did what he'd longed for her to do since he'd found her She opened her arms to him. For a long while they sat together in a close embrace. Then they came to their senses, brushed themselves down and walked slowly, arm in arm in the gloaming, back towards the comforting lights of the city.

Thirty-Four

1966

For several moments there was silence in the cosy sitting room of the cottage, then Mrs Kitto said in a low, heartfelt voice, 'Thank you, David.'

Belle brushed tears fiercely from her eyes. 'I didn't know that's what you did in the war, Dad.'

'No. I couldn't bring myself to inflict my experiences on anyone else. Not even Jill. What I've given you is an edited account, but, still, I felt you had to know, finally. I'm sorry if I've upset you.'

'I'm okay. Really. It's horrible. Dreadful that it happened to you. But it's history, it's gone.' She sighed. 'It's the other stuff that affects me. About Imogen.' She addressed Mrs Kitto. 'How did you know who I was?' she cried.

'Oh, it was immediately apparent. You look so like her.

And when you described that photograph on the beach at Kynance, a shiver ran through me.'

'A shiver?'

'I remember—'

'That photo, Belle,' her father broke in. 'When you stumbled on it I admit I was rattled. I didn't know I still had it, to tell you the truth.'

'Why would you have got rid of it?' There was something about the atmosphere in the room. A sort of tension.

'Because ... I can't tell you that yet. Not until you know the rest of the story.'

'Tell it to me then,' she commanded.

Her father and Mrs Kitto looked at one another, but before anyone could say anything further the telephone began to ring in the hall.

Mrs Kitto went out and they heard her answer it. 'Would you wait a minute, please,' they heard her say and she returned wearing a grave expression. 'Belle, it's Rain for you from the hospital.'

Belle rose shakily. She walked to the phone with a heavy tread and picked up the receiver.

Thirty-Five

When Belle returned to the living room a few minutes later, she was beaming with relief.

'He's better. Angel's better. He's going to pull through. Oh . . .' She sank onto her chair and briefly covered her face. 'I've been so worried, but he's going to be all right. Rain said . . . Well, not much really, just that he's out of danger and can come home soon.'

Rain had hardly been able to get the words out. She'd sounded confused and exhausted, had hardly made sense, but her message had got through.

'What has happened exactly?' her father asked, puzzled, and Belle explained.

'That's hair-raising,' her father said with a frown. 'To think you've been living with these people. They sound highly dysfunctional. That woman I met when I arrived . . .'

'Janey?' Mrs Kitto said.

'Janey. She appeared to be a sensible type, but the young man with her ...'

'Arlo.'

'Is that his real name? Barefooted, his hair a mess. And the older man, Sirius. An artist, I gather.'

'Oh, Daddy. They're not that bad.' She felt a strange need to defend them.

'And who's the young man who brought you here in the first place? That's not Arlo, is it?'

'No, his name's Gray. Gray Robinson. He's a musician and a good one. I'll introduce you to him. But I've got to tell everyone about Angel. Now.'

'I thought you wanted to hear the rest of the story.'

'I do, I do. Desperately. But I must share the good news first. That Angel's going to be all right.'

When Belle returned to the house only Gray was in the kitchen. She told him quickly about Angel, and then about her father arriving, which surprised him mightily.

'Where is he? Should I meet him?'

'Yes, of course. Oh, there's so much to tell you, Gray, but it'll have to wait. I can't stop, I've got to tell everyone the good news!'

She ran round locating everybody. Janey was upstairs lying on her bed and snivelling to herself, but her eyes brightened when Belle told her the tidings. Sirius had been hunched gloomily smoking in his studio, but he too cheered up. Gray told her that Arlo was outside tinkering with his motorbike and she asked him to go with her to speak to him.

She was still too cross with Arlo after their argument to want to be polite.

'Angel's okay. That's a relief,' Arlo said, when she'd told him, wiping his hands with a rag.

'Where's Chouli?' Belle asked and a shifty look crossed Arlo's face.

'Yeah, something's happened with Chouli,' he muttered, shuffling his feet. 'She gave me a note.'

'What do you mean, "something's happened"?'

'She said goodbye an hour or so ago and went off down the drive dragging her case. A car picked her up at the gate. At least, I heard the engine and the door slamming.'

'Where did she say she was going?'

'You'd better read the letter. It's about somewhere. Ah!' Arlo picked up a brown envelope lying on the ground. It was unsealed, had a slick of oil on it and was addressed simply to 'Everybody'.

It was a short letter, written in Chouli's round handwriting.

I can't stay at Silverwood after what happened. Janey and Rain, you know what I'm talking about. I've decided to have this baby, but I can't do it by myself. Mummy and Daddy will be angry but I think they'll help me. Belle, I can't thank you enough. You've helped me see straight. Gray, you've got a good one there – and keep on writing great songs. Goodbye, Arlo – do something proper with Silverwood, will you? The old place deserves it.

Yours,

Julia (NOT Chouli any more)

PS: Please give the enclosed to Sirius.

'Oh,' Belle said stupidly. She shook the packet and a thin white envelope fell out, addressed to Sirius and firmly sealed. She went inside and handed it to him wordlessly. From the sight of Sirius's face after he read its contents, Belle guessed it packed a punch.

'I'm glad Chouli's gone home,' she told Gray as she walked with him down to the cottage to meet her father. 'She deserves better than Sirius. She'll be all right now.'

Thirty-Six

The following morning gusts of wind whipped the clouds along, but it was bright and dry and Belle and her father decided to walk down to the beach together. He'd driven his car round to the cottage, where he stayed the night, and Belle got out of bed in good time and met him there. Mrs Kitto tactfully left them together to talk, but Belle's father couldn't settle. He'd sat down and laid a small blue hardback notebook on the coffee table, piquing Belle's interest, but instead of explaining its presence, he'd stood up again, reached for the photograph of Imogen and studied it before setting it down. After that he'd gone to the window to stare at the rear view of Silverwood. Belle joined him there. The racing clouds gave the alarming impression that the huge house was falling towards them.

'I'd like to go down to the shore,' he said finally, straightening. 'It was such a beautiful part of the coast, but after the war it was a terrible mess.'

'Oh, it's lovely now. Dad, I still can't believe that you lived here at Silverwood. I know you described it to everyone last night, but I'm still getting used to it.'

The father she'd seen in the Silverwood kitchen the previous evening had been a different man from the one she thought she knew. Still edgy, conservative in his views, a little stern, but kinder, and he had asked searching questions and listened to the opinions of others around the table. He'd got on surprisingly well with Gray, who had been polite while speaking warmly of Belle and passionately about his music. Later, when Belle and Gray were alone, she'd explained to him all that she'd learned about Imogen and suddenly everything felt like the great wave on the beach at Kynance, utterly overwhelming, and he'd held her closely while she cried, whispering words of reassurance.

This morning she felt a little better, but there was something troubled about her father and she guessed why; she felt it herself. He must unburden himself of the secret he'd kept from Belle all these years, the final pieces of the story of what had happened to Imogen, her birth mother.

She waited while her father shrugged on his jacket and pocketed the mysterious notebook from the coffee table, then followed him out of the door. The breeze smelled fresh and salty and made the blooms in Mrs Kitto's garden dance madly. They set off down the hill, her father treading cautiously in his polished brogues, she stepping lightly ahead, stopping often to wait, noticing with concern the stiffness of his gait. She'd not thought of him as ageing. When had that happened? Her own feet dragged at the thought, but after they passed between the tossing trees and the path levelled out, he walked more easily and her spirits rose.

'Ah, the new road the Americans built,' he murmured when they glimpsed it.

'Not so new any more.'

'I can remember all this when it was unspoiled green hillside,' he said with a sigh as they crossed onto the footpath beyond. When they came to the ridge above the beach he stopped and looked down, taking it all in. The tide was full and the landing strips almost covered. As they watched, the sun broke through cloud and the restless water dazzled with a million sparkling diamonds.

'They've tidied it up, I will admit, but it'll never be as it once was.'

'I think it's beautiful,' Belle said, slipping off her shoes. 'And it tells a story.'

'It certainly does,' he murmured. 'A brave one.'

They walked about, each lost in private reverie. Belle knotted her skirt and paddled in the gentle waves, her hair tossing in the wind. Meanwhile her father trudged the span of the shore with his hands in his pockets. She watched him shade his eyes to stare up at the ruins of the pillbox nestled among the trees on the promontory. Finally, he went and sat down on a flat rock at the far end of the beach. She left the water and followed to sit beside him. It was pleasantly warm in the shelter of the headland.

'Toffee?' he said and she took one from the paper bag he offered. They sat in companionable silence, enjoying the soft buttery sweets, and watching some gulls diving for fish. It was a while before her father spoke.

'Your Gray's not a bad lad. Serious about his music. Looked me in the eye.'

'I suppose that's a compliment, Dad.'

'It is. I'd much prefer that Duncan boy, mind you. Decent prospects as an academic.'

'Dad!'

'That's not what we came to talk about, though, is it? I hardly qualify to pass judgement on your life. But I do earnestly want you to be happy, girl.'

'I know.' She shuffled her bare feet. 'But I wish you'd explain. I do know that there was something odd about our family. I've known for a long time. From something I over-heard Aunt Avril say.'

'Ah, dear Avril. Her voice does carry, doesn't it?' was all he said after she told him what his wife's sister had said. 'I owe you an explanation and I'll do my best, but what I'm about to say to you is, despite the passing years, still painful to me.'

Belle nodded. 'I understand,' she whispered, 'but I have to know.'

'You should look at this.' He reached inside his jacket and brought out the notebook she'd seen earlier. He weighed it in his hand a moment then passed it to her.

'What is it?' She opened it and saw the owner's name. Imogen Johnson. Her married name.

'It's a sort of diary. She started it when you were born to record your babyhood. I knew she had it – she used to read me bits early on. It was rather touching.'

Belle turned the pages and read some of the entries: 'Baby is two days old and already changing. Her face is filling out and she's losing that yellowish tinge ... A week old today and Belle is feeding well. Her eyes are darkening now. They'll definitely be brown like her dad's ... Today I cut her fingernails for the first time. I wanted to keep the clippings but I know that's ridiculous. I love everything about her, she's so dainty.' Belle couldn't read on for tears. She blinked them away.

'You kept this,' she whispered.

Her father cleared his throat. 'Because it was all about you. This part, anyway. Later, she's written about me. It's not always flattering. I suppose you'd better look.'

The pages fluttered in the breeze as she tried to turn them. 'Not a good ...' She held open the pages. 'Not a good day today. Sometimes feel I'm trudging on hoping for the sun to come out ... Something I said upset him ... Belle said her first word today – it was "Dad". I wish he deserved it.'

Belle read a few more comments, puzzled, then closed the book and returned it to him. 'I'm not sure about reading it now. The bits about you don't make sense to me. I don't like them. Can't you tell me the story instead?'

He pushed the book back into his pocket, smiled at her and began.

'The day I married your mother was the happiest day of my life thus far. But for Imogen it was not without distress. She'd had to break off her engagement to Ned, you see.

'We married in her family's pretty parish church in Hertfordshire in January 1946 while a snowstorm raged outside and the congregation shivered in the pews. Her old schoolfriend Monica was bridesmaid. My old commanding officer, Robin McDougal, a man of my own age whom I admired, stood as best man. Apart from Imogen's family there were hardly any guests, only an uncle and a distant cousin on my side. But nothing was as usual with the postwar privations and nobody thought much of it. Imogen was sad that Sarah Summers was unable to attend, her excuse being that Matron had denied her the time off, but Summers had recently had bad news, the worst possible. Her fiancé had not survived the prison camp in Malaya where he'd been sent after the fall of Singapore and had died of dysentery in 1943. For two years she had been waiting and hoping in vain. Imogen's happiness had become difficult for Sarah, more so because of what she regarded as Imogen's betrayal of Ned.

'For Imogen, breaking off her engagement to Ned had been as painful for both of them as she'd imagined it would be. She would never forget the way Ned flinched as though her words were physical blows. She'd arranged to meet him in Falmouth, neutral ground, for a brisk walk in a park near the station. "I do love you, dear Ned, but not in the right way," she'd told him. "I thought I wanted to marry you, but I just can't. It's my fault."

'"It's Johnson, isn't it?" – or perhaps I must say Dalton to maintain my alias – "He should have stayed away. Why couldn't he have stayed away?" Imogen had wanted to tell him the truth, that it was before I'd returned that she'd started to have doubts, but in the end she couldn't – that would have hurt him more. Let him think it was me who'd cut the cords that had tied them. It would damage his pride less and I didn't mind taking the blame.

'"I'm so, so sorry," she said. "You won't feel like it now, but one day I hope we might be friends."

'"Don't be so sure," he'd spat out and it was her turn to flinch. "I can't believe that you'd think that. And don't come running to me later saying you've changed your mind. I've had enough." He spun on his heel and walked away. She stood stunned, her jaw hanging open. She'd never seen him so angry. About anything.

'When she recounted to me later that evening what had taken place I must say I was surprised at the strength of Ned's anger, but reluctantly admiring. "I didn't know the old chap had it in him," I told her.

'"Don't be flippant. I cut him to the quick. It was awful." And she broke out in sobs and could not be comforted. Despite this inauspicious beginning, our engagement and the early days of our marriage were very happy. And only eight months after the wedding we learned that she was expecting you, Belle. Such wonderful news.'

Thirty-Seven

September 1946

Imogen heard the front door close, laid her brush across the paint tin and called out, 'Oliver? I'm up here, darling, come and see.'

'Righto!' She heard his light tread on the stairs then his tall figure appeared in the doorway of the box room they'd started to call the nursery. 'Very nice,' he said, smiling. 'But I prefer you without the overall and the paint on your nose.'

'I meant the room, you daft thing,' she giggled, rubbing at her nose, and he gazed round admiringly at the fresh blue-green walls.

'The young 'un will think he's under the sea. Or in a forest.'

'Oh, Oliver, he won't have seen the sea to know.' They'd decided early on that the baby would be a boy.

'Plenty of trees round here, though,' he said, stepping carefully over the dustsheets to peer out down at the scrap of back garden where a pair of gnarly apple trees were bursting with fruit. 'And we'll take him to the beach as soon as he's old enough. My brother Andrew and I used to make smashing sandcastles with moats and channels and toy soldiers in the battlements. I—' He turned to her with a look of sadness. 'I say, I don't suppose that we could call the baby Andrew?'

'I don't see why not. I've always liked the name. It means "manly", doesn't it? D'you remember how the boys at Silverwood used to rag poor little Andrew Hood?'

'Calling him "Manhood"? That was quite erudite for them.'

In the September after their wedding they were over the moon to discover that they were to become parents. 'All tickety-boo, Mrs Dalton,' the doctor said. 'A baby in the cot for Easter.' She should take special care of her health, he went on, because of her past illness. She shouldn't overexert herself. Imogen had never recovered from occasional periods of breathlessness, when climbing hills, for instance, or struggling with heavy shopping, and shortly before the wedding she had consulted the doctor about it. Slight damage to the lungs, possibly mild asthma, he'd said. She hadn't wanted to upset Oliver by telling him at the time. It seemed like making a fuss and surely she'd continue to get better.

It was odd settling in Truro, renting this terraced house up the hill near the hospital but not being part of the hospital any more. Imogen had kept nursing until they married, and it turned out that, despite the rules, Matron had considered keeping her on, but Oliver hadn't liked the idea of his wife working when he could afford to keep them both. There was enough for her to do at home even before the baby started and then there was the attendant tiredness and morning sickness.

That was past, thank heavens. Three months pregnant, she still wasn't showing, though she'd had to start letting out her clothes.

Oliver was getting on well at the Cathedral School. There was talk of the deputy headship coming to him because the current incumbent was retiring in the summer. The headmaster valued Oliver's kind but no-nonsense approach with the boys apparently.

What nobody saw except Imogen were the dark moods of despair that overtook him from time to time and which she had no idea how to handle. It was hard always to know what caused them, these periods when he retreated into his thoughts and barely said a word to her. The silences could last days and she'd go about anxiously, trying not to betray how unhappy they made her. It appeared that he still managed his work professionally and could interact with the world outside the house. Only at home where, presumably, he felt safe, did he drop the front.

She tried to talk to him about it, how lonely it made her feel, whether he ought to see a doctor about the matter, but with limited success. Black thoughts were the problem, he said. Not about her. He'd always been prone to them, but since the war ... She wasn't to worry, but of course she worried. She was sympathetic. Losing his parents – she'd lost her father, too – and his beloved brother, the things he'd experienced in the war. She didn't dare admit Oliver's condition to anyone she knew. He'd be horrified. If the matter became public he might lose his job. Friends might recoil. Surely the sensible course was to sit out these patches of depression. They'd pass of their own accord. So many people were having a wretched time one way or another, trying to adapt to the peacetime world, it would be wrong to complain. Maybe, when the baby came, he'd cheer up, leave the past behind, become more hopeful about the future.

After all, they were fortunate. They'd survived the war. They'd found each other and were happy – most of the time.

~

1966

'You were born at home just before Easter,' Belle's father told her and he smiled, remembering. 'Our early Easter egg!'

Belle smiled in turn. 'I'm sorry I wasn't a boy as you expected.'

'Once we'd got over the surprise we didn't mind at all. Only we'd not thought up any girls' names.'

'Not Andrea instead of Andrew?'

'I don't know why we didn't think of that. You were beautiful from the start. So we called you Belle, and Mary after Imogen's mother.'

'Oh.' Another connection to Imogen, then she remembered: 'Mum's middle name is Mary, too.'

'Indeed, she has always been pleased about that link to you.'

'I'm pleased too. It was the name of the school as well, wasn't it?'

Her father nodded absently. 'I'm afraid the next part

is difficult for me to relate. I found out a great deal from Imogen's notebook here, adding it to my own perspective. I've brooded over it through the years, as you might imagine. It doesn't reflect well on me, Belle. I'm sorry.' He took a deep breath and continued.

Thirty-Eight

1947

Hardly any woman finds looking after a newborn baby easy, especially when it's their first, but Imogen at least had the advantage of her nursing experience. Her mother came to stay with them in Truro and Imogen was glad to see her, but Mrs Lockhart wasn't much help practically and dithered about, making endless cups of tea and grimacing at the bucket of dirty nappies. If they hadn't had the daily woman to assist with the laundry and the housework, Imogen wouldn't have managed as well as she did. Still, she felt a pang of sadness when Mrs Lockhart hurried home after a week with the excuse of a tight publishing deadline. Without family in Cornwall, Imogen felt isolated.

Despite the doctor's warnings her pregnancy had progressed without incident. During the final months she had been extremely tired and short of breath, but she'd rested frequently and once she'd been delivered of the baby she recovered quickly. Apart from a touch of wheeziness when pushing the heavy pram up the hill from the city (the pram a splendid present from her mother), she was otherwise fit and well.

With the birth of their baby, Oliver did indeed cheer up and for a while the three of them inhabited a cosy little world together. Imogen was enchanted by her tiny daughter and completely wrapped up in her. Oliver, being a man and completely unused to babies, held Belle awkwardly and refused to have anything to do with the messier side of childcare so it took longer for him to form a bond with his firstborn, but he got there.

The summer term, then the long holidays, passed. September came and with it, Oliver's new role as deputy head, and the dark times returned. Belle was teething and didn't sleep, which meant that her parents didn't either. Oliver's work meant that there were many evenings of marking and preparing lessons as well as weekend duties. Imogen tried her best to help, sometimes sleeping on a mattress in the nursery so she could attend to Belle without waking her husband. She put the baby to bed early and served dinner on time so that he should feel looked after. She couldn't help yawning with tiredness after the washing-up, though, and fell asleep in her armchair while Oliver worked. Often she'd go up to bed before him and rise early to send him off with a good breakfast. All her efforts, however, could not save him from slipping into a black mood.

This time the depression lasted months and was deeper.

Oliver plodded about the house as though weighed down by a terrible burden. Imogen felt she was watching her every word or gesture in case she said or did something that angered him. He never hurt her, not physically, nor did he say anything really cruel, but it was hard to live without his affection. She became afraid that others were beginning to notice. The wife of one of his colleagues asked her after the school carol service if he was unwell. If she invited anyone round to tea – a neighbour with a baby or one of her old nursing friends – and he arrived home while they were there he'd go upstairs without speaking to them and she'd be furious. That's when the arguments began.

'You need to visit the doctor, Oliver.'

'There's nothing wrong with me.'

'There is.'

'Let me alone. I'll manage it in my own way.'

'So you admit there's something wrong.'

'And what good would it do you if they said I was mad and locked me up?'

'Who are "they"? The doctor would give you some pills, advise that you rest.'

'Imogen, I have a job and responsibilities. The best thing is to keep going.'

'That's clearly not working. Trust me, Oliver, I know something of these things.'

He turned away.

In February 1948 heavy snow began to fall and the temperature dropped. The pavement outside their house became an icy slope. There were days when Imogen and little Belle were effectively marooned and Oliver had to buy what food he could on his way home. It was hard to remain cheerful in these circumstances. Their worlds grew apart. Hers was an indoor life, dark and cold and lonely. He was out all day with other people, busy and important, but when he came home he was either surly or silent. The thaw outside began in March, but the chill that had set into their marriage took longer to melt.

One morning just before Easter when Imogen was out with little Belle, she had a shock. They were coming out of the butcher's with a parcel of stewing beef when she saw a familiar figure watching her from the opposite pavement, hands in his trouser pockets, a small rucksack hanging from his shoulder. It was Ned. For a moment they simply stared at each other, then Imogen lifted her hand in hesitant greeting. At that Ned walked quickly across the road, dodging a bicycle, to meet her with a cheerful smile.

'Imogen, it's good to see you. Who's this little one?' he asked, grinning at thirteen-month-old Belle, who was sitting in her pram wearing a pom-pom hat and clutching a teddy.

'My daughter. I mean ours. Her name's Belle.' Imogen was flustered. It was the first time they'd met since their break-up and his friendliness surprised her.

'She's very like you,' he said.

Imogen laughed. 'That's what everyone says. How are you keeping, Ned? I didn't know you were still in Cornwall. The school moved back to Kent, didn't it?'

'Generally I'm not. The school moved just before Christmas

'forty-five. I had heard on the grapevine that you were still in Truro.'

'Yes, Oliver teaches at the Cathedral School. Another deputy headship in fact.'

The pavement was narrow in this part of the street and people were trying to get round them so Ned stepped off to stand in the road. 'Shall we walk?' he suggested and they began to amble along together, rather aimlessly.

'What's it like in Kent?'

'Everything was in a terrible mess as you might imagine,' he told her. 'Bomb damage to the dormitory block and the games pitches ploughed up to grow vegetables. Still, we're getting back to what passes for normal.'

They'd reached the cathedral and sat down on a bench in the little square outside. It was a breezy day, but the air was warm and the square bathed in sunshine. Ned appeared the same as always, Imogen thought, but she felt on edge, still full of guilt that she'd jilted him. Belle was playing her favourite game of throwing her teddy from the pram and she was glad to avoid Ned's gaze by bending each time to pick it up.

'Nice to have a little girl,' Ned mused. 'A change from boys.'

'Yes, girls are quite different. How are your family, Ned?'

'All well, thankfully.'

'Your brother – Vaughn?'

'He's still living at home.' This was said abruptly and Imogen did not pursue the matter, sensing some sadness there.

She restored the teddy for a sixth time and as she was leaning over the pram, heard voices and glanced up to see a crocodile of young boys in blazers and caps enter the square on their way to the cathedral. A couple of teachers strolled behind them, chatting, and she froze, for one was Oliver. He paused and smiled at her, then seeing her companion the smile vanished and his brow furrowed. He greeted her as he passed, nodded coolly at Ned, then waved at little Belle who cried, 'Dada, dada,' reaching out her arms to him. He hurried by to guide the pupils up the cathedral steps and Belle burst into furious shrieks.

Imogen stood jiggling the pram, trying to hush her, feeling more flustered than ever. Oliver was annoyed, she could see that. Ned, when she glanced at him, wore a faraway look, his lips pressed together. She knew that look all too well. It meant that he was at a loss. Belle finally quietened, distracted by a rattle.

Ned rose, setting his hat on his head more firmly. 'Oliver looked well, I thought. Look, I must be getting along. Meeting someone in fact. That's what brought me to Truro.'

He seemed reluctant to say more and Imogen felt she had no right to ask. Instead she fell into step beside him and after they crossed the main street they parted.

'It was good to bump into you,' Imogen said with false cheerfulness. 'Do send my best wishes to everyone at the school. Especially Miss Edgecumbe. I forgot to ask about her.'

'Miss Edgecumbe left the school. Didn't she let you know?'

'No, we've fallen out of touch. It's a shame, actually. I became rather fond of her.'

'Her mother died suddenly and she returned home to look after her ailing father. I'll find out the address if you like. It's in Kent, not far from the school. Mrs Forbes visits her quite often.'

'That's very kind. I meant to write to her after Belle was born, but somehow it never happened. I should have tried harder, I suppose . . .' She didn't like to say that she'd tried to put St Mary's School out of her mind because of Ned.

'Not easy with a new baby. If you want her address you'd better let me know where you live.'

'Of course. We're up the hill here in Truro, near the hospital.' She watched him write the address down on the back of a receipt which he folded into his wallet.

'There. All safe.'

They grinned at one another with their old affection. Perhaps, she thought as she toiled home up the hill, he'd forgiven her.

Oliver hadn't forgiven, however. When he arrived home later that afternoon, Imogen, in the kitchen giving Belle her tea, heard him shut the front door with an angry click. She called out, 'We're in here.' He did not reply. Instead he came and stood in the doorway to the kitchen and her heart plummeted to see his stormy expression. She scraped the last spoonful of blancmange from the dish, popped it into the child's open mouth and rose, untying her apron, to put the kettle on.

Oliver ruffled his daughter's hair and smiled at her, then disappeared off upstairs, still without speaking. As she wiped Belle's face then set her in her playpen, Imogen listened to his footsteps sounding through the ceiling and the hiss of water in the pipes as he washed. Tears gathered but she blinked them away. Suddenly she felt so weary that she slumped down on a chair and it was there he found her staring at the wall, unseeing, while Belle sat crowing and bashing a rattle on the bars of her pen.

'I'll pour my own tea, shall I?' he remarked, but she leaped up with a murmured 'Sorry' to do it. He took the cup from her with a 'Thank you' and left the room again. She heard him in the sitting room, tossing Belle's toys into a wooden box, the noise of each falling brick a reproach. Anger flashed through her, but she quashed it and instead took Belle upstairs to bathe her. The child was sleepy by the time Imogen laid her in her cot, switched off the main light and set the clockwork merry-go-round playing. By the time the silly tune slowed, Belle's eyes were fluttering and when they were tightly closed, Imogen withdrew, pulling the door to. She waited on the narrow landing for a moment, listening to the sounds of the house. The ticking of the bedroom clock, the rustle of Oliver's newspaper, the wind whistling in the chimney. All peaceful, but as she made her way downstairs she sensed a domestic storm was brewing and her stomach tightened.

In the kitchen she retied her apron and eased the pot of stew from the oven. When she straightened she saw Oliver enter, a glass of whisky in one hand. She set the pot on the table, which she'd laid with a red cloth and the mats with views of Cornwall that her fellow nurses had given them as a wedding present. She was turning to fetch the plates, still warming on the stove, when he spoke.

'You've some explaining to do.'

'Have I?' she said lightly, hanging up the oven gloves.

'What's he doing back in Truro?'

'If you mean Ned, then I don't know exactly. Meeting someone, he said.'

'You, I take it.'

'No, not me. I can assure you I didn't know he was here. We met accidentally. He was passing as I came out of the butcher's.' She took a ladle from a hook and began to spoon out the rich meaty stew. 'We could hardly ignore each other. Why should I want to? Heavens, Oliver, you're not jealous, are you?'

Oliver's face was suffused with colour. His anger was palpable. She felt afraid.

'Of course I'm not. It simply looked odd, that's all. Seeing you and him together on that bench having a cosy chat.'

'I assure you there's nothing for you to worry about. He's safely in Kent most of the time. I expect it was just a flying visit. Quite natural for him to have connections down here still, but this time it wasn't me.'

'This time? You mean there were other occasions?'

'This is getting ridiculous, Oliver. Sit down and eat, please. Shall I cut you some bread?'

Fortunately he obeyed and they sat in silence as they ate, both comforted by the hot rich stew that Imogen had managed to concoct out of the scraps the butcher had sold her. She went over the encounter in her mind. Who had Ned been meeting? What had brought him here? Then she remembered what he'd said about Miss Edgecumbe.

'Apparently she's left the school.' She told Oliver why. 'Ned's going to find out her address for me.'

'He knows where we live?'

'Yes, silly. I told him.'

Oliver glowered but said nothing more and Imogen felt herself relax. The storm had passed without much damage done.

The following day, when emptying a wastepaper basket, a torn-up page from a book met her eye. She fitted the pieces together and realized it was Ned's handwritten dedication from the front of the Cornish guidebook he'd given her. *How petty*, she thought, and tears rose to her eyes.

The promised letter arrived the following week while Oliver was out. Four sides of paper, she saw as she unfolded it. Excessively long for Ned. Miss Edgecumbe's father did indeed live quite near the school – she'd write to her there. She turned the page over and was astonished to read what came next.

'You'll forgive me for not explaining my presence in Truro and must have thought me odd. In truth, I had hoped to see you again and to make things right between us, but there was something I wanted to sort out first. And now I have.

'After we parted on such bad terms I was low, as you might imagine, but I picked myself up and went on as best I could.' Imogen squeezed her eyes shut briefly. Poor Ned. Then she read on.

'Just before the school left Silverwood I met your pal Sarah Summers in Falmouth and she remembered me. She confessed her despair over the loss of her Sam and there we were, a couple of miseries, thrown together. Anyway, I'll leave out the boring bits. Suffice to say that we kept in touch and began to meet up as frequently as we could. This time I came to Truro with the intention of asking her to marry me, and I'm delighted to say that she's made me the happiest of men by saying yes. God knows what she sees in me but there we are. We don't have a date for the wedding yet and her mother is dismayed about her only child leaving Cornwall, so there's much still to discuss. In the meantime I'll be coming down to see her as often as I can and I'd like to suggest that we all meet up. What do you think of that as an idea?'

'I really don't know,' Imogen whispered to herself. She was amazed but delighted at the same time. Good old Summers. She had hardly seen her since leaving the hospital. And good old Ned. Yes, she could imagine them together. What a lovely happy ending. But it wasn't unalloyed delight. She felt shamed that Ned was so forgiving of her having jilting him, and she had long ago worked out that Summers had cooled towards her because she'd been shocked that Imogen had dumped him.

She left the letter on the kitchen table for Oliver to read when he came home. After he'd done so he tossed it down with a harsh laugh.

'Does he really imagine we'd all forget the past and become great chums?'

'Oliver, that's unreasonable. Ned's never been at fault.' She had to admit though that the men had never been friendly. 'He's merely suggested meeting. Actually, I'd love to see Summers again. I miss her. I realize now that she always liked Ned and thought I'd done him a great wrong.

Understandable, given how faithful she was to her poor lost Sam all through the war and there's me chucking Ned aside like a flibbertigibbet. It's rather marvellous, don't you think, that she and Ned have come to love one another?'

Oliver paused, his mouth twisting in puzzlement. 'I don't understand you, Imogen. We think so differently.'

'Not about really important things. I wish we were happier, though. I don't know why we're not happy.'

'Of course we're happy,' he said, looking shocked, but he didn't sound certain.

She pondered this later when she woke before dawn and lay brooding as he slept beside her. Surely it wasn't differing opinions that kept them apart but a lack of care. Did they love each other? Of course she loved Oliver, and she sensed that even through the dark times she was his anchor. So often these days, though, he made her cross and miserable. Perhaps many marriages went through stages like this. Didn't they? No one ever said.

~

Belle's father's voice faded to a halt and for a while he seemed disinclined to continue. After a while he sighed and said, 'Well, I suppose I must go on, but it's hard to admit how neglectful I was, Belle, very hard. There's something more to warn you about. Imogen's notebook is no use after this point. I've had to imagine her feelings on that lovely July day in 1948 when we set forth with Ned and his Sarah.'

Thirty-Nine

'Hop in the back, ladies. Will Belle be all right on your knee, Mrs Dalton?' Ned's roguish tone grated on Oliver. Ned seemed very faux jolly today.

'I'm sure she will be,' Imogen replied. She climbed into Ned's ancient car and took her little daughter from Oliver. Belle snuggled into her as everyone else packed themselves in and the old car moved off with an alarming grinding noise. It was a bright Sunday in July, perfect for a beach visit. Imogen smiled at Sarah Summers sitting next to her on the shabby leather seat, but Summers was staring entranced at Belle, who admittedly looked sweet in the lilac sundress Imogen had made her.

Imogen glanced anxiously at what she could see of Oliver in the front passenger seat. He was sitting stiffly upright, but kept looking round at her, frowning, and she felt a bolt of exasperation. He wasn't even trying to be pleasant to Ned.

The situation was awkward, there was no denying it. Ned had insisted that the four of them – and Belle, of course – meet up as soon as the schools finished for the summer. The car was a recent acquisition, bought for a song from a colleague, but he'd given it a name and talked to it as it strained up the hill out of Truro: 'Come on, Freda!'

'She is a dear, isn't she?' Summers was talking about Belle and this time she met Imogen's eye and smiled.

'She's very good, aren't you, sweetheart?' Imogen kissed Belle's abundant dark hair with its lilac-coloured ribbon.

It was more than two years since Imogen had spent time with her old friend since leaving the hospital. They'd bumped into each other on occasion, but Imogen had been hurt by the other girl's frostiness. Now that Summers was safely engaged to Ned – she and Oliver had been invited to the wedding next month – she was melting again. She'd have to stop thinking of her as 'Summers' after that, Imogen thought. She'd practise saying 'Sarah' today.

They chatted easily, catching up with one another's news, with Oliver listening in. Imogen had known that Ned would be staying with Sarah's parents in Falmouth tonight, but not that Sarah would be giving up nursing at the end of July. Sarah spoke anxiously about the move to Kent after the wedding, worrying how she'd fit into the life of the school, but boasted that Ned had promised that they'd look for their own place as soon as he'd saved enough, then they'd try for a family. She'd miss Cornwall and her parents dreadfully, but one's husband had to come first, didn't he?

Imogen murmured that she supposed he did. In the front Ned was hunched over the wheel, taking the bends slowly, talking cheerfully to Oliver. She couldn't hear Oliver's replies and he kept glancing round at her. Sarah chattered on. Belle fell asleep with her thumb in her mouth in Imogen's arms, making delightful sucking noises.

After half an hour the road sloped steeply down. Shortly before they reached Falmouth, Ned signalled and turned sharp right, with another 'Come on, Freda' as they crawled up a fresh hill. Freda made it safely to the top and the road wound level towards the coast. There was the Helford Estuary. Soon they'd pass the lane that led to Silverwood.

Suddenly, Imogen leaned forward across the sleeping infant and spoke to Ned. 'Would it be an awful nuisance if we stop at the school? Do you remember I left a box of my things there?'

'Oh, Imogen, not now,' Oliver said.

But Ned had already slowed the car. 'We could,' he said over his shoulder, 'though I don't know what happened to them. Or indeed if there's anyone to let us in.'

'Never mind, they're not important. Just some old books and a few letters.' She sat back, resigned.

'And those photographs! We can try.' Ned seemed enthused by the idea. 'I'd like to see the place.' The turn-off down the lane was hidden by rampant greenery, but he took it expertly, and soon Freda was trundling through the tunnels of trees, rounding the bends that took them gently downhill and then between the gateposts to Silverwood.

'Lord!' said Sarah, who'd never seen the place before. It looked the same as it had when Imogen saw it last, the prefab classrooms still standing, although the gravel forecourt was threaded with weeds.

Ned drew to a halt and they all climbed out. The place had a deserted feel and there was an acrid smell in the air, like burning. There was no response to the slamming of the car doors and when Ned pressed the doorbell they heard it echo inside the house but no one came.

'Let's go round the side,' Imogen said to Ned.

'I'll come, too,' Oliver said.

Imogen passed Belle over to a delighted Sarah. Belle gave a wail, but Sarah shushed her whilst the other three walked round under the gateway.

The walled garden was overgrown and the kitchen door was locked when Ned tried it. They continued round to the back, then froze in shock and dismay. Where the eastern wing of the house had been was now a mass of tumbled, blackened brick and sodden charred wood, among which ruined walls, part of the roof and a chimney reached forlornly to the sky.

'My God,' Ned whispered. 'What happened?'

Oliver looked up at the main body of the house. Imogen followed his gaze. The windows were boarded up and fire had daubed the granite with black streaks like sooty tears.

'All right?' Everybody flinched in surprise. A grizzled fellow in overalls cupping a cigarette in his meaty hand was clambering across the debris towards them. Behind him, Imogen glimpsed a wheelbarrow piled high with bricks.

Oliver explained their presence. 'When did this happen?' he asked, hands on hips.

'Few nights ago in the storm.'

He went on to tell them in his soft country accent that he lived in a nearby cottage and had heard a thunderous noise above the sound of the wind. Shortly afterwards he'd seen a sheet of flame light up the sky above the trees. He'd set out to investigate, found this wing of Silverwood aflame and had hurried over to the neighbouring Trebah estate to summon help. With the assistance of a local fire engine, they'd managed to put out the fire before it reached the main house. Mr Penmartin had arrived the next day, found metal casings that led him to declare the cause to be an unexploded bomb and employed him to start clearing up.

His story told, the man returned to his lonely work. Ned, Oliver and Imogen wandered about for a minute or two, stopping occasionally to pick up an old picture in a frame or a hairbrush.

'The only good thing is the house was empty,' Ned sighed as he laid down a damaged bedside lamp. He dusted his hands and held Imogen in a level gaze. 'I don't think there's any point in looking for your box today.'

Oliver shook his head.

'That's what I was thinking,' Imogen said, eyeing the boarded French doors. 'Come on, I've held everyone up long enough.'

She followed Oliver, who'd started round towards the front of the house. Ned fell into step beside her.

'It's sad that Silverwood is wounded,' she sighed. 'It's a very special place and I was happy here.'

'Mmmm. Me too. Most of the time. The last bit was tricky, though.'

She glanced anxiously ahead, fearing that Oliver had heard. 'I'm sorry, Ned,' she replied. 'Have you forgiven me?'

He grinned. 'Just about. I have Sarah now and she's right for me. I see that now.'

'I'm convinced that's true,' she said sincerely.

When they reached the car, it was to find Sarah laughing over Belle's antics as she toddled around on a patch of soft grass studded with daisies.

~

Kynance Cove. A radiant sun, drifts of white cloud across a sky of endless blue. The party made their way carefully down the rocky path towards the golden sand and the dazzling sea, the salty breeze blowing the women's headscarves and lifting the men's hats, Belle shouting in delight from her perch on Oliver's shoulders. Imogen, a bag of towels on her arm, stopped occasionally to look out across the black rocks and the white-topped waves and defied anyone not to feel happy in a landscape like this.

Ned, behind, lugging the picnic basket, was singing 'I do like to be beside the seaside' with special emphasis on the 'pom pom poms', making Belle giggle and Sarah roll her eyes. Even Oliver filled with pleasure out here in the fresh air with the sun on his face. Oh, plodding old Ned had been right to bring them here. Perhaps after all they could erase the past and be friendly.

The beach was busy with visitors, but the tide had started to slide out and they hiked round a rocky outcrop to find a less populous area. There they set up camp right up against the cliff where the sand was firm and dry. Ned spread out a large picnic blanket while Oliver bashed at the poles of the windbreak with a mallet, Sarah poured coffee from a vacuum flask and Imogen tried to stop Belle eating sand. Then off with the infant's sundress and on with a pair of gingham swimming bottoms and a cotton mob cap. Oliver rolled up his trousers and carried his daughter down to the sea where he dangled her chubby feet in the waves, causing her to squeal with delighted terror. Ned brought out his camera and took snapshots. One of Imogen with Belle in her arms. 'I'll send you the prints,' he promised Oliver. 'We have a proper darkroom at the school in Kent. And I've started a photography society. The boys love it.'

A picnic lunch followed – Sarah had brought cheese sandwiches and salad and there were slabs of sponge cake made by Imogen with carefully hoarded sugar. Milk in a flask for Belle and tea in another for everyone else. Then Imogen produced a bucket and spade and Oliver and Ned built sand pies for Belle to smash, while Imogen and Sarah chatted, rolling their skirts above their knees to catch the sun. Later, Imogen rocked her tired daughter until she fell asleep, then wrapped her in a towel and laid her down in the shelter of the windbreak next to Sarah who was reading a magazine.

The sun was long past its zenith now but still dazzling, the strength of it disguised by the cool breeze. Ned's neck reddened, but Oliver had sensibly turned his collar up and was reading a library book. He had worn his air-blue shirt and linen trousers today because Imogen had told him they suited him and he was trying to please her. Ned, lumbering off to catch his hat, which the wind was bowling along the beach, reminded her of Belle's teddy bear.

Oliver looked at his wife and smiled at her and noticed

with dismay her hesitation before she smiled back. He ought
to smile at her more often, he decided, with a rush of love for
her. He reached for her hand and squeezed it gently and they
gazed into one another's eyes. All at once he experienced a
sudden certainty that all was well between them. He lifted
her hand to his lips and kissed her fingers one by one. When
he raised his eyes to hers desire flashed between them. Ned
was coming so they quickly loosed hands and he returned
to his book full of happiness.

Imogen glanced down at Belle, still sleeping, and tucked
the towel more closely round her. Sarah slept too, curled up
on her side, her head resting on her arm and her mouth open.

'I'll fall asleep in a minute, too,' Ned said, sitting down
again. 'A swim, perhaps, Im. Will you join me?'

Imogen glanced at Belle again. Not a flutter of her long
lashes or a twitch of her rosebud mouth. She was deeply
asleep. 'Oliver? Would you mind?'

'Why should I mind,' he said, still replete with happiness. 'You go.'

Ned disappeared behind a rock to change, but Imogen had
only to drag her dress over her head to be ready in the ruffled
navy swimming costume she'd bought specially for the day.
Oliver sent her a smouldering look and she giggled.

Ned returned in black trunks, which Oliver thought made
him appear a little tubby.

Oliver smiled at Imogen. She gave him a little wave, then
cast a last glance at Belle and Sarah.

'Two sleeping beauties,' Ned said with a smile. 'Come on,
race you.'

'Not if I can help it.'

Oliver watched as they ran laughing to the water.

Ned got there first, but waded in slowly, crying 'Brrrr' at the cold and rubbing his arms, but Imogen plunged in without fuss. She dived under a wave, then surfaced sleek as a seal and gasped, 'I won! I won!' Ned roared comically in response and started after her, but a wave broke over him and knocked him off his feet. She laughed at his efforts to recover his balance, then started to swim out, bobbing over the crests of the breakers towards calmer water.

Oliver shaded his eyes and watched their antics with lazy interest. He drew a pair of field glasses from his knapsack, unwound the strap and trained them on his wife. Imogen's movements were so graceful, he thought admiringly, as she coursed through the water. Stocky Ned, on the other hand, had the appearance of an awkward walrus. He lowered the glasses and returned to the book, but the sun was strong and the words were starting to dance on the page.

He sighed and gave up, lifted his face to the sun, enjoying its warmth. All in all, the day wasn't going too badly. He'd been dreading it, seeing Ned again, fearing it would stir up buried feelings. Jealousy, fear. Fear that Imogen would leave him. He'd always seen when he'd taught at Silverwood how close she was to Ned. She acted naturally with him, laughed and chatted, came alive. She'd never been quite the same with him, Oliver, her husband, but he was beginning to realize that this might be partly his fault. Starting today he'd try harder to be different, more loving.

He'd always wanted her, from the moment they'd met by

accident in that harbour-front café in Falmouth. The sympathy in her eyes when he'd poured out his grief about his brother. Seeing her up close, the sprinkling of freckles across her nose, the pulse beating in her upturned wrist as she'd poured the tea, and later that day, the tender way she'd helped the oil-soaked victims of the *Lancastria*, poor sods.

He'd felt such relief, such gratitude when, two years later, they'd met after the bombing raid on the hospital and she'd responded to his advances.

He'd been proud then of her achievements. She'd laboured so hard to become a nurse, had been more use than he had in those days.

But he'd played his hand badly, he wasn't sure why. He hadn't felt sure of her, that was it, and thought she'd pulled back too, her war work an excuse. He'd been a fool not to keep things going with her, to write more regularly. He'd lived in his head, become obsessed with proving himself in this war as she had done, to show himself as good as his brother Andrew. Even now he didn't know if he'd achieved that. When he thought about his time in France, which he tried not to, he thought he'd done no more than simply got through. He'd survived. Even that, he admitted now, was partly down to Imogen. Whenever he'd felt like throwing in the towel, he'd thought of her and made one last effort. 'No heroics,' he remembered she'd instructed him. He gave a flicker of a smile whenever he recalled this. His war had certainly not been about heroics; it had simply involved obeying orders.

Then for a long time after he'd returned home, he didn't feel worthy of her. All the things he'd seen and done, he could not forget. That concentration camp they'd liberated. He'd witnessed there the worst of what so-called civilized human beings could do to one another and felt tainted by it. Imogen had been right. He should have sought help to deal with his feelings, but what was he but one among many who were struggling. Even now he did not believe he was worth saving.

Maybe if he sought help their marriage would be easier. He cursed himself for all the unhappiness he'd caused by his moods, his silences, the petty jealousies. Yes, he would do something about it for the sake of their marriage, for Belle. God, how he loved them both.

He touched his field glasses to his eyes and looked out to sea. It took a moment for him to see her. There she was, thirty, fifty yards beyond the other swimmers. He followed her bobbing head, admired the elegant way her arms entered the water. She really was a long way out now, he thought with unease, but he supposed it was all right. The water appeared peaceful.

A movement by the windbreak caught his attention. Belle was stirring. Sarah, too, awoke and stretched her limbs. 'Sorry,' she murmured, sitting up and rubbing her eyes. 'I hope I wasn't snoring. Where are the others?'

Oliver pointed.

'Goodness,' Sarah said, squinting to see. 'I can see Imogen, but where's Ned?'

'To the left. Closer in. He's had enough, I think. He's heading in.'

Sarah rose, yawning, and brushed sand from her legs. Belle woke properly and cried out. Sarah bent and unwrapped her, made soft soothing noises as she changed her nappy, then passed her into her father's waiting arms.

'Shall we look for Mummy?' Oliver hauled himself upright. 'No, leave the strap.' He freed the field glasses with his spare hand. 'Now where is she?' he muttered, sweeping the bay for Imogen. 'My God, she's way out now.'

He hurried down towards the water with Belle, Sarah in pursuit. He stood in the shallows, staring anxiously out to the sea. Ned surfed a wave and surfaced near them, waist-deep, then seeing their agitation, turned to follow their gaze. He stilled, then plunged back into the sea, swimming for all he was worth towards Imogen's distant, flailing figure.

Bystanders noticed the little party's distress, began calling to one another and pointing. A burly young man plunged in after Ned, taking the breakers with ease, then ploughing out past him.

'We need the coastguard,' Oliver said, looking round wildly, despatched a spindly youth who set off obediently toward the cliff. Oliver handed Belle to Sarah and began to wade out into the water, but quickly retreated.

'I can't swim!' he cried to Sarah. 'My god, I can't swim!'

He lifted the field glasses once more and swept the horizon. 'I can't see her!' he shouted. 'Where is she?'

Far out beyond the waves he could make out Ned treading water and gazing around him with a bewildered expression like a dog that had lost its ball. Then slowly, steadily, he began swimming back to the shore in long slow strokes.

Forty

1966

'She'd gone. My beloved Imogen had gone.'

Belle's father's voice died away and for a long while there was silence as Belle absorbed the shocking fact of Imogen's fate. Tears filled her eyes. Slowly she became aware again of the playing of the breeze on her face, the rhythmic sound of the turning waves. She tucked a stray lock of hair behind her ear. A lump had formed in her throat that hindered her speaking. She reached for her father's hand. He clutched hers back and stared out across the water.

'I was there on the beach,' Belle said slowly. 'I was there with you, but I don't remember. Dad, I don't remember Imogen. I don't remember a thing about it. Even with the help of that photograph. It feels so wrong that I can't recall.'

'Of course you don't remember. You were only a baby,' he said softly, stroking her hand. 'You cried for your mother that day and for many days after and I felt utterly helpless. You simply weren't the same child. For a long time you turned inward, lost your cheerful nature. We just pegged along, you and I.'

'It's ... difficult to know how I'm meant to feel, what to say except that I'm so sorry that it happened, Dad.'

He put his arm round her and drew her close. 'I should have told you a long time ago, Belle. Jill wanted me to, but I could never bring myself. It would have shattered your safe world. She threatened to tell you, you know, on more than one occasion, but I was so angry at the idea that she never did. Poor woman, I don't know how she's put up with me all these years.' He smiled fondly.

'Because she's lovely Mum,' Belle said with a short laugh. 'You haven't told me what happened after, though. After you lost sight of Imogen. How long did they search for her?'

She felt her father breathe a deep sigh. 'The current had taken her right out to sea. By the time a helicopter picked her up it was too late to save her. You can imagine the confusion, us waiting and watching on the beach. Other people, complete strangers, were marvellous.

'I've not described to anyone since the inquest exactly what happened that day. Not even, in detail, to Jill.' His voice was heavy with sadness. 'It turned out that Imogen had been consulting the doctor again about breathlessness. Lung damage from her illness in 1944. The coroner recorded it a contributing factor. The funeral was dreadful; so was afterwards, trying to establish some form of normality.'

'Of course ...' she echoed.

'I employed a local woman to look after you. Kate something. Walker. Mrs Walker. She was fond of babies. Her own had grown up and gone.'

'I don't remember her either.'

'Nice woman. She was with us for a whole year. Then the miracle happened. I met Jill.'

'Mum. I know that bit of the story. You met on holiday, didn't you? In Wales. Was I there?'

'No. Mrs Walker took you for the week. I'd always wanted to see Edward the First's castles. Harlech, Caernarfon, Conwy. I rented a car and took myself off, stayed in guest houses along the way. I met Jill on the second day. I was reading a notice on a wall at Harlech, when something cold hit my cheek. When I looked up, there was a young woman eating an ice cream looking down from the parapet.'

'And she burst into giggles.'

'That's right.'

'And then she hurried down to apologize and you learned that she was on holiday with Aunt Avril and Uncle Vic, who were home from India on leave, and you ended up taking her to tea.'

'She was irresistibly pretty, Belle. Dark wavy hair, enormous blue eyes.'

'I know what Mum looks like, silly!'

'Only twenty-two, she was then. Too young to have seen the worst of the war and that's what was refreshing. She was happy, loved life. With her I could start again. Not forget, no, never that. I used to ask her why she would take on an older man like me and his motherless child and her answer was always the same. That she loved me. She loved me, Belle, with all my faults. It was marvellous. It still is. And she loves you – but you know that, of course. The first time the two of you met, it was wonderful. You toddled over to her at once and she lifted you into her arms and you laid your small head on her shoulder, your thumb in your mouth.'

Belle smiled tenderly at the thought.

'And I wouldn't say that it was easy after that, but everything was lighter. After we married she moved in with us in Truro, then we decided that it would be best to start again somewhere else. And since Jill's parents lived in Surrey that's where we ended up. I got the job at the grammar. We lived with them for a few months before we bought our current house. They were an enormous help with you and Jackie.'

'I miss Grandad so much.' Jill's father had died five years before.

'So do I. He was a fine man and I learned a great deal from him. He'd been in the trenches and I felt he understood what I'd gone through. Not that we dwelt on it much, but he'd pass the odd comment. As you know, he was a man of few words. He liked to show his love through doing things for people.'

'I suppose he wasn't really my grandad either.' Belle's voice cracked.

Her father caught her other hand and turned to face her. 'He was. You mustn't think like that. He loved you every bit as much as he loved Jackie. Your grandma does too. To her there is no difference between you.'

She bowed her head and nodded, knowing it to be true.

'Coo-ee!' They both looked up to see Mrs Kitto standing

further up the beach. Belle's father rose and Belle followed him to meet her. 'Sorry to interrupt,' Mrs Kitto said, 'but there's been a telephone call. It's from your mum, Belle. She and Jackie are at Truro Station waiting for a train to Falmouth. They'll need picking up from the station.'

'Mum's coming?' Belle's spirits rose.

'She said she might.' Her father twinkled at her. 'I telephoned her last night and gave her Miss Edgecumbe's number.'

'Mrs Kitto, Dad, not Miss Edgecumbe. Where will they stay? Not in the main house, surely?'

'Don't you worry about that,' Mrs Kitto smiled. 'I've three bedrooms and I imagine they'll be more comfortable with me.'

As they walked back up to the cottage together to collect the car, Belle asked her father, 'What happened to Ned and Sarah? Did they marry?'

'They did,' her father said. His pace slowed and she realized with dismay that she'd prodded another tender place. 'They still wanted me to go to the wedding, but I couldn't face it.'

'I went,' Mrs Kitto said and a soft expression stole over her face. 'It was a beautiful service in a parish church in Falmouth. And a reception at a local hotel. They looked very happy, I must say, and they were married by the very special man who later became my husband! The Reverend Charles Kitto.'

'That's where you first met him?' Belle's voice was bright with interest.

'Yes, along with his lovely wife, who, as it turned out, I

knew slightly from my nursing days. And after she died I wrote him a letter of condolence and ... well, this isn't the place for my story. We were talking about Ned and Sarah.'

'What happened next. I mean, do you hear from them?'

'Yes,' Mrs Kitto said, her eyes alight, 'Sarah and I became very close after my father died and I returned to the school for a while. She was lonely at first in Kent, having left her family and friends behind in Cornwall, but she eventually found her feet. We still exchange cards at Christmas. They have two children, both boys. And they still live in Kent. Ned's a headmaster now at a prep school near Tunbridge Wells.'

'Think what you like of me, but I couldn't bear to see them after that awful day,' Belle's father muttered. 'I always blamed Ned for what happened. He should have looked after Imogen.'

Belle glanced at Mrs Kitto, who said nothing. But then neither of them were in a position to accept or deny that Belle's father was right. Belle felt desolate. To think of all the years that had passed and her father still nursed resentment in his heart.

Belle and her father were quiet as they drove the few miles to the station. Belle was looking forward to seeing her mother and sister again, but she dreaded it, too, for she must regard them in the light of her new knowledge. Mum was still her mum, she told herself fiercely. Nothing had really changed. But of course it had. The unsettling words she'd heard Aunt Avril utter on her sixteenth birthday had been only the start. And now she knew about her real mother and the circumstances of her birth, she felt so much worse.

Imogen's story had touched her beyond belief, but Belle still found it difficult to feel an emotional connection to the woman and to deal with her father's obvious distress. It was all such a tangle. Just at that moment the strands of a song that Gray loved to sing crept into her mind, *'Only time will tell,'* it went, *'only time will tell.'* That brought thoughts of Gray with it and she smiled to herself. Before they'd left she'd slipped into the house to tell him where she and father were going. At first she couldn't find him and had called out, then followed the sound of his answering voice. He was in Angel's room chatting to Janey, or rather Janey was doing most of the talking while changing the bedding ready for the boy's return. Gray was busy tidying the shelves, arranging the books and the toys. A bright Indian rug from the hall covered the threadbare carpet. The window stood wide and the curtains billowed in the light breeze. The stale air had blown away.

'It's to welcome him back when he comes,' Gray explained.

'He'll love it,' Belle replied and with a rush of warmth. 'Gray, I'll explain properly later, but my mum is coming and my sister Jackie. Dad and I are off to fetch them.'

Gray looked surprised, but he smiled and nodded.

She turned to Janey. 'Will that be all right, Janey? They'll sleep at the cottage but it's quite a lot for Mrs Kitto to feed.'

'There's always plenty of food in the pot,' Janey said, looking thoughtful. Poor Janey, the good news about Angel had come as a massive relief, but this was tempered by Chouli leaving so suddenly. Janey had been quite upset, especially since Sirius had refused to discuss the matter. Belle still thought Chouli had done the sensible thing.

As her father drove, the lines from the song played in her mind. '*Time will tell . . . time will tell.*' There were things she had to do, to work out, to plan. And if her family were still here on Friday, perhaps they'd come to The Ship to hear her sing.

She smiled to herself as the car turned into the station yard.

And there they were, Mum and Jackie, waiting on the pavement with their luggage; Mum, neat and pretty in a linen sheath dress, smiling and waving, and Jackie, a self-conscious teenager in jeans, her shy grin half hidden by her long fair hair, and Belle waved back, her heart swelling with happiness. When the car stopped she jumped out and ran into her mum's familiar embrace where she felt perfectly at home.

Forty-One

Friday evening in Falmouth, blustery rain, mist over the sea, but it hadn't deterred the punters. The Ship was full of people divesting themselves of raincoats, shoving wet umbrellas in odd corners, crowding the bar. The air smelled of beer and tobacco smoke overlain with something headier and sweeter. And the noise! Chattering, laughing, the shouting of orders. At the far end of the overheated room, Belle sat with Gray and Stu. Gray's blond head was bent over his guitar as he tuned up and Stu, lamplight glinting off his round spectacles, was polishing his flute with a soft cloth.

Belle smiled and waved across at the Silverwood contingent. They had arranged themselves around two tables pushed together under the window. Francis, Sirius, Arlo, Belle's parents and Jackie, large-eyed, overwhelmed. Even Janey had come this time. The only ones missing were Rain and Angel. Belle had invited Mrs Kitto, but she'd demurred, saying it wasn't her sort of thing. And now the landlord rang a bell for attention.

'Shut it, all of you, it's time for what you came for and that's not just pints of Tribute! Girls and boys, please welcome The Witchers!'

Belle felt lifted by the swell of applause as Gray strummed an introduction and he launched into the first song. It was 'Love Among the Willows', the one she'd first heard him sing in that Derbyshire village pub, the Black Dog, all those weeks ago – another world, and it still wove enchantment round her, with its plaintive lyrics and the swinging beat of the chorus. The audience loved it and Gray smiled as they clapped, then he segued easily into a brighter number to which Stu played his flute and Belle sang a descant. It set the feet tapping.

After that he introduced Belle as 'my bewitching third Witcher'. The dreamy 'Silverwood' they sang as a duet with deep emotion, after which there was a respectful silence before the applause began, loud cheering coming from the Silverwood contingent.

Half a dozen more songs, a couple sung by Stu and Gray together, then Gray announced the interval. He'd hardly set down his guitar before a portly young man in checked trousers and holding a cigarette between his fingers pushed a way to Gray's side.

'Jerry's the name, Bill Jerry. Comus Productions.' He handed Gray a business card. 'Expect you've heard of us.'

Gray studied the card and passed it to Stu then looked up at Mr Jerry, brushing the hair from his eyes. 'I know who you represent,' he said, narrowing his eyes. 'Faery, is that right?'

'Faery, among others, yes. I like what I've heard tonight. Looking forward to the second half, but I need to rush off at the end. Thought I'd get a word in now. You lot fit what we're looking for. Come and see us sometime. Portobello Road near the Electric Cinema. Phone number's on the card.'

'Thank you,' Gray said, his face cast in pleased surprise. 'Thank you very much.' Stu passed back the card, which Gray slipped into his shirt pocket. The man winked at Belle, then vanished back into the crowd. The three of them stared at one another, but before anyone could say anything, Francis came across carrying two brimming pint glasses and a half-pint on a tray.

'Who was that character?' he said, handing round the drinks.

'Oh, just a band promoter,' Gray said airily, plucking the card from his pocket to show him. 'We might give him a call sometime, eh, Stu?'

'Fine by me!' Stu said in his quiet voice.

'Comus, eh?' Francis said wonderingly, turning it over. 'Means nothing to me.'

'They manage some big names,' Gray said casually. He sat up straight, took a long draught of beer, then smiled at Belle, his eyes glowing sapphires of satisfaction, and she grinned back. She hadn't heard of Comus either, but she knew of the folk band Faery and gauged that the encounter was important. 'Don't say anything to the others yet,' he begged Francis, 'in case it comes to nothing.'

'It must come to something,' Belle said with feeling.

Gray started tuning up for the second half and Belle's apprehension grew, for after the first song with Stu, it was her turn. When the moment came she took up her guitar and spoke out bravely. 'This is a song I've written myself. It's a love song and it's inspired by my time here. I think Cornwall's the most beautiful place on earth and, um, anyway, I hope you like it.' The crowd were quiet. The first chord sounded tentative, but as she played the introduction her confidence grew. She closed her eyes, took a deep breath, held the right note in her mind as Gray had trained her and began to sing. *'Whenever I hear your name/It takes me back, takes me back/To a war I did not want to fight/A love I could not bear to lose.'*

The words had come to her one night and as she'd dwelled on them the following day, the tune had started to coil around them. After that time she'd tested the harmonies out on Gray, she'd worked on it further until it was perfect. As she sang it now, her voice caught on the saddest phrases, conveying the full strength of emotion as she sang of a lost love. It was her only solo this evening and after she'd finished, it was as though the audience was holding its collective breath and only a glass clinked into the silence. Then someone – possibly her dad – began to clap and after that the applause was tumultuous. Belle blinked in delighted amazement.

The most nerve-wracking part of the performance over, she could now properly enjoy herself and together the three of them put their heart and soul into the final few songs.

After the encore – a short duet called 'Poles Apart' in which the tunes wove cleverly in and out of each other without quite meeting – people crowded round to offer their congratulations. Stu slipped off to the bar, where he sat eating crisps and chatting to fans, quite content.

Belle glanced around for Bill Jerry, the promoter, but he

had indeed already left. 'He went just before the encore,' Francis said as he swept them up to join the Silverwood party. Sirius, Arlo and Janey moved up to make room for Belle to sit opposite her family at one end of the table. Gray, next to her, reached for her hand. Belle sat bemused. The pride on her parents' faces was all she had longed for.

'I hadn't realized we'd been nursing such talent!' her father said, beaming. 'Can't think where you got it from. My family aren't musical.'

'From Imogen perhaps, don't you think, dear?' Belle's mum whispered.

Her father frowned, but then his expression cleared and he nodded. 'Yes, of course. Imogen had a beautiful singing voice. She loved the cathedral services,' and the tension left Belle's shoulders. Perhaps now they would talk about her real mother in a natural way.

Jackie, sitting between her parents with downturned mouth, said nothing. Belle gathered that their mum had now explained everything to her, but she wondered if Jackie had taken it in. Belle had been so intent on her own feelings, but it must be troubling for her fifteen-year-old sister to have learned such a devastating family secret.

'Jacks, shall we take Figgy out for a walk tomorrow?' she said gently. Jackie loved all animals.

'Oh, yes please,' Jackie said, her eyes lighting up. They held one another's gaze, and Belle felt an unusual urge to reach out and hug her sister, but satisfied herself by making their private childhood sign, a flicking motion using thumb and forefinger. Its origin was long forgotten but it was their version of a thumbs-up. Jackie smiled and flicked back. Whatever the precise biological nature of their relationship, Belle was determined that they should always completely and utterly be sisters.

Forty-Two

Long after Belle had said goodnight to her parents and sister at the gate of Mrs Kitto's cottage, and the other inhabitants of Silverwood had gone to their beds, she and Gray and Stu sat in the kitchen talking, too excited to feel sleepy.

Bill Jerry's business card lay on the table between them. Every now and then Gray picked it up and examined it as though it was something precious. It was, to him. As he said to Stu, it could change everything. Apart from Francis, they hadn't told anyone else about the approach. It was too new and fragile and the opportunity might vanish like a Cornish mist.

'If they took us on, they'd record our stuff. We'd tour and they'd pay for everything. At least, I think that's how it works, we'd have to find out. And we could divide everything by three.'

'It sounds wonderful, but surely you mean two, not three. It's you and Stu they want.'

'He said all of us, I'm sure he did,' Stu said warmly.

'If so, he was being kind. I'm not a proper member of The Witchers.'

'Belle, don't be like that,' Stu said. 'A girl singer is important, especially a pretty one.'

'That's exactly what I mean,' she said, triumphant. 'They'd want me for what I look like, not because I'm a musician.'

'You're both – pretty and talented,' Gray ventured.

'You don't understand, either of you.'

'I need you with me, right, and Stu agrees.'

'So you want me to go with you because I'm a girl.'

'We want you because they want The Witchers and that's you, Stu and me.'

Belle thought about this for a moment and despite everything couldn't help feeling a frisson of excitement. 'What if it doesn't work?' she said in a small voice.

Gray sighed and rolled his eyes. 'We can but try.'

There was no answer to that so they finished their tea and went to bed. Gray fell asleep soon after they turned the light out. Belle lay awake. She was overtired now, wound up. Too much was happening too quickly and there was so much she was unsure of. Top of that list was her future with Gray.

He loved her. She knew that by the way he looked at her, the gentle way he made love to her, his care. Yet he, the artist, the wordsmith, had never actually said the words to her, though she'd whispered them to him once or twice during their lovemaking. Tonight, they'd talked about the longer term for the first time, but it had been about their music, not about their relationship. It was no good. She must take responsibility for herself.

Up until now she'd followed where he'd led, trusting him. He'd brought her to Silverwood, portraying it as a Shangri-La, a paradise set apart from the world.

Now living at Silverwood had proved to be otherwise, with Angel ill, Chouli gone home and Rain's vision dimmed, Belle knew she wouldn't stay. She wasn't comfortable with the kind of life they lived, which to her seemed without proper purpose or foundation. The members of the community weren't equal. Janey and Chouli were exploited, the child neglected. Belle had begun to recognize that in many ways she was quite traditional. She liked a structured life and to be part of the world. She loved her family. Rain and Sirius and possibly Arlo were selfish at heart.

But what should she do? Part of her badly wanted to resume her university course, despite its frustrations, for life to return to what it had been, secure and structured, but that could never be. By finding out about Imogen, the structures of her life had been shaken. She hadn't taken everything in yet and she felt scared.

She smiled as she remembered how happy they'd all been tonight, eating together in the big kitchen, Mum asking Janey about recipes and growing tomatoes, Dad discussing contemporary art with Sirius, showing a knowledge she didn't know he possessed, although he still declared a lot of it 'rubbish'. Sirius didn't mind. He liked a good argument and didn't seem bothered if he didn't win.

Unlike her father. She understood better the roots of his

anger and bitterness now, though she wondered if he would
ever change. He'd been in charge of school discipline for too
many years and was probably stuck that way like an old tree
twisted by the wind. She was finding it hard, too, to come to
terms with his silence about the hidden years of her infancy.
At least in this she would receive plenty of love and reassurance from her mum.

An owl hooted in the darkness, an eerie sound, though
Belle was used to it now. Just as she had accepted that she
must leave Silverwood, she realized how much she'd come to
love it. She'd often felt directionless here, but she'd actually
learned a great deal about herself and about the adult world.
And she was in love for the first time in her life. Would she
and Gray stay together if she went back to her studies and
he went back on the road? That was another conundrum.
Nobody could work that out for her. She'd have to do it herself.

Restless, she rose and went to the open window, lifted the
curtain and leaned on the sill to breathe the cool night air.
It was a lovely night, with a moon veiled in a drift of cloud
rising above the cottage. She sniffed at a woody scent and
heard the owl again, further away this time. It was strange
to think that her mother had lived here, maybe in this very
room, and experienced it all first. Realizing made her feel
close to her in a way she hadn't before.

There were many ways in which her life had touched
Imogen's. Like her birth mother, Belle knew what it was to
love with a passion, to feel conflicted about what to do with
her life. She was still trying to accept that her beloved mum
Jill had not given birth to her or been part of her early infancy,

yet she couldn't remember Imogen in any respect. There was just that photograph of herself as an infant with Imogen on the beach. On the day that her mother had drowned.

Belle closed her eyes and rested her arms on the sill, trying to concentrate on the memory of the photograph in Mrs Kitto's sitting room. Perhaps by doing so, she'd remember Imogen. Rain had said she was good at sinking into a meditative state.

At that thought, her eyes flew open. The events she'd experienced in those sessions with Rain, when she'd felt as though she was swimming underwater, that others were calling her back . . . how disturbing they had been. Could they be connected to what happened to Imogen? Surely not. Belle herself had not been in the water then. She'd been on the shore, safe in her father's arms. But still . . .

The breeze picked up and she shivered, then pulled the window to and returned to bed. Snuggling up close to Gray, warmed by his body, she fell into a deep, dreamless sleep.

Forty-Three

Belle met Jackie at the cottage the next morning, a Saturday, and they took Figgy for a walk across pastures and alongside the river beneath tangles of trees. The path occasionally dropped down to one of the several small beaches that indented the bank and here the dog obligingly chased sticks that the girls threw into the water. Belle had always felt a mixture of affection and irritation towards her younger sister, and they rarely discussed anything important. The large age gap was mostly responsible. This time, however, a serious talk was impossible to avoid. Belle tried to reassure her sister that nothing in their tightknit family had really changed. Seeing Jackie brighten and lark about with Figgy on the journey back, Belle saw that she'd done a good job. Jackie was happy again.

It was Belle who must adjust. There was now a fifth presence in their family of four and it occurred to Belle that she'd always sensed Imogen's shadow. Since the secret had come out, the shape of this shadow was clearer. It was not a dark frightening shadow, but a sad ghost of one. She did not know if it could ever be laid to rest. Or should be. After all, now that she knew about Imogen as a person, she did not want to ever forget her.

So lost in thought was she that she mistook a turning and it wasn't until they arrived at the field with the standing stones that Belle realized where they were. With a delighted cry, Jackie ran towards them and began to caper among them like a child.

Belle followed, laughing. 'Watch out!' she cried. 'You'll be turned to stone.' Then seeing Jackie's confusion, she explained about the village maidens who'd been punished for dancing on the Sabbath.

Jackie grinned. 'I bet that's not true.' She must have heard enough extraordinary stories for one day. Suddenly she cried, 'That's our cottage!' and ran ahead with Figgy in hot pursuit.

Belle watched her lift the dog over a stile and trudged behind more slowly. When she reached the cottage it was to find Mrs Kitto in the kitchen brewing coffee, her parents and sister sitting at the table, Figgy lying panting under it. The cat watched proceedings from the safety of the window-sill. When Belle entered, everyone looked up with smiles of welcome.

'You enjoyed your walk, I gather,' her father said, then continued without pausing. 'Your mother and I were just saying that we'd better go home this morning. I'm on sidesman duty at church tomorrow and we're expected for lunch at your aunt and uncle's.'

Jackie screwed up her face in protest, but her father said, 'And yes, you do have to come. It's Uncle Vic's birthday.'

'You're welcome to come home with us, Belle,' her mum said gently, 'but if you'd prefer to stay—'

'Then that's fine,' her father finished. They looked at Belle expectantly while Mrs Kitto quietly poured coffee.

'Please come,' Jackie whispered. 'There's nothing to do at Aunt Avril and Uncle Vic's.'

Belle took a deep breath. 'I can't, Jackie,' she said. 'I'm sorry. Perhaps you'd sign his card for me. Oh, don't look so glum!'

To her parents she said, 'I'm not ready, I'm afraid. I've things to sort out here.'

Her father nodded. 'Of course. I half expected you to say that. Take all the time you need.'

Wow, Belle thought. He was finally treating her as a grown-up. 'I haven't forgotten about that university exam,' she assured him, 'but no promises.'

He inclined his head but said nothing.

The conversation turned to the practicalities of the journey. Mrs Kitto offered to cut sandwiches for their lunch. Jackie, her interest perhaps piqued by the Dancing Maidens, asked tentatively if they could stop at Stonehenge on the way and was surprised when her request was granted without their father's usual grumbling that they should go 'straight home'.

Heartened by this, Belle asked her parents, 'Have you got time to come to the house with me. I want to show you something quickly. It's to do with Imogen.'

'Of course,' he said. 'And we'd like to say a proper goodbye to your young man.'

'Don't call him that,' she sighed. 'It sounds so . . .'

'Old-fashioned? And I don't suppose you're "courting" either?'

'Dad!' Belle raised her eyes to the ceiling. 'Of course you can see him. Just don't embarrass me by asking what his intentions are or his prospects or anything like that.'

'I'm used to teaching young men, don't forget.'

'Gray isn't "young men". He's Gray.'

Her father raised his palms in mock defence. 'All right. I understand.'

'Good.' She grinned.

'You go with your father,' Belle's mum said softly. 'I'll follow in a bit.'

'It's much the same as I remember,' her father said, looking round. He and Belle were standing in the old library. 'But shabbier.' He ran his finger through the dust on a shelf. 'Housekeeping is not your lot's strong point, is it?'

'Never mind that. It's this we came to see.' Belle bent over the shelves of children's books and worked the hidden mechanism. The door of the secret room swung towards them and she smiled as her father's eyebrows shot up.

He followed her inside, wincing at the cobwebs. 'Good Lord, I never suspected this room was here.'

'You wouldn't have done. You'd left the school by the time Ned discovered it. The box of Imogen's books was over there. Ned left them in the library cupboard, but somehow they ended up in here.'

'I never asked about that box again. Where is it now?'

'I have her engagement diaries upstairs.' She told him about Arlo taking the box. 'He says there were photographs in it and he wanted to show Francis.'

'What photographs?'

'I don't know exactly. He was sort of shouting at me.'

'If you won't ask him or Francis then I suppose you won't find out.'

'Dad.' His clipped tones goaded her to say something that was on her mind. 'The way you described things, it sounds as though you weren't exactly kind to Imogen.'

They were standing close. He turned away, but not before she caught an expression of intense pain that crossed his face. *I've gone too far this time.*

He paced the little room, ducking to examine a hook nailed onto a beam, turning over the bedding with his foot. It was a while before he straightened, and then he did not meet her eye.

'Do you think I've not known that and had to live with it?' The voice was low, full of desperation. 'All these years I've regretted my behaviour. I took out my moods on her and refused to seek help for my difficulties. I was jealous of Ned, their easy friendship. I was starting to realize, to try to make good – and then it was too late. As I said, for a long time I blamed Ned for her death. It was he who suggested they swim, he who let her go out too far while he swam nearer the beach. But it was I who had never learned to swim and could not help. Do you know, there was a red flag flying because of the currents? I should have noticed it.'

'You can swim, though,' Belle said, puzzled. She remembered it was Gray who couldn't.

'Jill made me learn.' He smiled, then sighed. 'All these years of blaming others, and now I realize that the only person who needs forgiveness is myself. I must ask your forgiveness, Belle, and I should ask Ned's. I cut them dead, him and Sarah. They were grieving too and must have been hurt by my behaviour.'

'And me?'

'And you. You lost your beloved mother.'

'It really wasn't your fault she drowned.'

'It was my fault that our short marriage wasn't always easy.'

'But then you'd gone through so much. Perhaps you couldn't help it.'

'I should have done what she said, consulted a shrink about it. Instead I took it out on her. Our home was a haven, but I abused it. Oh, I've wasted so much time, Belle. All these years. But I've been lucky, too. I have your mum and you and Jackie and I don't think I've appreciated you all enough. But now I do and I must ask for your forgiveness.'

'Of course I forgive you, Dad. Don't be daft.'

'Do you?' He smiled at her and the tension left his face. He looked many years younger and with the light of his smile she saw how handsome he must have been as the young man with whom her mother had fallen in love. Love took away fear, didn't it, and love forgave. Belle stepped over and hugged him, pressing her face against his warm, wool-scented breast and, with a sigh of relief, he hugged her back.

'Do you know,' she said when they returned to the library, 'there's something important I do remember. Going to a big house with stained glass windows that threw coloured light over a wooden floor. And there was a Christmas tree covered in lit candles and a scent of oranges. Where was that?

'Your maternal grandmother's house,' he said at once. 'In Hertfordshire. I took you there for Christmas the year you were three and your Great-Aunt Verity was there, too with her husband and three grown-up sons, Imogen's cousins – I wish I hadn't lost touch with them.' He smiled. 'I liked Mrs Lockhart, your grandmother. She wasn't much good at mothering, but she tried her best with you. That christening bracelet you still have, I think. She gave you that.'

'Oh, Dad, I didn't know. It needs mending. I should have told you.' She sighed. 'I think I do just about remember her as a kind presence.'

'She was kind, yes. But much diminished by her daughter's death. Our visits were awkward, but I wanted you to know one another. She died when you were five. Left you some money in trust until you're twenty-one. That's when I was going to tell you about Imogen. When you were twenty-one. It's not a life-changing amount, but it is substantial. Her Norah Gentles detective stories did particularly well in America.'

'Oh, Dad!' Belle breathed, hardly able to take this in. 'There was one of her books in Imogen's box.'

'We have a few at home. Belle, I think it would be best to keep the matter of the money to yourself at present. You don't want anyone to try to take advantage. Not that I'm saying—'

'I understand what you mean,' she said quickly. He was referring to the inhabitants of Silverwood. The money wasn't to be hers for almost another two years, though, so it was safe enough for the moment. As they walked back through the hall she thought of something she'd do with it when she got it. She would give some to Jackie. That would be fair. Dad would advise her.

They found Mum and Jackie chatting to Gray in the kitchen. Or, at least, Mum and Gray were chatting and Jackie was listening and stroking Figgy, who had his head on her lap.

Belle hovered in embarrassment as her father asked Gray more about his musical ambitions, but she needn't have worried. New horizons motivated Gray to speak of his work with seriousness and technical knowledge. She could tell that her father was won over. When they said goodbye, she was surprised to see the men shake hands. Gray smiled courteously at Belle's mother and sister and wished them a safe journey. She left him standing at the kitchen window waving as she escorted her family back to the cottage to collect their luggage.

Mrs Kitto met them at the gate, her face alight with news.

'Angel is being discharged this afternoon. Rain rang to ask if someone would collect them from the hospital. She thinks around two o'clock.'

'Sirius is about somewhere. Or Gray would, I'm sure. And I could go with him. I'll run back now, shall I?'

Belle found Gray sitting at the kitchen table, reading a newspaper, and he readily agreed.

When she returned to the cottage, it was to find the car packed and her family ready to leave. Her father was frowning, which as ever made Belle feel that she'd done something wrong, but instead of making some biting comment he said gently, 'Your mum has had an idea and I think it's a good one if you have the time.'

'Tell me,' she said guardedly, though when he did, she smiled.

'Oh, Dad,' she breathed, 'I'd like that very much.'

Forty-Four

The ancient church of St Mawnan stood on the headland where the Helford River met the sea. It was a beautiful, atmospheric spot at the end of a narrow, winding lane overhung with trees; a place of perfect peace.

Belle's father parked the car next to the churchyard and set off on foot through a square-set lychgate. Belle, dawdling behind, glanced up to see words in Cornish inscribed overhead but, not understanding them, hurried to catch up with the others.

The old stone church building was hunkered above a rugged, grass-covered graveyard studded with lichen-covered tombstones. Belle's father followed a path around to the far side where Belle drew a sharp breath at the sudden clear view over the estuary, its restless waters glimmering in the sunlight. He paused, shading his eyes against dazzle to get his bearings, before setting off downhill towards a crop of more recent graves. Belle followed, but her mum and Jackie kept stopping to read inscriptions. She could hear Jackie's light clear voice remarking on the old names – Ebenezer, Hepzibah, Mercy.

Her father stopped by a smooth gravestone of light-coloured granite and stood, hands in his pockets, his shoulders hunched, gazing down at it, lost in thought. She crept up beside him and read the words on the stone. 'In memory of Imogen, beloved wife …' then her dates and a single phrase: *'And underneath are the everlasting arms.'*

'Her mother chose that verse,' Belle's father murmured. 'I had no idea what to put. I'd lost what little religious faith I'd had in France. Didn't think there could be any god if he allowed that suffering. But I wanted her buried here. She loved the river and I thought she'd have appreciated being near Silverwood. The rector was very understanding.'

Belle said nothing. She bent and scraped a strand of ivy from the base of the gravestone, then straightened and looked about. A gust of wind ruffled the grass, bringing with it the scent of the sea. Birds sang in the trees and a gull gave a single sad cry as it passed overhead. She squeezed her eyes shut briefly. She felt something released in her, a sense of peace.

'Thank you, Dad,' she said finally. He smiled sadly at her, then reached for her hand. For a while they stood together looking out across the water.

'We'd better go, I suppose,' he sighed. 'We've a long journey ahead.'

A few minutes later they dropped Belle at the entrance to Silverwood, getting out to hug her goodbye.

With a pang of sadness she waved them off, then she trudged down the drive towards the house. Imogen's grave was in a place of peace, but seeing it underlined that she was more than a character in a story. She felt aware that she was walking where Imogen and her father had once walked, viewing the front of the house as they had done, living where they had once lived. She'd not fully appreciated this before.

She sighed. It was time to fetch Rain and Angel. She hurried past the vehicles on the forecourt and round to the kitchen to look for Gray.

Forty-Five

'So your dad was going to tell you all this stuff sometime?'

'Yes.'

'Good. So finding it out wasn't my fault for bringing you to Silverwood.'

'No. I wanted to come, remember?'

'Yeah, you did. I didn't force you.' He flashed her a smile.

On the drive to Truro, Belle had shared the full details of Imogen's story, and Gray listened without comment. He could be very restful that way, she'd noticed. He didn't interrupt or ask stupid questions. It was easier, too, to talk in a car when they were next to each other, close, but not staring into one another's eyes. When she came to the end of her narrative he'd reached for her hand and shot her a glance of concern.

'I'm sorry if it was all a bit heavy.' She'd remembered too late that Gray's family situation was not exactly happy.

'I didn't mind.' He withdrew his hand in order to overtake a horse pulling a cart laden with straw. As the car crept by, bits of straw and dust whirled against the windscreen, almost obscuring the view.

'Your family are nice,' Gray remarked when they were safely past.

'They're not bad,' she murmured fondly. It was a relief that he'd got on with them. She remembered what he'd said about the photograph in her room at university. 'Bet you don't still think we're the perfect family.'

'No, that was just first impressions.'

'I don't believe there's such a thing though, do you?'

'Mine certainly wasn't perfect. You couldn't even call me and Mum a family.'

'Do you still see her?'

'Sometimes.' The engine was complaining loudly as the car climbed a hill. 'So . . .' he said, when it was quieter. 'What have you decided? Are you coming to London with me? I thought I'd go up next week. Tuesday perhaps. Stu's keen. Strike while the iron's hot and all that.'

'I still don't know for certain, but I think Mum and Dad are right. I ought to go back and take that exam I missed. Then assuming I passed all my other papers, I'll have options.'

'That's very sensible, but . . .'

'And perhaps I should ask to delay my return for a year. If I didn't want to continue with English Lit, I could try to switch courses. History might be interesting.'

'But will you see Comus and audition with us?' he persisted. From Gray's frown she sensed the importance of her answer.

She smoothed her cotton skirt and said uncertainly, 'If you both really think I'm up to it.'

He flashed a grin. 'Of course you are.' He straightened in his seat. 'You'll be amazing,' he said happily.

Clasping her hands in her lap, she gazed in silence at the passing scenery. There was a belt of trees behind a long low wall on one side, glimpses of a silvery river on the other, then a village of narrow terraced houses, followed by rolling farmland and a distant view of a church tower.

She'd said she'd go with him, but there was something missing. A reassurance she badly needed but lacked the courage to ask for. Was there something wrong if she had to ask for it? Next to her, Gray was humming to himself, probably a tune he was composing in his head, one forefinger tapping a rhythm on the wheel.

On the occasions she'd whispered her love, he'd only smiled with eyes that were sometimes as clear a blue as a summer sea, at others deep navy and inscrutable. How did you know a relationship was right? Her mum, Jill, and dad had known right away, it seemed. Imogen, her birth mother, had been less certain, made mistakes. Being with Gray felt risky. It might involve sacrifices she'd be stupid to make.

What do you feel about me? Am I special to you? She opened her mouth to ask him, but he was humming away, lost in his world and, anyway, the words dried on her lips. They would sound silly, needy, as though she didn't trust him.

They were on the outskirts of Truro now. The car turned right downhill past houses with gardens, a terrace of townhouses. Belle got a glimpse, between tall trees, of the nurses' hostel where Imogen had lived, before Gray swung the wheel to enter the car park.

They climbed out and walked together to the hospital entrance. Rain and Angel were sitting close together waiting in the reception area, holding hands, and Belle rushed over to them. And in her excitement she temporarily forgot her problems. Angel was well again, Rain looked herself again, and they were ready to come home.

Forty-Six

'You're quiet today, dear.' Mrs Kitto, rolling out pastry on a board on Monday morning, frowned gently at Belle across the kitchen table. 'I thought you'd come to tell me something.'

'I have,' Belle said, stirring her coffee, 'but it's hard to say. We're leaving tomorrow, Gray, Stu and me. Going to London.'

'Oh dear, I thought it was something like that. I'm not surprised, after hearing Gray's news.'

'It's a bit of a rush, though.'

'Strike while the iron's hot.'

'That's exactly what Gray said.'

'You're not happy about it?'

'I didn't say that.'

'No, but I can tell.'

'It's . . . a bit of a muddle. I don't really know what to do. I need to phone the university and arrange to go back and do that stupid exam.'

'You can telephone from here.'

'Thank you. It's long-distance. I'll pay for the call.'

'You don't have to do that.'

'I will, though. The trouble is, I don't know what to do longer term. What happens if Comus, they're the people who manage bands, do like us? What happens if they don't? I can't see the future.'

'None of us can do that,' Mrs Kitto said drily, sprinkling flour.

'But should I go back to university and finish my course?'

The older woman sighed as she peeled pastry off her rolling pin. 'I don't know, Belle. You'll have to work that out.'

'But I can't see what's right.'

'You have to feel your way.' Mrs Kitto surveyed her thoughtfully. 'Try not to close down options until you're comfortable with your choices.'

'Should I follow my heart or follow my head?'

'A bit of both, I'd say. But, Belle, no one else can make decisions for you.'

'It was all easier for your generation,' Belle grumbled.

'Possibly,' she said crisply as she flipped the pastry over. 'Possibly not. Remember we had the war. Two wars in my case. And they very much restricted my choices.'

'I'm sorry,' Belle murmured, remembering that Mrs Kitto's fiancé had died of wounds in Flanders. She'd had to work at the school, then look after her aged father and had not married until her childbearing years were past. Simpler, maybe, but not easier.

'Imogen's life was hardly straightforward, either. She may have loved working at Silverwood for a while and she certainly enjoyed nursing, but we were expected to do our duty in wartime. And think how your father's wartime experiences blighted their short marriage. Perhaps I shouldn't have put this so baldly, but I gather that he described it to you in those terms.'

'He did,' Belle sighed.

'Well then.' She turned away to rummage in a drawer, then began stamping circles in the pastry with a biscuit cutter. 'You're fortunate, my girl, having choices. If you complete your studies you will have more opportunities in life. If you don't marry and have children immediately, that is.'

'I don't plan to. Bringing up children looks difficult if Angel is anything to go by.'

'It is. My work as matron taught me that. I was always much admiring of the parents. Which reminds me. How's young Angel getting on?'

Belle swallowed a stolen scrap of sweet pastry. 'He's much better.'

'I'm so relieved.'

'Everyone's relieved. He's very pale and thinner than ever, but he insists on getting out of bed, even though he's supposed to rest, and plays with Figgy or follows his mother around. She's being very attentive to him. His illness really frightened her.'

'I can imagine.'

'There is something different about her. She told me and Janey that she made a bargain with her guardian spirit when Angel was at his worst. The deal was that she would put him first in her life. D'you know, she's going to visit the school in the village and see if they'll take him in September? She thinks he needs friends his own age.'

'That is a change of heart.'

'And she's signing up with the local doctor so Angel can have his vaccinations.'

'Excellent.'

'And she's going to help Janey more. They're working on a plan of the vegetable garden and there are going to be rotas. Actual rotas! And even Sirius will have to do his bit. But with Chouli gone and us on our way, there'll be more for them to do. Arlo's not been around much in the last few days and when he is he's acting most mysterious. I think he and Francis are plotting something. Francis is coming over later today and wants to talk to us all. I don't know why Gray and I are included since we're leaving, but apparently he wants us there. And Stu.'

'It sounds interesting,' Mrs Kitto said lightly. She finished laying the biscuit rounds on baking trays and dusted her hands.

Something about her tone made Belle narrow her eyes. 'Do you know something about this?'

'I might do,' Mrs Kitto said, flashing Belle a smile before opening the door to the oven. Belle felt a waft of hot air as the trays were slipped inside then the door shut. 'Then again I might not.'

'You are a tease.'

'Francis and I go back a long way. He often asks my opinion on matters to do with Silverwood. In fact I took the opportunity of challenging him in return. I asked whether

Arlo had given him the box of Imogen's possessions from the secret room and explained why I needed to know.'

Belle sat up, her eyes rounding. 'And what did he say?'

'He claimed at first not to know what I was talking about, but caved in when I persisted. Didn't say if he's keeping it, though, or why. You have to understand that Francis and Arlo are as thick as thieves, more like father and son than uncle and nephew. Francis not having married, and Arlo's real father having disappeared into the sunset, they've formed a close bond. Francis is very protective of him.'

Belle thought it made sense. 'I still don't understand why Francis would be interested in a lot of old books and photographs.'

'Nor me. Now I've told him that you're Imogen's daughter he may regard the matter in a different light. Whether that's a good or bad thing we'll have to see. But whatever happens, Belle, will you stay in touch? I should like to know how you get on in London or wherever you end up. I feel I owe it to Imogen. But also, well, I've become very fond of you.'

'And I'm very fond of you. Dear Mrs Kitto, thank you for everything.'

'It's been a pleasure.'

'There's one other thing I wanted to ask. What happened to Kezia, the maid, whose husband died?'

Mrs Kitto smiled. 'Dear Kezia. She married again. She and her husband run a hotel in Helston. I often call in to see her when I'm there. They never had children, but some people don't. It doesn't seem to bother her. Oh, my life!' Mrs Kitto snatched up an oven glove. While they'd been talking, a delicious buttery smell had been arising from the oven. Now she removed the tray of biscuits, all golden brown, and tipped them onto a wire rack to cool. 'Just caught them in time! Now, would you like a tin of them to take home with you?'

Forty-Seven

The afternoon was drawing on when the household assembled over mugs of tea in the kitchen at Silverwood to welcome Francis, their landlord. Rain and Janey, Angel, wrapped in a multicoloured blanket snuggled against his mother, Sirius, pulled away from his work and looking particularly surly, Gray, Belle, Stu and Arlo, who wore a secretive smile as though he knew what this was all about. A couple of loud bangs outside announced the arrival of Francis's battered Austin and caused Figgy to leap onto the alert. A moment later crisp footsteps and voices – one female – were heard and the back door opened to admit not just Francis, but a slickly coiffured brunette wearing a bold-patterned skirt and matching jacket and carrying a clipboard. She shied from Figgy's interested approach, then glanced around the kitchen with a bright pasted-on smile.

'Hello, everyone.' She had a cultured American voice.

'This is Miss Littlemore from the Carnoustie Ridgemore Arts Foundation,' Francis said proudly.

'Call me Clara, do,' the woman murmured to her stunned audience.

'Janey, I'm sure Clara would like tea. I know I would.'

'We only have goat's milk.'

'I'll take it black then,' Clara instructed and Janey rose without a word to fill the kettle. 'I say, you have a marvellous place here,' she said, staring at the painted clouds on the walls. 'Plenty of atmosphere.'

'We've put a great deal of effort into our work here.' Rain straightened, her arm round Angel, her nostrils flaring like an old warhorse smelling battle.

Clara smiled and blinked. Francis hastily stepped in, introducing everyone to the newcomer. Chairs were fetched, tea was poured, and everyone waited for Francis, sitting next to Clara at the head of the table and making ready to speak.

'Not to beat about the bush,' he said briskly, 'there have to be changes here. I hope that you'll welcome them and that we'll put Silverwood on the map. It'll come as no surprise when I tell you that we can't keep going as we are. The place is in danger of falling down and unless I start charging you some exorbitant rent I'm unable to pay the bills.'

'But we're unable to pay you any rent at all,' Rain said into the silence.

'Exactly. I had hoped that you'd do more with the place, a few repairs at least. Instead, I gather that some of you aren't pulling your weight.'

Belle noticed Rain and Sirius look accusingly at Arlo for sneaking. Arlo did not meet their gaze.

'I've thought about selling Silverwood, but my nephew has

begged me not to, so I've been exploring alternatives and I'm pleased to say that the Foundation is considering stepping in. Clara, perhaps you'd explain your vision.'

'We've been searching for a property like this for a while and think this is the perfect setting for what we want to do.' Clara Littlemore sounded as though she was reading from a script. 'The Carnoustie Ridgeway Foundation has been created by the renowned American businessman Mr Samuel Carnoustie Ridgeway in memory of his English wife Laura Carnoustie Ridgeway. Laura was a painter and musician and loved Cornwall. Mr Samuel Carnoustie Ridgeway wishes to explore the establishment of a special community here where artists, musicians and other creative individuals might live together in harmony, enjoying the simple life and being at one with nature while they pursue their artistic activities.'

'Mr Carnoustie Ridgeway is an extremely wealthy man,' Francis put in, his eyes shining. 'I gather his businesses include a chain of American funeral homes and a famous pet food brand.'

'He is also a man with a soul,' Clara said earnestly. 'And the Foundation would like to discuss the possibility of working with you all to develop his vision.'

Everybody looked at each other. Belle read the range of expressions. Sirius's wary, Rain shocked, Janey bewildered. Gray's was unreadable. Only Arlo appeared to be excited. Angel had fallen asleep with his head on the table.

'Belle and me,' Gray said, 'we don't know what we're doing yet, but I'd like to try to help.' Belle stared at him, astonished that he was becoming so purposeful, but he only winked at her. Beside him Stu nodded.

Sirius cleared his throat. 'It's all very well, a nice idea, but how would it work? I'm not a performing monkey. I need freedom.'

'Mr Carnoustie Ridgeway understands the ways of artists,' Clara assured him. 'Though there would need to be account-ability, someone in charge, if you like.'

'That would be me,' Rain stated. 'I have the experience.' She and Clara stared briefly at one another.

'Be assured, though, that our founder is an extremely generous man.'

'I'd like to help,' Janey said, 'but I can't go on doing everything I do now by myself.'

'Others would join you,' Clara stated enigmatically. 'Well.' She scribbled something on her clipboard. 'It seems that the response is positive. Now, I'd like to have a proper scout round if you wouldn't mind.'

While Francis and Arlo went off with her to tour the house and grounds, the others remained in the kitchen in ardent discussion.

'What the hell are we supposed to do?' Sirius growled.

'She said other people would join us. I don't like the sound of that,' Janey moaned.

'Hey, we're leaving tomorrow, as you know,' Gray said mildly. 'But as I said, maybe I'll be back. The idea has possi-bilities. What do you think, Rain?'

'Frankly, what else can we do but go along with it? Otherwise we'll have to give up, return to our old lives. I don't want to do that, so let's give it a try. If we're given a grant there's lots we could do. Build proper studios. Yoga. Country crafts. Animal husbandry and gardening, Janey. We could run courses. I can oversee it all.'

Sirius was still unsure. The arguments went back and forth. Belle and Stu listened quietly.

When the viewing party returned, bright-eyed, Sirius was saying, 'I don't get it. Wouldn't the Foundation want to buy Silverwood?'

'Let me answer that,' Clara put in. 'We would lease the house. The Foundation is happy with that, seeing as Francis doesn't want to sell.'

'There is one thing I haven't told you,' Francis said. He smiled at his nephew, who straightened proudly. 'Arlo here will be my representative. Estate manager, I suppose you might call him. It'll be good experience for when I'm gone and it shouldn't get in your way, Rain.'

Everyone stared at Arlo, then at Rain. Rain shrugged and everyone sighed with relief.

It was time for Francis to drive Clara to catch her train, but first he asked for a private word with Belle. Outside, Clara climbed into the car and he led Belle over to the goat pen so they were out of earshot.

'It's been good to meet you, Belle, and I wish you and Gray success with your endeavours. You have a great deal of talent between you and I hope you'll return to help out the crew, assuming everything works out here. I think it will. Clara's very struck by the place, though she says we'll need a surveyor to take a look at it.'

'We've been glad to be here. Thank you, but I want to ask you about something. It's —'

'About Imogen? I gather you're her daughter. I should have guessed, there's such a resemblance.'

'That's what Mrs Kitto says.'

'She's told you the whole story, she said.'

Belle nodded.

One of the goats was pulling at Francis's jacket with its teeth through the fence. Francis tugged the fabric free then said, 'I've got something in the car for you,' and she breathed in sharply when he lifted out Imogen's box. He brought it across and laid it on the grass.

'Oh, you did have it,' she said.

Bending stiffly to open the lid, he took out a thick brown envelope from the top and slid out two photographs. These he handed to Belle.

Belle saw with a jolt that they were both pictures of Imogen. In one, she was standing against a wall, wearing a shirt dress that showed off her trim figure. She was laughing at the camera. The other was a close-up. Belle stared and stared at the laughing face. In some ways it was like looking into a mirror. Imogen's face was full of life and vitality. *Do I really look like that?* she thought with awe. And finally she grasped what she hadn't been able to up to now. This vibrant young woman really had been her mother. Tears sprang to her eyes. 'Thank you,' she whispered to Francis. 'Thank you.'

'I ought to apologize,' he said and she looked at him, surprised. 'Let me explain.' He took the other photograph in which the full height of the wall and the edge of the sloping roof could be seen. 'This is the wing of the house that was destroyed. Look at that, lying right up there.' He pointed.

She looked closely. A long, cylindrical metal object with a pointed end was just visible above the lip of the gutter. 'Is it . . . ?' she asked frowning.

'It's an unexploded shell. And it's important because I've never been able to wangle compensation for the loss of that wing. I hope you'll forgive me because I need to borrow the photograph again to show the authorities. There's always been a suspicion that I blew up the wing myself to steal public money. Why I'd do something as stupid as that – I might have destroyed the whole house – they're not able to say. I'm not certain that it will work, of course, but Arlo spotted it and he likes to please me.'

'I see. So that's why Arlo took the box to you.' It was starting to make sense.

'I don't think it was just that.' Francis looked shifty. 'He's very protective of Silverwood, that lad, and loyal to me. Been dealt a bad hand by his parents. Maybe, now, he has a chance to prove himself.'

Belle nodded, guessing he was hinting at Arlo's dislike of her. She didn't like Arlo any better, but she was beginning to understand him and why he was suspicious of her. She had, after all, been critical of the Silverwood community. She looked at the photographs again. 'Mrs Kitto said that one night a German plane flew very close over Silverwood and dropped a bomb that exploded in a field. Do you suppose it was actually two bombs, but the second didn't go off at the time?'

'I think that's precisely what happened. Now, you take the box, Belle, and one of the photographs, and I'll have the other for the moment.'

She nodded and crouched to look at the contents. The books were all there and some papers. She would explore them sometime. Francis tucked the close-up of Imogen into the envelope for her and slipped it inside the box.

'You may not realize, but I spoke to your father at length when he was here,' he said. 'I knew your mother and was immensely fond of her, but had no idea, of course, that he hadn't told you about her. I'm glad that it's all out in the open now. He's a tormented soul, but maybe now he'll find peace.'

Belle nodded.

'Now, you won't want advice from an old fogey like me, Belle, but I'll give it to you anyway. You're on the cusp of adulthood and the future lies before you. Think about what's important in life and worth working for and the desire for that will carry you on. Me, I've wasted opportunities that other men would die for. I've always tried to help others though and there's nothing like going to bed with a clear conscience. Goodbye, Belle.' He placed the box in her hands and solemnly bowed his head to her. She watched his dignified figure as he walked away and climbed into his car beside Clara. He gunned the engine, waved to her and the vehicle bumped down the drive, backfiring as it reached the gate in a salute of farewell.

Holding the box close, Belle turned and went thoughtfully inside.

Forty-Eight

After supper that night, when everything had been washed up and put away, Belle left Gray with Stu, Arlo and Sirius, went upstairs and packed up her few things. She wasn't sure exactly where they would sleep tomorrow night or what would happen next. Gray had mentioned a friend in Bayswater who'd have them, but he was vague about details. In all honesty she wanted to go home at the earliest possible opportunity, but they needed to see the people at Comus and perhaps after that matters would be clearer. Perhaps Gray would come with her. She tried to imagine him in their neat suburban house. Her mother would put him in the spare bedroom to save Belle's maidenly virtue, that was for sure – she smiled to herself – but he'd liked her parents and would, she thought, put up with the house rules. They, in turn, would do their best to make him feel welcome. This, at least, was progress.

She looked round the bedroom, scattered with Gray's

things, but otherwise as bare as they'd found it. They'd been happy here in this dusty cocoon, getting to know one another. On top of that was the view. She wandered over to the open window and perched on the sill to look out. It was another glorious evening. The sky was streaked with gold and peachy drifts of cloud. Maybe Imogen had once stood here, admiring it? She'd miss this vista of fields and woods and the mist over the sea, Mrs Kitto's cottage in the distance, nestled amidst the trees. A crow alighted on a chimney, but after a moment it spread its wings and flew off, circled the garden then landed on a treetop.

Like the bird Belle felt unsettled, her way ahead unclear. It was an exciting feeling but overwhelming too. Yet whatever happened she'd be all right, she told herself. If one thing didn't work out, there would be something else that did. She must learn to rely on herself. Francis had said something useful yesterday. What was it? That it was helpful to decide what was important in life and worth working for and the desire for that would carry her on. She must be careful not simply to drift, she thought, with a brave little nod, or to follow someone else's dream at the expense of her own.

Feeling stronger, she left the window, thinking she'd go for a quiet walk. She stuffed a stray sock into a pocket in her rucksack. As she did so her fingers touched metal and she drew out the delicate gold watch which had been tucked away there forgotten since the day she came to Silverwood. She wound it carefully then smiled to hear it tick. It was working again. She fitted it onto her wrist feeling it was a sign that she was returning to real life. Then she rested the rucksack against the wall, and set off downstairs. Reaching the first-floor landing she paused, hearing a murmuring voice, and smiled. It was Rain, reading Angel a bedtime story. This was new. Something glinted up at her from between the floorboards and Belle bent to look. A sequin. One of Chouli's probably. No one had heard from her. Belle hoped she was all right. She continued down to the hall, then hesitated. The door to the library was closed. She went and opened it and stepped into the gloom. Her fingers felt unerringly for the hidden latch and the door to the secret room sprang open.

It lay bathed in the golden evening glow. The bedding had gone. Arlo had a new regime, it seemed. The floorboards were bare. Whether or not the room had a ghost, it felt peaceful now. 'Goodbye,' she whispered, and listened, but there was only silence. She retreated, carefully closing the door.

The hall smelled of paint – Sirius had left the door to the drawing room open. Presumably it would smell of all sorts of things if the Carnoustie Ridgeway project came about. She smiled to herself and entered the kitchen where the men were still engaged in earnest discussion. She heard the words 'World Cup' and 'Bobby Moore' and quickened her pace. Figgy lay asleep by the range and she managed not to disturb him as she let herself out by the side door.

At the far end of the kitchen garden someone was humming and Belle could see Janey's slight figure bent over the lettuces. The humming was new, too. Belle called a greeting as she passed and Janey straightened and waved. 'Just going for a last walk,' Belle said.

She moved slowly over the courtyard, wondering what the

new regime might do about the ruined wing. Perhaps they'd leave it, a dramatic part of the landscape. She imagined a drawing class grouped before it, sketching the jagged ruins that reached to the sky and the romantic cloaks of ivy and Virginia creeper. She walked on, thinking she wouldn't disturb Mrs Kitto this evening. Instead she crossed to a stile and set out across the pasture to see the standing stones for the last time. There she stood in the centre of the circle, turning slowly to see the world roll away on every side. Lit up by the dying sun tonight, the twisted shapes of the stones seemed vibrant, alive. Belle grinned and executed a little twirl, then a curtsey in their honour.

When she steadied herself and glanced up in the direction of the house, the low sun dazzled her and as she raised her palm against it, she caught a movement and blinked. The figure of a young man was walking across the field towards her. It was Gray. She waited until he entered the circle of stones and stood before her with a lopsided grin, his hands in his jeans pockets.

'I thought you'd come here. I saw you from the kitchen window.'

'Spying on me?' she said, smiling back at him.

'Of course.' He leaned and kissed her nose. 'I loved your dancing. Glad you haven't turned to stone like the others.'

'Then I'd have had to stay here for ever. I can think of worse places.'

'A little inconvenient, though. A disaster for The Witchers.'

'I'm glad to be needed.'

'Oh, yes, you're needed.'

'Really?'

He took both her hands and breathed in deeply. 'Very much.'

'So is it Gray Robinson of The Witchers who needs me or just Gray Robinson?'

'Both,' he said promptly. 'But let's see how we go. Stu and I will manage if it's really not for you.' He put his arms round her, drew her to him and kissed her fiercely, then he breathed into her ear, 'I love you, my Belle. Just in case you hadn't realized.'

He cupped her face in his hands. 'You didn't doubt it, did you?' His face creased in a frown. 'Belle? What's the matter?'

For her eyes were flooding with tears.

'Nothing,' she said, brushing them away, 'I'm just so happy, that's all.'

'I always want to make you happy, Belle.' His gaze was soft. 'But what happens if . . .'

'It doesn't matter. Stu and I will be okay, whatever. I love you.'

'Gray, I'm a bit frightened. Not knowing what's going to happen.'

'So am I,' he whispered, 'but whatever it is I'd like us to be together. This is not just about me and what I want to do. Since meeting you I've changed. For the better, I hope. Wherever the future takes us, I want to be with you. If you feel the same way . . .'

'Of course I do.'

'Then we'll manage somehow.'

With this reassurance Belle felt a great wave of happiness

wash through her. They couldn't see the future – no one could – but if they were committed to one another they could try to work it out. Their path ahead might mean give or take, sacrifices on both sides, but love was the most important thing of all, wasn't it?

She looked about at the standing stones, the dancing maidens frozen in time. Silverwood had been a place of stillness, of rest and reflection – at least, that had been her first impression – but she'd learned so much here too. Not just about Imogen, her birth mother, who'd followed her own path, weighing love against duty in time of war – but about what was important to her, Belle. True love couldn't be just a romantic feeling, it must be something tougher, deep-rooted. There was no place for jealousy or selfishness on either side. It would be hard, there was no doubt of that, but they could take things day by day.

'Come on,' Gray said. 'We've an early start tomorrow.'

She took his hand and they returned to the house together.

Author's Note and Acknowledgements

Silverwood is a fictional house, but I've imagined it to be a neighbour of the very real Trebah estate on the north side of the Helford River. Trebah's wonderful gardens run down along a valley to Polgwidden Cove, which was used by American forces as a launching site for D-Day. The gardens are open to the public and the price of a ticket includes access to the private beach. The breathtakingly beautiful Kynance Cove belongs to the National Trust but is open to all. Everywhere in Cornwall the sea should be treated with respect and warnings heeded. Its dangerous wildness is part of its beauty.

The original inspiration for *The Hidden Years* was a photograph of pupils from my father's old school, which was evacuated from Kent to Cornwall during the war. They occupied a rather grand modern hotel in Carlyon Bay on the south coast and despite the deprivations must have had rather a splendid time.

I consulted many books and websites in my research of wartime Cornwall and of the Royal Cornwall Infirmary, the old site of which finally closed in 1999 to become flats. I should particularly like to acknowledge: *Cornwall at War* by Peter Hancock, 'The Tragic Truro Raid of 6th August 1942' by Lawrence Holmes at www.rocatwentytwelve.org and *The First Cornish Hospital* by Dr C. T. Andrews. *No Time for Romance* by Lucilla Andrews and *One Pair of Feet* by Monica Dickens provided valuable background about nursing in this period.

Various people and organizations have been helpful during the writing. I wish particularly to mention Kresen Kernow (Cornwall's County Archive in their fabulous new building in Redruth), Jenny of the Tregolls Book Club and Debbie Spittle for sharing their memories of the Cornwall Royal Infirmary, and Liz Fenwick for her knowledge of the Helford River and general encouragement.

As ever I am thankful for my wonderful agent, Sheila Crowley, and her colleagues at Curtis Brown, for Suzanne Baboneau and Louise Davies, my amazing editors together with freelance copyeditor Sally Partington, and all others at my UK publishers Simon & Schuster, including Ian Chapman, Gill Richardson, Rhiannon Carroll, Amy Fulwood, Rachel Keenan, Sara-Jade Virtue, Sam Combes, Dominic Brendon and the tireless sales team.

My husband, David, continues to be marvellous and supportive – I don't know how he manages to put up with my periods of lost confidence and my insistence on visiting out-of-the-way places to research tiny details that don't make it into the book, but he does.

RACHEL HORE
Norwich, 2023